BROKEN TIDES

CAYLA CAVALLETTO

Edited by Megan Carver | Thorns n Roses Co
Cover Design by Katelyn | Design by Kage
Interior Formatting by Katelyn | Design by Kage
Proofreading by Cerra Cyrus | Lemon & Grain Co.
Published by Lemon & Grain Co. Crafted with care beneath golden light and wild ideas.

ISBN: 979-8-9937177-0-8

Printed in the United States of America

For more about the *Blade & Bonds* series, visit: caylacavalletto.com

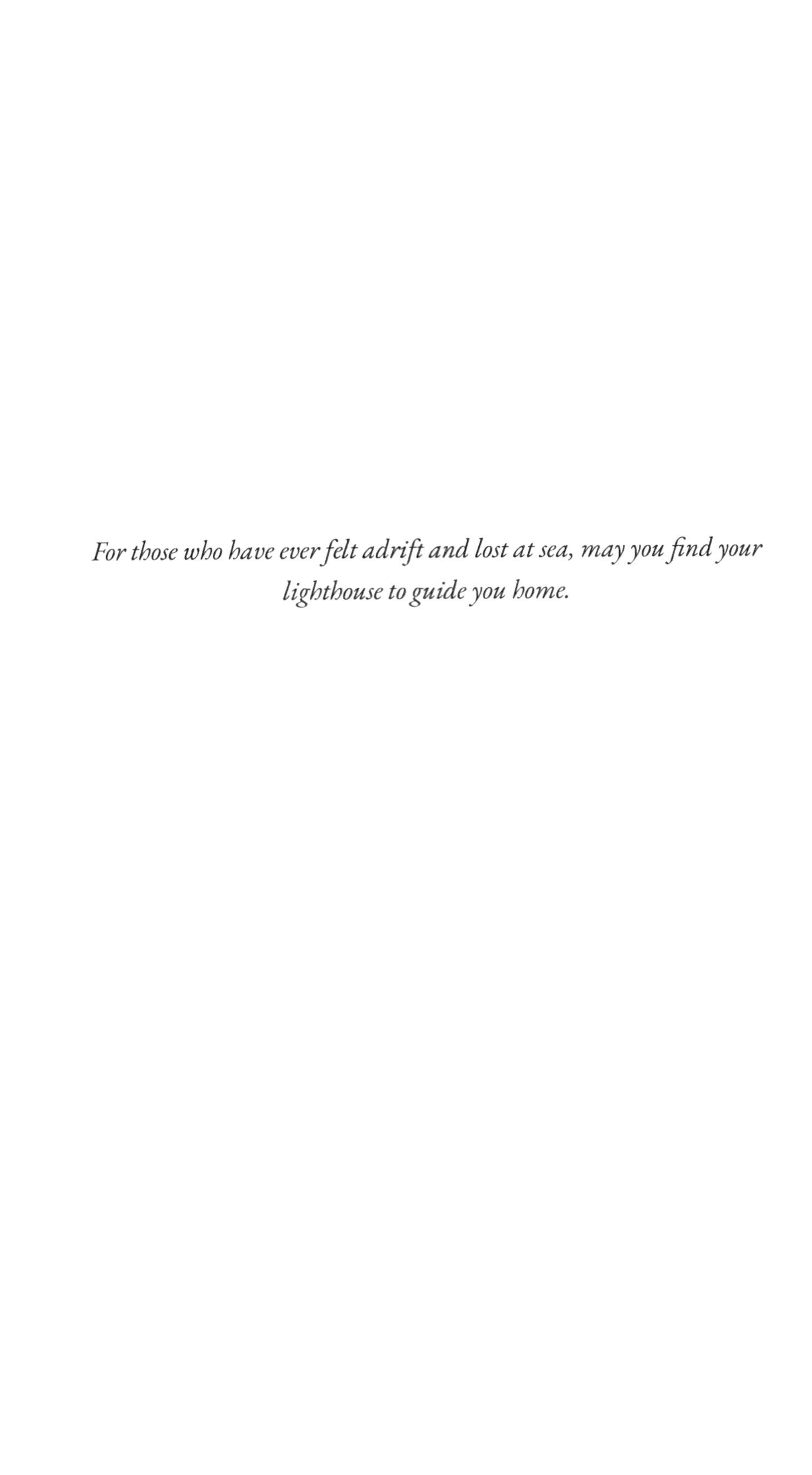

For those who have ever felt adrift and lost at sea, may you find your lighthouse to guide you home.

ELDRATH
ALLERIA
FALDO
LEFENDOR
DREAD FL
BAEL'THIREON
ARETHOR
N
E
S
W

EBYSSIAN SEA
BAUSTANTIA
SOUTHERN ISLES

PROLOGUE

*I*N *BAUSTANTIA, REPUTATION IS worn like perfume—heavy, cloying, and often masking rot beneath. Skyships may rule the skies, but it's whispers in the smoke-laced halls of the Merchant Council that steer the country's fate.*

No one is coming to save me. That kind of mercy hasn't ever been shown to me.

The docks reek of coal and blood—the first from the Skyship hovering above me. The second from the steady drip of foul liquid slipping down the blade haphazardly tucked into my belt. Shadows cast from the strange Baustantian lights lick around me, closing me in.

I appreciate their assistance. I can keep my Grit untouched, leaving me more in case something about this damned job goes sideways. And things always go sideways. With how easily I slipped into and out of Frando Solstairo's charming residence in the Palace District, I'm just waiting for something to barrel into me and send this job into a downward spiral.

The Skyship commander thankfully had no busybody wife, only a steady stream of doves to warm his bed each night. I'd spent the better part of a fortnight lingering on the roof of the building across from his tall, ivory and gold-plated home watching the comings and goings—and there has been a lot of coming—to find the best time to eliminate the head of the snake.

A sea trader spent more than a pretty platinum for my services. Only one instruction, though: take out the commander of the Skyships. The one protecting all the Baustantian sea merchants and preventing the Eldrathian traders from making port.

It had been far too simple. Wait for Frando's dove to leave him satiated and sleepy—courtesy of the Velvet Veil draught I'd had the female slip into the commander's wine—and then climb in through the window left open for the cool maritime breeze—and for me.

The dove had been all too willing to aid me. A few silver pieces may have helped my cause.

I smile to myself, gloved fingers tracing the handle of the serrated blade Laz gifted me before this job. He's only ever gifted two things to me: my brand and this blade. I should have drawn out the commander's death a little longer so I could have used my new toy.

Next time.

The Baustantian shadows turn from curious licking to an aggressive prod. The brand at my nape flares, stopping any concern at the change in shadows. *Fucking Laz.* My brand flares hotter. Somehow, even a continent away from the bastard and he still uses that damn brand to control me.

I peer down at the insistent tendrils at my ankles. Amidst the roiling, one shadow flips over, opening like a palm, and produces a yellowed parchment.

I blink. *The hells is that?*

The small shadow shakes the parchment at me as if to say, *take it!* No. Whatever it is, no. It lifts the folded paper higher. I stare without making a move to take the parchment.

If shadows could sigh, this one would, but I'd still tell it to shove off. Lazrik's notes rarely bring good news. The last note he sent me told me which poison would hurt the least to grab when Rafe had me pinned to a target with my own blades. I don't need another bedtime story, thanks. Finally, the shadow surges up and shoves the paper into my hand hanging by my side. The thing gives a satisfied, smug shake in my direction, then falls away.

Footsteps approach from behind me, stomping down the docks. I clench my fingers around the paper and slink into the darkness. I pick my way along the dock, avoiding the late-night dockworkers and guards going about their business. I pass ship after ship, trying to find the perfect one for escape.

No...no...not that one...no...Aha! That one.

Shoving the parchment into my belt, I slip through the shadows up the gangplank, but rather than traipsing onto the deck, I squat and launch myself at the side of the hull.

By the absolute tips of my fingers, I latch onto the lip of the open porthole. My boots scrabble against the side of the wooden ship as I haul myself through the window.

Probably could have planned this better. Do I know anything about this ship other than where it's headed? Not a chance. But since it's bound for Eldrath, more specifically the elven city Alverdine on the northeast point, I'm betting on it. Taking a minute on my hands and knees, I breathe a deep sigh of relief after feeling like I've been a bowstring pulled taut for too long. The silence welcomes me like an old friend.

I glance around the interior of the ship. Crates fill the entire hull.

What in Nythraxis' bleeding shadows have I stumbled into? Gold, bronze, and copper metallic feathers peek out from one of the wooden crates. The thing cannot be natural with those feathers—alive and yet perhaps not. I inch closer, only to stumble back when the creature squawks out a sharp cry, the sound like metal being struck upon an anvil. It echoes like a bell inside my skull.

The phoenix-like bird clanks its beak, tilting its head, and I swear if it sneezes fire on me, Laz will owe me a new pair of eyebrows.

Scrambling back away from the creature, my shoulders bump into another hard surface. Water sloshes, drips, then chills atop my brow, slipping over my Night Elf marking and down my cheeks. I crane my neck up, up, up.

An opalescent scale-covered head looms above me with eight long curving teeth extending from its jaws. The fangs are longer than my forearm and hand combined. A glow shimmers beneath the creature's scales, running in long streaks like its very blood glows within its veins and arteries.

It arches its neck in a graceful swoop downward, sniffing me. I clamber to my feet, caught between launching straight out the window I'd just climbed through and morbid curiosity.

Twin cyan eyes lock with my own. That echoing bell in my mind fades away, replaced by a longing, haunting croon, a song that should not be possible from such a creature. Its reptilian head presses down, coming into contact with my breastplate. It breathes again.

With a snort, it plunges farther down, stopping once it reaches my belt. I gesture in a small movement to the dagger still dripping with blood and whisper, "It's from someone allowing you to be smuggled."

The creature tosses its head and plunges its snout back to my belt with a harsh exhale. A ripple of paper fills the air. Oh gods. Laz's note. I pull it from beneath the leather around my waist, the yellowed parchment only slightly stained from the bloody dagger.

"Care for a bit of dock gossip, eh?" I say gently. The creature's eyes gleam as I unfold the note. Harsh lines fill the page. To anyone else, the lines would be the scribblings of a madman; but I've spent more than half my life reading these strange lines.

My eyes scan the note. Once. Twice. So many times the lines blur. No. No, he's lying. This must be a cruel joke.

Kira,

By the time this reaches you, Lachlan will already be gone—claimed by Vaeroth's Scales. They'll call it an "accident." A failed trial. Do you believe that? Do you think your brother—the boy who could outthink every instructor, who fought twice as hard to prove himself—would fall to some mere trial? I do not. They will bury the truth along with his bones if someone doesn't make them speak.

You were always the clever one. The one who could slip through cracks others didn't even see. If anyone can get inside the Spire, it's you. Find out what they did to him, who they sent him against, why they needed him silenced. And if justice is to be dealt, do it as only you can.

Come home, Kira. Bring the blade I gave you.

For Lachlan. For the brother who would have bled the world dry to keep you safe.

Do not fail him now.

-Laz

The world caves in. Air, light, everything good is ripped from me with those words. He can't be...gone.

Everything falls away, the haunting song of the creature in the tank, the clanging squawk of the metal phoenix, the rocking of the ship. None of it matters. Not without Lach.

They killed him. My baby brother. The only light in that damned Underbelly.

And I let him walk to his death.

I should have talked him out of that job. He'd been so set on going, so set on keeping me from knowing whatever it was that job had been about. Nythraxis take me, I should have sent him to the Conclave instead of letting Da keep him in the Underbelly with us.

A scream tears through my chest, but instead of rending the air with my hollow cry, the serpentine creature drops its jaw and releases an echoing shriek to mask my grief. I clamp my hand over my traitorous mouth at the same time the aquatic creature dips its head to rest upon my shoulder.

My body shudders under the weight of my sobs, but I can't be bothered to give a damn about crying right now.

Footsteps split the silence in the hull. A quiet creak and a sliver of light come from the top of the stairs at the edge of the room. The heavy head of the sea creature pushes on my shoulder, urging me to move.

I sidle along the edge of the glass tank and tuck myself into the shadows between it and the wall. Diving into my Grit, I wrap shadows around myself like a familiar blanket. The sea creature rumbles a deep, grating growl, its focus on the cracked door.

With a loud *snap*, the door shuts, cutting off the small sliver of light.

Thoughts come flooding back. Lachlan. Lach is gone.

And it's my fault. *My fault.*

The words beat sharply within my mind, again and again. My stomach roils and an ache swirls in my chest like a tempest, threatening to suck my heart straight to its depths.

Sleep.

I startle, searching for the voice.

Sleep, Wanderer.

I peer up once more through my shadows. The strange glow of the sea creature's eyes and veins greet me, and I have to fight the pull of my heavy lids.

CHAPTER 1

THE CRUMBLING STONE FALLING down the back of my leather jerkin is becoming more of an annoyance than I had anticipated. I hadn't *planned* to hide out in an alleyway behind barrels of ale, standing in puddles of—*fuck, is that piss?*

I sniff. *That's definitely piss.* Shifting my weight, I try to inch my boots out of the foul liquid without making too much noise. If I'm not careful, the Arethor Guard Warlocks prowling the streets will be able to sense the disturbance of the shadows. I hate Locks. As a procurer of desired items, they make my life so much more difficult.

Although, today the desired item isn't so much of a thing as it is an opening—an opening of the gates to Shadowspire Academy. Securing my spot in the Spire won't matter much if the Locks throw me in the stockade and ship me off to the Dread Flats. More like they'll live up to their common name and lock me away in a dungeon with one of their Demon Fate Threads. I'm meant for scaling rooftops, crafting poisons, and slinking through the shadows, not the hard labor of digging out opals and garnets or sowing the fields by hand. I'm even worse suited to tango with one of the unfortunate souls bound to a Lock. I shudder at the thought.

Diving within the golden well of Grit writhing in my chest, I call upon the power and slip further into the shadows. My body becomes nearly translucent in the darkness. As long as I don't go traipsing about in full daylight, people shouldn't notice me. Key word: shouldn't. This fun party trick got me into all sorts of trouble before the Rogue's Guild took me in for schooling and locked me away in the depths of the Underbelly to train with the rest of the dark dwellers.

"Come out, come out, little shadow." The words slink down the alley with all the syrupy sweetness of honey. "I'm sure the king will only ask a few questions and let you on your way."

Of course he will. He'll send me right on my way to meet the gods in Natharia so Vaeroth, the Crimson Judge, might weigh me against his Crimson Scales, whether I can pass onto the lavish afterlife or if soon I'll be chained to a Lock as their subject. And I already know there would be no unending flagon of mead waiting for me to revel along with the rest of them. No eternity in Nythraxis' chateau on his dusky vineyard.

Wrinkling my nose against the thought of the Crimson Scales, I thank the Gods I'm finally able to move enough to get the pebbles and sandy stone out of my armor.

I shift the leather jerkin protecting my chest and upper body. My leg plates will have to wait, leaving me stuck with a rock jabbing my thigh. They're adorned with the vines of the Elves that forged them, but I had them add small daggers and poison vials hanging off the vines. The plates match my bracers and some of the plate inlay of my chest piece. I look down and notice the heads of my vials peeking over the top of my belt, winking in the light. Might have to rethink their position or add a fabric cover before my next job. Their luster is just as likely to get me noticed as the poison is to help me in a bind.

I turn and grab hold of a notch in the wall, shimmying up the side of the tavern and swinging over the side of the red-tiled roof.

I choose my steps cautiously; too much noise and too much movement will cause my grasp on the Grit inside me to slip. Without that, I might as well be a figurehead at the bow of a ship, just waiting on the Locks to use their damned Demon Fate Threads to yank me to them.

Out of sheer habit, my palms find the handful of sheaths at my thighs and hips. Daggers are still accounted for, and that doesn't include the ones sewn into my chest armor.

Looking down, the billowing purple robes of the Locks snap angrily behind them as they storm away from the dirty corner I had just occupied. The taller of the two wears a gold medallion around his neck—a pledge to Vaeroth or the king, no doubt. He swipes a thick thumb over the metal, making dense, purple and black smoke ripple at his heels.

Not good. The swirling smoke clears enough for me to see the portal to the Void. The Warlock used a Demon Fate Thread to open it, summoning a void demon. Those things are like bloodhounds. If it catches the scent of my magic, it'll be game over.

"Find her, Ifan. Find that blasted Rogue," the Lock demands to his new charge. *So testy.* Even knowing its soul has been judged by Vaeroth and found lacking, I still feel bad for it being saddled with serving that *delightful* Human down there. "She knows where the Shardblade hilt is."

I can see the spittle flying from his lips toward the other Lock even as I perch above them on the rooftop. Disgust has me scrunching my lips and nose up. *Control yourself, Lock. You're supposed to be better than losing your temper over 'little shadows.'*

"Either she'll lead us to the hilt, or we'll take her to meet Vaeroth. Escape isn't an option," Ifan growls, flicking his wrist and summoning a void demon of his own. A shiver dances down my spine. Because I don't have what they want. I got rid of that thing as soon as I could.

The sinew and shadow making up the void demons' amalgamated form writhes and undulates as it shifts and shudders into this plane. Its skin, a deep, rippling black, doesn't just absorb the light—it consumes it. Only the faint glow of its piercing violet eyes betrays its presence within our realm. Not just a shadow, but a void where light simply cannot exist. The temptation to prod at their shadows with my own beckons me, but I pull my Grit closer to me, reining in the writhing tendrils.

Standing taller than any mortal, its elongated limbs end in razor-sharp claws capable of rending steel. It smells of stale decay and the air just after a lightning strike; the scent eclipses that of the fresh bread from the tavern below. Void demons are built for pursuit, their movements unnervingly fluid as they leave their master behind. From prior experience, I know they can cover obscene amounts of terrain with unnatural speed. But the fact that they can rebuild their bodies faster than I can even summon a nugget of my own Grit has me shrinking away from the edge of the roof.

Time to go.

That particular job will haunt me for the rest of my life. I shove it from my mind with no desire to revisit those demons that still live within my soul. My cloak swirls around me, as I finally turn my back to the two Locks still weaving their Threads down alleys, searching for me. Their murky grey and vibrant indigo lengths snap and stretch like predatory tongues, probing every shadow for my shape.

I'm not in any hurry to stick around and tempt fate, so I slowly skulk back away from the ledge, away from the horrific demons below. It doesn't matter how many times I've seen them; they still leave me quaking, whether from magic all their own or just the simple knowledge that they are a formidable threat.

I hop from rooftop to rooftop, the Spire looming over me in the distance. Fortunately, it casts enough shadow throughout the Trade District that the darkness naturally clings to me, allowing me to release the hold on my magical well.

Finally, I let loose a smirk, just like the one I unfurled the day I stowed away on a ship to cross the Ebyssian Sea. The Locks command the demons within the Void, so they might think they hold the power of the shadows. But these shadows? These belong to me.

The clamor from the weekly market drifts up to me. It's been an age since I've been in Arethor for a market. I've never had the pleasure of attending the first market of the season before either. The pink flower blooms decorate stalls and shop doors. Laughter dances across the breeze as children of all races run through the market, dipping below stalls and weaving through patrons while playing a ruthless game of tag. The smells from the food carts have me cursing the hard bread and cured meat I've survived on for Gods know how many years.

First market day comes with a celebration. The informal celebration of the vendors and the citizens acknowledges that days of prosper are on the horizon, followed by the celebration of the royals.

King Wilder will feast tonight. He and the rest of the pure races—Humans, Night Elves, Wood Elves, and Orcs.

The halves like me aren't welcome there unless we serve the king. However, that is a door I have no wish to open. I serve no one. As if the thought triggered the spell, my Rogue's Guild mark along the back of my neck burns. *Yes, yes, Lazrik. I haven't forgotten. I serve the guild.* Damned bastard made sure none of us would forget our place, gifting us Shadowbrands to mark our status in the Guild.

Truly, I have no idea if Lazrik can actually hear my thoughts through the brand, but I like to think he can. No one from the guild has ever gotten a straight answer from the master about what the brand fully does. What we do know is it allows us to track each other when Lazrik allows it, though he can always sense where we are. It burns occasionally, and my thought is that happens when old man Laz notices we've strayed from our mission, or he isn't quite pleased with our current objective.

The Guild doesn't force us to work solely for its purpose. As long as we report for the annual gathering of the Underbelly and pick up the occasional contract, we're allowed a bit of freedom to follow our own paths, which I'm currently taking advantage of. Though, this particular mission has been sanctioned by Laz, he'd hinted as though it shouldn't be official Guild business.

Laughter snags my attention, and I pause my steps before vaulting to the next building so I can peer down at the street below. A group of

Berserkers stride down the street, goods in hand. Not as bad as Locks, but when they are employed by the King? They're a bunch of blowhards.

Jealousy licks up my skin though, looking at their purchases. One holds a pastry dipped in chocolate. White, powdery sugar dusts the chest plate he wears. Another shovels a hearty stew into his mouth, gripping a loaf of bread underneath the bowl he carries. The second Berserker's long ears extend elegantly through his purple hair tied up in a top knot. His Night Elf markings bunch on his cheeks as he throws his head back in laughter at something the third Berserker said.

I let my eyes finally rove over the third member of the group. He's tall—taller than his companions. His silver hair is shaved on the sides, with strands flitting in the wind over his forehead. His cheekbones cut such a fine line, I could use them to sharpen my blades. One side of his full lips quirks up as he watches his compatriot's unbridled mirth. It isn't enough to cause his Night Elf markings to round the way the other Berserker's do, though. This elf's markings are intriguing: two distinct marks, each starting at his hairline and casting downward, one side through his brow and the other dipping around his eyes. They end in sharp points next to the corners of his mouth. Similar and yet singular in their swirls and whorls.

I bring my fingertips to my brow, feeling my own elvish marking. It's not nearly as pronounced as the Berserkers', each of them bearing the full facial markings of a pure Night Elf. My status as a half only affords me the small band of vines and whorls across my brow. My ears are too long to hide under my hair, much like my marking, and don't allow me to pass as a pure Human. But my ears are too short to be a pure Night Elf, and my marking too small.

My Shadowbrand burns at my nape once again. *Nythraxis, how did the nosiest bastard become the Master?* A smug little smile teases my lips at my invocation of the Veiled One's name. Lazrik fears if we use our God's name in vain too many times, he'll cut off a Rogue's access to their Grit. I think Nythraxis likes having his name invoked since he's forgotten by all except those that walk in the darkness.

I shake my head to clear it of the fixation on the Night Elf's face, my braid swinging and the metal spiked strap woven in hissing against my armor. I like my hair, but I refuse to let it be a weapon against me. I focus back on the group of Berserkers, trying to glean any information about them. Assigned to the wall? The keep? Possibly the Spire?

I creep closer to the edge of the roof line, dismissing my Grit's urge to slip back into the darkness. No one thinks to look up, so I can leer at the Berserkers in peace from my perch. My new vantage point allows me a closer look at the armor of the guards as they stroll my way.

Light glints on the tallest Berserker's armor, drawing my gaze to the crest on his breastplate—he's a captain.

The captain also bears the insignia of the Spire upon his pauldron. I eye the other two guards' shoulder plates. One, the pure Human's, shows a keep assignment emblem, and the second Night Elf's breastplate matches the captain's Spire assignment. Are they instructors? Curiosity has me leaning well past the edge of the roof to snatch up any more information I can about these guards.

Suddenly, a heavy *thunk* sounds followed by the tinkling noise of shattering tile. The golden pool of Grit bursts out of my chest, encasing me in darkness. The magical reaction happens in a heartbeat, but it's a heartbeat too late. My eyes collide with the captain's gaze below me, his glacial irises hard, and his smirk flattens into a hard line.

Despite being wrapped in the familiar cocoon of shadows, I feel no comfort. Only a sickening feeling in my gut, the hairs around my Shadowbrand standing on end, as the brand itself burns. Someone can see me.

My eyes flick rapidly through the market. The Locks must have found the traces my Grit left behind. As my eyes dance between the people milling about the market with baskets of produce on their arms, I don't find either of the Locks or their demon spawn anywhere nearby. Just townsfolk, not a care in the world marring their faces.

My brows draw down. *So who is watching me?* Finally, my eyes land on the captain again. Though his focus is back on his comrades, I feel a distinct tendril of Grit circling me. A sea-touched Grit unique to this Berserker.

That one is dangerous. The dagger tattooed on his ear and the hard lines of his face belie his power. Not to mention his two-handed, gleaming, rune-covered battle axe. I finally let my feet carry me through the shadows to the Spire without a backward glance.

CHAPTER 2

THE GLEAMING ONYX SPIRE looms over me, its Gothic architecture like creeping fingers reaching upward to block out the sky. I suppose I should be grateful since it offers me the ability to slink back into the shadows, but I do appreciate a clear sky every now and again. Unfortunately, the Spire ensures no one gets to enjoy an afternoon basking in the sunlight on a grassy knoll.

The image of the three Berserkers from the Trade District lounging on a blanket and sharing fruit off a vine pops into my head, causing a snort to escape my carefully constructed facade of indifference.

A Mage traipsing down the cobbled lane next to me casts a wary gaze my way. He pushes the blond, nearly white, hair from his forehead; clean face, round ears, and shorter than me. Human. He must be a Pure.

"Don't Rogues go to their own academy?" The question itself is innocuous enough, but I don't miss the underlying message: You don't belong here. Wide, copper-brown eyes meet the muddy-green of my own. "I mean, not that you aren't welcome. I'm sure you'd be an asset to the Guard." The Mage tears his eyes from mine and braves a glance over my armor.

Delight curls in my belly watching him take stock of how many daggers line my person—at least the ones he can see. The supple leather shifts and molds itself to me, and with how much I forked over for the pretty pieces of armor, I have to hold back my inner peacock wanting to preen under the Mage's horrified stare.

"In the Underbelly, yes," I say, and the words hang in the air between us. "Can't a Rogue serve the realm, or the king, or whatever?" The man shrugs and falls into step beside me, as though we're longtime friends making the historic trek to the Spire together. It's apparently a rite of passage for all the magic denominations besides Druids and Rogues. The Druids tend to stay within their Groves, tending the Verdant Flames and learning to control their forms before they are allowed into the world. Either that, or they choose to remain in the Grove as a protector of the Moon Pools, known for their healing powers.

Every other harvest, just after the turn to the fall season, the king's messengers push their steeds, be them riding rams, jungle cats, frost wolves, or horses, to the brink of exhaustion to cry out his royal decree: All of noble birth, those with their magic in their blood who can be spared, and those that hadn't been chosen as a child of the gods were to report to Arethor to serve the king. Citizens must report to either Ashford Keep or the Spire.

I question the legitimacy of the requirements. Who decides what professions can and cannot be spared?

I never understood the excitement about hiking to the academy for the first year of training, but I'd been a member of the Underbelly for far longer than most of these young bucks had been dreaming of the academy.

Like Locks and Berserkers, Rogues are dangerous when left to their own devices. We're shipped into the Underbelly of Arethor after our tenth winter. The Spire requires a minimum of twenty winters before they'll admit a magic user.

Grunts though? Ashford Keep will take the non-magic members of the guard after their fifteenth winter. Children—literal children—selling their souls for enough grain to feed their family. Risking their family lines being wiped from the history books should they fail.

I assess the Mage beside me, curious if he has just hit his twentieth winter and is eager to enter the guard. Or perhaps he's staved off his service in favor of other exploits. He teeters along, loaded down with a pack that's nearly a big as he is. His deep-blue Mage robes mark him as a Frost Mage, and boast an opening to the front revealing his chocolate brown breeches and sturdy boots.

At least he had the forethought to trade the typical Mage cloth slippers for boots before coming here.

He extends his right arm, seemingly for me to grip his forearm in a show of welcome and camaraderie. "Aster Hoarfrond of Alleria."

Without acknowledging the limb stretching toward me, I continue down the cobblestone road. "Did you think you wouldn't be allowed access to books while in the Spire, Aster Hoarfrond of Alleria?"

A cheeky smile lights up his face, transforming it from a meek, boyish expression to a sly, fox-like grin. "I was an Arcanist Archivist before this. Some of these are my own research, but others are ancient tomes of spells that might help me. At least I can go back to my research if I fail out."

I blink. Back to his research? He'd never receive credit for any of his findings. If he fails the testing and trials, all traces of him and his entire family would be removed from the history of Arethor. I shake my head—not my issue to worry about.

"Arcanist Archivist, say that ten times fast," I mutter to myself. A chuckle bursts out of my unwanted companion. I'm loath to admit the barnacle I've found will likely be a hot commodity if he's able to make use of all the information he's got stored away.

"Trust me, we've tried. Particularly when we were under the effects of too many flagons of ale."

Surprise washes over me like a bucket of ice water. "Who knew you stuffy Mages knew how to have fun?" I give in to the urge to elbow the poor kid. The force of my jab sends him careening sideways under the weight of the tomes filling his pack, and I yank him back by his collar before he can take out the beefy Berserker walking next to us.

"Aster, I thought Mages were meant to be ranged fighters. You're like a newborn calf on your feet." I mean for the words to be snarky, but my acidic tone is lacking, leaving only a friendly jibe in its wake.

"Oh, we'll do hand-to-hand in the Spire, but it's a last resort in case things have gone sideways or we run out of Mana." Aster pushes his long, thin fingers through his wild, platinum hair.

Right. Mages had Mana. I'd learned that early in the Underbelly—what power belonged to whom, and what it could cost you if you weren't careful. Mana fed the Mages, Clerics, and Druids. Grit fueled Berserkers, Paladins, and Rogues. Warlocks played a darker game, their Demon

Fate Threads tethered to life itself. Berserkers danced on the edge of Bloodlust—that was another tale altogether. But whatever your magic, let it run empty, and the fight's already lost. Regardless of the source, running out of reserves is an unacceptable outcome for any fight.

Grit and Mana could be treated like a muscle; the more you trained, the stronger and more stamina you had. But there is an inherent level of aptitude, just like with someone's musculature. Some beings are just naturally stronger or have more endurance, just like some Mana and Grit users are more powerful or can wield for longer.

It's on the tip of my tongue to offer combat training—I wouldn't even hesitate if he were a younger Rogue. But that's not why I'm here. Friends were not part of the equation I plotted out with Laz. A churning begins to simmer in my gut...Is this guilt? No, no. I don't do guilt. I stuff the foreign feeling down beneath a mental trapdoor to examine at a later date—a much later date.

The massive portcullis of the academy inches ever closer, giving a glimpse into the bailey when momentary gaps in the influx of new sacrifices—I mean, trainees—allows it. There's a small table just beyond the gate; a Human Arcane Mage sits in a wooden chair behind it, motioning one hand to control a quill flitting over a long scroll of parchment. She's recording all the names of the people who are somehow convinced that King Wilder is an honorable royal to serve.

It takes considerable effort to keep my face from contorting in disdain for the king whose sole focus is on some mythical spell that will allow him to gain the power of each of the deities. Our Paladin king has strayed from the Light. Thalos, the Iron Sentinel, is probably in his fiery palace in the sky cringing, watching this fool deviate from the Path.

A thin, raven-haired Warlock steps up, garbed in black robes with purple embroidery. Green flames lick upward behind him. I cast my eyes down and see the bony, three-foot-tall creature lurking behind him: an imp. The thing looks like someone desiccated a body, shrunk it to a third of the height, gave it a beakish nose, then set the whole thing on fire. Horrific little things, but they do pack a punch. I absently rub a spot over my kidney where I'd been hit with an imp's firebolt years before. Blasted Locks and their demons.

The Mage flicks her hand to jot down his name, barely giving him an ounce of her attention, as if all of these aspirants are beneath her. Her thick, cornsilk hair is twisted in some fancy braid at the nape of her neck. Instead of being swallowed in the traditional robes of her denomination, she's clad in a white tunic with a neckline that dips low enough for my far-from-virgin eyes feel scandalized while in the polite company of my poor companion. Plus, the corset cinching her waist and pushing up her ample chest is far from standard issue. Tight, mossy-green leggings round out the outfit.

"Since when did the king allow tavern girls to moonlight as Mages?" I murmur quietly to Aster. Sparing him a glance, I realize he's been gaping at the sheer number of other people filing toward the Spire. But the look that overtakes his features as he beholds the female Mage is one I won't soon forget. His lips part immediately with an audible, sharp intake of breath. His pale northern skin adopts the same pinkish hue as the sky before sunset, slowly creeping across his cheeks in the same slow manner as the sun dipping below the horizon. If his eyes get any wider, I might wonder if he managed to retract his lids back into his skull.

"I don't think we're meant to wear anything like that while in service to the king." Aster's voice climbs several octaves, his hand around the Arcanist's Eye pin at his throat. The way he's holding his cloak together makes him look like a duchess clutching her pearls.

"I'm not sure she cares what she's *meant* to wear, archivist," I tell him, a wry twist taking over my lips. The Warlock and his imp have long since climbed the stairs to the left of the table, entering the Spire itself. Only a handful of aspirants separate Aster and me from the table.

As I look to the second gatekeeper, my heart begins to pound out an erratic rhythm. An elf stands next to the table, assessing each aspirant, arms crossed across his breastplate, and the tip of an axe peeking peeks over his shoulder. As if his gleaming silvery hair didn't give away his identity, his distinct markings all but hit the last nail in that coffin that it's the same Night Elf captain I'd seen in the market.

While I don't think he knew that the Locks were hunting me during our *moment* in the Trade District, I can't be certain he didn't run into one of them between then and now. If they did, I'm sure there's a wagon and a set of riding rams ready to take me to the Dread Flats.

His icy glare finds mine over the shoulder of the Berserker ahead of Aster and me—the same Berserker Aster almost fell into when I'd elbowed him.

The scandalous Mage records the Berserker's name and sends him on his way, leaving the path open for Aster and me to step forward. My feet feel as though they're stuck in molasses solidified from the winter's chill.

"A Rogue and a Mage, how...quaint." Her words drip with more venom than I have concealed in my belt. The urge to fling a knife into the table between the awful woman's fingers zips along my limbs like one of Zorvyn's lightning storms.

"Better than a Berserker and a Mage. How common," I practically coo, scrunching my nose and forcing a dreamy smile. Aster chokes and sputters. I reach out and smack his back for good measure. After regaining his composure, Aster provides his name to the woman, but her hand never moves to guide the quill.

"We'll get to you in a minute. There are plenty of dithering Mages desiring to test into the Guard." She fixes me with an icy stare, the chill causing me to second-guess the Arcane symbol hanging at her throat. "*You*, however, are not a dithering Mage."

"I'm not." It's a simple reply. No response was necessary, but I will not be offering up any unnecessary information.

"I can only imagine you think entering the King's Guard will protect you. Who is it you're hiding from?"

"A great many people, probably." Though I know I should be cooperative and bland so no one takes note of me, I'm unable to fight the blasé tone and seemingly innocent head tilt.

My braid shifts across my back, and I know the second the tips of my ears become visible. The frosty Arcane Mage's demeanor shifts from mildly annoyed to blatant disgust. "Ew. A half."

"I'd think that was obvious from the markings, but if you're a bit slow on the uptake, the fault lies with you." I've had decades to learn how to deal with the overall nastiness shown toward halves. Unfortunately, people treat half-Human, half-Night Elves worse than any Orc half. Though, few Night Elves would be caught intermingling with Orcs outside of forced alliances and the most tenuous of friendships.

"Enough, Luella," the captain finally interjects. His voice booms like the sea rumbling over a rocky outcropping, with hints of thunder rolling in the distance. "Take the damn Rogue's name and be done with it." Luella rears back like the Night Elf struck her. My eyes narrow, flicking between the two. Are they *something?* What a stuffy pair they'd make.

"Kiralin Thorne, Blade Master and Poison Weaver of the Underbelly," I say. My eyes focus solely on the Berserker in front of me, the Mage still too busy huffing over the Captain's dismissal to notice our intense stares.

The same sea-breeze Grit from before licks up my legs, tugging at daggers and probing my armor. The smoky tendrils of my own Grit pour down from the magical well inside of me. They tangle with the Captain's in an effort to push the unwanted touches away.

Luella chirps something at Aster, who responds with some sort of placating remark. Neither of them are aware of the invisible battle occurring just feet from them. Only the most practiced in manipulating their surroundings with their Grit or Mana can sense the tendrils of other's magic when they are not fully channeling. From that small group of magic users, even fewer can interact with another's Grit or Mana.

The Captain poses more danger than I had originally thought. However, the breezy tendrils don't feel aggressive; they're almost *playful* as they loop and poke at my own. With great effort, I loop a tendril around the entirety of foreign magic and thrust it back to its master.

"I believe there's someone looking for you, Thorne," he murmurs as his Grit pools back. He obviously knows the Locks were after me. Why hasn't outed me yet?

"I suppose that's their problem if they haven't found me yet, Captain," I say, raising my chin in defiance.

A smirk barely tugs at the corner of his lips. "I suppose it is."

CHAPTER 3

THE SPIRE TYPICALLY SEPARATES the dorm rooms by magical denominations. The Berserkers together, the Paladins in another wing, the Mages closest to the library, the Clerics near the infirmary, and the Warlocks in the basement to cast whatever demonic rituals they do before bed.

No need to designate blocks for Druids and Rogues I suppose, since we rarely find ourselves as students of the Spire. It isn't forbidden for us to join, but neither denomination is common in the King's Guard, especially with our tendencies to find employment outside of the governing body of Eldrath.

Druids are not common outside of their Verdant Groves in general. Few even elect to seek homes outside of the elven cities that surround the Groves. They're also the only denomination that is not found outside the elven races, leaving them a mystery to all but Pure elves. Only in the rarest of cases has a half ever been revealed as a Druid.

Rogues aren't elite so much as we're *whatevers*. We just serve the guild. We're more likely to steal from the king than to serve him.

Wait, I stole from the king and now I'm going to serve him. *Nythraxis, did I just make a pun?*

Living in the Mage Quarter and sharing a room with Aster is going to ruin me. After our delightful encounter with the Arcane ice queen, they'd shuffled us through the bailey to another table where they'd unceremoniously dumped a sword and some crappy armor in Aster's arms. The attendant looked me over and grunted to follow the "walking library" to his rooms. Dutifully, I trudged after Aster toward the Mage Quarter.

"So, you're on the run?" I'd been waiting for him to make a comment. The entire walk through the tower I'd seen the questions trying to burst free from him. I'm more than a little shocked he's managed to hold himself at bay until now.

My new roommate sits on the small bed opposite mine. The room itself barely big enough to fit both of our beds shoved to the walls, two wardrobes, and a desk for each of us. The space between the beds is hardly large enough for either of us to stand, leaving Aster's knees nearly touching the edge of my bed as he perches on his mattress awaiting my answer.

"Does the upper echelon want us to snuggle while we sleep? Reach out and hold hands? I've seen closets bigger than these rooms."

The Frost Mage gives me a look, clearly indicating he noticed I didn't answer his question.

"Did you see all those closets while you were breaking into houses?"

I give Aster the blandest look I can muster. "That's usually where I put the bodies of the idiots that asked too many questions."

A sick thrill ripples through me when Aster blanches. "I'm only partially kidding."

His jaw snaps shut with an audible *click*, and he turns to yank open the top of his rucksack. He pulls out book after book, and I'm only able to understand half of the runes on the covers. Arguably, I know that he's just as equipped to kill me as anyone else I've encountered. But at the same time, Aster doesn't seem like the type to ever take the killing blow.

He's wasted as a King's Guard; his skills would be put to better use in the archives and researching. Though, Nythraxis knows what it is they research.

"Were you planning on wearing the same clothing until we're issued uniforms? Did you bring anything from home? Wait, do Rogues have homes or do you all live in the Underbelly?" The questions shoot my direction as if I'm in front of a firing squad.

"First of all, no, we do not all live in the Underbelly, but those of us that do are rarely home enough that it only makes sense to keep rooms there. Second of all," I pause, waving my wrist through the air, "I brought enough to get me by. I will not be wearing those awful things they call uniforms."

I reach into the pocket of shadow where I've kept my rucksack and tug it back into the light. I deposit it onto the bed, releasing the thin thread of Grit I've been holding onto all day to create the pocket.

The Frost Mage abandons his task of organizing his library inside the wardrobe—the sheer number of books consumes nearly all the space meant for his robes and weapons—and approaches me with a look of curiosity painted across his features.

"Fascinating!" He spares me a glance but reaches for my pack and waves his hands around the space where my shadow pocket had been. A chill overtakes the air, his Mana probing about. "Where does it go? How did you manage to create a portal as a Rogue?"

Oh, Crimson Scales, I've unlocked a monster. "I'm not an Arcane Mage; you should know I can't create portals." Aster's brows draw down into a harsh V, whether in thought or annoyance or maybe both, I'm not sure. "*But.* I can create a pouch, if you will, out of shadows. And with just enough Grit, I can then link that shadow to me for as long as I have enough reserve to hold it."

"Do it again," he commands.

It's as easy as breathing since I've done this so many times. Without a thought, the Grit that's already there surges up, meeting my request before my brain has even processed it. In that same moment, Aster lunges forward and plunges his arm into the shadow pocket.

"What the fuck!?" The shout makes the Mage jump, but he doesn't withdraw his arm from the shadowy space. I peer into his gleaming amber eyes, but he is wholly focused on the space where his forearm should be.

The same chilly sensation of his Mana twirls around the thread of Grit holding the pocket.

"Amazing...It's almost as if I can feel the magic creating the pocket, and yet it's just a ghost of a sensation. Like a thought just out of reach." He pores over the space where his arm disappears, and he must wiggle his fingers because they become visible, though they remain mostly transparent.

"The faster you move in the shadows or the louder you are, the more quickly the shadows unravel from around you. Or it takes more Grit than it's worth to stay concealed. It's why Rogues still have to have some decorum and training. If we were all a bunch of bumbling buffoons, we'd exhaust our Grit before our objective was ever complete. That, or we'd appear in the middle of a vault and have to kill someone instead of just slipping away," I explain when he looks at me.

Aster removes his hand from the pocket and thumbs his lower lip. "I wonder if Mages could create some sort of pocket this way or perhaps Berserkers and Paladins could use this trick to store things, like weapons?" His soft words soft have a meandering sense to them as he turns from me to pace the three strides to the door and back.

"Aster," I call. "You Mages can create actual portals to storage realms, so a pocket isn't quite useful, is it?" His face alights with a delight I'm discovering relates to all things magic and learning.

I release the Grit creating the pocket and begin the process of laying all my daggers onto the bed for sharpening, leaving only one that remains hidden down the spine of my leather jerkin on my person—a gift from Laz, though I can hardly remember what for. I rarely part from the inscribed blade and its beautiful hilt.

I smile at the small act of kindness from my mentor and pull the whetstone from my pack to sharpen the blades, even though they likely don't need it. Then I reapply the poison on two I'd used after leaving the ship I'd stowed away on. Fucking demons. When Aster's mouth opens to regale me with more of his working thoughts, a pounding knock at the door stops him.

While he steps to the door, my hands itch to slip my other knives back into their sheaths at my thighs.

Instead, I take a feigned casual stance, leaning back on the bed and dragging my blade along the whetstone simply for something to do. Before Aster even greets the visitor, I'm reaching for my Grit, resisting the call to disappear into thin air. Heavy boot steps pound as the hulking Night Elf from the bailey barges into the already-cramped room.

Something foreign curls in my stomach. My heart races, and moisture collects on my palms. Trapped. I've backed myself into a corner, and I didn't take the time to look out the window to see if that is a viable egress.

The choice rips from my hands when the unmistakable pressure of thousands of feet of oceanic depths presses against me. Invisible and yet immovable. I let my Grit slip through my control, coiling back into the well.

I try to thrash against the bonds, but it's no use. My inability to move and being at the mercy of the Captain overwhelms me, and I can't help the growl that rumbles in my chest.

"Breaking and entering as well as holding a cadet hostage, Captain?" I spit, fire lacing the words.

"Kiralin Thorne, Blade Master and Poison Weaver of the Underbelly," the captain purrs, ignoring my comment entirely. "And elder sister of Lachlan Thorne." The final words hang in the air. The abyss of grief in my chest tears open, threatening to suck me in.

He knows Lach? There isn't much I can do to get myself out of this situation without blowing my plan out of the water. I still need a way into the Spire. But Gods, how can I find out what this elf knows about my brother? There was someone inside the Spire that he trusted, someone he was working with, but I'd bet my hoard of coin it wasn't this pompous captain.

So, I try for bluster.

"I'd recite your own title back to you, but I don't know it. Funny though—you seem awful eager to remember mine."

The Berserker prowls forward with all the grace of a jungle cat, a quality afforded to pure Night Elves. He slips into my space, filling my vision while his invisible ocean holds me against my pitiful bed. The elf's previously smug smirk curdles into something twisted.

Is he disgusted by my insubordination? He had to know someone from the Guild wasn't going to simply fall into their rank of cadet like a baker trying a new recipe. Or is it the thought of Luella in bed? In either case, I pop that information into the back of my mind to use as fodder to push his buttons later.

"Captain Ironhart, to what do we owe the pleasure?" Once again, I'm reminded that Aster is not meant for the Guard. A diplomatic role would be just as easy for him to slide into as returning to the archives.

"We do not owe any pleasure to him," I bite out.

Ironhart leans over me, crowding my space further, filling my nose with the scent of leather and salty brine. A smirk slides back over his face.

"I'm only here to question a new cadet on their intentions. It's not everyday a Rogue joins our ranks, especially one whose brother died last year in a training accident while in the service of the Guard." The words are so casual, even as he drives a proverbial knife into my chest and twists.

I'm caught somewhere between an agonizing misery that threatens to break the dam holding back emotions I've buried, and the blazing rage tempting me to release my Grit to unleash hell on the dickhead elf in front of me.

"What the fuck do you know about Lachlan," I spit. His ocean-tinged Grit squeezes me in response, a reminder that I have no power in this moment or in the Spire. As a captain, he could easily turn me in to the

Locks or just outright murder me and say it was swift punishment for treason.

I have no doubt that the "training exercise" that killed Lachlan is a cover up; but a cover up for what? My brother might have been a Mage, but he was raised in the Underbelly like a Rogue. Combining that kind of magic with a Rogue's inability to let secrets lie can be a dangerous concoction.

Quite a concoction our parents created. Ma was a Mage, and Da is a Rogue. An outlaw Rogue at that. Da prefers explosions set to detonate at a precise time while he lingers in the shadows, avoiding poisons and blades like the rest of us *normal* Rogues.

The Night Elf shifts on his feet, drawing my attention back to him. "A few things. He's not my concern anymore though. *You* are." If I didn't know better, I'd think this elf is actually a Druid from the way he purrs and growls. "You might as well get out now. I could easily have you wiped you from the records…Well, I'm sure your tome-toting friend here could do it with some incentive."

If I was just here for a simple job, I'd certainly bail and go find someone else willing to pay for my skills. That's the thing about Rogues: We might always be on the lookout for a bag of coin, but at least we're upfront about it.

But the Guard? They hide behind noble bullshit and propaganda. I suppose that happens when you have a king that blatantly shuns half his population in favor of his precious Pures. I'm perfectly content being a hybrid. The vigor, lifespan, grace, and agility of an elf, but the hardiness of a Human and the ability to socialize. Elves can't socialize worth a shit unless it's with another elf.

If only that hybrid vigor could have helped Lachlan. Alas, he's probably in an unnamed grave somewhere.

The tendrils of his sea Grit slip just enough that I'm able to weasel my shadow-tinged magic between the spaces. Neat thing about shadows: they consume things they touch. With a sudden burst, I push outward with my Grit. All at once, I'm released from my confines.

Jutting my chin up, I face Ironhart. But where I expect to be met with shock, I'm confronted with an assessing smirk. Is this a damn test? What is he looking for? Mentally, I chart through all our interactions, but then I realize I have to go beyond the meeting at the gate. I have to think about what he could have discovered while I was peering over the roof at him the other night.

He's a captain, one that has access to friends in the keep and the wall—plus, there's the whole issue of Locks hunting me.

"Using the Spire to hide out from the Locks?" he asks. "I'll admit, hiding in plain sight is a novel idea. But if they find you, do you really think they'll leave you be simply because you're indebted to the Guard?" His carefully fashioned drawl is too intentional to be considered causal. All the same, it's hard to miss the distinct coastal accent peeking through his regimented tone.

A true Sea Berserker. So few of them remain in this realm, many lost to the more intense Bloodlust and Battle Rage Sea Berserkers face. They have a closer-knit bond with their God, Zorvyn. If he's one of them—fuck, he must be a couple centuries old. *Gross.*

His breath ghosts against my face as he leans in further. "This place is like a trap, and a little fox like you might think they have the upper hand. But you'll be caught all the same, chewed up, and spit out. Just like Lachlan."

Red eclipses my vision, and for all my supposed paragon of subtlety, I throw it out the window in favor of brute strength and anger. Driving forward, I fist the collar of his shirt and spin him around, pinning him to the wall as I free a dagger still tucked into the back of my leathers. Flipping the grip, I swing the edge of the blade up in an arc to meet his neck, the one bit of skin peeking out from his armor.

My mind races at his words. Maybe it was this fucking Night Elf who drove the sword through Lachlan's heart, or slit his throat, or tossed him off a cliff. I don't even know how my brother died. Some of the rage bleeds out of me, sorrow filling the space it leaves behind. A strangled scream rends through the air, and belatedly I realize it's my own voice I hear.

It isn't until I feel Ironhart gripping my wrist that I realize all my chaotic emotions have rendered me motionless. In that moment, the only thing I see is the blade only a sliver away from its intended target.

"He wouldn't have wanted this for you," Ironhart murmurs. *Wait, what?* This has to be a new technique to get me to crack. Nythraxis, I *am* cracking. "You won't find the answers you want here."

I tear my gaze away from the glint of the blade's edge back to his glacial stare. Beneath the whorls of his Night Elf markings, pain brims in his eyes. A pain that mirrors my own.

"Who did you lose to the crown?" I ask gently.

"Lachlan." His words shock me. Oh, Nythraxis' bleeding shadows, I had almost killed my brother's mate! I had known my brother found his mate, but he'd never revealed who it was to me.

"I'm so sorry! If I'd known who you were...Lachlan would tan my hide for thinking you killed him. Disrespecting a mate bond like that. A more pious person would go beg forgiveness at a shrine." I realize my knife still hovers over Ironhart's neck and quickly step back, distancing myself from him.

I glance at Aster. "That's what I should do, right? For trying to kill my brother's mate?"

CHAPTER
4

"Y OUR BROTHER'S *WHAT!?*" ASTER's pale face is stricken, his wide eyes darting between me and the other half of my brother's soul. His hand finds its way back to the All Seeing Eye at his neck for comfort.

Before I'm able to respond, Ironheart's laughter snaps through my panic and pain. Head thrown back, jaw dropped, unabashedly belly laughs.

He's...laughing? "How can you possibly be amused by this?" I bite the question out.

"Sails, I loved Lach, but certainly not like that. Caverns not twigs, and all," he chuckles, and has the audacity to wink at me. "Adrian, your brother's mate, is a Wood Elf—a Wood Elf *Druid*. He's been gone for a long while. He didn't quite take Lach's death well, as you can imagine." Ironhart scrubs a hand over his jaw, the calluses on his palms rasping against the stubble barely visible on his jawline. His expression sobers. "All the same, he wouldn't have wanted you to risk yourself here."

The words slice through any goodwill I may have suddenly found for the captain. "Don't you dare tell me what you think he would have wanted, Ironhart."

"I'm daring to tell you what *I know* he wanted because the blasted fool made me promise to Zorvyn I wouldn't let you go gallivanting through here like a Rogue in shining armor taking up his mantle." All traces of humor fade. He grits his jaw between syllables, as though each word takes an effort to get out. His lips curl back to bare his teeth with every syllable, the elongated canines peeking through. If I'd forgotten how primal and damn near feral the Night Elves could be, this was a stark reminder. "You need to leave, Kiralin."

His show of dominance with his teeth bared and hulking posture triggers my own instinct to submit, but I remain standing at my full height, forcing myself not to show my pitiful fangs. I refuse to give into those instincts.

"You don't know this brand of Lock. They don't just kill you, they *erase* you," he grinds out.

Aster appears in my peripheral, clearly having no knowledge of feral elves and their prey. He leans in, clearly curious about the newest bit of information. His earlier pallor all but gone. "I'm sorry, did you say erase? As in the memory of, or the body? How erased are we talking?"

Ironhart snarls at Aster, who jumps back, stumbling into the edge of his bed and landing in a haphazard heap atop it.

I turn and tell Aster, "Best not to approach elves from behind when they've got their fangs bared. Specifically Night Elves. Might as well spook a wild animal ready to tear into something."

Red creeps up Aster's neck, his ears highlighting themselves in pink as he waggles his head in a vigorous nod. "The elves in the Archives were all much more..."

"Refined?" I offer. Returning my focus to Ironhart, it's clear he's regained his senses. I've always found if I'm not maiming, injuring, or disposing of an elf, ignoring their temper-tantrums is the best tactic. Da always had issues with his little elf fits if anyone came after Ma, or when Lach and I did something he didn't particularly agree with. I'm sure Ironhart's issue falls under the latter, and as captain, he's accustomed to everyone falling into line.

That may pose a problem for me.

"Sit," the elf growls, the hard edges of his primal instincts linger in the words even after regaining his senses. If the first command doesn't work, sure just give another one. Despite the command chafing me, I follow the order. Ignoring too many of his commands runs the risk of escalating him to a Lunar Frenzy, where he would lose any semblance of humanity and control over his actions. His primal instinct, combined with his Berserker nature, would push him to revert to all animalistic thought processes. At that point, he'd basically be a rampant murderous creature of the night.

"Captain—"

"Matthias. You're Lachlan's sister, you will call me by my given name." His statement carries every bit of ferocity as his body just did a moment ago, but the tension wanes like the Lunar goddess is releasing her hold upon him.

"Matthias, let it go," I start again. "I'm not going to leave, but I am willing to listen to any orders you may give while I'm here…Within reason." I want to keep my tone gentle, but I cannot give in to the order he just gave me. I don't care if he promised Lach he'd force me out of the Spire. My brother was here for a reason; I need to know why. What was so important he was killed—erased—over.

More of the rigidity eases, but his fangs remain bared toward me, eyes flicking toward where Aster has arranged himself on his bed.

"Aster is from Alleria. Elves aren't common there, you know this." I learned with Da to try to jog his thinking, force his brain away from instinctual-driven paralysis.

Recognition slowly blooms behind the icy eyes. Finally, the last of the agitation in his form bleeds away completely.

"You'll follow orders?" he grinds out.

I hold up a finger to stop him. "Not quite what I said."

Matthias storms away from me with a heavy curse. "You're just as squirrelly as he said you'd be."

I shrug. "I am what I am." The captain stops and turns back, leveling me with a bored, unimpressed look that would give even Laz a run for his money. The guild master was previously the only one I'd seen accomplish the look while remaining somewhat intimidating. But with how old Matthias must be, he could have taught Laz the look.

Continuing, I lean against the wall. "I'll listen to whatever commands you dole out, and I will take them under advisement. I haven't needed a babysitter in all of my time with the Guild, so I doubt I'll need one now." Aster chokes and splutters, but Matthias continues to bore into me with that same intensity. Though no tendrils of Grit twine around me, I can still feel that same salty magic in the air. It's as though he simply oozes with the power, his emotions heightening the magical chaos of Zorvyn and his Waking Storm.

"If you don't get yourself killed, you'll be the death of me," Matthias says after giving me one last hard stare, slamming the door in his wake.

Not long after Ironhart left, a young page knocked timidly on our door, handing me a folded missive when he stuttered out my name. Barely over eleven most likely, no magic to speak of and headed for Ashford Keep when the time came.

"You're proving to be quite popular, aren't you?" Aster teases, poking his nose over my shoulder to read. "Commandant Megora requests you in his office?" His brows raise, and he strokes the eye medallion around his neck.

"Seems so. If they throw me out, leave the window unlocked for me, would you?" I grin at the Mage and slip out the door.

I stroll through the halls, wandering to the center of the Spire. I can only assume Captain Ironhart's superiors are just as pompous as he is, and would put their offices at the center of the place, or the top. The idea of climbing that many flights of stairs only to find out his office is on the first floor sounds worse than having to be here in general.

Luella, the surly Mage from the admissions table, lingers in the rotunda ahead of me, head bent together speaking with a Warlock. I stutter step and tuck myself closer to the wall. Is this why Megora called me into the office? Sending me to the dungeons already?

"We should have never changed the regulations around heritage for entry to the Guard. Halves could be sent to the infantry, magic or not," she scoffs. Heat boils in my belly. The words don't shock me, but they still tempt me to lodge a knife in the Mage's throat.

None of us chose to be halves, not that many of us would choose other parents. Halves are typically born to parents through a loving bond since our conceptions are much rarer.

The Lock hums in agreement and adds, "The disruptions in bloodlines do not make for Guards fit for power. Aldros has always been shocked the deities would ever favor those with sullied blood. Halves are not welcome within our ranks. The rest of the denominations would do well to weed out the rot."

I back away from the entry to the rotunda, creeping down the hallway at my left. Had Lach been killed for being a half? It'd been a long while since I'd witnessed *that* much hatred toward our kind.

Before I can sneak away, a robust voice stops me short. "Ah, Thorne, I'd just set out to look for you. Feels as though my page came back nearly an hour ago, I've been waiting so long." A tall, well-muscled Orc stands before me, bearing a set of long tusks from his lower jaw. Three gold rings adorn his left ear, marking three challengers he'd had to overcome when he requested his wife's hand.

Not a lick of armor in sight, only a finely embroidered shirt and pants that appear too tight for the bulging muscles of his thighs. Commandant, indeed.

He gestures for me to follow him through an open door, entering a room where the stone walls are covered by massive blueprints of the castle and keep, maps of the districts and cities as well as the continent, and various sketches of wanted persons.

Amused, I stroll toward the wall of wanted suspects, lips quirking higher with each individual I recognize.

"Looking for yourself?" he asks. I jump, realizing he's prowled up behind me. Glancing over my shoulder, I give him my best unassuming look. "You're not unknown to the Guard. That stack of papers contains all sixty-three warrants for your arrest. You thieves aren't nearly as slick as you think you are," Megora remarks drily.

The commandant gestures to the two chairs facing his desk while he settles into the plush arm chair on the other side. Paperwork litters the top of it, and my eyes flit from piece to piece, trying to glean anything of note. Easier said than done, especially when it appears the commandant's handwriting rivals that of most toddlers.

My fingers itch to set some of the papers in order. How can the man think in this disaster?

"Thorne." I bring my eyes back to his. "Don't go looking for trouble. Your brother's death is already a mark on our statistics. I wouldn't want to add another recruit death to those numbers." He levels me with a hard stare, lips frowning around the tusks protruding from his mouth. "Do you catch my drift?"

"Are you insinuating you'll kill me if I'm not the perfect Guard cadet?"

That frown tilts the opposite direction, leaving Megora with a grimacing smirk. "I'm insinuating that the Locks have a cell and torture table waiting for you in the king's dungeon, should you decide to play games. And once the Locks are through with you, the gallows awaits. It's up to you if you see your brother sooner rather than later."

CHAPTER 5

THE AIR WHIPS BY me, lifting the end of my braid and twining with the strands that have slipped free. Aster strides alongside me as we make our way across the sky bridge from the Mage Tower and library toward the central spire where morning formation will be. After today, once we've been fully enmeshed into the Spire, this is where we'll hand in any written work and where our physical training will occur.

The level of physical training relies solely on our weakest member as well as if any punishment is to be doled out, increasing our physical work for the day. Punish one, punish all.

It's the same methodology Laz uses in the guild. However, the intent of the Guard is to breed a sense of camaraderie. The intent of the guild is to create a sense of individuality among the group. The Rogue that causes the punishment is brought out to face horde. Every eye watching if they struggle or succeed, to see if they feel remorse about what they've caused. It's also a way to teach the new Rogues to blend in, to swim with the school, and to not draw attention to yourself. The best Rogue is one that slips below the notice of their marks and those around them.

I'm currently failing spectacularly at the last one. Aster is garbed in the distinct blue robes of the Frost Mages, the lower portion billowing around him as if he wears a cloak to reveal the gray breeches and sturdy boots beneath.

Shockingly, it isn't the Mage fascinated by the surroundings this time. It's me. I can't manage to tear my eyes away from the luminescent symbols in each stone making up the sky bridge. They line the edges of the structure and pop up along the center of the walkway every so often.

"You're gaping, Kira," Aster jibes.

"Okay, archivist, but what do they do? I've never seen so many runes in one place."

"Haven't you ever wondered why no one falls off these death traps?" Aster ambles alongside me without a care in the world. His tone reminds me of my lesson masters from childhood.

"Not really no. Then again, I'm not a bumbling tot that can't walk in a straight line." My boot covers another twisted shape as I cross the long slab of stone, a glow outlining the sole. I peer over the edge of the bridge.

The death would be instantaneous once you hit the ground, if you didn't die of fear on the way down. "So, if I pushed you off—"

"Please don't test that theory," Aster interjects sharply.

"—would you bounce right back, or is there some sort of invisible barrier?" I finish, undeterred by my companion.

"Well," Aster stops to inspect the nearest rune, "I'd think—"

An Orc Paladin in plate armor passes by me, and I take the opportunity. With a quick shove, I send the olive-green skinned woman toward the edge of the bridge.

Enraptured, I watch to see what, if anything, will happen. In quick succession, the Orc twists her body to meet my gaze as she careens to the edge and lets out a violent curse in her own language. But an invisible force shoves her back, directly into me.

"What in Thalos' shield was that, Rogue!?" The Orc's hand shoots out to grip my neck, the metal of her gauntlets rasping against my leathers.

"Testing a theory," I rasp out with a shrug. I know she can't kill me—it's forbidden within the Spire. Plus, without a direct order, it probably goes against her Light blessed beliefs.

"Kira, you can't go tossing people off the Spire!" Aster hisses, awkwardly dusting off the Paladin's shoulder. "Sorry about my roommate, she hasn't been around civilized people in awhile."

The woman turns her hard stare on Aster. "I've heard Rogues kill each other in training for fun, to reduce competition for contracts. Maybe we should adopt their ideology and get rid of the ones that don't belong."

Aster raises his hands in a placating gesture. "While that is an intriguing idea, I'm sure she'll be useful for spying on King Wilder's enemies." Neither of them seem to care that the Paladin's hand remains clasped around my throat, not quite hard enough to completely deprive me of air, but still enough to be a nuisance.

"Can you decide if you're going to try to kill me or not?" I force out, glaring at the Orc woman in front of me. I have to tilt my chin up to look at her full on. She has smooth, olive-green skin, high cheekbones, and golden eyes. Two small tusks extend from her mouth, giving her lips a permanent frown. She's shaved her black hair on both sides—leaving it long on top—though she has it tied up with a strap of leather and metal ring. This leaves her long-tipped ears exposed, each bearing rings and studs from lobe to tip. Two scars slash through her harshly angled eyebrows. She bears a wolf pelt cloak over her broad shoulders.

"An apology might be beneficial here, Kira. Have you heard of those?" Aster supplies.

I grunt out a huff. "Fine. I'm—"

"Save it." The Orc releases my throat. "I appreciate an unabashedly cutthroat woman."

A grin spreads slowly across my face as I rub at my neck. "I like you," I finally say.

"Tharava Wolfshield of Ostramma." She extends an arm toward me, and I grip her forearm in response.

"Kiralin Thorne, Underbelly."

"No shit." Her lips turn up in a savage smile. Yes, I think I like her very much.

"Are you adopting her too, Kira?" Aster laughs and shakes his head. "Aster, former Archivist."

A burning prickles at my nape. *Yes Laz, I know. I'm not supposed to be collecting strays. Just whatever it was Lachlan was after.*

CHAPTER
6

T HE BRAND I'M STUCK with is proving to be more of an annoyance than any sort of benefit. The blasted thing has been itching and burning and doing absolutely anything it can to draw my attention like a needy ex-lover.

Formation was a delightful affair in which the Spire's lieutenant eyed me far longer than he did any other trainee. Seems I'll be an oddity for the span of my time here, which hopefully isn't long enough for me to actually swear fealty and a decade-long contract to the king I'd rather throw off a skybridge.

The brand pulses at my neck again. *Yes, Laz. I know that would ultimately solve the problem, but it would only create more problems in the end.* Laz has never been quiet about his ultimate goal to unseat King Wilder in favor of someone more accepting of halves. My mission is more focused on why Lachlan was murdered in some great cover up, but the Guild isn't concerned over a single Mage.

Lachlan was my concern. Damn it, he's still my concern, even if his soul has been sent to be weighed against the Crimson Scales.

I stand against a stone wall with my feet crossed at the ankle. The mid-morning sun does nothing for the chill seeping through my leathers. Whoever decided to hold combat training on the rooftop courtyard must have been a sick bastard.

Stone walls enclose us, but the center of the roof opens to the air, and Arethor's notorious wind whips in a vortex through the massive courtyard. Racks upon racks of weapons line the walls. Great broadswords, crossbows, rapiers, and massive battle axes, though none bear the glowing runes that lined Matthias'.

My eyes flick from cadet to cadet, each one a member of my platoon. Not mine, really. Can't imagine leadership would want to put an individualistic Rogue as a sergeant for a platoon. I wouldn't set any good examples for the starry-eyed future Guards.

Plus, if Ironhart has his way, I'll be out of here and back to the Guild before the week is out. He'll have to try harder than a few grumpy words and wee show of his Berserker strength to force me away.

The cadets surround me, warming up and easily ribbing each other. Seems many have either formed friendships quickly or knew one another before arriving at the Spire.

Tharava stands a few paces from me flipping a small dagger end over end. She brought her own broadsword, which is currently strapped to her back.

"You gonna be able to keep up, half-pint?" Tharava calls to me over her shoulder. Aster's face pales and the easy grin usually consuming his features drops like a stone in water.

"Tharava! You cannot call people that. Ostramma might simply poke fun at someone's heritage, but...not here." Aster shakes his head.

Something warm pokes its head up in my chest at his defensiveness of my—

Nope, nope, nope. Push that back under the trapdoor where I keep my heart and humanity. Better to focus on the Orc's casual use of humor against my half status.

Tharava's dark brows slant into a V and her lips tug down farther into a frown, which draws further attention to the protruding tusks. She swears in Ostrammish. "Blood status was not my intention. She is small, is she not? How can a melee fighter possibly withstand battle if she is so small?" Tharava peers at Aster, assessing his stature. "You too are small. How has such a fragile race survived for so long?"

I grin, dipping into my Grit. With barely a thought, I use the shadows cast from the high walls to my advantage. I slip into nothingness, flit around her, and snatch her blade to press the flat of the dagger against her exposed throat.

"Appears we'll be alternating putting each other in deadly situations in this friendship, Paladin," I purr.

"You rely too much on shadows, Rogue."

I open my mouth to defend myself, but another voice calls out. "Just as you should rely on the Light to bolster your fighting, Wolfshield."

Ironhart's cloak swishes behind him in almost a choreographed dance. He strides through the group of Paladins and Berserkers lingering by the center ring. Nice of him to finally join us.

"The Rogue you are criticizing may rely too much on shadows to be effective as a Guard, but those shadows have served her well. She has more confirmed kills than the whole of your leadership at the Spire combined."

Well, fuck.

Forty pairs of eyes swing my way. Despite my racing heart, I lift my chin in defiance. I will not cow to these green cadets. My eyes remain trained on the captain—he's painting a target on my back.

The longer our eyes stay connected, the warmer my cheeks become. Blast his handsome features. He's just a Guard. A Guard *Captain*, at that. High cheek bones, curious markings, hair I could run my—*Nythraxis' shadows.* Heat creeps down my neck, and I tear my gaze away just as something flickers in his glacial stare.

"Carrying the mountains on his shoulder, that one." Thara's voice filters into my ear, and had I not been at least half elf, I probably would have missed the remark entirely.

I jerk a nod in response to Tharava, but stop my gaze from returning to Ironhart. His face devoid of any warmth. Whoever this elf was last night, the one throwing his head back in laughter, is gone. He's been replaced by a glacially cold captain taking delight in trying to intimidate me into leaving.

However, it doesn't matter to me if these greenhorns hate me or fear me. I'm here for answers; to finish whatever the hell Lach had been digging at. Then I'm getting the hell out of here. I'd never serve on the front lines or at the Keep with these idiots—not including Aster...and possibly Thara.

While I knew Matthias was an instructor here, I hadn't exactly thought he was going to be one of my instructors or constantly in my business after last night. I'd also wrongly assumed as a captain he had better things to do than teach combat skills to the cadets.

Ironhart whirls to face the weapons rack at the edge of the fighting circle. The lithe elf snatches a broadsword off the rack and tosses it blade first to the Orc closest to him. "Malcroft!" Ironhart's sharp command catches the Orc's attention with barely enough time for the Paladin to save himself from being sliced by the flying blade.

The captain's gaze weighs heavy on each cadet as he peers around the courtyard, his voice stern as he continues. "I am not here to coddle you. I am not here to teach you to perform pretty dances with blades suitable for the palace. I am here to teach you to stay alive. You will not hear me tell you that fighting with a blade or a hammer or a mace should be done without your magic. The Gods blessed you with this power. You will use it, or you will die."

A hint of an ocean sea breeze twists in the air, but Matthias doesn't seem to be grasping for his Grit. Perhaps he's showing that his Grit is just as much part of his fighting as his blade? Does the damned magic just drip from him, unable to be contained?

Malcroft, standing off to the side of the fighting circle, now holds the blade awkwardly. "Sir, I—I typically use a hammer, not a blade." He's ballsy, I'll give him that. With his thick stature, I can see why he prefers the hammer; it's probably easy for him to deal a good bit of damage and stop opponents when he has that much weight behind him. However, the same heft that the Orc puts behind his blows with a hammer could be put into slices with the great sword. He'd also have a better ability to parry blows.

From the corner of my vision, I see Thara nodding decisively, as though she too has come to the same conclusion. "Varek has always clung to that hammer because he never had to learn more than '*Orc angry, Orc swing,*'" she murmurs to me.

"If I wanted to know what you typically used, cadet, I would have asked," Ironhart drawls. It's a dangerous sound. It holds all the casualness of a comrade but all the underlying challenge of a superior wanting to put you into your place.

"I'd be better off sticking to what I know. I know the hammer. I'm better suited to help the king using my strength and my hammer." Varek's words are arrogant, bordering on condescending. He tilts his head to the side, which causes the strip of hair left in the center of his skull to flop to the side covering one amber eye. My eyes flare when he darts his tongue out to stroke up one tusk.

Is he ballsy or just plain mad?

"We can play your way, if you want to test this," Matthias says, gesturing back to the weapons rack. "Grab a hammer." He strides into the sparring ring, Varek armed now with a large war hammer. The Orc follows him on heavy boot steps, his feet thudding along the stone floor.

In a blink, Matthias advances toward Varek, one moment empty-handed, and the next his rune-covered battle axe slices though the air. I cannot stop the gasp that slips out. I hate to admit that his handle on his Grit is remarkable. I've met few others with that level of control.

Varek jumps backward and spins to the side, unable to bring his hammer up to block Matthias' attack in time. The Orc arcs his body back, leaving only the leather cord around his neck in the path of the blade. The single animal tooth from the cord slips to the ground.

"That's cheating!" Malcroft cries.

"Cheating? Or simulating what the real world is going to be like?" Matthias remarks, continuing his assault on Varek.

The Orc uses momentum to swing the hammer toward the Night Elf, but Matthias dips low and swings the weapon once more, aiming for Varek's knees. He won't be able to dodge this blow, and his hammer already curves in an arc above his head, swinging toward a target that isn't there.

Though Matthias pulls his axe up short and refrains from striking, I feel the telltale sign of him reaching for his Grit and see the wave of oceanic power lash at Malcroft's knee where the blade of the axe should have sunk in.

Varek utters a sickening howl. "You can't use your Grit! This is a combat training class!" He swings his hammer once more, face twisting into a mask of rage, teeth on display, which makes his tusks look all the more intimidating.

Matthias advances on Varek. I step closer to the edge of the ring, waiting to see what either of them are going to do. Matthias uses his Grit once more to push Varek toward the edge of the circle.

"Stop cheating, Ironhart! Fight me like a man!"

Shock ripples through me. Through the entirety of the group. "Use your damned Light, Varek," I holler to him. For a split second, I think he might listen to me, realize this is partially what Ironhart is trying to teach him. That combining his Light with his love of his hammer he might be able to withstand the shortcomings of the weapon, but alone the hammer is too slow to keep up with the speed of an elf.

"Shut the fuck up, half, and let me focus."

Red eclipses my vision. He did not just *fucking* say that. I snatch a thread of the shadowy Grit in my chest and step through the shadows to join the melee. Was I invited? No, but if the captain wants to simulate a real fight, it's rarely going to be a one-on-one fight.

I slip a dagger free from its sheath and jab forward in a quick movement, while gathering the shadows from around the room to twine at his feet.

Matthias drives his axe toward Varek's back, and the Orc stumbles toward me, tripping on the nest of shadows I've created. I turn my blade at the last second so I don't murder the kid but let the hilt of my dagger find its way to the soft spot in his armor.

"Dead." I glare into his hate-filled amber eyes. "I might be a half, but I can still kill you. Stop fucking acting like this is your backyard sparring ring and use the Light you've been mistakenly gifted with."

I look to Matthias' face over the top of Varek's shoulder, his expression unreadable. His gaze weighs heavily upon me. With judgment, approval, something else I haven't the faintest inkling what it could be. What I do know is that his presence is like a tether, as though my Grit recognizes something within him.

Varek commands my attention once more as he leans down into my space. "I don't need a nasty-blooded waste of space to tell me how to use my Light."

His foul breath cascades over my face, the stench like rotting corpses. With a quick flick, I spin the blade in my hand and rotate my aim down, letting the sharp edge drive through the soft fabric of his shirt and find purchase in his belly. Malcroft grunts, and I delight in the pinched expression on his face.

"If you'd used your Light, maybe you wouldn't have a poison-tipped dagger in your gut," I murmur the words as though we're in a lover's embrace. I yank my dagger back and wipe it on my breeches. "I'd say maybe a Cleric could heal you, but maybe they shouldn't waste their Mana on you since you won't be using your magic to protect *them* in a fight."

I shove at the Orc's chest. His face takes on a sickly pallor, and he stumbles backward out of the ring.

"Anyone else?" I turn to face my fellow aspirants and search their eyes. I want to know if anyone else is dumb enough to question whether halves have a right to be here. At the end of the day, it doesn't matter; I've already been branded as a member of the Rogue's Guild, spent decades in its service slaying monsters these pups wouldn't dream of in their worst nightmares.

I lock eyes with a lithe Paladin standing apart from the rest. Fine armor lines his figure. He crosses his arms over his broad chest. *Night Elves and their imposing statures*, I think with an eyeroll. He only winks and dips his chin in deference. My brow knits, but before I can give it any further thought, another voice captures my attention.

"You're as big a cheat as the captain," the Berserker with a mop of red hair spits from where he stands supporting Malcroft.

"If you think the king's enemies are going to fight fair and *not* use everything they have to kill you, you're deluded enough to think swimming to Baustantia through the North Sea is an option." Someone snickers from the huddle of Clerics. At least someone thinks I'm amusing.

"How do we know you aren't an enemy to the crown?" Varek grinds out while he grips his wound, sickly black blood seeping between his fingers.

"Time is ticking on that poison, Orc. If I was an enemy to the crown, I'd have shoved that blade through your throat and left you with a gaping hole where your windpipe sits. At least now—" I pause and level him with a sadistic smile, "—you have the opportunity to ask someone for help."

With a quick burst of Grit, I step through the shadows to end up back at Tharava and Aster's side. The former holds up her fist and forearm, which I smack my own forearm against hers. The show of solidarity fills me with a sense of rightness.

"That one's mother should have fed him to the wolves," she states drily. I have to bite my cheek to stop the laugh threatening to bubble out of me, though I don't think Tharava meant for it to be a joke. Aster's lost his battle with a smirk, both sides of his lips tilting up in an expression I did not expect to see on the mild-mannered Mage.

At my glance, he shrugs. "Wouldn't have been the worst thing in the world. Orc's often send their young out to the Frost Worgs to see if the massive wolf-like creatures will eat them or bless them."

I shudder, though it's no more barbaric than how I was raised. At least my parents hadn't trusted the things that go bump in the night to bless me. They'd simply believed Laz and his cadre had taught me well enough to survive. The scars lining my skin told the stories of all the times I almost hadn't.

After a moment, I recognize a sea-tinged Grit sliding through my shadows. It pokes, and prods, and *strokes*. When I meet the captain's gaze across the ring, there's something cautious there, something I can't name. And that unsettles me more than I want to admit.

CHAPTER 7

True Sea Berserkers are a dying denomination. Very few are left, having been hunted by the masses for their huge amounts of power. They can also be highly volatile creatures with moods and whims turning like the tides.

THE PUB BUSTLES WITH noise. The kind of noise I enjoy losing myself in, even just for a moment. The bard standing on a table at the end of the bar belts out a bawdy tune, and most of the patrons who've consumed too much ale chant along. I've frequented many taverns just like this; the only differences between any of them are the goofy names and maybe the ale and food available. In Arethor, apple mead from the Harsdred Orchards and beef stew are my preferred options.

The warm glow of torches and Mage lights cascade through the space. I sit in a corner with my back to the wood-paneled wall, one foot braced on the edge of the table. After being surrounded by cadets all day trying to prove themselves to their superiors—fucking Pures—I regretted the decision to join the damned Spire so I could find answers rather than just sneaking in. So, I marched down here to the Blue Rose so I didn't have to eat with the other cadets and could actually enjoy my meal without looking over my shoulder.

That last point is partially a lie. I still have to watch out for the Locks here. I'm still not sure if I should be proud or a little peeved there are sixty-three warrants for my arrest. Stealing, assassinations, the occasional Black Market deal. Only sixty-three? Rookie numbers.

At any rate, at least Locks don't like to have the type of fun found in places like this.

I catch the barkeep's hazel eyes and lift my tankard. The man is a common Human with no magic to be found, but I could argue the mead and the stew are their own kind of magic. The flavors explode across my tongue, and I haven't experienced a mead this smooth since I spent time in the Wood Elven cities.

"We ain't get a lot o' Rogues 'round here," a gruff voice says. The statement has me snapping my head to the side, eyeing the common Orc next to me.

"You do. You just don't see them," I reply. Another tankard of mead slides across the table, and I tip my head in thanks.

"I see you, don't I?" The Orc has long tusks protruding from his lips and a dark green complexion. His garb suggests he works in the mines just west of the city, soot and dirt covering every bit of exposed skin.

"Keep poking where your tusks don't belong and you'll wish you hadn't seen me." The long pull of mead I take slides down my throat with a pleasant buzz. I shift into a more comfortable position as I take stock of the people in the tavern. Mostly mine workers and other commoners from the city. I thank the Gods it doesn't seem to be a place the Guards frequent. As much as I could learn from the shadows surrounding hushed conversations of Guards off-duty, I don't feel like working tonight. If I did, I'd pick up one of the countless contracts available to me in Arethor. I just want to wallow for a moment in the regret of everything that's led to this.

The Orc, all but forgotten, finally glances at what's hiding behind the deep maroon cloak I wear. Wisely, he turns back to his own tankard. A loud *slam* resounds through the tavern, one punctuated by a steady beat of silence. It's as though the hands of a clock have simply *stopped*.

Two hooded figures stand in the now-open doorway, their purple robes encasing them in an eerie silhouette. I look past them, hoping I won't find any trailing demons, and Nythraxis must be smiling upon me because there are no signs of the void at the Locks' feet. Pushing their way into the space, a third figure is revealed. There is no mistaking the curly blonde Mage in her revealing dress—Luella.

Fuck. The Night Elf captain might be willing to keep my identity from the the Warlocks, but I doubt Luella would have any qualms about trussing me up like a prized pig and handing me over. I sink farther down into my slouched position, but I keep a close watch on where the trio sits. With a flick of her wrist, Luella summons three flagons and bowls, never interacting with the barkeep. She's missing out—he's delightful.

It wouldn't shock me if she doesn't pay for the food and drink she's just summoned from the kitchen. Although Mages can summon their own food, I've never tried it. Lachlan tried to convince me to taste the dishes he summoned, but the idea of food summoned out of Mana and nothingness was too weird for even me.

I feel as though I cannot tear my eyes away from the group. What are they meeting for? I thought she was merely an instructor for the Spire. I didn't think she was active duty of any sort. I shake my head at my own assumptions.

A solid warmth presses in against me without warning, and a shudder jostles the bench as someone settles beside me. I strangle my gasp before I make any sort of noise, though it would be gobbled down by the boisterous song the bard is leading. Without a second thought, I snatched the fork off the table and jam it into the newcomer's leg.

"Easy there, pisúlë," a deep voice rumbles. I wrinkle my nose at the elvish term, but leave the fork embedded in Matthias' thigh. I'd been forced to learn the bare minimum of Elvish, but this term was outside of my vocabulary. Also, why had he given me a special nickname?

"Can I help you?" I snatch my cup of mead off the table and bring it to my lips, all the while my other hand grips the fork, still pressing the tines of the silverware into his leg. My aim was dreadfully close to the juncture of his thigh.

"Push a little harder. I might like it." The glint of a fang snags my attention, and I can't help but openly gape at him. "Surely you know elves like it a little...rough."

Yanking the fork back, I set it on the table much harder than anticipated. The aggressive *thud* catches the attention of the Orc I'd been volleying back and forth with. He eyes the elf next to me but doesn't make a comment. Of course he doesn't, why would anyone question the massive elf who has at least a head and a half of height on me and Gods knew how much more muscle he had. I'm just a wee little half, no need to worry about me. The snarky thoughts have me biting back a snort.

Matthias raises a brow, but wisely doesn't make any comment.

My head drops back against the wood of the bench we're sitting on, and I let it loll to the side to peer at him. His features are cast in shadow from the hood of his deep green cloak resting over his head. The long points of his ears make the back of his hood sit at an odd angle, causing the corner of my mouth to quirk before I tamp it down. Though I cannot clearly see the frozen wastelands that are his eyes, I can certainly feel their icy trail as he looks me over.

I try to sound as nonchalant as possible, but annoyance creeps into my tone. "Is there a reason you're interrupting my evening of listening to raunchy music and drinking? Here to order me to leave again?"

"Never said I was here for you," he states.

I think back over my words. I guess I did insinuate he was here for me, but if he's not here to convince me to leave, then is he here with Luella? Watching her back? Or is he spying on the Locks? My mind cannot seem to fit the puzzle pieces together fast enough. I drag my gaze away from the breadth of Ironhart's shoulders when the barmaid deposits his own meal in front of him, and I bring my focus back to the Locks and the Mage.

The trio lean in close to each other and murmur in hushed tones. I'd have to be sitting on top of their table to hear them. The Mage lights—strange little fires powered by the tithe of Mana the Conclave forces their members to pay—cast long, thin shadows—they're too frail to cloak me if I dared creep closer. I shove that particular idea out of my mind. Besides, I'm not here to court Megora's wrath or a trip to the Flats.

"Tell me what they're saying," Ironhart demands as he bites into a hunk of...boar? He eats as though he'll never see food again. Perhaps he just eats like a Berserker. Grease slicks his knuckles as he gestures for me to speak, as though eavesdropping were as easy as asking nicely.

"How should I know? I'm only half Night Elf; you've better hearing than I do." I cross my arms like a petulant child.

"Zorvyn, do they not teach Rogues anything about actually using your Grit?" Matthias scrubs his hand over the scruff on his cheeks. I rear back to look at him, baffled.

"We use our Grit plenty, thank you kindly." Without warning, the ocean breeze I've come to associate with the captain dances around me only to unexpectedly dip into the well of magic in my chest. His presence slips over me like waves across the sand.

I yelp. "What in the blazes do you think you're doing!?" The sensation is bizarre, intimate—far too intimate. "Get out of my Grit!" I whisper harshly, but the tide is already pulling at me. Like a gentle hand offered to a wary animal, or a morsel of cheese to a hungry mouse.

A sound not unlike rocks rumbling together erupts from the elf. "At least you can feel when someone else is in your magic, with your lack of knowledge of how to use your own power, I didn't think you'd sense me."

Excuse you, brute. Does he forget I sent his magic back to him just days ago?

The tendril of sea magic is not unpleasant, and I'm not entirely sure I want to force him out. The magic coaxes my own. In my mind's eye, I can see my shadowy, yellow magic unspooling in my chest, rising to meet the cerulean Grit stroking at it.

"That's it." Matthias' words are almost a sleepy sounding murmur. Despite his quiet words, it feels as though he is all around me, holding me in an embrace. The smallest sliver of his Grit slips inside of the tendril that's unwound inside me, and together they plunge us into my shadows. Except...

I look up. Our bodies are not in shadows. Our bodies are across the room. The sliver of Matthias' Grit inside my magic surges, holding me tight to the cover we're in, despite my Grit thrashing to return to me.

Somehow, I'm within the shadow with Matthias' Grit, but I'm also sitting on the bench next to him. I watch as my body grips my cup takes a sip while Matthias appears to speak to me, but whatever he says is muffled, as though it's spoken underwater. I feel almost as if my corporeal body cannot pass it to my consciousness one down the line of magic.

How does he know this is possible?

The ocean magic surges again. It commands my attention, but once I refocus on the shadows I'm within, a gentle touch strokes my cheek. Does he control what this sliver of his magic does or is he simply trying to get his approval across? If I had arms in this form, I'd slap him away.

As it is, the tide of the ocean magic pushes me toward a different shadow, and I realize we've landed ourselves—or rather the tendrils of our Grit—under the table next to Luella and the Locks.

Panic surges in my chest. If Luella is good enough to teach at the Spire, she'll be able to sense the use of magic nearby. Even more so if she can recognize Ironhart's distinct ocean magic.

The gentle caress comes from his magic though. *Stop that!* Not that he can hear me, still I can't help but push the thought at the stupid sliver of Grit. The damned thing tickles me once more and then retreats, it's only trace the smell of the sea spray and the faint sensation of being rocked on a ship.

Without the distraction of the captain's magic, I can suddenly hear the conversation between the magic users at the table.

"—not just missing. It's here. Dazek and I felt its presence," the Lock closest to me explains.

"It's your own fault it was stolen, Rashvik." Luella's words have a cruel edge to them. As though she's taking joy in twisting the proverbial knife. "If the king learned it's been gone for over a year, all because his precious

Warlocks let some—" But before she can finish her thought, the first Warlock—Rashvik—smacks the table.

"Careful, Lu. You may outrank the new recruits, but don't forget who is in charge here, who actually holds the king's favor."

From my place beneath the table, I can see Luella's feet shifting. Why is she so nervous? Her hand slips beneath the table to grip her seat, a blue rim tinging her fingertips. *Nythraxis.* She's so worked up she can't control her own Mana.

"Without *me*, the Shardblade cannot be made whole. You Locks can try all the Demon Threads you like, but I am the only one who can perform the spell," Luella snaps. She wipes her hand on her skirt, and the magic snuffs out like she's dusted dirt off her fingers.

The Mage's words finally process and I snap back into my body with a grunt. Shardblade. They want to make the blade whole. *He* wants to make it whole. The king is going to end us. End the halves. With the blade made whole, he'd be able to. He'd have the power of the Gods.

My well of magic writhes like a pit of snakes. It beckons, calling to me, urging me to slip away. Join the nothingness so I can escape into a back alley, into the silence. Tingling rises from my fingertips, but I clench them into fists. If I can't see the Grit trying to escape, it means I'm not losing control.

My chest heaves. I can't get enough air. This blasted tavern is too stifling. Too many people. Too much noise. Gods, the noise.

But all at once, the bawdy tunes, the clink of tankards, and the rumbling of conversations is consumed by the ebb and flow of crashing waves. I feel as though I'm rocking in the hammock of the ship I stowed away on.

Breathe.

Air rushes into my lungs. I can almost pretend it's the clean, fresh air of the sea, not the warm, smoky tavern. Blinking my eyes open, I realize

I'm fully back in my body. I peer toward Matthias, still leaning against the wall next to me. How in Gods name did he do that? Before I can ask, amusement ripples through me when I once again notice the long points of his ear causing the back of his hood to sit at an odd angle.

"I guess Night Elves do have flaws," I say. Impulsively, I push the hood back and stroke a fingertip along the arch of his ear, the length of it nearly longer than my smallest finger to my thumb outstretched. I want to inspect the runes tattooed into the dagger following the curvature of it. A small notch mars the otherwise perfect curve. Matthias shivers and tilts his chin up, granting me access to look into his eyes. Their frosty depths blaze.

"Don't touch my ears."

Without another word, he stands from the table, flips a few coins onto the surface, and slips away toward the back door.

Tharava's right. He carries the weight of a mountain on his shoulders.

CHAPTER 8

THE SURLY ELF'S ABRUPT nature only intrigues me. I've flitted from alcove to alcove trailing him back to the Spire. The sounds of Arethor have fallen away, but the eerie calm of the Spire hasn't completely taken over yet. Matthias fills every sense: the whisper of his cloak kissing upon the stone; his sea salt and leather scent; that tall, broad frame stalking through the halls.

I reach for the next puddle of shadows to flit to, but I pull up short when he reaches a wooden door I've yet to come across. Violet magic pulses at its edges, with straps of metal lining the top and bottom. Ironhart drags the outer edge of one of his pinkies across a bared fang then wipes the crimson blood from the wound across the planks.

Purple light flares in a brilliant blaze before the door opens, and the elf slips out of my view. I stumble back, heart pounding. With a shake, I let my head fall forward and blow out a hard breath. Despite barely touching the mead, I feel fuzzy.

Air. I need air.

Looking across from my spot against the wall, I notice stone stairs rise and twist to yet another foreign hallway. Without another thought, I push off from the wall and bound up and up. Instead of the steps ending and dumping onto another floor, they continue to wrap in dizzying circles.

Nythraxis' bleeding shadows, who designed this fucking staircase?

With every step, my thoughts spiral further about the bizarre evening. Will Wilder end the halves? How can he get the Shardblade? I force my mind to stay away from thinking about the Berserker with the emotional awareness of—well, a Berserker.

Gods know how many revolutions I've taken by the time I brace myself against the wall, my clammy palm meeting the smooth stone and rough grout.

I take a few more steps and cast my hand back out to the wall, but open air swirls around my palm instead of the familiar stone. Thoughts of Berserkers, Wilder, and the Shardblade fall away. I have only a moment before I'm able to right myself, realizing the staircase has spiraled so high I've found myself above the Spire.

Found that air I'd been looking for.

I peer over my shoulder a few steps back, looking to an archway curving over the top of the enclosed staircase behind me. I turn forward and look up, but the evening fog rolling in from the harbor shields whatever hides at the top of the stairs.

What could possibly be so special it needs its own marathon of stairs?

Casting about my Grit, the magic slips over everything and nothing. That's just it: nothing seems terribly *special.* Two more steps up, and my attention snags on the tiniest bloom pushing through the stones.

Silvery tinged black petals unfurl under my gaze. Moonveil. The thing almost preens the longer my attention lingers, making the corner of my mouth tug up. The flower acts as a potent aphrodisiac when rubbed on the skin or an effective way to stop a lover's heart. I can't help myself, I snatch the bloom and stuff it into a shadow pocket.

"Need to spice up your after-dinner extracurriculars, Kira?"

I yank the blade tucked into my boot out and whirl to face the speaker. I barely manage to pull up short of piercing the hollow of his throat, but the adjustment to my trajectory sends me careening toward the edge of the stairs.

My head swims as I teeter on the edge of the step, only a stiff wind away from falling countless leagues to the unforgiving ground. As if seeing the very real possibility of my demise in front of me isn't motivation enough, the nape of my neck sears with heat.

I swear to every God, Lazrik. Now is not the godsdamn time.

Cold fingers scrape at my skin and latch onto my belt. I'm yanked unceremoniously backward only to land with a heavy thud on the ground against the stone steps. Pain flares in my neck again, only this time it stems from the whiplash. I'm only saved from cracking my skull when icy Mana cradles against my scalp.

I meet the copper eyes of my companion who stands above me, a cheeky smile lighting up his features.

"You'll be the death of me, Hoarfrond," I growl with only the faintest bit of bite to the words. "What are you even doing on this death trap?"

He extends a hand down to me. "Only a death trap for those who choose to walk the stairs. The shadows up above were getting a little…restless," Aster says with a curious look.

I let the scrawny Mage pull me to my feet and ask, "What do you mean, 'Choose to walk'?"

"Those who make the decision to use their feet to reach the observatory?" Aster drawls, as if I'm having a hard time understanding the common tongue. He switches and says something in Elvish. At my confused expression, he continues, "Wasn't sure if perhaps you'd understand in Elvish, since you're half el—"

I smack him on the back of his head. "Are you daft? Did the elders in the Archives hit you over the head with too many tomes?" A lock of hair flops over his eye, making him appear younger than he already is. "I'm sorry, did you say observatory?"

His smile turns earnest, and he nods. "Come, would you like to see?" Once again, he offers me his hand. And once again, I slide my rough, scarred hand into his smooth, delicate one. However, where I expect him to lead me farther up the winding stairs, he instead waves his other hand in a sweeping arc.

His cool Mana swirls around us and trails along the path his hand took. An archway shimmers into existence. Within the arch, a round room with massive windows and a large contraption waits, not unlike the ones found in the wealthy homes of Baustantia. A long tube makes up the majority of the contraption, but where the ones in Baustantia end with only lenses on either side, this one bears a platform the size of a large dinner plate next to it.

Aster tugs my hand and steps through the arch.

"What—oh, no. I'm good. I'll walk," I babble and pull back. My fingertips tingle where they brush the threshold.

With a smirk, Aster plants his feet and reaches his other arm through the magical door to grab hold and yank me to him. With all the grace of a drunken ram, I fly into Aster's chest, sending both of us tumbling into a heap of tangled limbs and knocked skulls.

My stomach roils, threatening a second showing of the evening's food choices. "Oh please, Kira. That was barely a blink. Not even a whole portal," Aster grunts from underneath me.

Only. Not even. I roll off Aster and lay flat on my back to wait for the world to stop teetering on its axis. The Mage stands, dusts off his cream linen pants, and adjusts the All Seeing Eye medallion hanging above his loose navy shirt.

With a flick of his wrist and a flare of icy Mana, teeny crystals lift off the platform. I loll my head away from the stars and clouds peeking through the opening in the ceiling to watch Aster work. "Now then," he says as he walks toward the large contraption. "Are you going to lay there all night? Your Grit is messing with my calibrations."

Mages. So temperamental.

I push my Grit back into the well in my chest. I hadn't realized it had spilled out during my tumble. Curious, I heft myself off the floor and take up a position next to the strange platform.

Nearly transparent, blue shapes take form above the grey disc. Before I can think better of it, I poke a finger through.

Whap!

"Ouch!" I yelp and rub the back of my hand. "You didn't have to hit me with a damn book!"

"Did you learn your lesson?" Aster asks, opening the book to some page with diagrams and scrawled notes. He arches a brow at me over the top of the tome.

"No. Probably not."

He sighs. "Here, be useful. Move that lever there." He points to the farthest upright lever, and I give it a gentle push. The whole contraption shifts slightly, but I stare at the strange shapes on the disc. They move and morph along with the odd tube.

"It's called a telescope," Aster says. "The gnomish engineers in Baustantia designed it. Though, the Mages here have added some magical touches to show the stars and planets upon this"—he gestures to the platform—"so we do not need to look through the lenses." He points to formulations, circling his finger as he indicates around clusters of stars. "Berserker's Crown. Harpoon's Last Strike. The Leviathan. Do you know much about the stars?"

I shake my head. They're just there. I never had any need or desire to know much about what lives outside our realm.

"Whole other worlds exist out there. They say the stars warn of storms long before they appear on the horizon—if you know how to read them."

I hum. "And do you?"

His gaze falls back to the stars hovering above the platform. "What had you so spooked this evening? Seems unlike you to unravel like someone pulled your Fate Thread."

My eyes snap to his, finding him already assessing me. Legends whisper of a time when Nythraxis controlled Fate Threads, before Vaeroth stole the tapestries of fate and connected them to demons.

"And just what do you know of Nythraxis' Weavers?"

He winks. "Not much more than the stories we're told as children. Nythraxis once kept an army of spiders at his command, weaving Fate Threads into tight webs and tapestries." He continues to watch me, waiting for an answer to his previous question.

"I needed air," I finally quip. That same brow as before quirks. "Fine. It started as needing a drink and spiraled out of control from there. I think a job from an age ago is going to come back to haunt me."

The scabbard down my spine pinches, and I reach back to grasp the hilt of the blade. Yanking it side to side, I readjust the whole thing, armor included. I sigh, the sheath has never quite fit right, but hard to turn down the only gift I've ever received. Plus, the damn blade is so pretty and balanced. It could have been a war hammer and I'd carry it for how much the perfection enticed me.

Aster watches me with a strange look but turns back to the telescope. "Storms often follow those who carry something of value. What is it *you* carry?"

"Nothing anymore," I scoff. "I only carry things of value long enough to line my pocket with some coin."

I tilt my head back to peer up at the stars. The next time Aster speaks, his words seem far too close. "Then you'd best keep an eye to the stars, Wanderer. Seems the storms may come for you. They chase souls not silver."

I can't help the grin spreading across my face, so I cover it with my hand while I peer at Aster. Standing in the courtyard, he's dressed in cream breeches, a blue tunic, and leather boots, which on its own isn't abnormal.

He's done away with the robes during the day since starting at the Spire and spending more time with Thara and me.

The abnormal part is the leather *harness* he's sporting. The straps crisscross over his chest and around his waist in a bizarre belt-bandolier combination. Small vials, not unlike my poison bottles, line the chest straps. Aster has been brewing concoctions in the wee hours of the morning, and spending all his free time in the stacks finding potion books. His all seeing eye pendant still rests proudly in the hollow of his throat, though now, he's traded his Mage's cloak for a white, ankle-length coat with a white fur neckline. Various chains link to odds and ends on his harness and coat.

To top off his bizarre new outfit, the short staff he's taken to carrying slots through a ring on the belt.

"Why is the Mage dressing as a goblin?" Tharava asks loudly, her brow furrowed and lips pinched. A bark of laughter escapes me.

"He does look like a goblin fresh off a zeppelin, doesn't he!"

Aster glares at us and with a haughty huff, pointedly says, "Goblins don't even exist."

He spins on his heel and his coat flares around him. I have to say, the drama of it all suits him. In the weeks we've been at the Spire, Aster has flourished into his own, and I've enjoyed prodding him along.

Unfortunately, my own mission has not gone much further than the information I discovered at the tavern. It's maddening. I feel as though I'm stuck in the mud and cannot climb out.

Other Guard hopefuls meander about the courtyard while we wait for our morning formation. The shadows slowly shrink as the sun begins to peek its way over the top of the towers. I'm not a morning person; it's a reason I enjoy Rogue hours. We operate predominantly at night or in the afternoon. None of this up at dawn bullshit.

I stretch my arms over my head, feeling like a cat waking from a long nap. Aster falls in next to me with an elbow to my ribs.

"Maybe if you'd stop sneaking out every night, you wouldn't be so tired."

"You leave at night?" Thara's blunt tone brings me an odd sense of familiarity. She'd fit right in in the guild.

I cock my neck and pull it in hopes it'll stretch out the crick from the punch the damned Paladin from last night landed. "I'm still a Rogue on top of everything else here. I have contracts to fulfill." I'd been reacquiring a diadem for a Druid last night. She'd been lovers with a Paladin, and the prick had kept it after she was called back to one of the Groves to protect the healing Moon Pool. The diadem is gorgeous, with some sort of green metal forged into vines, and small green gems delicately accent the circlet.

The diadem bears a level of importance to her for some reason—I didn't care to ask. My only concern was who had it and how do I get to it. Now it's back in the Druid's hands, and the slimy Human Paladin is only a little worse for wear.

"The Rogue sneaks out to kill people. The Mage lives in the archives. Am I the only one not falling prey to the stereotypes of my denomination?" Thara shoves at Aster's shoulder, and I let myself laugh.

"Oh, I'm sorry I enjoy finding ways to use my brain rather than just brute force like you two," Aster scoffs, tossing his head back with a haughty sniff, his new haircut adding extra flair with the flip of the tendrils.

I relax into the friendly banter the three of us frequently find ourselves in. An Orc, a Human, and a half Night Elf. An unlikelier trio no one would ever find.

Unfortunately, it seems any time I let myself ease into some sense of enjoyment, a pin is nearby to burst the bubble. A familiar moss-colored male approaches us, the damned war hammer still strapped to his back. Seems some of us will never learn.

"Ooh, look who's still playing guard. We have a running bet among the Paladins on when you'll finally tuck your tail and run home to your little underground cave," Varek sneers. His two lackeys smack fists behind him, their chortles like that of pigs too pleased with their muddy sty.

"Aren't all caves underground?" Aster asks. I can't help but chuckle, though I don't think he's intending to rile Varek further.

I push off the wall and widen my stance. "It seems to me, you should be the one running with your tail tucked. If I remember right"—I tap my forefinger against my chin—"you were the one on the ground in our last match."

"Only because you cheated, half-breed!" Spittle flies from his lips, golden eyes flaring, and he flings a hand toward me.

Thara shoves in front of me. She has half a head on Varek and substantially more muscle. "Why don't you see if you can handle me? I'm happy to play with my food, noble brat."

Varek steps back, bumping into his cronies, but Tharava prowls toward him. Her movements are all lithe grace, the same way Matthias moves when he's stalking one of us in the sparring ring. She only stops once she's toe-to-toe with Varek. He tilts his head up to meet her gaze, but his knees quake before he can lock them straight.

"Careful, T," Aster drawls as he pops an elbow onto my shoulder. "That one one might wet himself before formation's even called."

The female Orc tosses her head back and barks out the most unladylike laugh I've heard, the beads at the end of her hair tinkling. Before she steps out of Varek's space, she strokes a finger over his weapon. "I'd lob this into the Shavarion river and let it take the damned thing out to sea before you have to face Matthias in the sparring ring again."

Varek shoves forward, his shoulder colliding with Thara's bicep, but she doesn't budge. He hisses at me around her toned frame. "This isn't over, half-breed. You won't always have bodyguards around."

"I don't need—" The bells in the tower echo through the courtyard, and anything I'd been about to say is swallowed up by the crescendos of the morning formation call.

CHAPTER 9

WE'VE FILTERED INTO TIGHT rows and columns, Aster standing next to me, and Thara somewhere in the back of our squad. The hard stone beneath my boots combined with the tension of standing at attention has my muscles aching for a soak in one of the hot springs near the river. The sun shines down over the crest of the Spire walls, gleaming across the mass of guard cadets all standing stock-still. The bright rays make it difficult to tell who stands at the head of formation today, the one to call out any announcements or grievances.

I can make out the shape of Ironheart's ears and battle axe as he stands just to the right of formation, but at the head, it appears to be a…Wood Elf. One of the colonels? I shift, using the height from the Night Elf standing next to me to block the glare and look closer.

The captain's full lips are drawn into a flat line, his glacial stare darting from recruit to recruit, never lingering long. Once they land on me though, they hesitate. Something dark flickers behind his stare, and it seems as though he's trying to convey something.

I have enough elvish sight to notice the muscle in his cheek flutter, but then his gaze moves on.

"What is *that* thing?" a cadet whispers.

"Why are they here? They have no business here." another remarks.

"Oh Gods, its eyes!"

The murmurs around me grow, and the whispers take on a frenzied edge.

Colonel Nostros' voice rings out above the gathered cadets. "Attention cadets. Warlocks will sift through formation today. A Void Demons recently tracked the magic of a wanted individual to the Spire. Allow them through the ranks, Void Demons do not take being barred from their prey lightly."

With the sixty-three warrants Megora laid out like a card game in his office, I can only imagine I'm the wanted individual.

The muscles in my legs lock, anchoring me in place when all I want to do is flee. There are no shadows for me to slip into and disappear. The horrific demon is two columns away, and it inches closer with every heartbeat. Nikolai, a Wood Elf from the western edge of the continent, leans away from the wretched creature when it sniffs him. My mind flies through the past few days. Have I used my magic enough lately for it to smell me? I'd used my Grit during a match with Nikolai three days ago, slipping the dagger from his boot into my own palm to use against him.

The Demon crooks its faceless visage into Nikolai's neck, its long bony fingers ruffling through his clothes until it pulls out the very same dagger. The one I'd held. The one my magic touched.

Nythaxis protect him—and me. I shove every last bit of Grit I can find into the mental trapdoor I usually save for my "for-later" thoughts.

I focus back on Nikolai in time to see the Void Demon flick out its forked tongue to lick the dagger. Ew. I can't linger in the repulsiveness because Rashvik enters my line of sight, sweeping through the ranks like oil sliding over the side of a lantern.

"What is that?" Aster's question is laced with repressed terror.

"Nothing good," I murmur back. "Void Demon."

Aster turns his head just slightly toward me, his eyes wide. "*That's* what a Void Demon looks like?"

I swallow back the chuffing laughter I feel in my throat, because that is the exact response I had the first time I saw one. Drawings don't do any Void creature justice. The imps are far more gruesome and the Void Demons much, much scarier than the Archivists' drawings would have any of us believe.

The demon slides the dagger back into the sheath beneath Nikolai's cloak and lifts its head. The forked tongue slips out to taste the air, and I can't help but let my hand fall beneath my cloak to one of the Moon-blessed daggers. One of the few things that can truly kill something from the Void, for those of us without access to Arcane or Light magic. Rogues are just one step sideways from the Void, making it impossible for any of our magic to kill the demons.

Rashvik growls something in the demonic tongue and the creature suddenly moves with intention, shoving between cadets, its bony limbs pushing anyone in its way.

Me. It smells me. It knows I'm here.

Nikolai heaves out a breath as the Void Demon passes, and his shuddering breaths are loud enough to reach even my ears. My heart flutters in my chest to the beat of a hummingbird's wing flaps, but I force my breathing to steady.

What can I do? *What can I do?* The question repeats itself over and over in my head. The demon has already scented my magic. Even if I tamp all my Grit down, will the Void Demon smell it on Aster? Tharava? I've doomed all of us. I created my own problem by allowing myself to care for two other cadets, but shit—I'm going to have to choose between myself and them.

How many cadets would join in if I start a fight with the Locks? I'll have to get to the shadows at the edges of the courtyard in order to have any hope for escape.

Rashvik winds between cadets with more decorum than his demon did, but that doesn't dampen the sadistic glee etched into every feature. His purple robes flow behind him, black hair streaming in a direct mirror to his clothing. His eyes are rimmed in red from one too many Demon Threads pulling at him. Another Lock prowls on the outskirts of our squadron.

The Void Demon is only one row away from me now. The forked tongue licks out every few seconds as it scents each recruit to see if it matches that of its quarry. The closer it gets, the more Grit I let unwind.

"Which one, which one?" Rashvik's singsong question has the cadets in front of me shifting from foot to foot.

The clacking of his footsteps sends shivers skating across my spine. Next to me, Aster lets out a soft whimper. I want to comfort him, but I can't risk drawing the thing's attention even further. I chance a quick hand squeeze before I pull my arm back to its place at my side.

The demon is only two columns away now. Two cadets over. The breath in my lungs saws with each restrained heave. I'm sure every full elf in formation can hear the pounding in my chest. I stand stock-still, but inside, a tempest rages out of control.

The demon lets its head fall back; its tongue darts out to taste the air once more. In an instant, the gruesome head snaps in my direction. *Nythraxis, be with me.* The brand at the nape of my neck burns with an intensity I haven't felt since Laz seared it into my skin. *I don't have a whole lot of options here, Laz. I'm going to have to fight my way out and ask for forgiveness later for the shit storm I'm about to create.* The only response is a final pulse of pain.

Uncontrollable shivers start at my hands when the thing enters our row. I steel myself; once it makes its move to strike, I'll jam my dagger into it and shove poison into its hellacious maw before sprinting to the corner of the courtyard for the open door to the Mage's corridor. Once there—

Writhing void tendrils eclipse my vision. Looks like time's up on my planning. Long fingers stroke down the front of my leather armor. The almost loving caress has me clenching against the fear that's become a living thing inside of me. The demon leans into me and that wicked tongue slips against the bare flesh of my neck, leaving a tingling, stinging sensation in its wake.

Rashvik's steps quicken. "This one!? Is it her?" The last word is a purr. The sound grates against my senses and clangs around in my mind.

In response, the demon looks back to its master, but then turns back and drives its face fully into my chest. No doubt it can feel the pounding against my rib cage. I pray to all seven gods, though praying to Vaeroth for protection against one of his own creatures seems a little ironic.

I focus on the tempest of magic within me in preparation for what I'm about to do. I sway with the magic, like a ship in the sea. The demon turns back once more to face Rashvik. A nod is next, I'm sure of it. My fingers tighten around the hilt of my knife. The tongue tastes the air again. The creature's features slacken. I gulp in a breath of air. I'm terrified to move, terrified that my raging sea of magic will spiral out of control and consume me, terrified this thing will finally nod and seal my fate.

But it doesn't.

The Void Demon claws its face, and it chuffs aggressively. Spittle and hot breath blast across my face. Next to me, Aster whimpers again. Seems he's given up on showing a brave face. I don't blame him. I've seen these things countless times and they still instill terror in my soul.

And then...it pushes to the row of cadets behind me.

What the fuck just happened?

I have to fight my muscles' silent plea to collapse and sag. I don't buck against the crisp cool air my lungs suck in though.

A guttural curse draws my attention, and Rashvik stares directly at me. The smell of sulfur creeps its way into my nose at the same time a scratchy Thread winds around my legs, dragging itself up my leathers. I focus on the feeling of swaying in a hammock on a ship, the last place I felt some sort of peace before driving forward on this mission.

Letting my mind drift out to port, I keep the Grit that wants to fight the Demon Threads on a tight leash. With a flick of my eyes, I lock onto Rashvik's brown eyes, only to see the fluorescent green that rims his brown irises flare when he summons more of the Crimson Judge's power. His eyes narrow on me, but the rough magic extracts itself from my thighs.

"Something's...not quite right." He slides like water through the rest of our ranks, and I can't force myself to care who he's focused on now. As long as it isn't me.

I can't fight the pull to the dais where Captain Ironhart stands at attention, watching his fellow guards try to sniff out the thief. Sniff out me.

It has to be me they're looking for—or rather, the hilt of the Shardblade I stole for Laz. I hadn't realized a deity-blessed object would mark me so thoroughly.

Matthias' attention on the Locks and their demons finally wavers. The weight of his gaze settles on me, and the calm seas and swaying hammock inside me rumble into the rough waves of a choppy tide.

His lips curl just enough for a hint of one fang to peek out, but just as quickly as his gaze lands on me, it falls away, and his lips settle back into a harsh line.

"Are you sure last night's job went off without a hitch?" Aster's hissed words break through the tunnel vision I've had on Matthias.

"Ye—" The word halfway forms when a strangled scream comes somewhere behind us followed by the sickening thump of metal and skin slapping the stones.

CHAPTER 10

I COLLAPSE AGAINST THE stone wall of an all but abandoned corridor leading to the Mage's dormitories. I need to finish whatever it was Lachlan was doing here and get the hells out before I end up dead or in a torture chamber.

To the Void with whatever course I'm meant to be in right now. Drill and ceremony no doubt, because it feels like that's half of our training here in the Spire. How often are we actually going to march in formation and do whatever these ceremonies are? In reality, I think it's just a way to torture us.

Don't turn correctly? Run a lap around the courtyard.

Call the command for the formation on the wrong foot? Push-ups on the dais where everyone can see you.

Can't answer whatever inane question Ironhart or the instructor calls out? Squats while holding your weapon.

None of it matters to me, since I have no intention of being an actual Guard. I won't be stationed in the Keep having to stand at attention for hours on end or monitor the ridiculous banquets the king hosts. I won't be assigned to the Wall to protect the King from whatever foreign assault might happen.

King Wilder is more likely to face a rebellion from the races than a Baustantian invasion from the north.

"Kira?"

"Go to class, Aster." I'd heard him coming, but I made no attempt at moving. I'm still recovering from my heart trying to beat its way out of its cage.

"It's history. I could teach the class at this point. I've spent so much time in the archives researching the Arcane. Personally, I think they could benefit from teaching more about how our magic intertwines with the realm, but what do I know."

He's not wrong; he's mentioned he's researched the origination of the denominations. I think I tuned out somewhere around when the first Humans arrived on the shores of Eldrath.

I can't bring myself to remove my cheek from the cool stone; it's grounding me in the present, but I should probably look at Aster. See what his face reveals. Should. Want. Need. None of it matters at the end of the day. I have something to accomplish here, and really, I went astray sticking around this long.

"Darius is dead." Aster's words are gentle, but it's almost as if he's reading the words out of a book. As if he has no real connection to the sentence, instead of talking about the healer that stitched him up just last week. Nythraxis, what had the Void Demon sensed about Darius? "He can't have been wanted, right? There's no way he was moonlighting as...as, well, you."

I shudder. "I know. They had to be after me." Voices filter down the corridor toward us, and I snatch Aster's wrist to pull him toward an alcove behind a tapestry depicting the king in some battle he never actually fought in.

"I've been running from the Locks for years now, but lately they've been a little more...persistent in their search." After a pause, waiting for steps to filter away from our hideout, I continue. "They damn near caught me the day we joined the Spire."

Aster leans back against the stone wall, his ridiculous outfit consuming his big personality and leaving me facing a shell of him. "What is it you have that they want?"

It's the logical question to ask. A question I knew he'd ask me. It's also the question I don't want to answer. Not only because that information is dangerous, but also because it seems wrong to drag him into this. Lachlan was murdered because I'd shared information with him, and he went digging.

Ironhart must know something about all of this. Laz certainly knows. The brand burns as if in confirmation of that. He wanted to keep this one close to our chests, and didn't want to lay any cards on the table for anyone to figure out what we're doing.

So much for that. Whatever Lord or Duke I stole the hilt from apparently had an obsession for checking on the piece of metal far more often than I had anticipated. He checked often enough that the fucking Locks and their demons were able to get a magic trail to follow.

Maybe Varek's right; I do rely on my Grit too much.

"Kira," Aster says firmly with a gentle nudge to my shoulders. I shake my head and try to focus here, focus on the disaster I've found myself in.

"Right." I flick my braid over my shoulder, avoiding the spikes woven in.

"You're stalling."

"Of course I'm stalling!" The words feel obscenely loud in the tiny space we're in. "Gods, this has to be the mustiest alcove I've ever been in."

"Kira."

"Fine!" I throw my hands up. "I have—*had*—a piece of the Shardblade. The hilt," I hiss, but the sound feels like someone in the Berserkers' dorms could have heard it. Aster doesn't move save for the rise and fall of his chest. "Or rather, I stole it at one point."

His warm, copper eyes never leave mine, but the wheels behind them are clearly turning. Aster's fingers reach toward the All Seeing Eye pendant hanging on his chest. "Holy Lumeris." He breathes, and the words are barely more than an exhale. "The Shardblade is...*real?*" The last word is only audible thanks to my heightened senses.

I dip my chin once, unsure if I can trust my voice.

"I've read about it, but I always thought it was legend. Why do the Warlocks want the blade?" Aster's fingers twirl around the medallion. Bits of ice cling to the luminescent purple whorls of the design in the wake of his ministrations. "No, wait. Let me think about this." He holds up a hand. With a flail, he forces his way around the tapestry. "Gods, that thing was obnoxious. I can just seal us in a sound shield, Kira. We don't have to hide like toddlers behind curtains."

He waves his hand in an intricate twist, and suddenly, Aster's icy Mana slips over my skin, sealing us into the sound shield with a quiet *snick.*

"Anyways, the blade is said to have been forged by the Gods, yes? A weapon to unify their magic?" I shake my head, but before I can respond he forges on, pacing up and down the hallway. "No, that's not quite right. Lumeris, grant me recall. It was their answer to something..."Aster trails off as he thinks, beginning a series of movements with his wrists. "Perhaps a key? Yes, and the Divine Mantle?"

A tinkling sound fills the bubble we're in and a massive tome flares into existence in Aster's open palm.

"I thought you were a Frost Mage? That" —I point— "is clearly Arcane Magic."

Aster waves his hand in a *later* motion. "Right, here's the passage. Not Divine Mantle, Mantle of Dominion. Started with a D, I was close. Da, da, da...Yes, here we are. 'The Shardblade is the key to the Mantle of Dominion which grants the wielder rule over all divine magic.' Fascinating."

"Aster," I prompt.

"Sorry, so the Locks want this back because the King wants to control all of us?"

"Not just control." I shake my head, wishing it was that simple. "It grants access. Key, remember? Light, Grit, Mana, Demon Threads, all of it. Wilder could be a Paladin one moment, a Warlock the next. He could access all denominations within seconds of each other. He would become a God, essentially. The ability to snuff out life or grant it."

Aster blanches. His fingers are still flying over cream-colored pages of the tome he'd summoned from Nythraxis knows where with Nythraxis knows what kind of Mana. A portal realm? Did he finally figure out how to create one?

His hands stop abruptly. "That's why the king wants it. If the blade is completed, the wielder wouldn't just *become* the gods' equal. He'd *control* them." His eyes flick back and forth through space, as though reading off something I can't see.

His gaze finally lands back on me, where I lean against the stones next to the tapestry we'd hid behind. "Was that what your brother was doing here?"

"I don't know. That's what I want to find out. Why was he in the Spire? What was he looking for here or through the Guard?"

The air in the hallway feels heavy, all-consuming. Even though I want to take these steps to get closer to whatever it was Lachlan was after, this step feels like it's going to suffocate me.

Flicking the latch on the nearest window I shove it open and suck down lungfuls of cool air. The effect is instantaneous. The shroud of claustrophobia seems to fall away with every inhalation of sea-tinged oxygen. I'm almost baffled that the height of the Spire can do away with the smells of the town and leave only the briny ocean air in its wake.

Footsteps sound at the mouth of the corridor, but instead of turning and continuing away from us, they approach. Aster slowly closes the book, and his hands tremble, making him motion several times before he's finally able to dismiss the book back into the ether.

"Lachlan was a Mage, right? Let me help you." I don't have time to respond before Aster makes one more motion with his hand to drop the sound shield. I shiver when the icy Mana drops away from me.

Striding down the hallway toward us is Lyra Faelwyn, our strategies instructor. She bears the same rank insignia upon her collar Matthias does. The woman intrigues me, having climbed so high in rank as a half. Though she is half Wood Elf rather than Night Elf, so she doesn't bear any markings to establish her immediately as a half. Her long, red hair is tied into an intricate braid, small strands of silver beginning to creep in at her temples.

Faelwyn's amber eyes narrow on the pair of us as she assesses the entirety of the situation. Two cadets out of class, in an abandoned hallway. The swish of her leathers halts when she comes to a stop just a few paces from where Aster's sound shield had ended moments before.

"Almë anorë," Aster and I mumble in unison with a bow of our heads, granting Faelwyn the customary moon's blessing of the elves.

"Though I know Aster does not need a refresher in history, I've seen your test scores, Thorne. Awful bold to shirk the opportunity afforded to you."

"Yes, Captain." I learned with Lazrik a simple acknowledgment usually saves me from running my mouth or walking into further trouble.

"It's a bit of independent study, Cap." Aster winks at Faelwyn. "We were having a chat about the artifacts of Eldrath and their possible uses in today's society." Faelwyn thinks I'm the ballsy one, but in reality, it's Aster and his inability to keep a rein on his cheek.

"And what *exactly* are you two discussing?" She sinks into one hip, the leather and metal mix of her armor creaks with her adjustment. The addition of her folded arms just heightens her shrewd intimidation.

"Lost items. Magical items. Items that could potentially end the continent. Useful things, really." I can't help the dumbstruck look on my face, hearing Aster's tongue-in-cheek reply.

I swear to Nythraxis, he's going to get us thrown in the brig.

"And are you planning to use one of those items to end the continent, Mage?"

To his credit, Aster doesn't balk at Faelwyn's tone, which is icier than the ball of frost magic he's now tossing from hand to hand. "Quite the opposite. We were also discussing some battle theory—which perhaps you'd be able to lend your expertise on—of how one would stop an opponent were they able to wield the magics of all the gods if one of those artifacts granted that capability."

Faelwyn's brows raise a fraction of a hair, before she settles her face into a mask of contemplation. "We should be lucky if no one ever puts *that* artifact back together, Hoarfrond. If they did, Elyndra save us." She shudders

"Wyn?" She lifts her head to gaze past us. I follow her line of sight, only to find Matthias standing in the doorway at the end of the corridor. Though he isn't wearing all of his armor, his form is just as imposing, especially when combined with the harsh cut of his brows when our eyes clash. The air shifts between us, shadows in my veins prickling. My chest tightens, caught between dread and something else.

Faelwyn—Wyn apparently—nods to the pair of us as the Berserker strides through the hallway toward us.

His presence overwhelms me the closer he gets. His Grit beckons to my well of shadows, his scent fills my nostrils, the sheer size of him seems to take over a corridor that felt expansive only moments before.

As he sidles up next to Faelwyn, his linen shirtsleeve scrapes along my own for a moment. Sparks dance along my nerve endings when the back of his hand knocks into mine. I suck in a sharp breath at the strange sensation. For the barest heartbeat, I swear his fingers flex toward me before he jerks them back, like he'd touched flame.

Wyn nods at him. Turning to us, she says "Tulya as elen, you two," before they depart down the corridor.

We mumble the elven goodbye in response. The hall feels too narrow, almost suffocating with his scent pressing in on me. I'm grateful when Aster speaks. Anything to distract from the way my pulse stutters.

"What denomination is sh—" Aster's question dies on his lips when a large panther materializes a step behind the Wood Elf. Black gives way to moonlit silver along her neck, the scruff standing out like a storm, the mane atop a body that's broad as a horse. Her ears sweep long and keen, tufted tips flicking as though she hears everything, from my heartbeat to the scampering of her prey three leagues away. "Is that a freakin' jaguar?"

"Lefendorian panther," I murmur. "She's a Ranger. Chosen by the earth herself."

Faelwyn extends her arms and wraps Matthias in a tight embrace as they walk. Something sharp coils in my stomach. Jealousy, maybe. Or just disgust. Definitely disgust.

Because why should I care if Captain Faelwyn tucks herself against him like she belongs there? Why should I notice the way his head dips close enough to catch her words? I don't. I absolutely don't. *Ew. Are they an item? I had such respect for her.*

Even as I think the words, I can tell I'm forcing them.

CHAPTER II

CONVINCING ASTER I'D BE fine going out alone tonight was almost as difficult as convincing my father Lachlan was safe coming on jobs with me. The Void Demon search still has the kid on edge, and I don't blame him. I've all but shirked my duties to the Guild this week. Taking this job was partly from guilt, but mostly due to the searing pain on my neck that has become my constant companion.

Lifetime of servitude to the Guild in exchange for what? I think, leaning against a pillar inside an upscale pub near the Keep. *So I can spend my nights pretending to be a bodyguard for some Lord in hopes he'll cough up whatever it was Laz traded my services for?* This was not a voluntary contract by any means.

A string instrument plays somewhere from the front of the tavern, but it's so faint I could be imagining it at this point. Aimlessly rolling a poison vial between my thumb and forefinger, my gaze wanders the room. This is by far the least dangerous 'post' I've ever had, and for the least dangerous creature. Adjusting my feet for the umpteenth time in the last hour, I try to get comfortable; but there's no comfort offered to the help here.

A group of Wood and Night Elves sit in the corner likely celebrating the moon phase, or an eclipse, or a falling star, who knows. I scan their faces and ears—all Pures. No surprise there. Halves can't afford this place on the meager coin we earn in piddling jobs.

Getting a little bitter in your old age, Lin. I can all but hear my brother's chiding tone. Lach was Pure passing though. He looked Human enough with our mom's ears, and his status as a Mage kept him protected from the elitists. How he managed not to be cursed with a half's Night Elf markings and ears proved he had all the luck.

A few tables away from the elves, a Human couple leans over the candle between them, the man feeding his partner something off a spoon. *Good for you, buddy.* I continue my perusal but find only ordinary people. I catch the waiter out of the corner of my eye and wonder if I could convince him to bring me a snack, or the very least, fill my waterskin.

Doubtful, since he's turned his nose up at me every time he walks by. I want to blow on him just to see if he'd be mortified my half air touched him. I bite back a snort at that only to swallow the whole thing when Faelwyn and Ironhart stride through the door one after another.

No one comes to a place like this unless they're obscenely wealthy or trying to impress someone. Matthias must be trying to impress Faelwyn, perhaps even to get her to accept a mating bond? Makes sense that he was so on edge that night in my dorm. I don't move from my position next to the lord's table. They'll either see me or they won't, and it doesn't matter to me in the slightest.

However, as Faelwyn leads Matthias through the tables, she seems oddly intent on where I stand in the room. My eyes meet hers from beneath my hood. The instructor is dressed for battle, not a lavish meal. Her chest plate gleams in the light, muscular legs wrapped in leather guards, and a long sword peeks over her shoulder. Behind her, Matthias wears a tunic the color of the pine trees surrounding Lefendor, chocolate-colored breeches, and an intricate elven belt holding an array of daggers and knives circles his trim hips. He's dressed for...a casual afternoon?

None of this makes any sense. Speaking of nonsense, apparently I'm obsessed with who the damn captain is mated to.

Faelwyn's giant cat is nowhere to be seen, but I don't trust that the thing won't pop out at a moment's notice. Pushing off the pillar, I roll my shoulders and move between the two instructors and the lord behind me. Though, I doubt he's their intended destination. I can't imagine they'd have any business with the poor, spineless bloke behind me.

As that thought crosses my mind, Faelwyn steps in front of me. Apparently, I've been mistaken. "Move, Thorne. We need to speak with Lord Preshkin."

"My Lord?" I call over my shoulder without taking my eyes off Faelwyn. She may be my instructor by day, but my current allegiance is to the Guild and by proxy, Preshkin.

"Yes, yes, Kiralin. I've been waiting for these two."

"Of course you have," I mutter under my breath, stepping out of the way. Faelwyn climbs into the raised booth behind me with the same grace as the Lefendorian panther that probably lurks somewhere in the dark nearby.

"What was that, Kira?" Matthias peers down at me, stepping into my space. A hint of a fang pokes his lower lip. My brows furrow.

"Why is it you are always around?" I hiss. I keep a tight hold on the shadows that beckon to me. I cannot seem to do anything in this city without this damned elf being there. "Did you know I was here?"

A line forms between his silver brows. "Can't imagine why you'd think I'd follow you here and fabricate a meeting with Preshkin. He's such a riveting conversationalist." With those final words, he brushes past me, his chest pressing against my shoulder, the familiar sensation of rocking waves and sea breeze air tangling with my legs.

Preshkin calls for one of the servers to bring a round of drinks and a tray of clams for the table. His cold blue eyes land on me briefly, and he barks, "Keep the lingering ears away from the table while we chat, dog."

A growl forms in the back of my throat; the feral nature of my heritage and the wildness of my denomination threaten to have me bare my sharp—albeit small—fangs at him. I may guard people, fetch things, and track them...shit, maybe I am a dog. Still, he has no business calling me one. I'm grumbling to myself about slimy noble rats when the server appears holding the clams and a bottle of wine. The Human casts a wary eye my way. I realize my sharp canines are still half borne, and in an attempt to ease the server's fear, I force my lip to lower from its curled state.

"—bodies have been showing up to the bailey in Faldorin for over a week! Daily we'll find decayed corpses, rotted as if they've been dead for—"

"My lord," I call, trying to keep an even tone despite whatever I had just overheard. Half decayed? Has to be the Locks, right? They're the only ones with ties to the Crimson Judge that could use magic like that. The alternative would be someone is holding onto the bodies long enough for them to decompose. Bile crawls up my throat at the thought.

The server places the seafood onto the wide round table followed by hefty pours of mead into the goblets for Preshkin and the two instructors. The server slips away without a second glance at me. Shadows dance across my skin, and I let them slowly consume me. I don't need to be wholly seen in order to keep potential eavesdroppers away. The darkness comforts me as much as that lingering ocean breeze, though that must be in my head because I can't feel any of the Sea Berserker's Grit in the air.

"What exactly do you think I could do about it, Faelwyn?" There's a solid *thunk,* but I don't turn to see what the Lord smacks against the table.

"Send out more guards. Guards that aren't magicless. You're sending them out against an unknown force to die, Preshkin." Her reply is all sharp words and harsh edges.

"We don't have any magic users in the ranks. You keep your precious King's Guard here, leaving us in the other cities to fend for ourselves with no magic."

Who? I want to ask. Who are you fighting out there? Why isn't Wilder sending people to help? I file question after question away in my mind.

"Fend for yourselves?" Matthias scoffs. "You *lords* are the ones who chose independence from the crown. Your choices have left you on your own."

"Get off your high horse before you fall, Ironheart. You're no more loyal to that bumbling buffoon than I am. The elven nations are as independent as those in Baustantia, and neither gives a shit about the king. Perhaps you forget you're expendable," the lord says with a snort.

Faelwyn cuts back into the conversation. "What else, Preshkin? Is there anything else about the bodies other than being...decayed?"

Peeking over my shoulder, Faelwyn leans so far onto her elbows on the table, she might as well climb onto it and sit there. Preshkin's attention is zero'd onto the wood elf, but I find Matthias staring back at me. I fight the desire to whip my head back around. The comforting sea breeze surges around me, but the only indication gives me that he's aware I can feel his magic is a wink before he refocuses on the discussion in front of him.

He slips a nimble finger along the curve of his long, arched ear that extends well past his hair. A sea breeze tickles along one of my sad, short ears, and I fight the urge to bat away his damned Grit.

Preshkin lowers his voice. "There are carvings in the bodies. In the chests."

I gasp. Not at the information—I've seen worse. Shit, I've done worse. But Preskhin's voice is not where it should be. His voice is coming from my right, as though he's speaking directly into my ear, rather than behind me.

"I'm not certain if the words are a poem, a prophecy, or nonsense. But each body has a verse and every four bodies, it starts over." I startle at the words. Prophecies died out with the Seers. They used to live along the icy shores of Alleria and Baustantia, hiding in plain sight as fishermen and women. But above their campfires, the smoke would dance and wind its way into verses and figures, giving hints to outcomes that may happen.

From my other side, Faelwyn gives a low hum. "What do they say?"

"The strength of many shall bow to one, after two become one, blade and soul twice undone, a shattered fate made whole once more chooses the fate of the endless war." Preshkin recites with a distant edge to the verse. I repeat the chanted words in my head, committing them to memory.

A slip of Grit squeezes at my forearm, and I spare a glance toward the table once more. Preshkin's lips draw into flat line in a direct mirror to Faelwyn, though her brows furrow in contrast to the weary look on the lord's face. Matthias simply stares at me. Something I can't quite decipher dances in his eyes, but it challenges me, dares me to say something, do something. I simply shake my head, thoughts swirling like a tempest too fast to catch and leaving me with nothing to do but hold tight to the mast in a ship stuck at sea.

I may have no idea what's being referenced, but I know someone who might.

CHAPTER 12

T HE HINGES OF THE wooden door creak loudly, despite my best effort to sneak into my shared room. The flickering candlelight peeked under the door before I'd entered, leaving me to assume Aster had fallen asleep.

"Back early this time," he drawls from his position lounging on his bed. A large tome with a moving eye on the cover blinks at me. It hovers in front of him, a purplish wisp of magic holding it aloft. Aster flicks his hand, and the eye peering at me narrows before the page of the book curls and turns.

"Ignore the blasted time; how in Nythraxis' shadows are you using Arcane magic? You're a Frost Mage!" He'd done it once before with the sound shield. My thoughts stutter. Are blinks and portals Arcane or Frost? I didn't think Frost Mages could make portals. How did I grow up with a Mage and not know how their designations work?

That same purplish magic zips past me and closes the door to our room with a quiet *snick*. "Yes, I am currently a Frost Mage," he replies absently.

"Aster, I don't have the energy for your riddles or your new *don't-give-a-rat's-ass* persona." I level a tired glare at him and flop into my desk chair to pull my boots off.

The floating tome snaps shut, and dust particles coat Aster's cheeks, leaving him coughing. A laugh burbles out of my throat. He may change his wardrobe, but he's still the same goofy tome-laden Mage I met walking along the road.

"Well, that certainly ruins your new identity." My body molds itself into the chair despite its less than comfortable form. Can't complain too much, it's more than I was afforded when training with the Guild. "*Anyways,* are you a Frost Mage or an Arcane Mage?" I loll my head against the back of the chair trying to make sense of the conundrum that is the man wiping dust off his face and tunic.

"I was born an Arcane Mage." He doesn't follow up his statement, but sighs when he meets my eyes. "I found a way—a spell—that allows me to channel Frost magic. It's much more unassuming for me to be a Frost Mage than an Arcane one, and it allowed me to study some of the Arcane texts and spells that are forbidden from those of that denomination because they might misuse them."

I blink, my eyelids feeling like they're moving through molasses in winter. I've had so much information shoved into my head tonight, my head feels like a wardrobe with too many clothes and nothing more will fit.

"But—what? Why don't all Mages do that then?" Mages weren't like Rogues; we simply specialized in training, be it poisons, daggers, out-maneuvering our prey, sleight of hand, pick-pocketing, you name it. Mages just simply...were. They were born as a Mage. They couldn't change what they were when the inclination struck.

"It's forbidden." He's matter of fact. His eyes bore into mine with an intensity I feel deep into my own Grit. The chilly, fresh aura of his Mana unwinds slowly, revealing the purple hue and sweet scent of the Arcane Mana hiding beneath the Frost. "To hold two derivatives of Mana is thought to be too much magic for any of us to channel. I was simply researching the ancient Mages, the first Mages to form the Orders. From there, I tested my theories. It's like an alchemical process: create theories, test theories, see results. Only instead of creating potions and remedies, I allowed myself to use a second derivative."

Aster flicks a hand in a complicated loop, and ice winds through the air before forming into a crystalized shape of an arctic seal found off Alleria's coastline. With a circular rotation of his fingers, purple energy swirls around the ice sculpture.

A *pop* resounds, then a frosty breeze pushes toward me. I whirl my head. The seal rests on one of my leather-bound journals with the purple Arcane magic giving the sculpture one last caress before it fades out of sight.

Gods, the Mages could be nearly unstoppable. Pairing multiple forms of magic together could yield incredible results. Or incredibly dangerous ones.

"Are there more—" I'm not quite sure how to phrase that. More what? Like him? More remarkably powerful Mages that could take down the entirety of the realm? Shivers dance down my spine as another thought blasts through. "Can you...could you channel fire if you wanted?"

Nythraxis save me if tri-wielding Mages organize and decide to take over the continent. Aster barks a laugh from where he still leans against the wall, his legs splayed on the bed.

"Definitely not. It nearly killed me to use Frost the first few times. It was like trying to ride a horse full speed down a mountainside while battling Ironhart in hand-to-hand combat at the same time. Mentally and physically taxing, and one misstep means death."

"Why, then?"

A coy smile blooms across his cheeks. "Knowledge. I had to see if it was actually possible."

He's nuts. Naturally, I'd befriend the craziest aspirant. No one in their right mind would risk—that's not quite true. How many times did I nearly kill myself making poisons and trying to test them?

Two peas in a pod we are.

"Have you shared this information? Did any of the others in the Archives try to channel another derivative?" I ask.

"No." He shakes his head. "I wasn't sure who to trust with the information."

Suddenly, energy simmers in my veins with no outlet. A band wraps itself around my beating heart, squeezing it tight. Was this what happened to Lach? Did he try to use a second derivative? I ignore the burning behind my eyes and shove the feelings burbling in my chest into a box, imagining myself back on that ship, rocking gently in the water, sea spray coating my cheeks.

I raise a brow. He meets it with a sheepish grin. "You're like a sister. You wouldn't betray me, right?"

The words are a dagger to the gut. A sister. I was a sister once before. It left me broken and battered, but isn't that how I've been seeing Aster? Almost like a Lachlan stand-in?

Looking back at Aster; he looks so young, so innocent. Like a small cub or pup with eyes wide staring back at me. It reminds me of the familiarity and hope that used to dance in Lach's eyes.

"Yeah," I choke. "Yeah, I suppose you can be my little brother. You certainly come with enough trouble, don't you?" My words find strength the more I say, and maybe it's the Crimson Judge's blessing, but a touch of woodsy Mana that feels just like Lach's twists its way around my hand and squeezes. Maybe it's Lach's way of saying I need Aster just as much as he needs me.

"What had you coming in here like a bat out of the hells?"

I wave him off, the night weighing heavily on my shoulders and my bed calling my name. "Will that thing last? Or is it going to melt and ruin my notebook?"

With one last wave, the seal is covered in a shining pink magic that leaves a shimmer behind but no change to the animal itself. "Should last even if you're sent to the Dread Flats."

"I'd be more worried about the Guild sending an assassin after me for not making one of my deadlines." I kick off my boots and leave them haphazardly next to my desk. "Though, I do have nightmares about being trapped in the Dread Flats mining for opals."

Aster blinks in rapid succession. "Opals aren't native to the Flats. You'd be mining for Moonstone. Different luster, different hardness—anyways. I can't decide if mining is barbaric, inefficient, or somehow disturbingly practical. Oh, your eyes are glazing."

CHAPTER 13

T HE SOLES OF MY boots click against the boards of the docks. Last I'd been in Arethor, I'd found a dealer of…illicit items. Perfect place to collect a few items I might need, and a trip to the docks always results in delicious information. Sailors always seem to have loose lips the eve before they board their ships to distant shores.

Light glints off the turquoise sea, but that isn't the shine that burns my eyes. Countless coins have been embedded into the docks and the pier.

Only the newest of them still shine. Fucking sailors. *Fucking Berserkers.* Their patron may not be as ruthless as Vaeroth, but his temper rivals that of any of the deities.

Anxiety prickles my fingers. Slipping to the side of one of the market stalls lining the dock, I flit my eyes from person to person. I find no overt threat. Only sailors half-gone on ale, evening doves looking for a bed to warm, and merchants hawking their wares.

So what has my hackles raised?

I catch a Human's's hazel eyes beneath a dark hood. She winks at me, twisting her hands in a quick motion—the customary silent acknowledgment of the Guild—before she slinks away and scurries up the side of a lodging house. *Holli?* Can't be. She's...dead.

Shadows bend around her, obscuring her from the rest of the docks. I wonder what contract she picked up that led her here. A sliver of Grit roils in my chest, tearing my attention away from the other Rogue. Pain lances down my thigh.

Nythraxis, what is happening?

I look down and find my leg unscathed, but my mind jumps straight to some Lock weaving a Demon Fate Thread around me. Alarm bells toll in my head. Shadowy Grit rises to meet my call, unfurling in my chest, and I slip back into the shadows next to a market stall.

I blink and find the scene of the docks has changed.

Heavy water droplets pour from the darkened sky. Arethor's glinting docks have disappeared, giving way to algae-covered pillars. I shake my head, but nothing moves. A weighted, burning Grit fills me, undulating and writhing. Red tinges just the edges of my vision.

Rage and grief loom inside of me. They war for dominance. Unfamiliar calluses line my palms that scrape when I drag them down sodden pants.

Pants with a hole in the left leg. Skin puckers beneath the jagged opening in the breeches.

Weighted steps pound against the dock, and the vision turns. A hulking Orc strides closer, crimson skin faded from sun exposure, shining under the moisture of the rain.

Nythraxis' shadows, a crimson. A Blooded. They haven't ventured from their southern seas in close to a century. Shock and awe raise my brows. Laz told bedtime stories about the blood-cursed Orcs. Their ancestors dabbled in magic found within their own blood. Magic that allowed them to channel things that shouldn't have been possible. Things outside their denominations. Their race shunned them, and though the practice of blood magic has long since faded, the color of their skin has not.

"Captain," he calls once he's only steps away.

I tilt my head in acknowledgment. "Commander." The commander adjusts the sword at his hip, the ruby catching the light in a dazzling spray.

"How was the voyage?" Despite the conversational tone, the red at the edges of my vision pulses. I clench my jaw against the words wanting to spill out unfiltered.

"Long, sir. But I hope to rest these aching bones with a trip to Bael'thireon. I've not seen my kin in nearly a decade." My heart stutters to a stop—my own, not this vision's heart. A decade without family. My chest ached for this poor soul.

I shake my head trying to clear this vision, but nothing moves. I glimpse the docks in Arethor for a breath before it fades away again.

Dark brows the color of rich soil draw down. "Nae, son, it's the heart of raiding season. Ye've responsibilities here. Ye can't be leaving us here. Ye've a ship to command. Or have ye forgotten I made ye captain this season?"

I grit my teeth hard enough a creak resounds in my skull. The sea rages just off the docks, the Maelstrom churning farther out. Ocean water sprays as the choppy waves lash against the docks. My chest heaves as I fight the boiling in my blood. The red tinging my vision threatens to overtake my sight.

I breathe in jagged pants, focusing all my attention on the jagged broken tusk on one side of the commander's mouth. "You'll survive a handful of raids on the Baustantian shores without me at the helm. I'll pay a Mage to portal me there and back. You'll hardly know I'm gone," I say, each word clangs around my soul.

Something pulls me to Bael'thireon. Some tether yanking me home. A terror. A melancholy. A strange grief that only stokes the flames of the terror. Even Zorvyn seems to urge me home, the tumultuous Grit rocking and swaying harder than the ships stuck in the Maelstrom. The Grit's roiling is an altogether uncomfortable feeling—it never rages like this.

"Ye're nae goin'," the commander growls. An air of finality settles in the space between us as he turns on the ball of his foot and begins to stride away. "Be on the deck before the sun reaches its peak, captain."

Bael'thireon and Zorvyn pull me home, but duty holds me in place. Forces my boots to follow the commander to the gangplank. Each heavy footfall resounds like a toll of the gallows' bell.

I stumble, nearly toppling a stall laden with meat pies and sweet pastries. The keeper hollers a wildly creative insult in my direction, but I drag myself down an alleyway where the shadows beckon me.

I'm losing it. Losing whatever sanity I have left. Seeing things, *feeling* things, that aren't there. I feel for the potions around my waist, but none have come unstoppered. Can't blame my sudden waking dreams on that.

I'm no Druid. I'm no seer. I reach for the shadows, their comfort surrounding me as it always does. But something niggles in the back of my mind.

They won't be able to protect me from the unraveling inside.

CHAPTER 14

THARA ELBOWS ME IN the ribs, and I yelp. Every other Guard aspirant turns to stare at me, including Varek, who curls his lips in a sadistic grin. It takes a great effort to keep my hand from flipping my middle finger at him. The Grit in my chest swirls, coating my limbs in a buzzing power, begging to be released on the Orc.

"Do you have a comment, Thorne?" Faelwyn's sharp words cut through my stare down with Varek.

"No. Simply a seatmate that can't keep her elbows to herself," I say dryly, knowing full well she elbowed me because I'd been nodding off. I hadn't slept last night after whatever vision or hallucination had plagued me at the docks. My jaw tingles with the urge to yawn, but I bite down on my molars.

A growl bounces off the wood paneled walls, sounding as though more than one large jungle cat prowls the room. Black dissipates to a silver scruff that juts out almost like a lion's mane, though much shorter. Her ears come to long points almost like the Night Elves, tufts sticking proudly out from the ends.

Cadets shift uncomfortably in the seats lining the long tables, including me. It's an unnerving feeling knowing a predator lurks in the shadows, one more powerful and lethal than you.

Faelwyn slices her eyes toward her feline partner, a soft smile touching her lips. I wonder what it must be like to have a creature that relies on you just as much as you rely on it. A being you trust, that brings you contentment.

My mind drifts to the fox playmate Nythraxis sent me as a child. Araya; one made of shadows and mischief. It's been ages since I've seen her. A hollow pang twists behind my ribcage.

"As I was saying, the first trial is nearly upon us. This is a test of your bravery as well as the strategy and combat skills we've instilled in you over the last few months." The Wood Elf meets each of our gazes, her lips drawn tight, no trace of the warmth that had touched her features just moments ago.

A hand shoots into the air. What are we, twelve? Still in our primary trainings, raising our hands to ask questions? Samson, a Human from one of the western coastal towns, sits near the front of the room surrounded by his fellow Clerics. Unsurprising, the healing folk tend to stick together.

"Yes, Sam?" Faelwyn calls on the Cleric with a kind of patience I've yet to experience. But perhaps that is the blessing of a Cleric. We all need them at some point, and thus they're afforded more leeway than the rest of us.

"What is the task? Are we"—he gestures to the group of healing students—"expected to fight like the rest of them?" The same hand he used to encompass the Clerics waves in the general direction of the grouped Berserkers.

"Yes, Sam," Faelwyn repeats in a gentle but firm voice. "What happens if you're sent on a patrol and your partner goes down? Are you going to ask your opponent if they'd mind taking a quick break while you help your partner? They won't wait for you to heal whoever you are with. Have you forgotten already about siphoning? You're expected to fight just the same as any Berserker, any Mage, any Warlock, any Rogue." She looks at me with the last word. We haven't crossed paths outside of class since the night at the upscale mead house—I've made sure to avoid her and her jungle cat.

Anytime I hear their six combined footsteps, I find somewhere else to be. Matthias certainly knows I heard what was said. He'd cast some sort of magic to allow me to hear through his own senses, which seems wildly outside of Berserker magic. But hells, Aster can channel both Arcane and Frost Mage magic, who is to say the Sea Berserker doesn't harbor some secret that allows him to cast...I don't even know who can cast magic like that.

I add that thought to the growing list of things I need to talk to my roommate about. I still haven't brought up the bizarre lines carved into the chests of the dead guards in Faldorin The knowledge about his second denomination of magic still sends my mind into a tailspin, but the more I think about it, the more I think about Lach, and maybe—

"No, Varek. You won't be given hints as to what the challenge is prior to the trial. No one out there will give you hints of what might go bump during your patrol." She motions to the three large windows as she speaks.

Four trials over the course of two years. Countless written exams. Stints of training in the Keep, the Wall, the Spire, and wherever else Wilder deems the Guard necessary. All to have steady pay and minor recognition for services rendered to the crown.

Varek mumbles under his breath, cursing the Spire for lack of preparation for their recruits.

Nythraxis knows we never had help in the Guild before any of our tests. And Laz thought up some truly horrific things to put us through.

I take the path along the sparring ring, each step kicking up the chaos still spinning through me. By the time I reach the upper courtyard, I have to stop and exhale, like maybe that'll steady me.

Gods, I'm a shit Rogue. Well, am I a shit Rogue or did I make friends with someone who doesn't care about subtlety? My nose wrinkles at the memory of being called out by Faelwyn. I snarl at myself and lean over the railing, taking in the view as I mentally berate myself.

I'm out of touch with my training; I ought to go in search of someone to actually spar with rather than relying on these elementary-level classes to keep me sharp for however long I'm within the Spire.

"Look, fellas! The half-breed's gone feral." Dragging my gaze down, I find several Warlocks leering up at me from the second level.

They want to see feral? I bare my teeth at them in response to the heckling.

"Worse than the Berserkers with how uncivilized they are," another Lock spouts. "Remind me, what is it farmers do to their stock when it threatens the bloodlines?" He taps a long, spindly finger against his chin and snaps. "That's right. They *butcher* them."

Rational thought flies out the window, and I plant a foot on the railing.

Fingers wrap around my ankle, stopping me from launching myself into the Lock combat course below.

"Perhaps you'd like to enlighten your captain on why all halves should be eradicated, aspirant." Faelwyn's tone borders on frigid but holds all the authority of her rank. Her earthy magic vibrates along my leg where her grip holds true.

An arrogant slant to the Lock's lips hints at his thoughts, but the next words leave no doubt. "Halves always look like they want power when they shouldn't have it. You're just mistakes the Gods missed. It's our duty to our kingdom and to our patrons to erase you from this realm."

I start at his word choice. *Erase.* Hadn't Matthias mentioned Lachlan had been erased rather than killed?

A heavy growl rumbles behind us, Faelwyn's bonded obviously not taking to the tone and the words any better than the Wood Elf herself.

Before she can do anything reckless and risk her position, the Warlock instructor finally calls out, "Eyes forward, aspirants. You'll never achieve anything of note if you stand around mingling with the halfbreeds."

The instructor summons a green flame and bends it to his will while calling advice and orders to his charges, but the flame holds no interest to me. What's left in its wake, however, does.

Decay.

Rot.

Withering death.

All the greenery has faded after being touched by the flame. My eyes snag on the poor bluejay caught in the crossfire, it's feathers now curled and wilted. The body swells and bursts in seconds, maggots springing forth. Something that held life only a heartbeat before now appears to have died weeks ago.

My eyes meet Faelwyn's, and we share a look of abject horror. There can be no mistake now; Locks must be behind the deaths in Faldorin.

CHAPTER 15

MY FOOTSTEPS ECHO AGAINST the stone wall of the suspended hallway, sounding as though an army of Rogues walk through this abandoned corner of Shadowspire, instead of just me. Between steps, I swear the faint crashing of waves reaches my ears, but I know that's just me longing to give up on this mission and escape to another place.

On cue, the shadowbrand sears my skin. *I'm not going anywhere Laz. I'll find out what Lach discovered and why he died.* I slip a hand to brush over the raised skin, wondering what it looks like when it burns. Is it red to mirror the fire it unleashes upon my skin, or does it darken with the shadows of its name and our denomination?

The day wanes as we creep toward the morning of our first trial as guard aspirants. Aster wasn't in our dorm room, and the only places I can think he'd have escaped to might be the library or perhaps the greenhouse several blocks toward the Garden District. A quick peek into the first-floor library reveals it's empty, so I turn my feet toward the gates only to be stopped by a hulking Berserker.

My heart takes off at a quick gallop. The day wanes as we creep toward the morning of our first trial as guard aspirants, but nothing says I *can't* be out of bed and lurking the halls. He's the one lurking in this situation. Something hot slides through my veins though. He seems to turn up at every corner. Every time I peer over my shoulder, there he is.

"Captain." I incline my head in the tiniest bit of submission that might play to his dominant elven nature. I catch the slight flare of his nostrils and a peek of a fang. He might not admit it, but his damned feral nature likes seeing me submit. With no one around, I let myself peruse his features. It's a guilty pleasure, but who could blame me? He looks as though he should be one of the figures above the Moon Pools the Druids protect so fiercely. Statues of Gods and Goddesses and heroes carved into stone, forever cast in their most beautiful light.

His elf markings, loathe as I am to admit, are stunning, and the urge to see his bare chest rears its head. If only to see if the legends about Sea Berserkers' having their own markings upon their torsos is true. He's recently chopped his silver hair, which fills me with a pitiful sorrow that those front locks won't fall in his face while he demonstrates new maneuvers in combat training. His notched ear faces me when he tilts his own head, revealing that curious tattoo upon his ear.

"Pisúlë," he says in a dark tone. I wrinkle my nose at the foreign elvish word. "We have unfinished business to discuss." He folds his arms across his chest, biceps bulging under the dusky blue tunic he wears. The arched brow he gives stretches the scar slanting across his face, a testament to the battles he's waged and survived.

"No, thanks," I say in my most polite voice and stride forward with the intention to step around him. I do not have any business with the captain, and I do not wish to have any business with the captain. Involving anyone employed by the crown in any of my endeavors risks the commandant's wrath, a life in the brig, and my status in the guild.

The brand on my neck blazes to life, and I bite my cheek to stop the yelp from escaping my lips. *Blasted Laz! Stop burning me anytime I think of the guild and my purpose at the academy! Better yet, stop bleedin' burning me!* My steps falter, and I can't stop the hand that flies to my neck, nails scraping at the offending mark. The fire that licks down my neck worsens, as if it senses Laz's agitation with me and my lack of progress.

"Do you have a lingering injury, cadet?" He moves closer while I remain rooted to the stone floor. His boot steps thud heavily against the ground, so much louder than my own. Gods damn Berserkers. Each long-legged stride sends a chilling thrill through my body.

Ignoring his comment, I force my reluctant body to move away from the elf, but his status as a Pure offers him faster reflexes than my own. He whips his hand out and grips my elbow, his touch alarmingly cool against my bare skin. But even more jolting is the soothing caress at the nape of my neck; Ironhart's Grit is unmistakable. It feels as though I've submerged the brand in one of the Druid's Moon Pools and let the healing properties wipe away all the pain.

"Don't do that!" With a jerk, I step away from him while his hand falls to his side, but the gentle undulations of his Grit remain.

"Do what?" The sharp curve to one of the corners of his mouth betrays his innocent question.

"Use your damned Grit to do whatever it is you're doing." His magic coasts up my neck and into my hair. It weaves through the strands, then dances down my spine over the aches and pains he's caused in combat training. Clenching my jaw, I bar the sigh in my lungs that threatens to escape. I swipe at where the magical ocean touches my flesh, as if I can wipe away the sensations and stop the heat building in my belly that has nothing to do with the Shadowbrand.

"Feel better?" Matthias' lips raise a fraction, giving me a glimpse of his sharp canines, but I yank my gaze away from his face to stare straight ahead. My vision fills with the broad expanse of his chest. A bandolier loaded with daggers curves across the hard planes.

With a shove, I'm finally able to force my way past him. "It's not your concern, Captain. I have somewhere to be."

A harsh breath is the only response, until his footsteps fall into rhythm with my own just behind me.

"I have nowhere to be. Sounds like a perfect time to have that little chat." A humorless chuckle skitters over my flesh. The sound ignites things in me I've long since excised from my conscience. Things I have no time for. Things that slow me down, that cause hesitation. Things that will get me killed in the Guild. "Lachlan was in over his head, and if he'd asked for help sooner or sent word to the Guild, he might still be alive."

"Fuck. You." Any fire, any flame, burning and building inside me peters out in an instant. What right does he have to comment on Lachlan? The fucking Pures always acting as if they know best. Who was he supposed to trust? How was he supposed to rely on anyone here? The Guards' black and white way of life is a direct antithesis of our own. We are the gray.

"I'm not trying to speak ill about him. But, Gods, I wish he'd come to me sooner," he growls the words like they physically pain him as much as they do me, each word striking me like a shard of glass or dagger driving into my back.

But the pain hits me differently; because he went to Ironhart. Why didn't he just send word to me? I'd have died in his place. Gladly. I'd have sold my soul to the very God whose disciples I hid from. I'd serve one of those foul creatures Vaeroth loves just to save Lach from death. He was supposed to outlive me. He was supposed to do great things. How was I supposed to go on without him?

My thighs shake, knees threatening to give out. The burning behind my eyes I've fought for months teases with moisture in the corners. I couldn't cry here though. We do not cry in the Guild. We barely mourn our dead. We carry on and this—this is not carrying on. This is breaking.

Stumbling steps take me to one of the arched openings in the wall, where the cool breeze kisses against my skin. True cool breeze. No Sea Berserker necessary. The pieces of myself I keep strapped together with armor and sheer determination threaten to fall apart.

My body—my emotions—fighting to do anything but what I wish for them to do is unacceptable. Yet the sob that wrenches itself from my throat bounces through the open hall. The echoes remind me just how unsatisfactory my actions have been, including this one.

"I failed him." The words pour out in a jumbled mess. "We were two halves of a whole, but he was the better half."

"I hear you, pisúlë." I appreciate the lack of placating comments. There's no *I'm sorry,* no *it's going to be okay.* It's almost refreshing.

"I let him come here. I'm just as guilty of his murder as the one who held the blade." Moisture claws at my cheeks, dripping down upon my cotton shirt. Each droplet like a tiny dagger, piercing my soul and any shred of dignity and hope I have left. I'm losing my mind to hallucinations, why not lose these too?

What hope do I have of achieving whatever it was Lachlan set out to do when he was the one selected for this job? He was always the more logical choice because he was, well, logical. I can analyze a situation and find the best route to lead me to what I want; but Lach could see a situation and plan twelve moves down the road for an outcome needed years from now.

The world was a game of chess for him, moving pieces here and there, a sacrifice made for the best gain. Someone getting the drop on him is unfathomable.

But here I stand, without him. I've kept myself exhausted, busy, and distracted, so I never have the opportunity to accept life beyond him. We may have been separated by age, but we were like twins, merely born in different times. Of one mind. Of one heart and soul. Perhaps we were lucky, sharing this unbreakable bond, but standing here with the cool breeze lifting wayward strands of hair from my braid, I realize how fragile that bond was.

The same cooling presence wraps around me, but rather than a simple caress at my neck, it envelops me into a hug. I can't remember the last time I'd felt the comfort of a hug. Has it been since I sent Lachlan away to Shadowspire? No, I don't think anyone offered affection this way since his death. A gentle stroke cups my face. I finally tear my eyes away from the void I've been staring into, only to fall headfirst into the glacial pools peering down at me.

"You do not wear the guilt of his death. It is shared by several, but you are not within that company. Mourn him. Grieve him the way you haven't allowed yourself to, but do not weigh yourself down with the pain that comes from holding onto guilt you have not earned."

Each word he speaks falls like a quiet hammer strike, tearing away at the horrific creature eating at my soul. For the first time in years, I let my guard down and weep. And he holds me through every tear. I allow myself the brief respite his sensitive touch offers, and the violent sobs abate little by little.

Although I feel like a ship lost at sea, he offers me a safe harbor to moor in, even if only for a moment.

CHAPTER 16

THE COBBLESTONES RISE AND fall unevenly beneath my feet, and it takes an effort to keep myself upright as I continue toward the greenhouse. It shames me to admit that my emotions have taken the helm. I breathe a sigh when no flames lick down the back of my neck.

Ever the faithful shadow—which should be my title—Matthias treks on silent steps just to the side of me. Not necessarily as a companion, but neither ahead nor behind. As though we are two individuals carrying on in the same direction with no tether tying us together, but I still swayed as that same ship afloat in his safe harbor. Or perhaps he acts as a breakwater, offering me shelter from the storm.

And yet he allowed for the storm to enter into the harbor initially. Nythraxis, I need to spend some time in the shadows for comfort instead of relishing in the sea breeze that seems to find me at every opening in the Spire. With every passing day, I sound more and more like the Sea Berserker standing next to me.

As we stroll down the lane, the buildings fall away to make space for lush gardens. Pinks and blues unlike anything that existed within the Guild reach upward, their blush and orange colors blooming in the darkness almost like candles from inside. Something warm battles the icy sensation lingering in my chest. Aster must have stopped here before continuing to the greenhouse.

His Arcane magic could help speed along growth, or it could give magical properties to the petals of these flowers. It seems to leak out of his hands without him even realizing it. Then again, the Mage can't pass a wilting leaf or struggling sprout without helping it along, which is why I have to laugh at the persona he wants to portray to the rest of the Guard.

"What will you do when you finish Lachlan's mission? Go back to the Guild and stick to your own?" Matthias' words pick at a concern I've scarcely thought about for fear of what I might discover if given too much attention.

My stride stutters to a stop. How do I respond to that question? Despite standing taller than humans, I've shrunk to the size of a bug upon the ground, the emotions, the stakes, everything around me is larger than anything I could ever overcome.

In the shadows cast upon the street from the moon and ornate iron Mage-lightposts, part of me yearns to turn away from it all, to disappear into the darkness cloaking the street only broken up from the moon and ornate iron Mage-lightposts. In another life, I could have been a simple Human or a simple half with a potion shop. But Nythraxis wove the threads of my destiny though so there would be no escape for me, until Vaeroth calls me to weigh myself on the Crimson Scales.

In a rare stroke of luck, Aster saves me from answering. In a peaked archway, he stands, resembling a statue from one of the temples in Cathedral Square. Intricate whirls and swirls of the iron frames make up the greenhouse, making it hard to follow where one ends and another begins. Leaves extend from the design like a mystical plant from a far-off realm. Gazing through the windows, glimpses of tall, leafy trees and blooming bushes beckon and bid me to sit in the woven wood chairs, surrounding an ode to the Druids' Moon Pools.

The roofline matches the peaked doorway, and while I can only imagine the grandeur the building has during the day, to see it in twilight, the time of my father's people, causes my heart to squeeze in my chest. In an instant, I long for places long since crumbled, for forests and gardens filled with long-eared folk dancing, the bluish gaze of the moon kissing their purple-tinged skin.

Warmth pulses in my chest as I let myself weave my head to a beat lost to us, only heard by the most ancient of the elves. My chest rumbles on a purr, a noise I've never emitted, never had the contentment inside me to elicit such a noise. A sound of elves truly pleased with themselves, their surroundings, their *mate.* Some piece of my consciousness cries for the thing I can never have. That piece of me knows Nythraxis did not weave the tapestry of my destiny to include a love beyond that of the Guild, Laz, and Lach.

"You can feel it, don't you," Aster calls, his voice surprisingly stoic. "The call of Elyndra."

Heat prickles my neck at the way his words strip the moment bare, like he's peeled back the curtain between us and laid the call of Elyndra open for all to see.

A sudden loss fills my very bones when I tear my gaze from within the greenhouse to meet the Mage's amber eyes. "She calls to your Night Elven ancestry. Just look at him," Aster says, his eyes narrowing as if he can see the threads of moonlight tugging at us both.

I don't have to look, though. Something within me, the thing attuned to his Grit, feels him swaying along to the music those ancient elves danced to. Nature's call. Need slips through me, controls me. It's like a sentient creature of its own. Pushing and pulling me to bridge the gap. To seek out my kind and revel in the moonlight. My hand crosses the distance between us, in search of the comfort of his safe harbor.

"Few hear her anymore," Aster murmurs, and I realize it isn't just Matthias he's studying—it's the chord thrumming between us.

Matthias surges into my grasp, whirling me around. We follow steps to a dance instinctually, one forgotten to time's passage. We float upon a cloud, twirling under the soft gaze of the moon and sharing her embrace in each other's arms.

Matthias' strong grip tethers me to him. His breezy Grit worms its way inside me once more, calling to my shadowy pool. Only too ready to play, my magic winds back around his, nestling in it the same way I've pressed myself against the hard planes of his chest with no care for the blades just inches from my flesh.

"Pisúlë." My nose doesn't wrinkle this time. That soft thing Laz once beat out of me opens a sleepy eye in my chest, and I revel in the feeling.

"Vael'astor." The word tumbles from my lips. Its meaning unknown to me, but a flash in the glacial eyes staring down at me has a smile blooming right along with the cozy feeling in my chest. I yearn for the days when Papa tried to teach us his mother tongue, but I never was a good student.

Everything around us blurs, falls away, until all that matters is the music, the broad hands upon my spine and my cheek, and...him.

A breath later, he's wrenching away from me. Matthias' chest heaves beneath his shirt, the motion causing a purple light to glint off the daggers adorning his bandolier.

My mouth opens and closes in rapid succession, like a fish out of water. Air saws in and out of my chest. I feel as if I've just finished a fight with a demon, energy sizzling across my skin and down each limb. Yet I mourn. A mourning so unlike what consumed me after Lachlan's death. It overwhelms me, and for the second time, tears well and prick my eyes. It's as if I'm missing a limb, the very core of my being.

The Grit that had only moments ago found a home inside a sea cave offered by his magic retreats into my chest, but a piece lingers, refusing the call to come home. A part of me feels its refusal and loss like a betrayal, but a quieter part of me understands its desire to say wrapped up in the soothing comfort.

"Fascinating." I whip to face the voice. Aster...He holds his hand aloft commanding his Arcane Mana to form an undulating pink and lilac colored circle around Ironhart and me. Aster, who should never have had any reason to reveal this part of himself, now stood bathed in his own forbidden glow—and it was my storm that dragged him into the open. "You should be safe from Elyndra's pull beneath this shield."

I shake my head like a dog, as if it will release the confusion both from what had just happened but also from the scene in front of me. Grit unwinds in my chest without hesitation and plunges us further into darkness, extinguishing the illumination of the greenhouse and the Arcane circle looping around the Night Elf and me.

"No need, Kira. It's done. I can't un-ring that bell," Aster says. I don't find any resignation or regret lacing his words. With the shadows eclipsing all light, his face is as hidden as his emotions.

I can't help but feel like a metaphorical pin cushion for the emotions assaulting me from every angle. Guilt, elation, comfort, shame, and loss. And now, I am to blame for revealing Aster's most guarded secret. If I hadn't chased the ache in my chest tonight, if I'd stayed in my room like I should have, Matthias wouldn't know about Aster's Arcane magic. My secrets are a weight I can carry; his was never mine to gamble with.

First Lachlan, now Aster—how many people would bleed their truths because I couldn't keep mine contained?

"Well, this night has been fucked sideways," I grumble. "Should have just waited in the dorm for you." I throw my arms up and walk to the edge of the circle Aster has encased us in.

"That should keep the goddess' influence from pulling at your baser natures." He nods at the floating purple stars and sparkles.

Boots scraping at the cobblestones draws my attention. Ironhart aggressively scuffs his feet, as though to wipe them from mud before entering a home or ward off a chill. He refuses to look my way, his head tilted back toward the cloudy sky overhead. A *boom* sounds toward the port just moments before a flash rends the dusky sky. The smell of rain fills the air, warning of the coming storm.

"Zorvyn wishes to play tonight. If you wish to stay dry..." The elf dips his chin toward the doorway Aster still bars.

CHAPTER 17

IRONHART LOUNGES UPON A chair woven from the very bark of a tree that has wound its way around the greenhouse, as if it nominated itself the king of the greenhouse and seeks to connect with each of its subjects. A benevolent king from the way each bloom, each frond, turns its head to seek out its loving leader's touch and gaze.

The captain appears more royalty than guard in this moment. Aster, on the other hand, lost his new wardrobe somewhere for the night, choosing to wear an unadorned peach-colored robe, though his All Seeing Eye medallion never seems to stray far from his chest.

The Berserker stares at the Mage who peruses the plants near him leisurely. While something unknown brews between the two of them, I sink upon a cushion near the wide pool in the center of the foliage. Raindrops patter against the clear panes and streak down the sides of the greenhouse, as if racing to the soil.

Aster breaks the quiet atmosphere. "Is he really not going to ask?"

"Probably not," Ironhart drawls before I have a chance to open my mouth.

The ever-affable Mage's laughter bounces from window to window, filling the cozy space with mirth. The captain readjusts in his seat with a sharp exhale. "In truth, your secrets are your own. I have no wish to collect more than I already hold."

What *exactly* does that mean? Before I can wonder further if he holds secrets beyond Lachlan, my status with the law, or knowledge of what I once possessed, I stop myself.

Of course he has secrets, Kira. The man holds the rank of captain. He didn't arrive there by accident and probably picks up more information simply existing in his rank than I do on a single reconnaissance mission.

"Even still. Aster—Gods, I can never atone for this." My braid slides over my shoulder, the hidden spikes scratching along my shirt as it goes.

"You worry too much. This brute over here seems to give fewer shits than Varek with that stick shoved up his ass." His Vaeroth-may-care tone eases some of the tension driving my shoulders up, but Ironhart remains still in his chair, features drawn. "Think he can hear us?"

I drop my head to one side and rake my gaze over the Night Elf's form. An electricity vibrates on his skin, causing the smallest of tremors to rack his honed muscles. The longing I'd felt from moments ago outside the greenhouse slithers its way through Aster's warding magic.

Here beneath the moon, Zorvyn's storm magic and Elyndra's beloved nature still beckons the feral nature in me. Matthias pulls at me, even as he sits stoically without granting me even a speck of attention.

Get out of my head, Elyndra! Nythraxis is my God. I am no child of yours.

A creeping vine from Matthias' tree weaves its way upon the earthy floor to skitter across my breeches and tickle at my legs.

Well, screw you too, Elyndra.

After batting away the offending vine without damaging it, I dip my fingers into the cool water next to me and fling a handful of water toward the hulking Berserker.

My lips part on a silent gasp when the blob of liquid veers sharply left and splatters against the wide leaf of a fern.

"Fucking Sea Berserker," I mumble to myself. "Listening but apparently too wrapped up in himself to pay attention to our lowly aspirant drama." I roll my eyes with a shrug.

Aster finally abandons the spot he's been rooted to, striding toward me and settling upon the top step of the pool. He pulls up the hem of his robe and dips his bare feet into the clear waters.

"Oh, gross! Why don't you have shoes on?" I scrunch my nose while watching the bits of dirt float away into the pool.

"It's called grounding, haven't you heard of it? Besides, it's not like anyone drinks this water." He settles back onto his hands after securing the bottom of his robe into his belt to allow himself the freedom to enjoy whatever grounding is.

"You're making that up. I might have grown up in some dark, dank Underbelly, but I've been around the continent, been to Baustantia, and I've not once heard of someone 'grounding.'"

He huffs. "You're obviously hanging out with the wrong folk, Kira. "

A protest forms on my lips, but the cheeky smirk that unfolds the same way a leaf might melts all my arguments. I shove his shoulder, and he just drops his head back, that smirk widening to a full grin. "You tricky little shit."

"Come on, take off your boots. Feel the earth beneath your feet." He taps the tip of my shoe where my feet are crossed. "You too can wash your feet in the Goddess' pools."

"I'm probably on her shit list already for either daring to be a half or not giving enough credit to my Elven side. Probably depends on the day." I raise my eyebrows and flash a wan smile. His expectant face never changes, so I set about unlacing and removing my boots and stockings.

Skipping the whole grounding thing, I slide my feet into the pool right alongside his. A tingling chill has me dropping my own head back on a sigh, and with that one exhalation, the tension bleeds away from each of my limbs. The weighty sluggishness gives way to a cool, floating sensation.

This must be what a dip into a Moon Pool is like. The world knew of their healing properties, but whispers danced in backrooms about slipping into the silky waters for a pleasure swim. To enjoy the kiss of something goddess-touched upon your skin.

"Why did you come out here tonight?" Aster's words are neither accusatory nor chiding.

I choose to stroke his already inflated ego, saying, "I need your expertise on something." Aster wastes no time in ribbing me.

"I love when I know more than you about something," he croons. His eyes crinkle at the edges, cheeks bunching beneath them.

"You know more than me about anything that comes from a book. Don't start with me." I snap my hand out to ruffle his hair, the same way I used to ruffle Lach's. Something like bitter chocolate coats my tongue, but I fight to stay in this moment. Emotions have stolen too much from me tonight, and I won't let it steal this moment of peace.

"*Anyways,* what do you know of prophecies?"

"Are you asking me to explain them to you? Like how they work?" He raises a single brow, head tilting like he's trying to discern if I truly don't know what a prophecy is.

"No, you dolt. Like have you studied them in the past?" He nods. "If I were to have heard one—" Fabric scrapes across wood and boots thunk against the soil.

The back of my neck prickles a half second before the sound reaches me. My shadows twitch as though something vast and familiar stalks closer, my pulse syncing to the storm's rhythm. I don't need to look to know it's him.

Matthias drops beside me with a weight that makes the floorboards groan. His shoulder nearly brushes mine, heat radiating from him like a furnace. I yank myself back after realizing I'm leaning into his warmth.

"You're supposed to be pretending we don't exist, Captain."

"I'm not your captain tonight." The words coil through me, low and rough, sparking a question I don't dare voice. If not my captain...then what?

It's on the tip of my tongue to ask what he is, but his stare prevents the question from ever forming.

"Go on." The rough edges of his words scrape at the lingering pull between us, like blunt knives against a rope. They may not sever it, but it still frays some of the strands.

I relay the prophecy to Aster.

The strength of many shall bow to one, after two become one, blade and soul twice undone, a shattered fate made whole once more chooses the fate of the endless war.

For a long moment, only the harsh patter of rain and occasional boom of thunder fills the space. The moment stretches on and on, until I'm sure Aster won't respond. But finally, he leans forward to rest his elbows on his knees.

His icy Mana tickles my feet in the pool. His hands move rhythmically, and curiosity drives me forward to inspect his actions. In the water floats a brick of ice, but with each motion of his hand, a tiny piece chips away. Like some sort of magical manual sculptor.

"Can't you just create the sculpture?"

"Yes. Now, hush. I'm thinking." He continues to chip and chip away at the block. With rapt attention, I watch each piece fall back to the pool and disintegrate with no inclination toward what the piece will become. I needed a hobby or something better to do with my Grit than maim and murder.

"You're far more trusting than he was," Matthias says. I don't have to ask who he's referring to.

"I wasn't always, but I do recall someone telling me once I didn't have to go this alone." I offer a small smile, and the look he gives me in return mends some of those frayed strands.

We linger as the rain slows, the storm losing its edge. Aster stands, silent and distant, his hands folded behind him as he slips out of the greenhouse. The unfinished ice leviathan sags in the quiet aftermath, melting by degrees—its features dissolving as he vanishes into the mist.

CHAPTER 18

"**N**ervous?"

Pulling my attention away from the row of poisons in my belt, I consider Thara's question. I am, but not for the reasons she or any other aspirants are. I've sent plenty of Void Demons back to Vaeroth, but any of the demons we face today could be summoned by Rashvik or Dazek or any number of the Locks working with Luella.

The commandant knows about my crimes against the crown, but only a handful know exactly what it was I took. Laz better have that damned Shardblade hilt locked away even deeper than the Underbelly. Hopefully the greedy bastard hasn't sold it.

We stand in a darkened vestibule outside the arena typically reserved for the king's entertainment. Gladiator fights, chariot races, typical monarch festivities with no regard for pain and suffering involved in the events. Aster drew the short straw and entered into the trial first, followed by Varek, a Cleric, and a Fire Mage. The numbers dwindle, leaving me and Tharava with a handful of other aspirants to pace the ornately decorated room.

A group of antsy aspirants seems like a gamble on whether we'll break something like bulls in a china shop.

I shake my head. "You?"

"Very much so." I study the female next to me. She's painted her face and chest in the traditional red war paints of her people. Strong lines accentuate her facial structure and the Blood markings adorn her skin with dots, whorls, and lettering in a language unknown to me. The designs are not unlike the Night Elven markings. With a pang I touch my forehead, the weaving black and indigo lines that make up the crown of thorns imbued into my brow currently on display with every wisp of hair pulled tightly away from my face.

Thara bats my hand away. Her short tusks pull at her frown, which only makes the look she gives me harsher. "Orc halves are revered. Hybrid vigor makes them strong. Makes them resilient. The best of both kinds. All full-bloods should want the abilities afforded to the Var'Shakar."

My hands pause over the sheaths at my thighs. I cock my head, brows furrowed, and search Thara's gaze.

"'Blood-blessed' in my tongue." She flashes a row of pointed teeth at me, the war paint bunching on her cheeks. "Our Var'Shakar lead some of the most elite warbands. They are offered the first selection of Great Wolves to ride."

"Blood-blessed." I chew on the word before it rolls off my tongue. "Var'Shakar." The word unlocks something inside me. My Grit giving a content wiggle in my chest, but the feeling reminds me of the piece that still refuses to come back to me from the Elven captain.

Thara reaches over to push the strands of hair covering my shortened curved ears. "Today, you are Var'Shakar. Not half. You fight for two peoples." Her choppy accent forms harsh edges around every word, and each one carves into my soul. Faelwyn appears in the now open doorway, calling the Orc's name. Thara dips her chin. "Gol'kash tavor. Go with honor."

She picks up her broadsword and leaves me staring after her as her feet pound against the floor. Thara hammers a cadence against her chest with her fist, humming and chanting in her native tongue. The rhythmic beating charges the expanse between the few of us left.

It builds and builds, the electricity in the air crackling and popping before she crescendos in a battle cry upon entering the arena, leaving an empty static silence in her wake.

Cadet after cadet leave the vestibule after Faelwyn calls their name. After what feels like too long and not long enough, she calls mine. I swagger toward her, leaning into my experience in the guild to bolster my confidence. She casts her eyes over me, in the same silent check-in she offered to every cadet before me, then steps aside to open the door into the arena.

Energy buzzes along my skin as I step into the stone-walled arena, bright with sunlight. Gritty sand crunches beneath my feet with each step. The sharp change in lighting burns my eyes, and it takes several blinks for me to finally take in the scene before me.

A crimson pool lays just inches ahead of me, but the dry earth soaks the lifeblood like a welcomed sacrifice. Sidestepping, I cast about without finding any trace of the demon I'm to face. Atop the stone walls, tiered balcony seats fill the entire arena, save the farthest edge of the oval. A covered dais stands above all else, likely where King Wilder presides during events. The single throne with a gold-wrapped frame and mauve cushions must have been pushed back to allow for the commandant and instructors to oversee the trial. Luella, clad in dusky-pink robes, stands with her hands clasped behind her. She's flanked by Dazek and another Lock I've not seen before.

He wears the customary purple robes, though in contrast to Dazek's hood, his robes peak in a high collar to frame his head. The rich color of his clothing offsets his sallow skin, made all the more stark with vibrant, crimson irises that pierce me even through the distance between us. A gold belt circles his skeletal waist, orbs and vials hanging from chains. Light glints off the fiery token resting on his breastbone, but I can't figure out what the symbol is through the black and orange tendrils undulating within and around it.

Nythraxis' shadows save me. *Who is that?* Three quarters of the length of the arena separate us and yet his Fate Threads weave around my legs like an oily cat. Even in their cool, soulless depths, his Fate Threads ignite an icy burn through my leg plates in their wake. The distance should be too great for me to feel his magic. I cast a wary gaze back toward the Lock.

A shiver skitters down my spine, knowing that Dazek and a Lock more powerful than him will summon the demons I'll face.

"You've got this!" Aster's voice pulls my attention. He sits on one of the stone benches in the first row of the tiered seats, leaning forward on one elbow. The other punches the air in quick succession. I flip him off, but he simply blows me a kiss. Warmth blooms in my chest. He tries far too hard to fit into the norm, but his attempts ease some of the anxiety.

Tharava perches next to him. Neither look too worse for wear. Dirt smudges Aster's cheek, and ash covers most of the exposed skin and war paint on Thara's left side. Other cadets surround them; I sigh when I see Varek and his cronies several rows behind the rest of the group.

They ignore my presence, but that suits me just fine.

"Come now, Thorne. We've not got all day." Commandant Megora stands in full armor, as if he's the one fighting these demons instead of managing them from a distance.

Once I stand beneath the dais, Megora speaks again. "Your first trial marks a historic day. The first Rogue to set foot in the Spire as an aspirant." Chewing my cheek, I stop the grin from forming at the acknowledgment I'm the first Rogue to *legally* set foot into the Spire. "Warlock Captain Aldros will oversee this trial alongside his compatriot, Demonier Dazek."

My lips part. Demoniers were rarer than rare. Only a handful existed as Vaeroth's chosen. They could summon demons far more powerful than they had any right to. Demons that ought to be left in the deep reaches of the Void. Demoniers had once raised full-fledged armies of demons on their own. Elves and Orcs from centuries past had all but eradicated them on the sole purpose that one demonier could level an entire city on a whim.

Dazek sneers down at me, his visage matching Luella's glower. They, along with Aldros, are a trifecta of magic, one I have no intention of taking on. Aldros steps to the edge of the dais, assessing me. I resist the urge to stand taller, to fist a dagger, or reach for the vials of poisons littered throughout my armor. His Fate Threads wander like fingers across my chest armor and prickle at my neck.

Did he do this to all aspirants or am I receiving special treatment?

"Kiralin Thorne. I've heard of you." The silkiness of his voice is sickeningly smooth and just as repulsive as his Fate Threads.

"Can't say the same." I spit the words before I can think better of it.

Crimson eyes flare in acceptance of the proverbial gauntlet I've thrown onto the warm sand. "The rules are simple. Fight, kill, or be killed."

"Just another day then," I drawl.

"Perhaps."

Behind Aldros, Dazek weaves his hands in a complicated dance. Roaring drags me away from the dais, back to the arena behind me. The very seams of the cosmos rip apart, red and violet lights hiss along the edges of the hole in the world. Air rushes out of my chest, and my heart clangs wildly against my ribs like a runaway horse.

Rogues have a term for a target that's a flight risk: rabbit. And that's exactly what I want to do right now. I want to rabbit out of this arena. If a demonier is summoning something from Vaeroth's realm, I want to be on the other side of the continent or at least on my way there.

Aldros speaks again. "There is to be no outside interference. If either of them"—the pounding in my chest stutters. *Either of them!?*—"deems you too weak to fight, your place at the Spire and your life are forfeit."

Oh, good. Death is my fate if they kill me, or deem me worthy of death. Pretty sure I'm worthy of death already, but if Nythraxis hasn't woven my ending into his tapestry yet, I refuse to let Vaeroth change that.

The air itself seems to shiver at the open, a swirling black portal creating a vacuum for all warmth and light. Willing myself to stay rooted to the spot, I watch as something from within the inky darkness moves. Finger by finger, the thing wraps its claws around the very edge of the portal, creeping into the arena.

Too many joints make up each of its limbs. Onyx skin consumes the light around it. Shadows would not save me here. Shadows require light; this is the antithesis of light. It finally unfolds itself from the rift like a mangled marionette with strings cut, leaving pieces and limbs hanging at impossible angles. Angles that should only exist on battered and broken bodies.

With a sickening crack, those limbs snap into place almost like a carpenter building a piece of furniture. Eyes—if they could be called eyes—beckon me into their sunken, swirling pools of mist. I stare into pits made from the very Void itself.

While I was focused on the first demon, the second slithered out of the portal. Just as grotesque, it shifts in rapid succession from plumes of smoke to beast. Its shape never lasts longer than a breath, each beast different from the last.

I'm fucked.

These are not mere Void Demons.

This is a death sentence.

Through the billowing, smoky body of the second demon, I make out Aster rising from his seat, his long fingers wrap around the railing. He's shucked off his ridiculous overcoat and abandoned his staff, a look marring his face that's out of place for him. His lips are drawn down, and his brows crease together. He lifts his hand only for Thara to yank it back to the railing. She says something to him, but it's lost to me.

She crosses her arms, but a word forms upon her lips as she looks back at me. *Var'Shakar.*

Yes. I am Blood-Blessed. I have the benefits of the elves and the Humans. I can—

The demons breathe in synchrony.

A wet, hungry sound echoes around me as if I've already been consumed, rotting within the pits of their bodies. Scorched metal and something fouler, *older* than death spills into my lungs and sends me coughing.

The pair stills and they sniff, tilting their heads. Searching. Seeking.

At last, the maws where their mouths should be open in soulless, empty smiles.

"We know you, *thief,*" one of them says, though neither's mouth moves. I cannot feel the magic from these demons, and the lack of sensation sets my teeth on edge. I slide two daggers from their sheaths, ignoring the commentary. I can't imagine they know me, and I need all my focus to figure out how I'm supposed to stop a damned wisp of smoke with a blade. I'd have better luck damming the river with a piece of chiffon.

Shuffling above me draws my attention. Faces tilt down from the benches, each locked in rapt attention to the demons. But confusion laces their curiosity and morbid scrutiny. Aster looks past the demons toward me, jaw dropped and eyes wide in alarm.

Not good. Assuming no one else's demons had a little chat with them.

Marionette creaks and ambles in a circle starting one way while Smoke slithers opposite his companion. I have no choice but to remain still, listening, waiting.

"You reek of stolen divinity."

Divinity!? How was I supposed to know the damned hunk of broken metal was divine?

Lead fills my boots. I cannot move. My vision clouds as panic sends my breathing into a frenzy, but my focus snags on movement in the doorway I came through. Faelwyn and Matthias lean with feigned casualness against the stone walls. Meeting a glacial stare for the briefest of moments, an ocean current pushes my feet.

Nythraxis, if any of the other onlookers can feel others' magic like I can, I'm dead. Gallows be damned, these two will drag me through the rift Dazek left open.

The two demons converge, Smoke wrapping around the limbs of Marionette—as if this wasn't nightmare-inducing enough. With the pair now conjoined, I begin to circle the demons.

If I can at least sever Marionette's head, that's one problem solved. Smoke is only ever solid for heartbeats at a time. How does one kill smoke?

"Nervous?" The demon's voice sounds eerily like Thara's just before she entered the arena. I should have said yes.

"Biding my time," I snarl. With a yell, I swoop forward. Pride surges through me when my blade connects with leathery flesh. A gods-awful screech rends the air as searing pain lances through my hip.

I stagger away from the demon pair. The dagger in my palm slips to the sand. Thick black blood drips like cold honey from a wound on Marionette's hip. I fight to block out the pain threatening to blind me, wiping my hand against my hip expecting to find blood. But there's nothing there. No tear in my breeches. No damage to my leg plates. Nothing.

The same smile touches Marionette again. "I know what might help you." The voice is like shadows personified. Airy, whispered, raspy. "Knowing how Lachlan died." In an instant, Lach's voice echos through the darkened arena.

"Lin, why didn't you save me? You sent me to die!" Tears smudge the edges of my vision. My fingers fumble when I yank another dagger from a sheath at my ribcage. With all the grace of a first-year trainee, I lurch forward in a wild flurry of attacks. Each slash connects against Marionette, slipping through the smoky armor provided by the second demon.

With each attack, the demon must somehow return the blows, cut after cut. But the pain is nothing. It matters little to me. Over and over, Lachlan's voice cries out my name in increasing intensity. Stumbling and wobbling, I retreat to circle the demon again, careful to avoid the rift, lest I tumble into the void from my own stupidity.

This may be the fight that kills me if the pain is any indication. I'll lose too much blood before I ever finish off Smoke. I pull at my Grit, urging the shadows to encase me, to press at open wounds, but it doesn't respond. Again, I beg my magic to do something, just hold in the blood weeping from my body. Still, it doesn't move.

Do something! I cry internally.

"Kill us, and the secret dies with us."

Salty air and cool water wiggles between my armor and skin, washing away the pain. I don't care if Matthias' inability to follow rules set by his own chain of command gets me sent to the brig. At this rate, I just want to survive. I'll thank him later.

When I don't respond to the demons cajoling, it dives forward. I retch at the smell, intensified by the blood leaking from its open wounds, and throw myself into a dive roll to the side. Sand plumes up in a cloud obscuring my field of vision. I cast my Grit out, the tall seating offering me that saving grace, and search for the demons.

"You're afraid of losing him too, aren't you?" Words whispered along my shadows reach me like water poured through a pipe.

A limb reaches through the cloud to scrape down my arm. In a move drilled into me by Laz, I snatch the end of the claw and use my other hand to drive my blade upward through its forearm from underneath. Pain erupts in my own arm the moment I thrust the dagger through. Ignoring the boiling agony pouring over my arm, I yank my dagger toward me with every bit of strength I have. I don't have time to consider if the mechanics will work the same as on a person.

I grit my teeth against the grotesque sensation, telling myself I'm cutting through the tendons and muscles of game animals. My blade slips free at the joint between the wrist and the arced claw. I wrinkle my nose, not quite what I wanted. I'd used that maneuver on a Baustantian human, tearing out their radialartery just before it broke off into the interosseous artery. I'd hoped the vascular system of demons would be the same, or that I could have severed whatever the connective tissue demons had around their carpals.

I clutch my arm to my chest with no care for where the blade fisted in my hand goes. My fingers loosen and the slick hilt slips free. And that's when it occurs to me: *Our pain is linked.*

I have somehow taken on this creature's pain. That should be beyond any magic of a demon. Matthias' Grit wraps its way around my arm like a splint, licking away my pain and supporting the limb that throbs as though it's been ripped off.

Marionette totters wildly, flailing and flinging black ooze in every direction. It leaves a gruesome painting on the stone walls and sand beneath us, the one arm dangling uselessly. I seize the opportunity to attack as Smoke retreats to the opposite side of the arena. I brace for the pain that will surely follow when I take the killing blow. I'll likely die from the pain when I feel like I'm severing my own head.

Legs pumping harder than I've ever pushed before, I drop the remaining dagger in my other palm, its ooze-covered handle slipping away with a thud on the sandy ground. My good hand reaches for the serrated blade sheathed against my spine. With a final drive, I shove my shoulder into Marionette's abdomen, and we both go careening into the ground.

With a guttural roar, it claws wildly with its remaining intact upper limb, making contact and tearing at my skin. I shove and strike, blocking the reciprocated pain with each blow. Thoughts eddy through as I attack.

There will be no justice for Lachlan's murder.

I straddle the demon's chest.

There will be no more late nights talking with Aster.

Blade at the demon's throat, a scream tears my throat like razor blades on the first saw.

There will be no exploration of Matthias and why my Grit has chosen him over me.

Excruciating pain explodes as I sever the demon's windpipe.

And there will be no redemption for me.

Air leaves my lungs for the last time.

One last drag of my blade, and the head of the demon tilts back and rolls to the side, connected only by frayed pieces of skin. I, too, fall to the side, slumping into the dirt. My blade falling free from the tight grip I'd held it in.

Death. That shall be my next journey. Did Nythraxis weave this fate for me? Will he welcome me into his great Gothic chateau? Perhaps Da is right and it's surrounded by vineyards. Maybe Nythraxis offered Lachlan a place there and I'll see him soon.

Tears well, and I seek out Matthias across the arena. His face is an impassive mask. Completely unreadable. Agony lances my heart. I know it was only the magic of Elyndra last night, but all the same, I had hoped our connection was real enough that he'd feel something about my death.

Smoke looms above me, only it isn't a smoky wisp of a demon. The nightmare dripping foaming liquid from its jaws now has the head of a wild boar. The front legs morph into that of a bear and the hindquarters of a bison, like something from a horrific children's tale. Its six tusks curve sharply and end in vicious points, all longer than my forearm.

I'll be home to Nytharia soon. Home to my God. I cast one more glance to Matthias, holding his icy gaze. I don't have the strength to channel or say anything, but perhaps this will be enough. I should have thanked him for watching out for Lachlan. Even if...

"Vael'astor." My lips wrap around the foreign word one last time. No sound follows. Matthias' glacial eyes crack, emotion I can't quite read contorting his face for the briefest of moments. He pushes off the stone, but a shadow wraps around my body—one not of my bidding.

The demon above me lowers its great head, preparing to impale me upon those grotesque tusks. With a great heave, it rams forward. Grit overwhelms me, dragging me just out of the way of its strike. Smoke's tusks bury into the ground where my body had once been, his snout inches into the sand.

I look inward to see my Grit unwound in a useless pile. It has already accepted we're going home to the land of infinite shadow.

But a cool breeze urges me to my feet. Pushes me. Refuses my own reluctance to live. Matthias' Grit guides my hand and drives me toward the boar with all the ferocity of a Berserker lost to Bloodlust. Slipping one more dagger from its sheath, his magic shoves the blade into the demon's neck, still solidified in its beast form. Animalistic eyes widen at the blade protruding from its body before I wrench it free.

I fall back. My ass hits the ground hard and I land on my back, knife falling to the blackened dirt. I'm alive.

As though moving my head underwater, I turn to the demon. *"You cannot outrun fate, dangerous little shadow."*

With one last feral, unhinged smile, the swirling pools of the void disintegrate, leaving nothing but the memory they existed and the faint traces of the dark magic they held behind.

CHAPTER 19

> *Deities are finicky things. Please them, and their descendants and disciples shall be rewarded handsomely, but even the smallest slight can result in a fate worse than death. Injure their pride, and even being forgotten in the Void will seem pleasant.*

Silence reigns in the arena as I gather my blades from the sand. The wind halts, and the noise of the city outside the walls fades. The only movement is my own. The only sound that of the limping scrape from my labored steps. The sun practically blinds me once the rift closes, releasing the chokehold it held upon the light in the arena.

I wipe the blades on my sleeves before sheathing them with all the care I'd show a piece of garbage. I'm too tired to care. Too drained.

Too alive.

That's the whole of it. I'd made my peace about leaving this world behind. Lachlan is waiting for me.

But only the night before I'd promised Aster I'd protect him as if he were my brother. The gentle simmer at my neck reminds me I have other obligations I can't simply abandon in favor of Nythraxis' vineyard chateau.

"You're dismissed, Rogue." Luella's high-pitched voice reaches me as though she stands in the arena with me. An amplification spell. I'd be able to hear her just fine without it, but of course, she uses her Mana at every turn.

I wave a hand in acknowledgment and trudge to the wall beneath Aster. A rope ladder hangs limply from the railing. I stare at the fifteen feet it spans. It might as well be Rianta Kai—tall, jagged, and merciless. Lach and I used to dream of climbing that mountain back when the Olythim range was nothing more than a smudge of blue on the horizon from Lefendor, the only world we knew back then. Now the real thing looms much closer—and the climb feels no less impossible.

My arm dangles at my side. Despite the knowledge that I did not shave off half my hand, the pain lingers and leaves me with the sensation of a phantom limb. Fuck that ladder. I'll just wrap myself in shadows and sit on the ground. I move to lean against the wall, intending to slide down and barricade myself in the dark, but Aster's chilly Mana sidles up my good arm.

An icy staircase leads to the tiered seats. It's crude and rudimentary, nothing like the sculptures he creates at any opportunity, but function before style and all. Tilting my head back, I meet his concerned stare. Offering him a grateful smile, I haul my beaten and broken body from the pit.

With a mumbled thanks and curt nod, I continue past the railing and up the stairs, directing myself to the last row in the first bank of seating. The wall will support my weary body, and the canvas overhang grants more shade—an opportunity to replenish my Grit.

I force my feet to climb the stairs, which might as well be a mountain considering the effort it takes to heave myself up them. My knees buckle once I've made it to my destination. Dusky-green hands slip beneath my armpits to steady me.

"You are," Thara murmurs, "the most valiant fighter I have ever beheld, var'shakar."

She eases me to the bench. My head cracks back against the stone, but the pain is the least of my concerns.

Someone up there knows about the Shardblade. How the fuck do they know?

It's been too long since I've talked to Laz. If I can escape tonight, I need to send a crow to him. Beg him to talk to me or reassure me he still possesses the hilt. Reassure me I wasn't out here risking my neck for some broken piece of metal he smelted into an earring or chamber pot.

Just my luck all of these people are hunting for something I stole, and my employer turned it into a chamber pot.

A humorless laugh escapes my lips. Aster startles at the sound when he eases down beside me. He rummages around in the small purse dangling from his belt. He pulls out two stoppered vials, one filled a with deep cerulean liquid with white speckles, and the other half-full of a crimson, almost blood-like substance.

"Painwake and Bloodbind. You'll hate both. One to numb the pain. One to stop the internal bleeding."

"Is there anything you don't do?" I roll my head toward him, the effort to lift it seeming too great to even attempt.

"Can't dance. Can't sing. Being a bard isn't in the deck for me."

Sand crunches in the distance. I suppose whatever poor soul followed my dramatic exit must be entering into the arena. Nythraxis bless them.

The shiny gleam of Paladin armor fills the archway from the staging area. The Night Elf Paladin, Taigh, steps from the gateway to the vestibule in the arena. Lithe muscles roll when he draws the heavy broadsword from his back. I tried to pick the blasted thing up after sparring with him once—I'd barely managed the weight.

I'd seen him during formation and combat training, the same one that offered me deference after my spat with Varek—silent, focused, always the last to leave the field. His jaw slackens upon seeing the carnage I've left upon the sands. Both demons' bodies still rest where they were slain.

I try to lighten the ordeal I'd just endured. "No one around to clean up the mess?"

Aster hesitates, but Tharava answers for him. "We fought Void Demons. They—"

"Evaporate upon death. Yes, I'm familiar." She glares at the interruption.

"They only had us fight one demon, a lesser demon. Not two servants of Vaeroth himself."

I finally unstopper the vials and put both to my lips simultaneously. The combination is wretched, but the potions' magic gets to work immediately. The vise around my lungs loosens, and I breathe in deeply for the first time since entering into the trial.

The burning around my neck cools as I gently sip air down. Aldros gives Taigh a much gentler version of the speech he gave me. No mention of impending death. Even adds a well wish at the end.

Bastards.

All of them on that damned raised dais, acting as though they are gods, kings, the ones to choose who lives and dies. It's not lost on me, however, that I have played a hand in many individuals' deaths. Severing the life thread is not my first choice, though.

"One demon." My brain finally processes what Thara said.

"Aye."

"The fuck did I do to earn myself a damn near passage upon Vaeroth's ship?"

A grim-looking demon enters from the gate opposite Taigh. Seems Dazek would not be opening any rifts to the Void for the other aspirants. Taigh brandishes his twin short swords. He's a formidable opponent, having spent time before coming to the Spire as part of the militia for his lord.

The fight is over in mere blinks.

"This—this is what they had you facing?" I bark out a laugh that borders on maniacal. Aster eyes me as if he's wondering whether I've devolved into madness.

Perhaps I have.

Neither says anything.

Sweat cools into icy pin pricks upon my skin. Taigh climbs over the railing after managing the rope ladder with no hesitation. He scans over the gawking aspirants, his eyes never lingering on any for long. Lifting up and up, he finally connects with my gaze. The Paladin treks up the stairs, passing Varek, who calls out to him to join his cadre on their bench. Taigh waves him off and continues upward.

He stands in front of me, blue-streaked, raven hair slithering out of the band holding it back, and dips his chin to the bench below us.

I mirror his movement, dipping my chin. He takes the seat, facing sideways with one leg on either side, the leg closest to me stretched out to accommodate for the higher level. "Captain sent this."

Taigh extends graceful fingers my way, a small scroll no bigger than my little finger pinched between them. I search his gaze but find no hidden agenda lurking, so I pluck the rolled parchment from his grip.

"You kill those things?" the Paladin asks. I nod, not trusting myself to speak to him quite yet. We've never spoken outside of passing commentary. I know nothing about him outside his denomination, name, and where he hails from. "Glad they didn't send one of those big bastards after me. Wish I could have seen it though."

He crooks a grin at me, the elegant features of his race transforming into a boyish charm. "Cap's my brother, if that's why you're looking at me like I've handed you a snake rather than a note from Matty."

The parchment slips through my fingertips at the same time Aster's head whips away from where another cadet struggles in the arena. "That old grump has a brother? No less a normal brother?" I rasp a chuckle at Aster's questions.

Taigh doubles over his outstretched legs, unabashed laughter ringing out. He does bear the resemblance of Ironhart. Wildly different hair colors, one silver as the moon and the other blue and inky like the far reaches of the deep sea. Opposite for what their denominations should call for. The Paladin ought to have hair like liquid light.

The elf winks one moss colored eye. "I'm the better looking one. No need to study me that thoroughly while we both have clothes on."

This draws Thara's attention; she says nothing, but glowers at the brazen statement. I don't fight the grin this time.

"Are we taking in another stray?" Thara asks drily.

"I think so," I reply.

Taigh looks between us before retorting, "Is this because I'm his brother or because you want to see me naked?"

My grin stretches wider, but I only waggle my brows. Taigh chokes when Aster opens his mouth. "I wouldn't be opposed. Our room is open."

Our laughter mingles, but next to me, Thara bumps into me with her shoulder and jerks her chin. In the arena, a Mage lays prostrate on the sand. Crimson pools around blackened, charred skin. Her face bears claw marks and hangs in ribbons from her skull. Unrecognizable. Blonde hair withered before our eyes into gray strands before disintegrating into ash, picked up by the wind only to disappear as if it never existed. Remnants of a rust-colored robe splay at her sides. The burnt color a cruel foreshadowing to her demise.

"Fallon," Thara says. I should feel bad I don't know her, but I've already let myself care too much about too many people here. I had no intention on staying, and if these *strays* as Aster calls them grow too close, they'll only end up as collateral damage when I do what I was sent here to.

"That's not a demon kill," I breathe.

Aster shakes his head in small jerks. "No. She burned herself out."

I've never witnessed someone channel too much magic. Especially not battle magic like this. Shadows don't burn Rogues when we use too much. We become perpetually stuck within them. It does not kill us, but we become specters. Not quite part of the Void but not quite part of this world either. Nythraxis refuses to let a Rogue enter the chateau if they fall prey to the shadow's lure, but should they ever make it to his realm in the Void, they are permitted to roam the vineyards.

Aster worries the All Seeing Eye in his hand, mumbling beneath his breath. "She'll be barred from Lumeris' library. The doors won't open to her. She'll—she'll be lost to the Void with Vaeroth," he says, stumbling over his explanation.

I suck in air on a silent gasp, mirroring Taigh's expression. The gods and goddesses who refuse their descendants entry to everlasting rest sentence them to an eternity as one of Vaeroth's playthings—be it demon or training dummy.

Aldros peers down into the arena from his perch, no emotion on his face. As soulless as the Void itself. Something churns in my stomach at the way he watches this unfold—not with grief, not even with interest. Like he's seen this a hundred times. Like he *planned* for it. He makes several aggressive, sharp movements with both arms. A rift opens in the arena, pitching the surrounding sands into darkness.

I press back into the stone behind me. Pain erupts from the invisible wounds across my forearm, chest, and back. Air refuses to enter my lungs. I can't suck it down. My throat doesn't exist; my head sits in the sands next to Fallon's grisly, blackened body.

"Nythraxis' shadows," I murmur. I have to get away. I will scale this entire colosseum to escape encountering another of those Marionette demons.

Before I can move, long spindly fingers creep through the tear in our realm. One by one, they straighten and curl, like sentient beings seeking their prey. How quickly had Lumeris renounced his claim upon Fallon? Did Aldros speed along the process, acting as a ferryman for an unclaimed soul?

Aldros is just as soulless as the demon emerging. I can't rip my attention away from the rift to see his face. I am commanded by the demon. Its existence carves through all bonds. It beckons, urges, enthralls me the way the deep sea calls to a stone dropped from a passing ship.

I must go to him.

Go with her.

His creature draws its head through the portal at long last. Its great, twisting horns swivel when it inhales deeply and shifts its focus upward, up the balconies. Ice slides through my veins, yet it's colder. Frostier than Aster's ice. Aster. I knew someone who shared that name once. He was kind, inquisitive. But the master of the Void, his mind is much more curious, far more than the All Seer.

I step forward to go to the one who calls me. Unlike the poor demised demons left to rot upon the earth, this creature has red within its eyes. With no lips, rows upon rows of pointed teeth gleam like polished onyx in the starry twilight now apparent in the Void rift.

The rift gapes. The demon watches me. I shake my head at my own foolishness for having been afraid of what lies beyond.

Then I taste sand in my mouth. I feel a crack in my ribs. I hear Taigh's voice—faint. Far. Taigh?

My legs try to move forward, but tangle with resistance, as if a cat weaves between them. I blink down to find the offending feline, but only shadows whirl. Pesky things. I kick at them, hoping to bat them away. Nythraxis has some nerve keeping me from my God.

The black tendrils resume their efforts with a renewed vigor, and Zorvyn's tide laps along my fingers, my ankles. Why do these Gods feel they have claim over a disciple of the Crimson Judge?

Blazing agony rips through all thoughts. Every injury I've suffered today barrels through all my awareness. Oily magic that can only belong to a being of the Void lances against my forearm, ripping it open, only for it to sew itself shut again with the black magic.

My knees crack against the stone steps, the sound ringing out as though it's been amplified by some sort of magic.

But an inferno of heat and light scorches my thigh. A sharp contrast to the dark pain still screaming in my arm.

Despite the excruciating burn upon my skin, the tether between me and the greater demon in the ring severs as if it had truly been a physical rope pulling me to it.

Shocked back into my body and senses, I shake my head and realize I'm at the railing—I'd been walking toward the arena.

I almost fall back when someone catches me. I finally look down at my leg to see Taigh's hand resting upon the breeches beneath my guards, glowing with a golden light. Shadows inch up my leg, dimming the Light Taigh is using to keep me grounded. My back rests against his chest, and I turn my head back to look up at him. The muscle in his strong jaw flickers rapidly, but he doesn't focus on me. He directs his ire to Aldros with zero regard for the consequences of doing so.

The demon, unperturbed by the break in connection, wraps its spindly hand around one of Fallon's ankles and drags her toward the still-open rift with a wet, scraping sound.

I fall sideways onto the bench, but Aster and Taigh catch me before I hit the stone, hauling me onto it properly.

With a shaky breath, I mutter, "I think I'm ready for this day to be over."

CHAPTER 20

Children bearing the same lineage can still result in different denominations. Even children of parents who share the same denomination can result in one that differs from their lineage. The Gods care not for how bloodlines work.

IN THE GREAT HALL, cutlery clatters, goblets strike the wooden tables, benches scrape the floor, but no jovial conversation or chatter. Silence holds court this evening. Although our squadron was selected for the Void Demon trial, each platoon and company faced a trial of some sort today.

Numbers in each company of the Spire deplete after trials. No one can escape the natural order of things, and when training for militaristic operations such as being a guard, there are bound to be dropouts and those who did not pass. I couldn't fathom the shame they'd feel. Dropping out meant their entire family line would be wiped from history. Ceremonial swords? Those belong to the crown now. Land? Belongs to the crown. Everything down to the spoon their mother stirs her tea with would become the crown's property.

However, in all the whispers I had collected for Lach before he set out and before my own arrival, death in the Spire is rare. Yet Vaeroth claimed a soul today—and nearly claimed another.

After Fallon's death, six more aspirants fought their trials. Four succeeded. Two yielded and were sent back to their villages with all the shame one could expect for failing to do their duty for their kingdom. Shame and the weight that their return wipes their family from the history of the realm. Just souls in the sands of time, swept away to be forgotten tomorrow.

I stare down at my uneaten roasted lamb and root vegetables on my plate. A combination of exhaustion and the lingering sensation of the grip the Void held on me left my stomach in knots.

I had bartered with a Cleric from Thara's village to heal the wounds that were untouched by Aster's potions, trading several vials of my precious poisons for his healing Mana. While it made my body whole, he'd given me a grim look when I mentioned the sensations of the wounds I'd inflicted upon the demons reflecting in my own body.

He couldn't fix those.

Like a nightmare, I'd have to forget those on my own.

Abandoning my cold meal, I extract the rolled up parchment from Ironheart where I'd stashed it within a used poison vial on my belt.

The scroll, only slightly damp now, shows no signs of damage. Through exposure on Laz's command, I'd built up a tolerance for the poison that burns flesh on contact, and the residue from the nasty substance barely bites at my skin—no more than holding my hand above a candle for a breath.

I unroll it to see what is so important he revealed his relationship to Taigh. I stretch the note between my hands.

Training yards, after the seventh chime. He'd be proud. Eat. You'll need it.

I cast my gaze about the great hall for the elf, but come up empty. The wheels in my head turn slower than usual, and it takes me a moment to realize he wrote the note hours ago and he cannot see my resistance to the hearty meal in front of me. With a resigned sigh, I accept defeat at the hands of a piece of meat and a few vegetables and dispose of them for the kitchen staff to feed to the pigs or whatever it was they did with scraps.

Aster and Thara had eaten directly after returning to the Spire, and Taigh went in search of a Humans Berserker he claimed used her Grit in bed. Thara had cut him off with a glare and a hard shove. I'm thankful for their absence since it makes slipping away to the training yards behind the Spire much simpler.

Leaving the great hall, I keep to the shadows, pulling my Grit quicker than normal from where I hold it inside me like a beloved stuffed animal. I meld into the shadows wholly; the twilight amplifies my denomination's ability and the Night Elf proclivity for the darkened hours.

My thoughts wander as I make my way, feeling aimless despite my known destination. I haven't been on steady ground since I set foot in this blasted city. From the Locks chasing me, Matthias' initial outburst in my dorm, the witch hunt with the demons, these blasted flashes of memories that don't come from my own mind. And all of it ending with today's tangle with death. I shake my head and weave my shadows tighter around me, holding my Grit close. Perhaps it will please Nythraxis to know I'm internally snuggling the gift he's blessed me with, thanking his shadows for buying Taigh time to keep me from my demise.

The Cleric healed the wound Taigh had given me too to break whatever hold Vaeroth held over me.. I'd almost asked him to leave it, as a reminder of how close I came to tumbling right over the railing and into the Void.

Grass squelches beneath my boots. With no one around, I put less care into my footsteps. Casting my Grit out to feel for others, the breezy sea air that kisses my cheeks alerts me to Matthias lingering at the edge of the space, toward where the Spire gives way to the river.

His broad back faces me, silver hair gleaming in the moonlight. He's abandoned his intricate axe for a sword with a wicked curve and glinting hilt at his hip. The absence of his preferred weapon offers me the ability to slide my gaze over him the same way I'd appraise a jewel to pilfer. His shoulders would make any farmer envious of their strength.

Matthias has traded his typical long-sleeve linen tunic for one that leaves his forearms bare, corded and roped with sinewy muscles. Winding and elaborate designs snake along his skin, starting at the middle of his forearms and disappearing beneath his clothing. I long to follow its path, to see the rest of the design. Are they the markings of the Sea Berserkers? Or did he draw them himself?

"Come," The captain says, turning his head, the moonlight gilding his features in silver. Night Elves are stunning creatures, but this Night Elf puts them all to shame. I'd only seen their High Priestess once, but I'd argue his beauty, as rugged and untamed as it is, outmatches even hers. The notch in his ear catches the light and my attention. I can only imagine what might cause such an injury to an elf. One with access to Clerics who might be able to heal him without leaving a scratch so much as a chunk of his ear missing.

An image flashes before me of a sailor on the docks. A young sailor begging for his life. I blink and Matthias fills my vision again, only for the strange sailor to call me back. He holds a sword in this vision. A vise snaps around me, leaving me with the helpless sensation of being unable to move. Sucking in a sharp breath, my nose fills with the briny smell of the docks...or Matthias? My head swims trying to parse through what's happening. A blazing slice to my ear tears a gasp from my throat. My fingers jerk to the curve of my own ear, but I find it intact. Unmarred.

Nythraxis, I need sleep. I'm hallucinating.

"Pisúlë, come," he repeats. I startle at his soft words and fall into motion. As I draw nearer to him, the missing piece of Grit wiggles and dances, reaching out to me; but it never makes a move to leave Matthias.

The sound of babbling water fills the air. This river feeds the bay and winds through the city. But even from the Spire, the crisp scent of the sea reaches me.

I stand beside the captain before asking, "Does the water call to you? The way shadows and poisonous plants beckon me?"

"Yes. I've felt their call today. And the shadows." Though he doesn't look at me, I can feel his awareness skip over my skin.

"About that, can I have my Grit back?" I grind my teeth together. I sound like a child whining for a lolly my ma took from me.

Ironhart's cheeks bunch with a soft smile. The sight sends me back a step. He's a Berserker, a surly bastard who hoards more secrets than the vault beneath the king's keep. Soft smiles do not fit him. "Stop that," I mumble. His smile merely blossoms into a true grin. Fangs on full display, he casts that feral expression down to me, lashes kissing his cheeks on a slow blink. The Night Elf markings ripple while he tries to ward off the grin that broke through the dam blocking his emotions.

"When you give back mine, I'll give back yours. You've had mine since the tavern." I frown. I don't have any of his Grit. I never decided to keep a piece of him inside me. Wouldn't I feel if he'd left a piece of him in my well of Grit? He shakes his head. "It's not in your Grit, the way you left yours nestled in mine."

"I didn't *leave* my Grit in yours. The damned piece refuses to come back. Like a hussy in search of a handsome creature to warm her bed."

"Calling me handsome, Thorne?" His lips twist in a wry smirk.

"That isn't what I said. Don't put words in my mouth to stroke your own ego." He parts his lips to say something, but I hold my hand up. "Don't. Gods, don't. I walked right into that one."

I plop down onto the grassy bank. A chill seeps through my thin breeches, but I relish in the sensation. It reminds me I'm still on this plane. I didn't succumb to whatever force nearly sent me through the rift.

Ironhart folds down next to me. His effortless grace emphasizes my Human side's lack thereof.

"My Grit just...is. It's like the air or the sea spray. You'll feel it upon your skin. In your heart, if the ocean calls to you. In your head when your thoughts drift to the sea." His eyes drift shut, and his magic rises around us like the tide. Something in my chest yearns for the lap of waves and the roll of a ship on a long voyage.

"I can feel you within me, pisúlë." One large hand grips his tunic over the base of his ribcage, where the hard bone gives way to supple muscle. "Here. But my Grit feels itself within you in here." His hand drifts to cover his heart.

When I don't answer—because what do I say to that?—he leans back and points to the sky. "See that star? The bright greenish one with three stars arced over it?" He waves his hand in a semicircle. I hum an acknowledgment. "Sailors call that Zorvyn's Leviathan. See the stars that coil beneath? When the Leviathan is in the sky, it's the best season for sailing, but"—he flashes me a boyish grin, looking so much like Taigh in that moment—"when he casts his gaze to the east, calm seas are coming. Those are the best days to take to the seas."

For a moment, I'm back in the observatory high above the Spire. Trying to find the constellations Aster was searching for answers in.

"I've never heard of the Leviathan. Wait, I take it back; Aster mentioned it in passing. I only know of the Anchor and the Helm." Both constellations contain directional stars sailors follow depending on what ocean they sail.

Matthias turns slightly and waves an open palm toward a shape I can't figure out. "Those are the Drowned, but these you might find interesting. The Wanderer and the Sentinel." He gestures to one side of the sky then the other.

The stars of the Wanderer glow faintly in a sprawling expanse of sky. "See there? She's reaching out her hand. Legends say she's always reaching for something we can't see. Vaeroth cursed her soul to wander endlessly after she dove into forbidden knowledge and magic. She carried the ocean in her heart and though she wasn't a child of Zorvyn, he blessed her, offering the opportunity to wander among the stars instead of the Void."

My heart stutters several times through his description of the constellation. Wanderer. That word. That name has followed me in strange places. The young leviathan on the ship from Baustantia. Aster. Now, Ironhart. I force my breathing to remain steady and brush a tendril of hair from my cheek, anything to act as though his words haven't affected me.

"The Sentinel, that cluster there, is bound to the edge of the sky. Duty bound to guard the horizon from the creatures of the Void that long to slip out when the sun dips and allows darkness to reign. He once protected the Wanderer, but his sword was called to protect the Drowned instead of following his Wanderer."

His chest rises and falls with each breath, head tilting to the sky, offering the moon a chance to shine upon his cheeks. Matthias comes alive at night; an energy buzzes about him, infecting me with the same vivacity. As beautiful as the stars are, I refuse to miss a single moment of the beauty in watching an elf spin tales about the stars.

"Once every few decades, or centuries—Zorvyn is a fickle God at times," he whispers the second bit in a conspiratorial tone, "the Wanderer and Sentinel meet during a Fated Eclipse. Zorvyn offers the Sentinel a chance to connect with his lost love." Breath saws in my chest. Ironhart searches the sky, eyes flickering between the Sentinel and Wanderer. His figure would match the constellation, if he only raised a sword.

It's on the tip of my tongue to ask him about his lost mate. Only someone who'd lost their love could see themselves so deeply in the tragic story.

"If that's not the most heartbreaking tale I've ever heard. You must be a delight on dates, Captain." I jab an elbow into his side, attempting to lighten the tension hovering above us.

"Date? Never heard of it." His lips curl into a brief grin.

Silence descends between us for a beat.

"So, you have a brother?" I ask.

Laughter booms. It sends a warm feeling through my chest. I'd like to bottle that sound, replay it when the world seems dark.

"Bleedin' Taigh. Biggest mouth in Bael'thireon." His brother's announcement had shocked me. Though, in hindsight, I don't know why. I'd imagined Matthias as a singular entity. One day he simply just came into existence. No kin. No ties. No history. He just came to be.

I scrape my thumb along the point of the sheathed dagger at my thigh, trying to keep the laughter at my own idiocy at bay. Up until recently, Matthias had been a whisper of help inside the Spire from Lachlan, then an instructor, and now...I'm not sure what category to box him into.

"Why are you keeping your relationship to him hidden?" I stare out into the darkness, watching the flickering light-bugs blink in and out of existence.

"Easier for the pair of us. No one suspects favoritism, and he's able to make friends and allies without anyone trying to leverage him against me or me against him."

Jostling my head back and forth as though I'm volleying his answer about my head, I consider his words. Would I have offered Lachlan the same opportunity? We were a package deal; take one, the other came running along after. The only exception being his departing from this world.

"If I'd had to enter the Spire with Lachlan but act as though we were strangers, I don't think either of us would last a day. I suppose it's an admirable thing, Captain, to offer your brother that courtesy," I say, no judgment hiding within the words.

Behind us a whippoorwill trills its twilight song, and in an even more shocking reveal than the revelation of Matthias' brother or his astronomy lesson, he purses his lips and returns the chattering birdsong.

"Speak of the devil and he shall arrive," Matthias grumbles.

"You'll end up in Vaeroth's grasp, brother, if you liken him to a lowly Paladin." Taigh's boots scuff along the gritty dirt until he meets the grassy bank we've settled on.

"Maman would drag me back from the Chasm of the Void if I left her with just you for company."

My head jangles back and forth as I watch the brothers toss jibes at each other as if they were sparring. My heart squeezes in my chest, and it's as if I'm missing a limb. Something vital to me. Not unlike the sensation I'd endured in the arena thinking I'd torn my own hand off.

I jam the unpleasant sentiments deep down inside, past the well of Grit, past my heart, past everything. I shove them so far down they might as well be lost to the Void, but still my eyes tingle and prick, blurring my vision.

"Finally going to show her? Tell her, Matty." Taigh's words pull me back to the present. He must have sat down next to his brother while my thoughts drifted because he lounges with sprawled legs and upper body leaned back onto his elbows, as though we're sitting on a sandy beach watching sailboats drift by.

"Don't want to. Doesn't matter," Matthias growls.

Taigh eyes him warily. "You need to. It concerns her."

Me? Why me?

CHAPTER 21

IN THE SPAN OF a breath, Matthias has Taigh pinned on his back. One arm presses against his brother's throat, fangs bared, fire burning in those glacial eyes. A feral growl vibrates the air, Lunar Frenzy magic rife within the sound.

To his credit, Taigh just laughs, not a single ounce of fear lining his features. Despite the Paladin's mirth, steel slides into my limbs when I move into a crouched stance, ready to insert myself into the fray.

"Do you fight like this often?" I ask, trying not to let my voice waver. I finger the hilt of a blade, weighing the consequences of stabbing an instructor, much less one my brother was apparently fond of.

"Only every other week." Taigh winks from beneath Matthias. He's not as broad as the captain, but they are evenly matched in height. His dark, bluish hair contrasts his brother's silver-tinged strands. Related and yet on opposite sides of every spectrum.

"Let me up, you big brute." The slim elf shoves at the feral one pinning him down, hands splaying across his chest. Matthias snarls in response, teeth snapping dangerously close to Taigh's throat.

"Matty, you know I can't submit to you. I'm fightin' the best I can. You need to let me up before I lose it and challenge you over something I don't even want." Taigh's accent thickens, his coastal heritage clipping words.

Confusion laces my thoughts. Challenge? Over what?

Taigh meets my gaze, hints of his own fangs starting to peek out below his trembling upper lip. Is he fighting the instinct to bare his fangs at his own brother? Not that I could blame him for the instinct or for not wanting to fight over whatever the hell has Matthias in this state.

Taigh's eyes plead with me.

"Ironhart," I call softly. His focus stays locked on his brother, but the Berserker stills the shaking in his limbs. "Look at me, Matthias."

His head turns slowly, but his arm stays rooted into place on Taigh's throat. A single lock of hair flops over his forehead, not quite long enough to cover his eye like before—which I hated to admit I missed. Lead fills my veins, and I fear I might actually need the dagger I've secured my fingers around. The icy color of his eyes has been consumed by a pool of molten silver. An undulating metal that's left nothing else. No pupil. No iris. The whites completely gone.

I'll be paying Elyndra's temple a visit after yet another encounter with this particular elf and her meddling in my damned life. Not to worship or give thanks and praise, but to holler at her. Nythraxis protect me from her and from whatever has Matthias wholly drowning in a Lunar Frenzy.

Matthias fixates his attention on me, his show of dominance bearing down. I tilt my head and show him my neck. I'll be submissive to him in this moment—pride be damned. Taigh might have been a stranger to me this morning, but Ironhart's his brother. How can I let him be killed by his brother? It'd destroy Matthias. I've borne witness to the pain weighing on him over Lachlan. I'm not sure he could possibly cope with his brother's death, much less at his own hand.

An increasingly familiar ocean breeze swirls around my torso, flitting over my exposed neck like the wings of a butterfly. I inhale sharply when the breeze strokes my cheek, feeling entirely too solid as though it's an extension of Matthias' fingers.

Without my permission, a word rips from my throat, from my soul. One I'd uttered once before slips into existence again, without my knowledge of its meaning. "Vael'astor."

Matthias pushes up onto his hand, forearm finally releasing his brother's airway. His chest heaves, fangs still bared, eyes still eclipsed.

I repeat the word, knowing I shouldn't be speaking Elvish when I have no idea if I'm swearing fealty to him, calling him some rude name, or any number of compromising alternatives.

Matthias sinks back onto his haunches. His snarl diminishes with every surge of breath from his lungs. Though the aggression in his expression wanes, the dominance and fangs remain. Tension bleeds away from my own limbs, and I step toward Matthias.

Again, the word lingers in the air between us when I whisper it. My pulse thunders in my ears. At this point I can't even hear the word I'm repeating over and over again. Am I even saying it out loud anymore, or has my heartbeat turned into some chant I can't decipher?

Matthias rises from his position over Taigh, who remains still as a corpse beneath his brother. With all the grace of Faelwyn's jungle cat, Matthias prowls toward me on silent footsteps. My breath stutters, and I stumble backward.

The distance between us closes, and with each step he takes, something within me builds, the kernel of his Grit inside me seeming to surge and roar like the tide during a storm.

What is this feeling? Gods, does every elf feel like this when the dominant males lose themselves to the moon? Thank fuckin' Nythraxis' shadows I'm only a half.

My own Grit reaches tendrils out to the Sea Berserker's rampaging Grit raging inside of me. I urge my Grit to keep wrangling it. Go! Go, go, go. Stop this madness inside of me.

But then I realize it isn't wrangling it. My Grit caresses his in long, loving strokes. A sensation along my cheek mirrors that of the mingling Grits. The same way lovers might stroke each other. The inky magic winds around the cerulean Grit in lazy loops, brushing close as if it craved acknowledgment, hungry for a touch that would never come.

Heat blooms in my belly. I yearn. I ache. Him. I need him.

Oh gods, no.

Why is my magic reacting this way? Elyndra, stop!

Matthias looms over me, startling me from my mental delve. Tremors writhe through my limbs. One massive hand reaches up and a callused finger trails along my neck, the same path his Grit stroked only a moment ago.

"Gods, your submission," his tongue caresses one fang then skims his full bottom lip, "is better than any mead, any substance." Matthias' light touch transforms into a gentle grip around my neck.

I need more of his touch. More of his heat. Before I can stop myself, I press myself toward him, aligning with the hard planes of his body. The moment I'm nestled into his embrace, starbursts erupt beneath my skin.

Home. I am home. Still holding my neck, he anchors me to him, eyes boring into my very core.

Diverting my eyes, I count the pulses in my ears, focusing too hard on making sure I'm still breathing.

"Pisúlë."

Something snaps inside of me. The tremors cease. The pounding eases. And the sorrow that has been a constant companion evaporates.

A deep yearning replaces it all. A homesickness. For...him.

With the same burst of speed he'd shown pinning Taigh, Matthias tears his hand from my neck and retreats, vanishing like a specter. Past Taigh, the training yard, and all the shadows I reach out.

The only indication he still exists at all comes from the scrap of my Grit within his chest. The scrap I can feel within him now that seems to be just a bit bigger than before.

I whirl to pin Taigh with a steely look. "What was that?"

"I wish I could tell you."

Hours later, heat still lingers in my belly, a restlessness I can't settle. I've sparred. I've run. Without resorting to drinking, only one cure remains: fucking.

The bathhouse for the Spire has long since been abandoned for the evening. Rows of copper tubs and wicker side tables fill the rectangular room. Tiles line the floor, cool against my bare feet.

I've left my boots by the door with no desire to track dirt and grime into the clean space. Turning the knobs, water cascades into the tub. As I watch the steam curl and rise, I shuck off my clothes haphazardly, kicking them toward the table. Bottles of soaps and oils sit on the table, but I add nothing to the water.

Instead, I step in and revel in the biting sting of the heat. It's been too long since I've sat in a tub and enjoyed the stillness that comes with submerging yourself in the cozy embrace of it, preferring the efficiency of showers or resorting to frigid rinses in rivers and streams while traveling.

Though hot water cannot fix my longing for release; agitation still rolls within me. Gritting my teeth, I close my eyes and drop my head against the lip of the tub. Molten silver giving way to glacial depths stare back at me as soon as I close my lids. I wrench my eyes open, but the feel of his hand around my neck comes next. My own fingers trail the same path his had, down my neck, going farther to trail across my collarbone.

Need pools and surges within me. I don't want to need him, but I crave relief. Giving in to this here in this tub doesn't mean giving in to him, right? So much for logic. It flees with every heartbeat as my fingers slide to the swell of my breast, teasing under the water's surface. Goosebumps chase in their wake

My heaving breaths and the falling water echo through the vast space. I hook a leg over the edge of the tub, allowing the stream of water to create a delicious pressure against my exposed core.

I groan from the sensation and drag a hand to my breast to grip and squeeze, rolling my nipple between two fingers. I imagine his fingers against my skin, rough and thick. Moans bounce around the bathing chamber.

My head tips to the side along the edge of the tub when my other hand dips to my core. I stroke against my slit, rolling my hips. Gods, I wish I had something other than my own fingers. All I can do is picture what Matthias might look like. Valleys and mountains of muscles. A thick cock.

Wimpering, I find the tight bundle of nerves at the apex of my thighs. Matthias' name falls from my lips.

"Oh fuck," someone growls. My eyes fly open to see the very elf of my fantasy looming over the edge of the tub. He appears just the same as when he'd left the riverbank. Down to the harsh lines of his expression.

Gods, my imagination pulled no punches in creating this vision of him. In the quiet solitude of the bathing chamber, I allow myself to fully peruse him. To admire the firm set of his shoulders, the tapered angle of his waist, the thick bulge hidden within his trousers. Oh, hells.

I plunge two fingers into my core. Matthias' lips part in a mirror of my own expression. His hand finds the front of his pants, cupping the growing bulge, a growl rumbling through the room again.

Who knew I'd find the possessive elven sound so fucking hot? I moan in response and work my fingers in and out, reveling in the warmth spreading through me, sharp and wanting.

"Spread yourself. Let me see that pretty cunt," he purrs. I follow the imaginary order, using two fingers to separate my lower lips. He groans, the sound nearly real with how visceral I respond to it.

I swirl my fingers around my clit again in tighter and faster circles. Release is just out of reach. My imaginary Matthias grinds his palm against the growing bulge in his pants. I grin wickedly, even though he's not real. I love that I can make my fantasy version of Ironhart squirm.

"Gods, look at you." Heat smolders behind his eyes, locked onto my form. Tension fills his form, but he never takes his eyes off me while I drive my fingers into my core over and over again.

"Come for me, darling. Let go." His words finally send me over the edge, free falling into a pool of pleasure. I shatter, crying out as the waves wrack my body. I writhe and moan as bliss consumes every ounce of my body.

I ride the high of the release my body has begged for, that has been building with every battle of wills I engaged in with Matthias.

My chest heaves as I come down from the ecstasy. Matthias smirks and shoots me a wink. "Thanks for the show. I'll see you in the training yard."

He disappears without any further indication if my mind truly created some version him or I've lost my marbles. I blink into the space he'd stood, left feeling confused but satisfied. A combination I'm unsettled by.

I sigh; might as well take advantage of the empty baths and scrub myself. Laughing at myself, I realize the water's nearly at the edge of the tub since I left the tap running.

Only you, Kira, could possibly create a sexual fantasy so vivid you forget to turn the bath off. I'd love to have to explain to Megora why I'd accidentally flooded the bathing chamber.

'Er, yes, commandant. I was so wrapped up in thoughts of fucking the captain I forgot to turn the water off. My sincerest apologies.'

CHAPTER 22

S LEEP CLAIMS ME AFTER my trip to the baths, but the dream realm leaves me restless, thrashing and tangling myself in the blankets. I can't shake the heaviness weighing on my chest. It yaws like an open chasm. Grief. Such a profound grief. Nythraxis, it's as though I slaughtered a whole city.

Salt burns my tongue and throat. A strong gust tears at the strands of my hair. I startle at the white-blond wisps streaming in front of me. The angry sea snarls at my back.

Voices roar over the crashing tide, urging and beckoning me to finish this. But what? Casting my gaze about, I look down to find a young Human heaped into a pile at my feet. Barely into his second decade, if that. His pupils flare when his eyes meet mine, lids peeled back in abject terror. His worn boots scrabble against the wooden planks of the dock.

Realization dawns on me—he's the same sailor I'd seen just hours ago.

I roll a shoulder trying to relieve the tension, but a weight drags my arms down. Tearing my gaze away from the young man, I find I'm holding a strange weapon. Not any of my daggers. No, this blade curves out in both directions with a central hilt. Like two curved rapiers fused together. Waves and ships glow in a strange etching on the blades alongside runes I do not recognize. An extension of my arm. Both of them, as I find I carry a second strange double ended glaive. Though if I stand them on end, they might almost tower above me.

"Finish him." The words echo in my skull. This is not our way. I'm no executioner. My mind reels with the foreign sensations and thoughts, wondering whose memory or vision I've invaded. But the perfectly balanced glaives, the moon-spun hair, the heavy grief threatening to split my chest in two, all remind me that I am a guest in this vision.

I kick a thin, short sword to the Human that reeks of desperation and horror. He snatches the blade, planting his other hand to shuffle to his feet with the same grace as a seal on land. Something rumbles in my chest. A laugh? A growl? Some sort of misplaced admiration for the young warrior trying to meet Vaeroth on his feet rather than the flat of his back?

Twilight hair flops over one of the kid's eyes, sliding out of the customary horsetail most young sailors prefer. He lunges for me. I dance out of range of his blade, tapping the edge with my strange weapon. Though, as foreign as the blade appears, its weight and the ability to strike in multiple directions with barely a thought tempts me to find a smith as soon as I wake.

"Stop toying with the traitor!"

Pain blooms at the tip of my ear, raw and real. I snarl at myself for allowing the fight to go on this long. I've prolonged this longer than I should have. Knocking the short sword aside, I step into the young sailor's feeble guard and drag my blade across his throat. Thick rivulets of blood stream from the clean swipe. The sharp edge of the blade glided through his skin like the keel of a boat through the sea.

His fingertips touch the wound and the steady flow of his lifeblood. Bringing his crimson stained fingers up to eye level, he stares as though he cannot believe Vaeroth's ship has come to take him to the Crimson Scales.

Unable to wait the handful of minutes for the God of Death to claim him, I reach for my Grit. A Grit so different from my own. It crashes into his lungs like a riptide to fill them with seawater. Another stone adds to the weight of my grief as I watch the life bleed from his eyes.

Gasping I sit up in bed, as though it were my own lungs that had been filled with sea water. I claw at my throat and try to remind myself it was only a strange dream. A strange dream I'd somehow seen bits of near the riverbank.

"Can I interest you in a sleeping draught?" Aster's sleepy slurred words pull me out of the nightmare-induced panic. I mumble a refusal and my thanks and flop back onto my pillow, praying to Nythraxis sleep doesn't claim me again tonight.

Nights later, my mind still won't stop spinning with questions. I've spent too much time buried inside my Grit, yanking and tugging at the larger piece that refuses to mind its leash.

I wander the dark halls mindlessly, not in the mood to slip down alleys or seek out a tavern, but too wound up to rest or fall asleep. Aster kicked me out of our shared room after I'd paced the laughable length, plopped down onto my bed, only to move to the desk, then resume pacing, and repeat for the better part of an hour. I can't stand any stillness. Something inside me bucks against it. I blame Elyndra and whatever Elven magic she's wrapped me into.

I collect nightshade bloom at the edge of the Mage Quarter, tucking it into one of my shadow pockets. The urge to collect ingredients for my poisons guides my hands more often than not. That shadow pocket rivals any herbalist's shop. My feet carry on down another hallway, turning when my Grit senses another poisonous plant. I tug on my magic, trying to spool all of it back into the well, but the damned strands yank back.

Excuse me, I am the master of my magic, not the other way around.

I tug harder. The shadowy Grit writhes and shimmies like a dog not quite finished with its game. A distinctly elven growl slips through my lips.

I like the stillness. I thrive in the quiet motionless period where I lay in wait for my prey. I like the stalking and the hunting too, but to play the game of logic and outfox my target is what gets my heart going. The rush of knowing I'm in place, waiting, enduring the adrenaline pumping higher and higher, waiting for the footsteps, listening to the breath of relaxation just before making my move.

This? This is not stillness. Pandemonium reigns within me. An upheaval of all my carefully crafted calm waters. Fucking Lachlan. Why did he have to make this damn Berserker promise to watch out for me?

Why would he even ask that of him?

I yank a Penance Lily from the ground. The stark white petals with red veins hide a vicious pollen within. They're beautiful on the outside, and vicious when needed.

I tear myself away from the patch of dirt outside the Paladin Quarter, still drifting with no end goal.

I curse Laz again for sending me here, for sending Lach here, for not telling me more about what he was doing here, for leaving me high and dry. Where is he? The burning has lessened in the last week. Have I been forgotten?

My feet drift past the wide colonnades, the floor beneath me tilting toward the Spire's quieter halls. A pebble clatters along the stone floor of the hallway. I freeze. I've been careless. Aimless wandering while my thoughts also wander off? Dangerous.

Breath halts in my chest while I assess my surroundings. Mage lights flicker overhead, lighting the open archways. Jasmine saturates my nose, and I wipe at it, the smell overpowering everything else.

Sucking in a deep breath, I try to cleanse away whatever plagues me. Moss? What is that smell? Something almost akin to the canals below Arethor.

No.

Jasmine.

It's jasmine. Not the stale water.

The Clerics use jasmine. Crushed petals amplify their healing Mana. They can also weave it into talismans to ward off corruption, be it of the magical variety or otherwise.

I blink and the Mage lights warp into torches. Black shadows writhe and undulate across the stone walls. Footsteps thunder to my right, and I whip my head that way. My vision stutters between the Spire and some strange tunnel leading to Nythraxis knows where.

Swirling thoughts slow momentarily, allowing me to piece information together. I'm on the ground floor with the open archways, jasmine plants or the smell of crushed jasmine permeates the air, and a waterfall. Trickling water and splashing drowns out any noise from outside the Spire.

The Cleric's Wing.

"We've been betrayed!" The coastal accent that laces through the shout has me scooping up a heaping mental handful of Grit. Seeking out the quiet calm of the shadows to ease the galloping of my heart.

I fist the dagger at my thigh and wait. My brows rise. Shit. What if it's me they've discovered? An alarm bell tolls in a haunting echo, knocking loose the spiraling thoughts as they form.

Think, Kira! They already know you're here.

Elves and Orcs and Humans battle around me. Die around me. They crash to the hard ground in heaps, leaving pools and spatters of crimson on every surface. Dread curls in my gut. I've not borne witness to a bloodbath such as this in a very long time. And even that could not compare to this.

It's a slaughter. There's no other word to describe this. My mind works overtime to make sense of the scene of warriors pouring through hallways and tunnels only to be cut down and slump into piles of bodies.

Another shout comes, but this one rattles around my mind like the alarm bell. A voice within my mind. It's not my own, and not Lachlan's. Not...Matthias'. On stumbling steps, I stand and move, but fall into the stone wall.

Steel flashes before my eyes. Silver hair. Glinting armor. Voices deeper than thunder reverberate around me. The gruesome, familiar spatter of blood sprays against my cheek. I swipe at my cheek, desperate to rid myself of the sensation, but no crimson stains my fingertips.

Metal clangs, and I whip my head toward the sound, leaving a dizziness from the wavering visions before me. A man—no, an elf—drives a sword with a wicked curve in an artful slash toward a figure. The elf howls a word I don't recognize.

Footsteps approach, coming from the open doorway at the end of the hall. The elf and figure disappear. Though the ring of the elf's cry still echoes in my ears. I pant as though I'd been the one locked in battle.

What is happening to me? My hands tremble thinking of the madness that seems to be creeping in.

I take stock of the physical world around me. The things I can see. What I can smell. I lock my mind onto the sterile scents emitting from that hallway. Jasmine overtakes the tangy iron scent of the blood from the vision.

I'm not there. I'm in the Spire. Not a battle. I touch the stone pillar next to me. The rough carved edges biting into my palm, reminding me where I am.

I peer farther into the Cleric's Wing. Through the entrance, a mosaic depicting Lumeris and his Starlight Vigil peeks back at me. While nothing can compare to the legendary properties of the Moon Pools, the Cleric's Starlight Vigils over combat victims and those with nearly fatal wounds are breathtaking to behold. The All Seer and Elyndra working together to grant new opportunities and snatch back life threads cut too short by Vaeroth.

A massive black, fuzzy head emerges, blocking my view of the mosaic. Following closely behind, Faelwyn fills the doorway.

"Kiralin?" Faelwyn's traded her usual teaching garb for leathers, her panther sporting a leather strap around her chest and over her shoulders. My brows draw down. A desire to inspect it closer sparks, but I rein in the urge in fear the enormous beast will flay me if I start poking and prodding.

"You look as though you've seen the end of the world." The half-Wood Elf looks at me, eyes full of understanding and a shared sorrow.

"Perhaps I have." I can't stop the words before they tumble from my lips, splaying themselves on the ground between us.

"Is this about your brother?"

I startle when the panther stretches its front paws in front of her, each the size of dinner plates with claws like curved daggers. She leans back into her haunches and yawns. Though the sound can better be described as a combination of a yowl and a growl. The oversized creature settles onto her belly.

"Oh hush, Gwyn," Faelwyn chides, but her tone is neither chastising or annoyed. A thick affection laces each word, punctuated by her warm gaze. "Acts like we rode across the continent instead of running a few mounted drills in the training yards. Ironhart, Milsap, and Zandeer would be ashamed of you."

My confusion must be plain as day across my face because she clarifies. "Milsap and Zandeer came from the same province as Ironhart. They went through the Spire together however many decades or centuries it was ago." She waves her hand dismissively, as if she can't be bothered to keep track of their history. "In any case, those three, outside of their duties, are hardly seen apart."

I make a noncommittal noise and move to step around the half-elf.

"Is this about what you overheard with the lord?" she asks. My steps stutter, but I shake my head, although that winding and confusing prophecy still wreaks havoc on my thoughts. I haven't been able to discuss it with Aster, and I feel woefully unprepared to make any intelligent jabs at what it hints at.

Faelwyn's eyes meet mine. The colors of irises have begun their seasonal shift. The Wood Elves are so deeply in tune with the plants and creatures within the forests that their eyes change to match their tree-top cities.

"Are the Pures giving you a hard time?"

Nythraxis' shadows. I don't need a mentor. Frankly, I don't want one. I've entered my third decade and I've survived this long without a mentor outside of Laz, who's conveniently abandoned me.

Her gentle tone chafes at me. I reach a thumb toward the dagger on my thigh, seeking its familiar edge through the sheath. Biting words wait at the tip of my tongue for the command to strike forward and lash out. I hold them at bay though; despite her needling I'm curious to see what she intends with this conversation.

Our interactions outside of formal classes are practically nonexistent, save the singular run-in when Aster revealed his Arcane magic. Plus the strange meeting in the restaurant with Matthias and Lord Preshkin. The urge to buck against the kindness she's attempting to show me throbs like a bruise.

"Did you say mounted drills? Do you ride her?" I jerk my chin toward the slumbering creature, her sleek, black fur reflecting the moonlight. Gwyn tilts her head, and the light catches on the points of her elongated canines curving viciously past her jaw.

"Why ride a horse when I can fight atop my greatest partner?" Some warm affection exudes from her, the emotion woven through each word. "The harness there allows me to sheathe weapons and gives me something to hold onto," she says, pointing to the strap I'd eyed initially.

Faelwyn strokes a hand along Gwyn's back, stopping to scratch her nails in one particular spot. Gwyn rumbles with all the force of a rockslide. "The Pures were horrible to me when I first came here. It's not so bad for the halves without magic. They get by with the Pures without issue because all common folk share the same struggles. But add in a little magic? It creates an air of superiority. Each denomination thinking they're better than the other." She finally tears her focus away from Gwyn's purring form to cast me a knowing look. The temperature around me plummets with her stare.

"Toss in a king who only values the Pures and outright refers to us halves as *dirty,* and you'll end up with a society Void bent on eradicating those without the preferred blood status. I've been gifted with the trifecta, a half chosen by Elyndra and blessed with the ultimate companion."

I blink in slow motion. Several times. What am I meant to say back to that? I understand the sentiments, but who is this Ranger? We share no bond. Our only connections being the Spire and part of our blood status.

How the Rangers in general are treated is abhorrent. The Gods' Chosen—those born with magic and blessed by the deities—loathe the Rangers, feeling as though they are a threat to their status in the deities' eyes.

The only Gods' Chosen who welcome Rangers with open arms are the Druids. They are Elyndra's other chosen, which is probably fortunate since the Rangers also reside within the Groves that house the Moon Pools.

"The Gods don't care what blood runs in your veins, only what burns in your heart." She taps Gwyn on the shoulder, which reaches Faelwyn's hip even in her prone position. "Don't forget you have the option to break any of their noses if they choose to mouth off." She smirks, a memory flitting across her eyes.

"That what you did?"

Derision braids itself into her laugh. Her slim, dainty features twist into a sneer, but she says nothing more. The giant cat lumbers to its feet, and they finally sidestep me and walk off.

I stand rooted long enough I may as well be one of the many statues filling the Spire. My stillness veils the turmoil inside, only exacerbated by Faelwyn and the words she's spoken.

The Gods don't care what blood runs in your veins, only what burns in your heart.

Embers crackle in the hearth of the Mage quarters' common area, casting a warm glow and pleasant heat where I've sprawled on the chaise lounge next to it. Aster sits tucked against the window in the chair next to a tall bookshelf. Taigh sits on the ground, leaning against the chaise with one leg cocked at an odd angle, tossing a leather ball from one hand to the other. He'd been humming a bawdy tune for the last hour, but he pauses to look back at me.

"Kira, all day you've been looking at me like you want to gut me or kiss me. Could you decide which one it'll be?" Taigh tosses the ball in a high arch and waggles his brows at me.

I pause my game of flicking my dagger end over to catch the hilt or the blade. "We could make a wager on it, if I catch the blade, I'll kiss you. If I catch the hilt, I'll gut you."

Taigh's ears curve back over the chaise hovering above my extended thigh; they remind me of his brother's growled warning not to touch his ears. I can't help but wonder if that's a personal preference or are they ticklish or something?

Sheathing my dagger, I lean forward with a peek toward Aster, who is wholly engrossed in the text in his lap. Perfect. My lips quirk up. Though, I can't imagine Aster would fault me for testing a theory.

"Taigh, you're always going on about how irresistible you are. Got any proof to back that up?" I ask with a mock innocence.

His fangs glint in the light as he says, "Sweetheart, I have a trail of broken hearts from here to the Baustantian border, and you want proof?" He chuckles darkly.

Resting my chin in my cupped hand, I reach forward with the other. "Let's see just how unflappable you are, then." Before he has a chance to question me, I stroke along the curve of his ear until I reach the soft point.

A growl fades into a moan upon his lips. Heat flushes my cheeks, but like a moth to a flame, I do it again. Taigh's hips jolt and buck, his mouth falling open. His twilight-tinged skin at his neck tinges crimson.

With a strangled sound, he tears away from his relaxed position, quickly standing and dropping his ball. He stares at me, pupils blown wide, fangs on full display. "Bleeding *hells,* woman!"

I huff a laugh that's somewhere between embarrassed, fascinated, and morbidly aroused. "Oh gods! You should see your face. What happened to all your talk?"

He glares at me, but no heat backs up the expression. His lips quiver until they bleed into a chagrined smile. "You're a menace," he huffs. "A cruel, beautiful menace. Do that again and I won't be held responsible for what happens next."

My laughter fades to a smug smirk. "Cruel? I barely touched you. Nythraxis' shadows, you elves really are sensitive about your ears." I roll my eyes at the drama of it all.

Taigh retrieves the leather ball and resumes his position on the floor, strategically placing his hands in front of the bulge in his pants. "Run around touching elves' ears often, do you?"

"Only the ones that share your blood apparently," I snipe back. Taigh grins wickedly, mischief dancing in his mossy eyes.

"Oh, Matty would absolutely melt if you played with his ears long enough." Taigh begins to toss the leather ball again, leaning back against the chaise.

My finger hovers above his ear once more, debating stroking his ear again for the sheer curiosity of it. He suddenly stops his tossing and eyes me out of his peripheral before I can move further. "Noted," I say with a resigned sigh. "I suppose I've tortured you enough for one night."

The elf goes to turn his head, tip of his ear brushing my finger as I pull my hand away. He shivers and says darkly, "Hardly torture, but don't expect me to sit still should you want to try it again."

I jump when Aster closes the book he's been perusing with a snap. "Do I even want to know?"

"Nope," I reply brightly. Matthias might kill me when he finds out I played with his brother's ears, but it'd been worth it.

CHAPTER 23

I FLOP BACKWARD ONTO the bed, and Aster barks out a warning to mind my shadows and Grit or else it will affect the potions brewing on his desk—and mine. He'd taken over my rarely used desk, claiming I'd used his potions so he deserved to use my desk.

I sigh and shift on the cot, wishing I could be like a dog and simply shake to alleviate the stress and tension writhing within my body.

"Do I need to find a Cleric to put something together for you to calm you down?" Aster glares over his shoulder at me, waving one hand in a circular motion to control the glass rods stirring in beakers and cauldrons while the other adds bits of Nythraxis knows what into a vial.

A myriad of aromas meld in the room to create a nasty perfume that I'd happily gift to Varek, telling him it would attract power and authority.

"Aster, how are you expecting to sleep with all of this?" I flail my hand around the room.

"You're being a crybaby." Aster doesn't even bother looking at me this time, just glances down to check something in the heavy ancient tome next to his alchemy set.

"I miss my rooms in the Underbelly," I lament half-heartedly.

My roommate clutches at his chest dramatically, leaving red dust on his billowing shirt. "Wouldn't you miss me if you were back in the guild though? How can you ever survive without me now?"

"Yeah, yes, I'd miss you," I say without taking my gaze off the knotted panels in the ceiling above me. I kick my boots off, the loud thunks startling the Mage. The heat in our room weighs upon me, and if I didn't think Aster would be weirded out, I'd strip off my breeches and tunic and lay atop my blankets in my breastband and knickers. Aster's purple flames may be tiny—nearly insignificant—but the heat they emit fills the room.

"You're more worked up than an Archivist realizing their theory has been disproven. What's going on with you?"

I sigh and wriggle my legs only to roll onto my side. Aster throws his hands up, muttering something about finding the ingredients for a sleeping draught.

"I think I've gone and fucked it all up, Ast," I mumble, the words barely audible. "I haven't made any progress toward what Lach was looking for, which means Laz is going to send an assassin after his assassin because I'm not working fast enough, and everything I do ends up in more questions than answers. My Nythraxis cursed Grit won't respond to me and is living inside the Captain of the Guard, who definitely knows more than he's letting on about Lach's death and the Shardblade and just everything. There's also apparently a piece of his Grit or pieces inside me...I don't know. I just want a moment of stillness."

The words fall like pouring rain, hammering against the floor between us. My breath saws against my throat.

The sharp, glassy clinks of the stir rods slow as they scrape the bottom of the beakers, coming to a halt when Aster's movements stutter, falter, and his arms fall to his sides. He gapes at me.

"This, this right here is why you shouldn't bottle things up." The lanky Mage sinks into his desk chair he'd shoved out of the way earlier. He shoves both hands through his floppy hair and releases a prolonged groan. "What am I going to do with you?"

Sitting up, I reach for the dagger and whetstone next to the bed. I can't think without doing something, and I can't very well pace in this minuscule room. Besides, Aster's kicked me out once before for my inability to sit still.

With a flick of his wrist, Aster sends my dagger and whetstone into a portal. "Hey!"

"If you keep sharpening that blade, you're going to end up with a needle instead of a dagger."

I pull a thread of Grit and open my shadow pocket, retrieving another whetstone. I scrunch my nose at my friend, the same way I did when Lachlan tried to mother hen me. "Give me one of your blades then."

He obliges me, but gives me a frank look. "Your Grit is inside Ironhart? And his is inside you?" His eyes take on a hazy look, the copper looking rusty as he delves into the mental archives, or library, or whatever was inside his mind. One thumb trails over the All Seeing Eye medallion he's slipped from beneath his shirt.

If only that eye could tell me which way to go and what to do, because Nythraxis sure isn't sending me any omens or directions.

"Fuck. I don't want to talk about it, Aster," I mutter as I begin to sharpen.

"You're the one who's acting all moody and opened up the conversation."

"Because you asked! And I'm always moody!"

I laugh at the ridiculousness of this whole situation. Three decades on this realm and I'm asking advice from a Mage who's only seen the inside of the Archives. I'm losing it. A gentle simmer flares along my neck. *Yeah, fuck you too, Laz. You don't have to agree with that thought.*

Apprehension coils like a snake in my chest. "Have you ever heard of someone's magic doing that before?"

"Their Grit staying behind in someone else?" he says, still mentally turning pages.

"Yeah. What am I even supposed to call it?" I reply

"Lumeris, it sounds almost like soul magic, the melding of two souls. But then you've gone and skipped the whole intimacy and courting bit, haven't you?" A blast of anxiety sucks my air from my lungs. How the hells do you explain something that shouldn't exist? Grits shouldn't be mixing, right? If Aster hasn't heard of it, I can't imagine it's a common phenomenon. "What does it feel like?" he asks, his copper eyes clearing.

I chew on my thoughts and reach toward the larger nugget of Grit inhabiting Matthias' sea of Grit. A singular, shadow-tinged gold chunk floats in the azure ocean. The increasingly familiar breeze swoops along my skin. I startle at the gentle rocking sensation within my magic. My Grit feels like a boat cradled by the gentle waves. I cast my reach farther, the most distant tendrils of my magic touching the edges of his ocean.

I suck in a breath. The calm waters affectionately caressing my Grit become more and more tumultuous the more distant the waters. They deepen to nearly black, though the color is not that of Nythraxis' shadows, but of Zorvyn's anger. Like the sky around the somber constellations Matthias had shown me.

Awareness tickles my mind. Mirth that isn't my own tilts my lips upward. Somewhere a lute trills in the air. Shuffling through my thoughts, I can't remember Aster telling me he played, but the boy has enough hobbies it doesn't surprise me he can play. The airy music gives way to a male chuckle. Warmth flares in my belly, bubbling like a kettle left over a flame too long.

Gods, if I'm having some sort of reaction to the fumes of Aster's potions, I'm going to castrate him.

Beneath the bubbling and flipping in my stomach, a yawning pit opens and floods my senses with a heavy, misery-tinged guilt. *Hello, friend. I'll take that bubbling amusement back.* I'm accustomed to the sickly, oily feeling of guilt licking over me constantly. A beast living within my belly, consuming each and every joyous moment or feeling. This, though, isn't mine; only small traces of Lachlan's loss exists in this yawning pit.

Rubbing a hand on my breastbone, I beat away the misery.

"Kira?"

With a jump, I focus on Aster. "What?"

"What does it feel like?" he repeats slowly, as though I hadn't understood his question the first time.

My lips part on a heavy inhale, but I'm sucked back into the warm ocean waters of Matthias' Grit before I can speak. Blinking rapidly, I try to focus on the scene filling my vision, but it doesn't make sense. A large goblet of mead rests on the table between my fingers while I spin the cup in circles. The amber liquid inside sloshing dangerously close to the edge. Two other goblets fill the table, along with more plates of food than I can comprehend even consuming.

Looking up, the two Guards from the Trade District sit opposite me—well, Matthias, as I realize I'm seeing what he is seeing. Sweet oaky maple bursts over my tongue. I suppose I'm also tasting what he's tasting.

The idea of Matthias going out and drinking, reveling with friends baffles me. Same as thinking about Laz anywhere except behind his desk or on the sparring platform. It's just not right.

The purple haired Guard—an elf—flashes a cheeky grin my way. Matthias' way. Gods, my head hurts trying to keep this straight. Conversation hums around us, the clinking of glasses and cutlery a constant punctuation.

"Would you stop spinning that?" The Human Guard slaps a hand over the rim of the goblet. "You've been fidgeting since you sat down."

"I don't fidget." Shame washes over my skin.

"You do when you've something on your mind," the elf Guard says with a sly grin. "Or someone."

"Someone, Zandeer? The unflappable, unshakable Ironhart? Interested in something other than Taigh or the Guard? Impossible," Milsap chortles and lifts his tankard into the air like a lighthouse keeper raising his lantern.

Matthias yanks the cup out from below the Human's much smaller hand and pours a hefty swallow down his throat. The liquid is cool against my throat, soothing even though the mead isn't physically touching my throat.

"Tell us. Is she terrifying? Snare you within her web?" Zandeer waggles his amethyst-colored brows, flashing a salacious smile to reveal white teeth and pointed fangs. His Night Elf markings favor one side of his face rather than both lend an eerie expression in the dim lighting of the tavern.

The deep, gravelly timber of Matthias' returning growl rumbles in my chest, sending my belly into a routine of flips as though the boat of my Grit in his ocean teeters on the edge of capsizing. "You've no idea."

Zandeer throws his head back, laughing. His long hair swishes back and forth with the motion. "Zorvyn's sails. I'm bloody glad she terrifies you. Might keep you from being a grouchy old bastard with only your axe and your pride for company one day."

"I'm only just now an adult in the elven cities. Just because Humans are considered adults before their twentieth turn, doesn't make me old." Matthias argues, focusing on his Human companion. His red hair flies out at all angles, wild and untamed like the Grit oozing off him. I wrack my brain for the other name Faelwyn had mentioned earlier this evening. Milford? Milsted?

"I think it's too late for him, Mil."

Milsap! This must be where they scampered off to after whatever drills they ran with the Wood Elf.

Milsap chuckles. "You're probably right. Should we end his misery? Send the poor old boy out to pasture?"

"Aye. We can replace him with Taigh once he completes the Spire."

Zandeer sobers after the back and forth with Milsap, focusing his mossy eyes on Matthias. "You feel her, don't you?" he murmurs.

The weight of his stare weighs upon my shoulders, and I slump...or Matthias does. I struggle to differentiate between the sensations I'm experiencing through him and the ones I'm experiencing still on the bed in my dorm room.

Milsap chuckles darkly. "He can feel her, al—" The Human Berserker grunts and jerks backward, spilling his mead down the front of his maroon tunic.

"Enough." Matthias slams his goblet down and shoves his chair away from the table.

"When you're ready to face it, we'll be here to make sure you don't mess up the one thing truly yours, Cap." Zandeer says, barely loud enough for Matthias' elven ears to catch above the din of the tavern.

He turns from the table to leave, but as he does so, awareness prickles over me, over my tendril of Grit within him. Can he sense I'm somehow seeing him? Feeling him?

A wisp of sea-touched magic seeks out my shadowy Grit strokes along the side of it and curls into the little boat it's made in his ocean.

The sight is so shocking, I tumble out of Matthias' consciousness and fall back into my own in a dizzying nosedive.

With a wheeze, I flail and crash off the bed onto the hard ground.

"What the *fuck* was that?"

CHAPTER
24

A STER STARES DOWN AT me, kneeling above me with blond locks of hair framing his face like a halo gilded from his Mage lights.

"You're quite pretty, you know that?" I say as I stare up at him.

"Bleeding Eyes. Did you hit your head that hard? Nythraxis' shadows consume your brain while you were in that coma?"

Reaching for my Grit, I wrap a shadow around myself like a blanket and revel in the familiar comfort.

"Kira, as fascinating as I find it to watch you snuggle a living shadow, can we please revisit this so I can fully experience it? Now let go of the shadow so I can check you over." He pauses briefly. "Should I call a Cleric?"

I shake my head. No. No Clerics. I don't want to bring anyone else into this. Whatever this is. My stomach roils and threatens to expel everything I've consumed this evening. I tamp it and my feelings down into a footlocker. Maybe I can send that down whatever connection I share with Matthias and he can sink it to the bottom of the ocean of Grit inside him.

I nod. Yes, yes. That's an idea. I like that idea.

"Yes, you want me to call a Cleric?" Aster pulls at his hair and grips the All Seeing Eye with his other hand. "Why am I even listening to you? I'm calling a Cleric."

I want to shove him away. To tell him it's none of his business, that my shadows will give me what I need. But the bed frame is cold against my back, and the ache behind my eyes feels older than my own bones. How much longer can I keep pretending I'm fine? Aster moves to stand, but I wrap slim fingers around his wrist.

"Please," I choke out. "No Clerics. I'll tell you what happened but no—"

"Alright, alright." Aster smooths my hair back from my face. The act is tender, loving, so reminiscent of Lachlan, and I bite back a sob.

The footlocker I wanted to send Matthias' way bursts open, and emotions wrack my body with the force of a torrent. I shudder beneath their force, but Aster doesn't leave me. He doesn't back up. He just keeps stroking my hair.

He pulls my braid, but a yelp sounds when, I assume, he touches one of the spikes on the strap I weave into it every morning.

"Blast it! I forgot even your hair is dangerous."

My breath wheezes in and out as I choke out the words. "I miss him, Ast. He was my everything. My best friend. My counterpart. My best friend."

Aster mumbles his reassurance while cries, whimpers, and truths fall from my lips. I don't know how much time passes, but when my body finally stills, Aster wipes the tear tracks away with his thumb.

His cheeks bunch when he flashes me a sorrow-filled smile. "I have to say, I thought you were talking about the captain for a moment."

The watery chuckle his words cause bounces off the four walls in the tiny room, filling the space with a tenuous levity.

"No." I push up from my sprawled position and lean against the bed frame. "He's a whole different beast. One I don't have any clue what to do with."

Aster climbs onto my bed and puts one leg on either side of me. "I'm going to take out this dreadful spike, and you're going to tell me everything." I open my mouth to deflect, but he stops me. "No, Kira. Enough half-truths and skirting the whole story. You're telling me all of it."

My teeth click together when I snap my jaw shut. Lach was the only one who ever knew everything. In the year since he's been gone, so much has happened that I can't even say he knows everything anymore. I've felt joy, laughed, moved forward, and my brother lays somewhere, forgotten and rotting.

"Hey. I'm not replacing him, but you can't unadopt me now. I'd like to see what it's like to have a sister to annoy." Aster pulls the tie from my braid and unravels the strands, tugging gently on my hair just to drive home his point. "Plus, I might not have known him, but I'm taking on his role in your life to make sure you don't take yourself too seriously."

"Gods," I breathe. "You'd think Vaeroth sent him to you so he could instruct you on how to be a little brother."

I let him continue his work. To his credit though, he doesn't push or pry, just lets me parse through my thoughts on my own.

"Earlier, when you asked about how it felt? I mind-melded or something with Matthias."

"*Ooh*, it's Matthias now, is it?"

I jab an elbow back into his shin. "I'll dislocate your kneecap next, you little shit. Shouldn't you focus on the mind-melding part instead of his name?" Reaching over to the nightstand, I feel for my comb and wrap my fingers around it, brushing across the smooth bamboo tines. Aster takes it from me and trades the spiked leather for it.

Spiraling into my thoughts, I scrape my thumb along the pointed edges of each barb. "I was in his magic at first. It's the same feeling I've been getting lately of an ocean breeze, or a salt spray on my face, or the rocking of a boat, but so much more. I was in an actual sea. The waves rocked me. My own magic became a boat held safely behind a breakwater, kept apart from any storms."

I pull the words from inside, unsure how I feel about pouring them out instead of stuffing them back in. Aster glides the comb through my hair with the same care and dedication he offers to his potions. He doesn't yank or tug on any of the snarls that have found their way into my hair; just continues his gentle strokes and offers me a quiet *hmm*.

Forging on before I lose my nerve, I continue. "But then I *was* him. Seeing what he saw. Feeling what he felt. Tasting what was on his tongue."

The comb halts. "Do I want to know?"

"It was just a drink, you heathen!"

The comb resumes its motion. Aster's silence stretches on and on, long enough to hear the sound of snores from the next room . Aster's fingertips move up to my scalp, continuing their dance upon my skull.

"Did he know you were there? Could you communicate with him?"

Peering over my shoulder at him, I shake my head. "No. Well, I didn't necessarily try to say anything to him. I was a little afraid of what was happening." Pausing, I waffle about whether I should mention the conversation. "He was with two other Guards. They were discussing…me I think? Some sort of obsession or connection Matthias has with a female and one of them asked if he could feel *her*. One said they'd be around to help when he was ready to face it."

I pull away from Aster's ministrations to face him fully, still sitting upon the floor. Wide eyes and flushed cheeks, I press further. "Face what? Me? Another woman Matthias has collected and ensnared?"

Aster's eyes crinkle and lips part, but I shove him before the snarky comment can jab me. "Leave it, Hoarfrond."

I've been a lot of places in this realm and seen a lot of things, but I know when my knowledge is outmatched. I'm not afraid to ask someone else who might know more. I just need that person to actually ask instead of finding a roundabout way to acquire the information.

"I have a theory, but the pieces don't line up quite perfectly. I don't want to lead you down the wrong path, so I'm going to keep it to myself for now." His brow furrows the same way his lips pucker in thought. Copper eyes roam over me, as though my physical form holds the key to why his answer doesn't quite match the problem.

Sagging under the weight of everything, I push my hair out of my face. "Same as your thoughts on the prophecy? Don't want to steer me wrong?"

"Something like that," he offers with a soft smile.

At that, I finally feel my shoulders relax. Everything bleeds out of me. Tension. Stress. Every emotion that's rolled through me in the last several days. It leaves me slumped on the floor, an empty husk, hollow and useless.

"Up you get. You'll feel better after sleep."

Aster tucks me into bed and returns to his potion making. Staring at the ceiling, I can't help but question what his theories are and how dismal the end results must be if he doesn't want to share them.

Exhaustion lines my limbs and my consciousness. The emotional outpouring I'd suffered with Aster the night before has left me drained and off-kilter. A feeling I'd rather avoid in the future.

I watch aspirants trickle out of the training yard after finishing up the late afternoon combat drills. Dappled light casts long shadows through the spacious area, fenced in by low wooden pickets. Various weapons racks are positioned throughout the yard, swords and axes back in place after the late session.

Targets and dummies are scattered about. I chuckle at the sword still stuck in the side of one, abandoned by its user. I snag the falchion sword from the burlap dummy and rotate it in my grip a few times, testing the weight. The broader end takes a moment for me to adjust to. It's been too long since I trained with longer blades. I've let myself become complacent in my Spire training.

Warmth touches the back of my neck, but its gentleness opposes the typical pain associated with my brand. Fresh brine fills my nose. *Matthias.* His magic must be acting up inside me, though I don't feel anything within my well of magic.

Glancing behind me, I find the tall elf lingering on the edge of the training yard. His stare trails over me, leaving goose bumps in its wake despite the heat from his Grit. As though he can sense the impact, his stoic expression gives way to a quirked lip and a blaze in his eyes.

Without saying a word, Matthias turns away and stalks through the open portcullis. I shake my head, returning my attention to the target in front of me, I resume drills I'd thought I'd perfected years ago. Though, it's as if I'm brushing off the dust from a forgotten tchotchke.

But even as my limbs follow along with long ingrained drills, my head seems tied to the Berserker stalking through the Spire hallways. My consciousness splits, one part controlling my swings and imagined reposts, the other watching Matthias bob and weave around aspirants, coming to a halt when Luella steps into his path.

"Hells, Thorne."

I whirl with a yelp, leveling the falchion toward the speaker, the tip resting in the hollow of their throat. "Thara!" I yank the blade away from her vulnerable skin. Only the slightest scratch left on her throat.

"It's no wonder you stick to daggers in training. You flail about like a fledgling with that sword. Come on then. Let's spar." Thara draws the massive longsword strapped to her back. The wicked blade glints in the setting sun's light, the ruby in the hilt twinkling as she readies herself.

Thara doesn't give me a moment to ready myself or take on any sort of defensive stance. She drives forward with all the vengeance of one of my marks.

"Nythraxis, Thara—Wait!" I heave out. I pull at the threads of myself still tied to Matthias who's been drawn into some sort of argument with Luella. The Paladin gives no leeway, slashing hard again and again. I nearly lose my head when I almost don't block her overhead strike.

I dance to the side, out of reach of the savage blade. I yank harder, Matthias' deep words from his conversation with the Mage rumbling in my chest. Thara charges forward with her sword raised, in the way only Paladins and Berserkers can accomplish effectively. At the last second, with only a breath between her blade's edge and my clavicle, she flips her wrist. The hilt I'd admired when she'd drawn her weapon crashes into the junction of my neck.

My head snaps sideways, pain erupting in a biting explosion. Stars cloud my vision, and I struggle to stay upright as I stagger away from Tharava.

"Pay attention!" she barks. Shame blooms on my cheeks. I'm fighting like an adept in the Guild that's never seen a blade, not like a trained fighter who's spent decades honing my craft.

Tharava flips her blade and moves once again into an offensive attack. I move to feint left, attempting to trick her into a strike. Yet something shifts in my chest, like a loose puzzle piece wiggling into its home. Liquid fire pours outward from my Grit and I burn, an inferno blazing out of control.

Time slows. The world itself slows. Sounds fade away. Tharava's movements, formerly blurring with the speed of her swings, slow and leave her looking as though she's trudging through molasses. And it becomes clear to me I've made a mistake: The feint opens me up to a brutal slash, one Thara prepares to deliver to my vulnerable 'lickies and chewies' as Lachlan used to call my vital organs.

All at once, sounds rushes back to my ears. The creak of the portcullis chain. The babble of the river down the way. Tharava's hitched breath as she anticipates my feint, but now the mistake in the feint no longer exists.

My body moves, and I plant my feet. Without any hesitation, I deftly swivel into her guard, my blade meeting her longsword with a spectacular clash. The sound of the collision resounds through the training yard making my arm vibrate, but the sting I'd anticipated and braced for never comes.

Thara stumbles back, her wide eyes mirror my own. A Paladin's strength should overcome that afforded by my denomination. Rogues rely on wits and shadows rather than the brute force of an ox.

Dropping the falchion blade in the dirt with a muted thud, I stare at my hands, eyes flicking between them and the Orc approaching me with apprehension in her gaze.

A breeze whips through the yard, my skin cooling beneath the flutter of air. Shadows overtake the fire in my veins, as though beckoning it back to the well.

Shivers run through my body at the loss of heat.

"What in the hells was *that?*" Tharava asks, a mix of wonder and apprehension filling her question. She waves a hand over her rib cage, fuchsia waves rippling across her torso.

"Shit! Did I hurt you?" I reach out, but quickly yank my hand back. I'm not idiotic enough to think touching someone else's magic is a good idea. Paladins' magic is some hybrid of Mana and Grit, allowing them the physicality of a Berserker with the healing abilities of a Cleric.

Unsteady feet carry me away from Thara, until the backs of my legs collide with the low fence. I sink onto it, letting my gaze follow the Orc as she pursues me to where I'm slumped on the wooden rung.

Once the magic fades, she waves me off, ignoring my question. She prowls toward me, a curious predator assessing a potential threat. Thara's lips flatten as best they can around her short tusks, the ivory color gleaming in the setting sun. She doesn't reiterate her question, but instead allows for it to linger in the air between us.

"I don't know." My answer is simple because it's the truth. It's hard to evade the question when I don't have any idea what I'm evading.

She grunts and dips to collect her sword. With practiced movements, she refastens it to her spine and says, "Don't know? Or don't want to know?"

I appreciate Thara for the fact that she doesn't ever mince words. They come out guttural in her tongue, sounding harsh and snappy, but she says what she means. Unlike the Mage I live with, who sometimes tells me one thing but means another. I hold no fault against him for it because I doubt he does so maliciously. Words said between Mages, especially those within the Archives, can be twisted and turned until they have no semblance of their original intention.

I hike a shoulder up. "More that I don't understand it." She dips a chin in sympathy. "There's something I don't seem to be grasping the purpose of. A link I don't think is meant to exist."

"With a Berserker." A statement. Not a question. She sinks onto the fence next to me, her height still towering over me, blocking the sun and casting me in comfortable shadows. The sun's darkness mingles with my Grit, offering its strength and replenishment.

I flash a wan smile, no sign of teeth to be found. Just a paper-thin look shielding the emotions swirling inside. Thara doesn't return the smile but looks at me with probing eyes.

"Don't run from whatever this link is, var'shakar." I open my mouth to argue, but she forges on. "Better for you to control the fate of it than someone else, deities included."

The shifting sands I've been standing on seem to solidify, reminding me of the earthy grounds surrounding my home in Lefendor. My stomach doesn't swoop like I'm standing on the edge of a tower, waiting for a breeze to push me off at any moment.

A tap on my forehead brings me out of my thoughts. "This. This crown, is it a mark of some sort of royalty in your past? A sign of your status in the Rogue's Guild?"

I bark out a laugh. My Night Elven markings only ever draws curious questions from Humans and Orcs. Both factions of elves know that the partial crown upon my head is the mark of a half, one side of my face deemed worthy.

"If I have royalty in my blood, the Gods have a sick sense of humor." I trace a finger along the path on my brow I once spent too much time scrubbing and scraping at, trying to remove all traces of my half status. Laz found me once with a pair of shears in my grip, shaking while I stared at myself in the mirror, trying to buck up the confidence to chop off the tapered tips of my ears. Too long to be Human, too short to be Night Elf.

I shake my head. "Royalty is chosen by the Gods. Revered. Blessed. No, Tharava. I was abandoned by all Gods but Nythraxis. No royalty lives in my veins, and the only safety I'm offered is that of the shadows."

We sit in silence for a moment, lost to thoughts within our own heads. Her words, gruff as they are, ring out clearly. "Zorvyn hasn't abandoned you either." She pushes off the fence, strides away a handful of steps, and turns back with a beckoning toss of her head.

A loving stroke brushes against my cheek, then cups my chin and lifts it gently. I hadn't realized I'd hung my head during our last exchange. The sea breeze, though much more solid than a simple wisp of wind, caresses my brow with a sensation like a kiss upon my mark, then fades away.

I fist the canvas bag of vials as I stalk through the Underbelly. Like most things in the Guild, the stone walls leach warmth from my body. Nothing warm and fuzzy down here other than the strange creatures lurking in the dark.

I slip around the corner, down a hall, and past the wide room full of tables with Rogues lounging about. Daggers, fist-load weapons, throwing stars, and every kind of sword fill the surfaces. The quiet snick of whetstones against steel underlines the din of Rogues swapping stories and gossip.

"Lin!" The shout draws my attention toward the bar top. A short female with porcelain skin perches on the leather-topped stool: Holli. We share a mutual respect for each other, but I only accept her invites to drink half of the time. She never ceases to extend the invite, and for that I'm grateful.

I incline my head her way in acknowledgement, but Laz waits for me in his quarters, so I don't have time to laze about with my colleagues. The brand at my nape flares, and I wrinkle my nose before striding past the revelry.

Murmuring greets me as I round the corner of the wood paneled hallway. I strain to make out what Laz is saying.

"...don't care what they think it's worth," Laz's voice, low and edged, slithers through the crack in the door.

Someone chuckles—a sound bordering half-charm, half-threat. "Value's in the hands that can keep it hidden. And in the right hands, it can buy more than coin ever will."

Rafe. What in the Void does that mean? What job does Laz have Rafe doing?

The Guild Master hums. The scrape of wood against the floor forces me into action. I move the last few steps to the door and rap my hand against it twice. The hinges creak from the force of my knock. With the door opening farther, I let myself in.

Laz in all his long-limbed glory perches at the front of his desk. A bottle of maroon Bloodwine sits next to his elbow with a half-full goblet hanging precariously from his fingertips. A lazy grin takes over his full lips when I cross the threshold.

Laz has always been the epitome of male beauty. Despite the scars littering his forearms and the few that have found their way onto his neck and face, I can easily admit when I first came to the Underbelly, I found myself pining after him. Long dark hair, fierce amber eyes, and a meticulously trimmed beard made him a sight to behold. Even still in his fifth decade—or perhaps older, I've never had the gall to ask how old Lazrik is—I'd still consider a tumble in the sheets with him.

"I'm not sure if I should be offended at the attention you give your Master, sweetheart," Rafe drawls. I tear my gaze from Laz to fall upon my lover. He winks, his lashes kissing his high cheekbones.

Rafe lounges in the wide leather chair Laz keeps tucked in the corner of his office. One leg drapes over the arm of the chair, his black breeches hugging every muscle and contour of his lithe form. Under my scrutiny, Rafe's tongue darts out to wet his lip.

"You've done well, Kira," Laz says, pulling my gaze back to him. "Thought it was time you carried something worthy.

Leaning back against the door, it snicks shut. My mind filters through Laz's words, not quite able to keep up with whatever line of thinking he's gone down. Worthy? What does he mean? Laz leans back, his free hand disappearing behind the desk. The drawer slides open with hardly a whisper.

Eyeing Rafe, he shrugs a shoulder and drags a hand through his red hair, letting it fall loose around his shoulders. Clearly he's not at all bothered by this conversation. Glad I'm the last to know whatever the hell is going on.

Laz withdraws his hand, pulling out a stunning serrated blade. The blade itself bears a vicious curve to the end with jagged teeth winking in the light. My mentor flips the blade end over end, catching it by the tip to extend the hilt in my direction.

I arch a brow. "Nothing in this life is free," I tell him. My hands stay by my side, still clutching the canvas bag. The proffered hilt tempts me though. Smooth in all the right places, rough in some, just the way I like. My poison vial and dagger design wrap above the grip. And is that...?

"It is. The smallest compartment to add in a poison for the perfect application during a fight." Laz grins at me.

"The first blade you didn't have to steal," Rafe says. "Consider it earned."

Without me making the conscious decision, the vials clink as the bag slips from my grip. I look down to see Rafe's Grit cupping my precious poisons, but more alarmingly, I find my fingers already wrapped around the sturdy handle. I've never held such a finely-made blade. One so perfectly balanced. My Grit hums in my chest.

Mine. Besides scars, it's the only thing the Guild has ever given me. The only thing Laz has ever given me.

The serrated blade sits in my hand. The one Lazrik gave me in the Underbelly, forged to fit my grip as if the steel itself knew my name. Rafe's smirk. Lazrik's grin. The weight of it—balanced, perfect, mine.

I shake the memory off, but the feel of that hilt still burns against my palm. Tharava may believe the Gods did not abandon me, but the only things I can trust in this world are a blade and my Grit. Even my Grit seems finicky these days.

Something about Rafe's involvement with this gift doesn't sit right. Especially not after the way we left things, with me walking out while he found his cock inside that Warlock.

But even still, I can't bear the thought of tossing the blade. With a swipe of my thumb over the concealed poison well, I slip the blade back into its sheath.

CHAPTER 25

THE TORN SHIRT FROM the Void Demon Trial—along with several pairs of breeches I've ignored for a month now—rest upon my cot while I fight with the needle and thread. Scraping against the glass window tears me from my mending. With a huff, I toss the offending items back into the basket. I'd rather just buy new ones anyways.

I hesitate before moving toward the noise, trusting my senses less and less these days with the visions taunting me. The scrape comes again. With a deep breath, I beg Nythraxis to keep my sanity intact.

Looking toward the window, I can see warm sunlight gilding the edges of buildings and trees with its warm embrace. Jays twitter their morning tune, and the last chill of night fades away with every inch the sun reclaims from the moon. But none of that captures my focus or my surprise.

That belongs to the wispy shape on the ledge, rubbing itself against the pane. Eyes that rival the pale blue of the brightest flame narrow on me in an unsatisfied glare. A poofy, gray tail flicks this way and that while the shadow beast clings to the thin ledge. Tilting my head down, I thank my patron god for the sole fact that the noise was not in my head.

The indignation in the fox's expression makes me chuckle. She can't really fall and die since she's made of shadow, but the fox is clearly angry I haven't let her inside. So she shoves all four paws onto the small sill.

Amusement unfurls in my belly. True amusement I haven't experienced in ages. With eyes crinkling and biting back a smile, I hurry to the window.

I check to see if the beast's scraping has woken Aster, but his snores answer the question for me. He can sleep through anything, but he also casts a spell to create a constant loop of rain sounds in our dorm at night. He says it helps to drown out any noises from the other aspirants. I slide the window open, and the shadowy fox pushes its nearly-translucent whiskers forward in a smug grin.

She steps forward, and my lips part when I see the entirety of her body. "Araya! What happened to you?" I whisper-shout in equal parts horror and awe. Made of Nythraxis' own shadows, she'd started trailing me when I was barely more than a child wandering around the Underbelly.

Then, she'd been wholly black and mostly transparent, the only color her fiery eyes. Araya pins her ears in shame. Almost asking, *Don't you like it?*

Her body still shimmers like the night sky, but a blanket of inky constellations now trace her side. She stares at me proudly, the stars extending to her brow in a simple downward curved arc with a line between the two points.

Extending a palm, I reach out to her, and she surges forward. Despite her writhing shadows and wispy state, her fur slides through my fingers as corporeal as if I ran a hand through Matthi—no, I steer my thoughts firmly away from anything suggesting I might be running hands through an elf's hair.

Araya purrs when I scratch beneath her chin. It's hard to comprehend that my shadowy friend has changed so much in so little time

"What's brought you so far from the Underbelly, sweet girl?" I coo.

In answer, she kicks out a back leg. The scroll tied with shadow above her paw becomes visible, the shadows receding just enough for me to snatch it off of her. Once freed from the duty of delivering a message, Araya shakes out her celestial coat and hops onto Aster's bed, curling inside the curve of his legs.

"Betraying me for my roommate in the span of a few minutes?" I huff a laugh. "Typical."

Her thin, silvery whiskers wiggle in a fox-like laugh. Little traitor. Unrolling the scroll, I sink onto the bed.

Loyalty is a precious thing, little shadow. So easily given, so easily torn away.

The Guild does not forget its debts. Nor does it tolerate loose ends.

You carry something that does not belong to you. Perhaps you've forgotten who you owe, who gave you the skills you now wield so carelessly.

You have until the next moon to prove where your loyalties lie. Otherwise, they will be decided for you.

Do not make us come looking.

The bottom of my stomach drops out and my lips part. Roaring fills my ears and drowns out all sounds of rain from Aster's spell and his incessant snoring. Laz is going to kill me. If I can't figure out what the hell Lachlan was doing, he's going to kill me.

But surely he knows my loyalties are with him. I know I've taken my sweet time figuring out what Lach learned while he was in the Spire, but it would have been helpful if Laz told me why in the blazes he'd sent my brother here in the first place.

All the same, my mind whirs trying to decipher what he's referencing. Everything I "carry" has been earned with my own blood, sweat, and tears or bought with money from my own contracts.

All the spinning of my thoughts leaves me adrift, dizzy and nauseated.

"Hey, hey." A creak of the cot, then warmth on my shoulders. "Slow your breathing. Kira, you're going to hyperventilate." Small gasps give way to panting slurps of air. I push them down, refusing to give them space in my already crowded mind. Emotions fill every nook and cranny inside me, something I haven't experienced since I was a child, still seeking comfort in my father's arms.

This warning is more severe than anything Laz has ever done—at least with me. I've only received minor slaps on the wrist, no cut of profits or confined to my quarters. After being in the Guild so long, Laz usually leaves me to my own devices.

"They're going to turn me out, Ast. I'll never see them coming. He'll send the shadows after me. Turn Nythraxis against me. You'll wake up and I'll be murdered in my bed."

Aster rubs a hand up and down my back soothingly. "Who exactly is casting you out?"

Araya slips between us, her shadows deathly cold against my skin and yet their comfort is unmatched. Aster tries to leap away from her, but before he can, I hand him the letter. Wrapping my arms around Araya, I scoot back on the cot to lean against the wall. Aster's eyes scan back and forth once then twice and a third time.

"I don't understand. What do you have that they want back? Why do they think your loyalties have changed?"

If only I knew, I'd be able to dig myself out of the shallow grave I've found myself in. I shake my head and shrug. The very seams of my world are unraveling, and I can't do anything to stop it. How am I supposed to follow his instructions when all Laz gave me to go off was "Your brother died in the Spire. Figure out what his mission was and finish it"? My mission derailed somewhere along the way with training here—for a position I don't want, by the way—and the side gigs I've picked up. It's resulted in discovering a prophecy I don't know anything about or what to do with.

Coincidences don't exist though. There has to be connection to Lachlan with the prophecy, especially knowing that Matthias is intertwined with that Lord and had ties to Lach.

I groan, only to startle Araya. Her whiskers turn down when she bares her little teeth at me. "Honey, you can't stay with me." The translucent fox makes a *mrrt* noise and readjusts herself in my lap. "Araya, it's safer for you in the Underbelly."

Her paintbrush tail whips aggressively, smacking me in the chest.

Aster looks between me and my longest companion. "Why can't she stay? She's shadow, yes? Does she eat? She can live here." He looks at me with earnest eyes, like a child begging their ma to let them keep the stray cat from the alley.

"She's not exactly…natural." I give my roommate a wry smile. "Besides, I'm not a Ranger. I'm not meant to have some Gods-blessed creature following me around."

Aster crouches next to my cot to peer at Araya, who leaps off my lap and turns about for him to inspect. She preens and prances, extending her neck and flipping her tail elegantly. The loss of her chilled shadows in my lap leaves me with the sensation I'll simply float away without anything grounding me.

"These constellations are incredible," Aster breathes. "Did you cast her from your own shadows?"

"That's the thing. I didn't create her. She's one of Nythraxis' own shadows." I debate on telling him more, but it's already out of my mouth before I can stop it. "She's been around forever, but the constellations are new. She used to be like any shadow, a void of light."

"Fasci—"

"She's not something for you to study, Ast," I snipe with a hard look.

He raises his hands in defeat, but Araya butts her small head against his palm. I can order her away as much as I'd like, but at the end of the day, I know she's going to do whatever she pleases.

"Now that our new friend's residency is settled, let's tackle the other problem here." He all but claps his hands together, like the problem ahead of us is a molehill rather than a mountain.

"We're not going to fix this here and now. I don't even know how to fix this or where I went wrong." My head thuds back against the wall, and I give Aster a long look. He perches on the edge of his own cot and brushes his fingertips over Araya's fur while she rests two paws on his legs and shoves her face upward trying to boop her nose against his.

Sunlight fully cascades through the window now. Dawn gives way to morning sun, the quiet peace of the early hour overtaken by the hustle and bustle of Spire workers and the city around us.

"There is someone who might be able to point you in the right direction," Aster says, trailing off and giving me a knowing look.

Matthias. It always comes back to the Berserker.

Turns out the giant Sea Berserker can be slipperier than an eel. Despite lingering after classes, lurking in the mess hall, and wandering the Spire, I haven't been able to corner the elf. I kick out at a pebble, making it skitter across the stone floor as I trudge down the hallway. Nythraxis' blasted shadows, he's always around when I don't want him and never when I need him.

I've no idea where to search next, but I need to decide as I approach the main foyer of the Spire. All the hallways meet here to dump everyone into the courtyard. I cast out my Grit, searching the immediate areas of each hallway. One by one, the tendrils of shadow come up empty. I approach the archway of the foyer and almost stumble when the last shadow reports three figures skulking my way. On quiet steps, I slip behind the column forming one side of the arch. The angle of the sun breaking through the massive courtyard doors affords me a plethora of shadows to conceal myself in.

"—still no sign of it?" Luella barks in annoyance. Her voice grates like nails on a chalkboard. I cringe, reminded of one of my instructors in the Underbelly who would drag a dagger down his chalkboard if he caught anyone sleeping during our courses.

"We have to be close. The demons whisper that one of the junior class aspirants reeked of Voidium. The only thing on this plane made of Voidium is the Shardblade," comes the quiet response. Dazek? I can't place if it's the Demonier or a different Warlock. Robes whisper against the ground, footsteps echoing in the wide chamber.

I hold my breath and send a prayer to Nythraxis for protection should they choose this hallway.

"Close isn't good enough! Aldros' patience wears thin with you, and the king is growing weary of your excuses. He's given us until the equinox to deliver the shard. Your usefulness might be coming to an end." Luella's Mana washes over me in a prickly, biting sensation. I shiver and fight the reflex to wipe away the magic.

"Perhaps we'll have to extract the hilt from someone's hands. Preferably once they're stiff with rigor," the second Lock purrs.

My joints lock, almost as if rigor has taken hold despite my heart still pumping. Rooted in place, I push back against the roaring in my ears.

Footsteps halt. "Start with the Rogue. The girl knows something. Mind yourself though, I've noticed shadows have a tendency to slip through your fingers." One set of steps stalks off in the opposite direction.

A grunt echoes through the space, accompanied by the sound of someone forcefully grabbing someone.

"Find the damned Shard. Kill the girl. I don't give a rat's ass how it's done, Nadil. That Mage will not kill us. I'm not dying for a fat sod on the throne either." Another shove, and then there's nothing but the tread of footsteps growing fainter, leaving me in the silence.

I sink farther into the shadows. My breathing slices through my chest in ragged heaves. I don't have what they're looking for. Haven't had it in over a year, and yet I'm going to be the one fighting for my life against the Locks and Luella. And Aldros, apparently.

Gods. Even the thought of his sallow skin and red-rimmed eyes sends a skitter down my spine. I release my Grit with a heavy sigh.

Apprehension coils in my gut. I ought to just cut my losses, board a ship to Baustantia, and open an alchemist shop. Remedies can't be all that different from poisons, right?

"You always this bad at eavesdropping, or am I just lucky to catch you this time?"

With an undignified squeak, I whirl to face the speaker.

Hair the color of twilight flops over one mossy green eye. Twin pointed canines glint in the low light of the hallway with Taigh's impish grin. He leans against the wall a few feet from me, arms crossed against his broad chest.

Amusement dances in his eyes. The carefree confidence he exudes is a direct opposite to the broody, hot and cold nature of Matthias. His easy expression leaves me cautious. Between his relationship to Matthias, his trial fight in the arena, and his history, I know he's dangerous. You don't make it this far without being a little lethal.

Shoving my apprehension and anxiety out of my mind, I force a smirk. "I though sneaking about was my job, Paladin."

He shrugs, the movement rippling across his chest. His grin widens, and his fangs take on an intimidating shine. My head begins to dip in submission to his Night Elf dominance, but I fight it at the last second, pulling my gaze back to him. Something flickers in his eyes before he blinks.

"Didn't have to sneak. You looked ready to bolt, practically ignoring the world around you. I'm just curious what's got you so worked up." He juts his chin toward the archway. "Who are we spying on?"

Taigh creeps closer and pokes his head around the pillar. He sighs. "Empty. No fun for me." Recovering, he jabs an elbow into my side. "So," he presses, "who were we listening to?"

I open and close my mouth several times, unsure of what to say. Taigh is an unknown to me. Sure, he's Matthias' brother, and against my better judgment I trust the Captain, but should I trust him?

Seeing my hesitation, Taigh arches a brow. "You know, if you were anyone else, I might be suspicious."

"And if *you* were anyone else, that might worry me," I volley back.

His brow drops and he rakes a hand through his wild hair, laughing that unabashed belly laugh. "I like you, Kiralin. You keep things interesting around here." He strides forward and links his arm with me, steering me toward the front gate. "Now, let's see if we can't intrude on a captain getting an ale and then you can tell me why you look like you've seen a ghost."

Among the Halves—those of mixed heritage, too Human for elves, too elven for Humans—there exist hidden places, havens carved from the bones of old cities and whispered of in cautious voices. These sanctuaries, known simply as the Crossroads, are neither governed by kings nor claimed by guilds. Here, debts are paid in favors, truths are traded like coin, and the weight of one's bloodline matters far less than the strength of one's word. The only Halves safe outside of the Crossroads are those with Orcish heritage.

T AIGH STEERS ME THROUGH the courtyard and down the cobblestone lane leading to the Spire. Shadows stretch before us, cast from the truly massive statues of various *heroes* of Arethor. I roll my eyes; their heroes are all Pures. All Paladins and Clerics. My eyes flick to the statue farthest from me: a stunning white marble figure with robes carved into a billowing flare, and a single hand raised with a flame wrapped up his arm. Upon his brow, an All Seeing Eye burns in perpetual purple.

"Do you fancy Mages, Thorne?" Taigh teases, still dragging me along.

"Not usually." I arch a brow up at the elf. "Why, trying to find your way into my breeches tonight?"

He wags his brow, smirk turning feral. He gives a shimmy of his hips when he says, "Tempting, but I've got a holy reputation to uphold. Paladin and all that." He winks. "Besides, I prefer a proper challenge. You'd have me on my back too fast."

"You know what, Taigh?" I say between laughter. "I think I like you too."

The elf takes a sharp turn down an alley I've shockingly never stumbled down before. A rat scurries past and ducks behind a stack of crates. I shoot the Paladin a dubious look to which he returns with a smirk and a shrug.

I dig my heels in. A tavern with rats isn't uncommon, but an alley with rats? Discreetly, I sniff. If there's even a hint of piss in this alley, I'll duck into the shadows even if I have to take Taigh with me.

No piss, but...I breathe deeply again. Something else fills my nose though. Succulent, savory meat. A spice I haven't experienced in ages. Bright aromas of vegetables. And another smell I can't quite place.

I must resemble a scenting hound with the way my head tilts back and my nose turns toward where the smells drift through the air. I gravitate farther into the alley where the odors become more intense. But where is it coming from? Stone walls reach upward like a funnel guiding me to the back. No doors in sight. Overturned crates litter the passage, but the faint clink of glasses and scrape of cutlery reaches me.

When I turn ask Taigh what he's playing at, my eyes falter on Araya. She lingers in the darkness, her tail flicking, blazing eyes focused on the elf.

In her static state, I have to strain a bit to make out her form, but the new addition of the constellations on her body make her an easier mark to find.

Though as I trace the stars upon her body, they wink out one by one, only to be replaced by a new pattern. I furrow my brows, trying to make out the new constellation. Something niggles in the back of my mind, but Taigh calls my name.

He stands with one palm upon a wall, gesturing to a stone door he opened while I studied Araya's new stars.

"Ranger as well as a Rogue? Haven't heard of that before." Dark brows slant in confusion. Multiple denominations are impossible. A Paladin and a Mage combination? I shiver. A Rogue and a Cleric? Fuck. I can only imagine what a Lock combined with a Berserker would be like.

"I think you've hit your head one too many times there," I drawl and stride toward the open doorway.

Taigh gestures to where Araya perches on an overturned crate. "Is she coming wi—" His words die when she winks out of existence. "What the fu—"

He's cut off this time by an angry shout to close the door. I snicker and pass him by. The decadent smells from the alleyway bombard me along with warmth from a blazing hearth. A scrape of stone against stone follows behind me, and Taigh's presence encroaches, making my proverbial hackles rise.

With hasty steps, I move to the side, putting my back to the wall. With a quick scan for threats—or more specifically, Locks—I force my shoulders to lower from around my ears. The hole in the wall I'd been expecting encompasses a much bigger space than it would appear to from the outside. My brows raise while I take in the enormity of the place. Tables upon tables fill half of the room, there's an open area for musicians to play, and booths line the sides. But what shocks me the most are the barrels hanging from the high ceilings on the second half of the room. Three of me standing atop one another could fit inside. A circular bar holds shelves of every alcohol and beverage I can think of and those I've never heard of. The barrels, with their massive spigots, hang around the bar hovering just over top the stools.

My lips part on a silent gasp when the bartender raises a hand and the lever on the tap turns on its own, releasing a flow of amber. With another flick of his wrist, the liquid arcs into a large loop before splashing into the tankard he holds. Violet eyes mine, and the Mage winks at me before slinging the tankard down the wooden bartop.

The Orc at the bar waiting for the ale stands shorter than most, tusks much smaller. A half, I realize. He grins at the Mage behind the bar, they exchange words before the Orc saunters back to his table with several beverages. His companions are a mixed bag of Pures and halves. My brows raise, and I widen my eyes, partially in shock and partially as though it will help me take in more of this impossible scene in front of me.

"Matty!" Taigh hollers across the room without a care.

My shoulders creep back up to their original position. In the time we'd walked from the Spire down to a random alley, I'd forgotten we were meeting his brother. Forgotten I'd been looking for him in the first place. Add in the shock and awe upon walking into this place, and I'm lucky I haven't forgotten my name.

Matthias lounges in an armchair next to the hearth. Orange light dances across his features, bathing him in an otherworldly glow. His features slacken when he finally raises his gaze from the drink he's clutching. I stumble because my gaze no longer holds Matthias. Instead I feel myself slip into his sight—

A black braid, nearly identical in color to Taigh's, slips over her shoulder. Warmth stings my cheeks, but not from the flames at the fireplace. I rake my gaze over the Rogue, appreciating the way the leather jerkin clings to her breasts and waist, watching her powerful legs right her frame after her stumble.

Vibrations rattle my rib cage and I hike my upper lip, baring my canines. My blasted brother grips her arm and slips a hand to her lower back to guide her to me. Taigh signals to Derrick behind the bar for another round of drinks, never faltering in his steps.

With every step, my pisúlë closes the aching distance between us, the nugget of her Grit swells within me.

"Did you forget how feet work, Thorne?" Taigh teases, and I jolt when my vision returns to my own body.

Nythraxis' bleeding shadows. I need to figure out how to stop doing that. I accept the metal tankard and greedily gulp down the fruity beverage—only realizing halfway through that I didn't watch it being prepared. *Idiot.* I pause, sniff the drink, but detect nothing.

I might have some innate trust with Matthias, but it would be far too easy for him to exploit that link. Factoring in Taigh's easy nature and the inability for anyone to dislike him, I groan at my own complacency.

Unease ripples through my chest when Taigh thrusts me in front of his brother. I'm overwhelmed with the urge to bolt, to reach for my magic and slip off into the shadows.

"You, little brother, are a pain in the ass," Matthias grunts, looking over my shoulder to the raven-haired near-clone of him.

Taigh says nothing, but I find the same mirth in his eyes that I often see in Matthias' gaze. He sinks into an oversized, gold-colored armchair, the furniture releasing a poof of air with the sudden weight.

The Berserker's deep grunt wars with the roiling emotions that batter against my senses. How can he be so unaffected when I feel like a kite whipping in gale force winds, my string ready to snap at a moment's notice.

I remain standing between Taigh and Matthias. Only two chairs exist in the sitting area next to the fire, both now being occupied by Ironhart siblings. I stutter on that thought, though.

"You're just mad Maman had to get out all the imperfections on you before having her perfect child." Taigh's tongue darts out, but when I flick my attention to Matthias, I catch the tail end of him rolling his eyes.

Deciding it's safer to focus on Taigh, I attempt to sate my curiosity. "Do all elven siblings needle each other like this, or is it unique to the Ironhart elves?"

My knowledge of Night Elf culture is surface-level at best, with most Pure Night Elves I've interacted with being Rogues first and foremost. The thought reminds me of the Guild and Laz's accusation of my disloyalty; it's like a knife in my back.

The sudden agony calls to mind why I went looking for Matthias in the first place. As loath as I am to ask him for help, he's my only connection to Lachlan in this place.

Standing above Matthias, I fish the note from my pocket. The brooding elf doesn't deign to move his outstretched legs when I deposit the parchment into his lap.

He eyes me, assessing everything from my expression down to my boots. Matthias sets his tankard on the side table opposite of the fireplace.

"Passing notes like we're in our first year of education?" Despite his careless words, I can sense his tension as though it's my own. The small kernel of sea magic thrashes within me.

"Just read the damn thing, Ironhart," I snap and drop my arms from their folded position to finger the knife sheath at my thigh. As observant as ever, his glacial eyes track the movement, the stare heavy upon my skin.

Long, elegant fingers pluck the rolled note from where it rests on his thigh and open it. His eyes flick back and forth over the short paragraph, lips drawing flatter and thinner with each passing moment.

He pushes out a weighted sigh. "Lach had a theory I think is connected to this."

I wait for him to continue and grit my teeth when his lips remain shut. Irritation gets the best of me, and I shove a boot against the leg of his chair, scooting him closer to the fire. The scrape of the chair legs like a warning bell.

Matthias braces his feet against the floor to stop his movement and shoots me an annoyed look, his Sea Grit inside me undulating with tension. Shaking my head, I try to shove my shadows over the watery magic.

"You stole something precious for Laz a few years back," Matthias' words bear no question. Words stated as fact. "Something the king searches for now. Something even the Warlocks believe an aspirant possesses."

I nod.

"Though you delivered it to the Guild, Lachlan thought you still had it. Unknowingly."

I splutter at the insanity of what he's saying. There's no way I still possess the Shardblade hilt. I haven't seen it since I gave it to Laz. I should have questioned his interest in the damned broken blade, but I'd assumed it had to do with vengeance or snubbing some lord.

"I don't have it. I gave it to Laz and that was the last of it." I snatch the tankard Matthias abandoned, gulping down the remaining liquid.

Taigh shoves out of his chair, making an excuse to refill our cups. Matthias pays him no mind, his gaze still boring into me.

"I think you do. I think Lach was on to something, and this note is evidence of that." He looks back to the flames and readjusts in the chair, reminding me of a dog shaking off the tension building in their body.

My mind flails wildly through every interaction with Laz. He told me he'd auction the hilt off. I didn't even know what it was or how important it is. Yet here I am the one holding the bag. The hilt. But with every encounter with the Locks, I get closer and closer to thinking something isn't quite right with the whole ordeal.

The night Laz pressed the blade currently strapped to my back into my palm surges to the front of my mind. The metal warms me through my leathers, like it knows my mind is starting to churn. Like it was *waiting*.

I used to think it was some trinket, a relic meant to be sold to the highest bidder. But the longer I'm here—the more I learn about the Shardblade—the less that story fits.

Could the blade they gave me have been something more? Something already reforged, or worse... something they never meant me to understand?

Why didn't he trust me with this knowledge? But he trusted—

"Wait. Did Lazrik send Lachlan to the Spire to collect pieces of the Shardblade?"

Matthias scoffs and rubs a hand over his stubble, but when he flicks his eyes back to me, the ale in my belly curdles. Fear slithers through my veins. "The Guild never sent Lachlan here."

My heart stutters. Time stops. I can't even create a response because nothing adds up anymore. My lack of response doesn't faze Matthias as he forges on.

His lips tilt down at a harsh angle with each word he forces out. "Your brother was searching for something on his own. A relic. *Codex of Severance* he called it. Before coming to Arethor, he'd found a dangerous spell. One he didn't talk about, which for a Mage is unheard of." The smile he sends my way bears no warmth, no joy, and his eyes remain impassive. "Lachlan was under the impression the codex was the key to stopping that incantation being used. Just before his *accident,* he'd mentioned the Shardblade."

Leaning forward, I brace a hand on the brick of the fireplace, staring at the flames. "What in the hells did you get yourself into, Lach?" I mumble, lips barely moving to utter the words.

"Your brother got spooked just before he died. He'd overheard someone in the Spire talking to the Warlocks about securing the Shardblade. He'd assumed for the king."

"Stop," I rasp. Hearing my brother's actions and failures laid out in sequence before his death pains me more than I can handle. It tugs at the locks and latches of the footlocker of emotions I bury within my chest.

"Kira, you need to hear this. It's *you* they're hunting. *You* they will kill next." Warmth surrounds me, different from the blaze of the fire. This warmth bears an icy bite. His breath skitters across my neck, over the small points of my ears. "Lazrik is playing his own agenda here. He's made you a pawn to a game you don't understand or know the rules of. Sending you with whatever piece of the Shardblade you stole—ballsy, but he doesn't know you've started to learn the game."

At Matthias' words, pain surges from the back of my neck, blinding me to everything but the white-hot, searing pain. My head falls forward and cracks against the bricks, but the scrape of the rough surface pales in comparison to the brand. Fingers bent into claws, I scrabble and maul the nape of my neck.

Callused fingers grip my flailing hand, preventing me from continuing to maim my skin. A cold anger slithers from my well of Grit. It seeps into my bloodstream and leaves me with hazy, red vision. Though for a moment, I see the back of my own neck. The angry, raised lines where my nails dug in. The harsh jagged rune of my brand glowing a vibrant maroon.

Matthias' other hand yanks the back of my collar down. In short, rapid bursts, his breath blows against my neck, heating and cooling my skin in a dizzying contrast. "What in Zorvyn's high seas is *that*?" Despite his harsh, growled words, his fingers release my collar to gently stroke over the wounded skin.

I peer back over my shoulder at him, and my eyes flare when I catch sight of his expression. It's the same look he'd turned on his brother when he'd pinned him by the river. Fangs bared with his lip curled in a snarl, pupils blown wide, the whorls of his markings bunch with his growls. I fight against everything in me from ducking my head and avert my gaze in submission. His nimble fingers move to the raised, angry lines of the brand. Gentle as he is, another wave of agony explodes through my body.

"Please, vael'astor, stop," I cry, loathing the sound. A single tear escapes and slips over my cheek. He tracks the movement like a hawk watching a mouse scurry through a field. When he resumes tracing soothing patterns along the side of my neck a safe distance from my brand, I breathe a sigh. "It's my Shadowbrand. Lazrik marked all of us."

He presses closer into me, dipping his head farther to speak into my ear. "That's no brand. That's a leash."

I pull my shoulder away from his chest and pivot, avoiding the hearth. Gazing up into his face, I search for any signs of deception. "What?"

He arches a single, dubious brow. "You think he blessed all his followers? It burns only when you wander off his objective, no? Why did it burn when I spoke his name? Spoke of his treachery?" His tongue darts out to coast over his lip. I track the movement, my brain latching onto any distraction from this wild revelation. Somehow, this elf finds ways to constantly bombard me with them.

"He owns and commands all of us. How else do you keep a bunch of thieves and assassins in line?" The defense sounds hollow even to my own ears.

He shakes his head. "A mark of loyalty wouldn't react like this. A brand to injure the bearer when they learn the wrong truths? Defy orders? That's a warning system. He tethered you to him or whoever owns him."

Matthias vibrates with rage. His Grit undulates and serpentines around us like a viper coiling, preparing against an attack. Even though his magic spirals out of control on the defensive, he remains over me, one hand planted over my head on the brick. Matthias takes one step forward, leaving only a sliver of air between us. I feel the heat from the stone of the hearth behind me, keeping me in place.

Tension still leaves him as rigid as one of the statues outside the Spire, but the link within our combined Grit alerts me of some change. A change in his breathing. A deep inhale through his nose. He's scenting me. Shock flares in my chest. What does he think he's doing?

"Vaeroth had better prepare for a series of deaths if they come for you. The Locks. The Guild. The damn king himself." A low snarl punctuates his threat. His previously soothing hand fists in the loose hair at the base of my neck, a gentle sting accompanying his vicious movement.

A dark emotion crosses his eyes, but something softer pushes it out. His hand moves to cup my cheek, yet it hovers just shy of my skin. Lightning sparks in the space. A war within himself rages plain as day upon his face.

He's holding himself back, but why? Gods help me, a part of me wants to see him unleash himself. I want him uncontrolled.

I swallow against the lump in my throat. Tilting my chin up, I bring our faces closer. His breath warms my cheeks. His glacial eyes have taken on the color of the ocean during a storm.

"You don't have to protect me on my brother's account. You have your own brother who needs you more than I do." The words physically pain me to say, but they're the truth. Risking himself, his position, for an ally's sister is foolish and unnecessary. Lachlan's death weighs on my conscious enough as it is; Matthias' death would be like tying an anvil around my neck before being shoved into the ocean.

The grief would consume me.

Matthias' sharp exhale commands my attention. His lips part to argue likely.

"Well this is tense," comes Taigh's cheerful drawl.

Matthias shoves away from the bricks with enough force pieces crumble and rain down at my feet. He rolls his shoulders and neck in a circle. My heart pounds and I'm left with the same sensation as when the adrenaline flees after a job—like an empty husk. Taigh smirks like a smug cat and flops into his armchair once again, setting the three tankards on the side table next to him.

"Didn't mean to stop whatever this was," he says with a waggle of his brows and waves his hand between us. I flick my eyes to where Matthias seethes toward his brother. "If you're done making eyes at each other, should we maybe discuss the Locks sniffing around for halves?"

I scowl at Taigh and the clear amusement rippling across his features. He hides his grin behind one of the tankards. Blasted little brothers.

Matthias cuts off my excuse by clearing his throat, finally straightening after releasing the pseudo-Lunar Frenzy from his form. Studying him, his expression is carefully blank, all traces of the near feral aggression and rage erased.

He looks at his sibling, and begins to explain. "We weren't—she needed to know."

Taigh lifts a brow at his brother, clearly unimpressed with his answer. "Right," he says, drawing the word out in multiple syllables. "And it just so happens you needed to be nearly stroking her face to get your point across." My cheeks burn hotter than my brand ever has, and I duck my head to hide my face. "Brother, if you keep looking at her like that, she's bound to ask questions you don't want to answer."

A muscle flickers in Matthias' jaw. "Leave it alone, Taigh," he snarls.

"What questions?" I interject, ignoring the captain's clipped words.

Taigh stands, picks up his tankard, and runs a hand through his hair, that same cheeky smirk plastered on his face. "It's nothing you won't figure out soon enough on your own, sweetheart." He slips a finger down my jaw then claps his brother on the shoulder and saunters off, whistling a jaunty tune.

I slump into the chair Taigh vacated, the weight of everything revealed tonight combined with whatever the hells that exchange was bears down upon my shoulders. And the realization that now I have to find this blasted codex. It's all suddenly too much for my body to carry. Matthias stands stockstill staring after the Paladin swaggering out of the tavern.

"Should I worry about fratricide?" I ask. The murderous stare swings my way, and I shrivel before the carefully blank stare returns.

CHAPTER 27

Necromancy and the creation of necrotis has waffled between forbidden and celebrated over the thousands of centuries magic has been around. Necrotis have no true emotions or thoughts. They are influenced by their creators. They cannot make decisions and so they are an extension of their creator's will. This is their biggest advantage and disadvantage.

THE SCRATCH OF QUILLS against paper fills the large, stone-walled classroom. A hazy, golden glow casts eerie shadows through the room, the drawn shades leaving only the Mage lights to illuminate the space. A thick tension shudders around each aspirant in anticipation of the next trial lurking just around the corner.

A hand swipes out, scattering my notebooks across the floor. From my seat, I stare up into Varek's algae-hued eyes. His self-satisfied smile contorts around his tusks, the expression leaves him somewhere between smug and jarring. I've been fortunate in avoiding him this long, but my luck has finally run out. It seems to be doing that a lot lately. Void Demons, the Guild's note, and all the revelations from Matthias that have left me feeling adrift and untethered.

"You're not nearly as remarkable as your reputation boasts," he sneers. "Who'd you blow to get in? The commandant?" I roll my eyes. Refusing to take the bait. He lets out a dark chuckle and leans forward, but the room itself seems to close ranks around us, listening for his next words. "Not even Megora would be interested in your vile mouth. Though I know who might."

Muscles coil one by one, waiting for him to say the wrong word. Waiting for the green flag to end his pathetic life. "A certain captain seems to have a penchant for collecting dirty things. Useless things. Using them up and tossing them away. Wonder when your turn to be tossed out to sea will be."

My chair clatters to the ground, and before he has a chance to move, I wrap a hand around one of Varek's tusks. With a vicious kick to his knee, I yank his tusk and slam his chin into the desktop. He cries out, the crack of his landing resounding through the space. The momentum from the throw allows me to swing around to his back and press on the back of his other knee until it buckles. Enjoying the sick sound of his knee crashing to the stone floor, I throw my weight forward and press his head into the wood, still holding onto his tusk.

A victorious smirk spreads across my face, baring my small fangs. He howls and thrashes his arms, but I'm just out of reach. Using my free hand, I slip a vial from my belt and unstopper it. It drips along the back of his tunic, hissing with every point of contact before I let a puddle of it pour over his axe.

The liquid rolls over the edge of the blade and down to the skin of his neck, where it leaves grotesque red welts in its wake. My smirk grows into a savage grin, knowing his pain is only beginning. Each welt will pop and breed more until his entire body is left covered and aching, the cycle repeating until he's sought help from the Clerics.

But the real beauty is the concoction's corrosive nature. It'll eat at the metal of his axe and, hopefully, leave him without a weapon when he needs it.

"Thorne, if you're done toying with your classmates, would you mind unhanding him so I might begin?" Faelwyn's calm voice reverberates through the room. I unwind myself from Varek and tuck the vial into my sleeve to conceal it, hoping my constant exposure to the mixture will offer me a bit of protection, though the salve to ease the welts waits for me in my shadow pocket should I need it.

As I release his tusk from my grip, he jerks, and the tip snags across my palm. I bite back the curse; Varek stands, shooting me a vile look of a combination of self-satisfaction and loathing. Though I rein in my temper that wants to continue this, he lets his loose and shoves me on his way past.

I stumble backward, and my back collides with someone's chest. A set of mossy-green hands wrap around my shoulders to steady me. I mumble a quiet thanks to Tharava and right my chair. One hand clenched in a fist to stop the blood from dripping, I reach with the other to snatch my notebooks off the floor.

"Now, if that's settled, survival is more than strength on the battlefield." Faelwyn's sharp gaze bores into each aspirant as she walks across the front of the room. "Survivors are not mere warriors and fighters. They are first and foremost strategists."

The Paladins and Berserkers balk at her words, but the casters—the Mages, Locks, and Clerics—nod, a knowing filling their eyes. "You must know when to hold your ground, when to fight, and when to wait. You must also understand when retreating means winning, because not every battle is won head-on. Poor planning will result in more deaths and more losses than a poorly skilled combatant."

Faelwyn stops pacing in front of the broad table at the head of the room. With enviable grace, she leaps onto the desk and settles into a comfortable position, Gwyn appearing from thin air at her feet to lounge. The panther bears no leathers today, but the thought of the lithe elf riding the giant cat into battle brings a genuine smile to my face. She must be a sight to behold. The *pair* of them must be truly incredible.

"Some of you fight without planning in general, simply reacting and acting on instinct. Your death looms closer than ever if you continue to fight like this. We're playing a game of strategy here, where we must plan a handful of steps ahead of your opponent. You want to use your instincts? Use them to outwit your opponent and figure out their moves before they make them." Faelwyn pauses her gaze on me, and it's as though she's intending the words for me and me alone. Like she's urging me to dig deeper, reminding me of our last encounter. I can't help but wonder what strategy they chose to deal with Preshkin's shriveled corpses.

"Your combat training with Captain Ironhart later will focus on opponents who do not feel pain, do not tire, and do not hesitate. You'll be unable to read these combatants. Those of you who react in the moment may find this exceedingly difficult."

Are they really going to pair us against demons again? Those are the only creatures who don't feel pain, unless the Warlocks are dabbling in necromancy. I wonder, do necrotis—the corpses raised by the Locks—have thoughts?

I shake my head, ridding myself of the bizarre line of thinking. I've been around Aster for too long.

Faelwyn's gone mad. Bits of wood? Surely she's not intending for us to swing around at sticks? I haven't whacked a dagger at a branch since Lachlan and I fought imaginary foes in the woods behind our cottage in Lefendor.

While I keep my amusement and skepticism locked away, others outright snicker or question the sanity of the instructors at the Spire. Loudest among them, unsurprisingly, are Varek and his entourage. They resemble a pack of hyenas rather than a group of aspirants.

"Laugh all you please, but I don't think you'll find these branches as comical once Luella has had her way with them." Matthias leans casually against the low fence surrounding the practice yard.

The grating, high-pitched giggle floats through the air. The entirety of the class turns to gaze at the archway leading to the bailey. Beneath the raised portcullis, the light-haired Mage saunters, her plum skirt swishing against the cut grass leading to the training yard. Her proud stride eats up the distance. Before she even crosses the boundary, she waves a hand. Sticks strewn about next to Tharava wiggle and writhe against the ground. With eerie scrapes, they drag themselves toward each other, stacking and weaving into a grotesque form. They pile and pile until they've exceeded Thara's stature.

Once an ambiguous visage forms, the branches snap and break into a long sword. The wood figure takes a few practice swings, the same as any of the Berserkers or Paladins do before sparring with a new weapon.

Murmurs break out among the crowd. Apprehension weaves through the aspirants, leaving anxiety and curiosity in its wake.

Tharava doesn't seem to share the same qualms as the rest of the aspirants. After assessing the bizarre woven labyrinth of branches, she dives into an offensive. She doesn't hesitate in her movements, driving forward with exacting precision. She dances below a horizontal strike the wooden figure attempts to deliver. My brows pucker, noting Thara hasn't reached for her magic or her weapon.

She kicks one leg out, snapping her boot against the joint midway down the creature's leg. A sickening crack resounds, but Thara anticipates the stagger that comes next, placing her forearm in just the right spot to provide a bump stop for the figure's limb. Apparently though it does not experience pain and cannot be read for decision making, certain things will always have the same reaction. The jerk to the back of the figure's wrist from Thara's well-placed arm causes the branches holding the hilt of the wooden sword to split apart.

The blade drops into Thara's waiting hand, and she uses the weaponized branches to lop off its head. Without pause, the sticks crumble into a pile, raining down like a summer storm. Even the wooden blade within Thara's hand slips apart and leaves her holding one single branch. She looks like a toddler Mage practicing their first spells with a guiding rod.

"Well done." Faelwyn's clear voice cuts through the heavy silence left in the wake of Tharava's fight. "She strategized, she planned, and she executed."

Luella, now perched upon the fence between Faelwyn and Matthias, flicks a finger. Another of the grotesque creatures twists itself together. I wrinkle my nose at it; they're mockeries of Elyndra's creations. They warp the beauty she weaves in every leaf, tree, and bush into something vile.

Though this one differs from Thara's and carries a serrated blade longer than my forearm, its jagged edge drips dark, sap-like resin.

Calculating eyes dart my way, and Luella's hand waves the figure toward me. Where the first had swung like a drunkard, this one moves toward me with purpose. Fast and low. Tharava had no chance to snag her weapon, but I don't squander any time with the seconds afforded to me. I yank two daggers from their respective sheathes at my thighs, their cool hilts and familiar weight a comfort. I don't waste the energy or time with practice swings; these two blades have been my constant companions for years, decades even.

I fall into a combination of strikes so ingrained they require no thought at all. I hop over the kick it sends my way and slash forward, one dagger after another. Edges of blades bite into the wood, but the construct pays them no heed. Skitters of knots harden like iron beneath the bark. Splinters float down from its hip. Without any pain forcing it to stop, jump, or even falter, the wooden construct forges on. The hilt from one dagger slides free from my palm when I bury it too deep into the wood.

This isn't working. On instinct, I drift a hand to my belt, fingers curling around the top of a vial until I remember poisons won't help in this situation.

The barest hesitation costs me. The serrated resin-knife bites into my leather jerkin. With the force used to yank the blade free, I stumble into the open arm of the creature. It wraps around me, drawing me in. I frantically search for some way to get out of this, a pocket to drive my blade into. Terror claws at my throat when I come up empty.

No. No. This is not how I go. I've never found myself in a situation like this—this dire. How did I let this happen? I have too many threads left tangled and untied to die at the hand of some stick figure. At the hand of Luella.

I reach for my Grit in hopes to find some use for it, but it lays coiled around the sea-tinged nugget that grows ever larger, reminding me of the leviathan I'd met on the ship back from Baustantia.

Obstinate Grit be damned. My mind delves to a darker place.

In the Underbelly, Rogues have whispered about the Gambler's Edge. At our core, Rogues are risk takers, bettors. The Gambler's Edge can sap large portions of our Grit to give us extra strength, enough for an all or nothing Nythraxis-blessed attempt to save ourselves. Gods, I don't want to use it. No Rogue will shame another for surviving because of the Gambler's Edge, but no one praises the use of it either.

My cheeks burn just at the thought of anyone knowing I used the Gambler's Edge. That I would ask Nythraxis to roll the dice for me and my life.

I reach into my Grit, but stop short of scooping up and forcing the heaping amount I'd need to call upon Nythraxis. In this moment of panic, I instead coax and cajole the scrap of Matthias' Grit in my chest. I wait for its response, but the wooden construct tightens its hold upon me. With a blade creeping far too close to my lickies and chewies for comfort, I writhe within the grip, pleading to Matthias' magic to do something, anything.

Begrudgingly, it creeps toward me at an agonizing pace. After a laborious trudge through my own shadows, a comforting sea breeze rushes through my veins. I gasp when a blazing heat follows quickly behind the cool ocean air. A band squeezes my chest, and my muscles lock.

A red haze descends like a veil dropping over my face. Recognition flares: It's just like when I'd shoved Thara halfway across the training yard. A fire fills each limb; I force my upper arms out against the branches holding me in place and am rewarded with an echoing *snap*. A heavy *thud* follows the initial sound. Nythraxis, please let that be a limb. I twirl away from the construct, and in a moment of Grit-fueled adrenalin, I grasp the wrist and pull off the other arm. This limb separates into its individual sticks and branches. They sink to the ground in a twirling spiral, residual leaves floating and whipping.

Unexpectedly, the creature snaps its head down. Pain blooms behind my eyes. The construct's crown of spiked, thorned branches digs into my own crown of thorns markings. It heaves and tugs, our faces flush, my eyes boring into vacant depressions of wood. Another yank frees the thorns from my brow.

Warm rivulets stream down from the wound. Matthias' magic surges, taking hold of me. In a vicious swipe, I drag my remaining dagger through the wood forming in the thing's neck. For a brief moment, wicked sharp teeth bare at me in a gruesome smile though nothing connects the head to the body.

Looking at it gives me the sensation of looking in a mirror. Crimson slips down from the thorns upon its head and pools within the holes where eyes belong.

The moment breaks, and gravity takes hold of the severed head. As it falls to the packed dirt, Matthias' magic recedes like the tide, returning to its home nestled in my own Grit.

I heave a deep breath and whirl to face the row of instructors. Droplets of blood fly in an arc with my movement, leaving a cool trail down my face and dripping off my chin.

A slow clap erupts from behind the training yard's fence. Pale hands collide together, jewels glinting off the dark metal rings upon his fingers. Sallow skin pulls taut across high cheekbones and contrasts with the dark hair that hangs straight as a true blade. My lips part catching on the ears previously hidden beneath Aldros' hood at the trial.

Chills raise the hairs on the back of my neck, my focus on the questionable Shadowbrand there. I should never have come here. All I've done since I arrived in Arethor is question the things I held to be absolute.

In the deep recesses of my mind, Lachlan whispers, *Good. Keep questioning.*

"And that, aspirants, is a spectacular example of survival rather than strategy." His eyes flick from the aspirants to Matthias to me before continuing. "And the reason why Rogues are more suited to...*thievery.*"

My tongue darts out and swipes a droplet of blood. My eyes connect with Aldros'. Four gnarled fingers grip the top rail of the fence. With a heave, an imp—Aldros' I assume—leaps into a crouched position just to the left of his summoner. It bumps his shoulder with its head in a move not dissimilar to the loving affection of a cat.

Anxiety pools in my belly. The imp and Aldros refocus on me. Something twitches in me, a vibration rolling through each limb. A shock wave.

An all too familiar agony rips through me. I'm back writhing upon the arena floor. My bicep burns, the skin flays off, and a hoarse cry lodges in my throat. Cocking its head, the imp smirks at me, and half of the rows of jagged, pointed teeth flash.

A warm cloth brushes against my senses. A cozy blanket on a cool evening. Long, callused fingers cinch around my arm. They steady me, but more, they give me something real to focus on. A thumb scrapes along my shirt. I hate the sensation, but at the same time, the longer it goes on, the more grounded in the present I become.

"Yes, well. A delightful contrast of fighting styles." Faelwyn, the diplomat, splays her hands. Gwyn swings her head to the imp on the beam. In response, the demon waggles its fingers in a mockery of a wave.

A resounding gasp flutters through the yard when Gwyn opens her maw and snatches the head clean off the imp. Its body disintegrates in a heartbeat. I can't stop the grin when the panther breathes the black smoke of a void demon returning to the ether from her nose.

Faelwyn smacks Gwyn's rump with all the force of a newborn batting at a toy. She's fixed her face into a semblance of contrition. I bite my cheek to keep from laughing when Aldros snaps, "Contain your beast."

"I mean, you can summon another one," she calmly replies.

Aldros pushes off the fence rail and stalks through the crowd, bumping into whichever aspirants don't move fast enough. His long robes billow and snap with every step he takes. A trumpet to herald his departure as much as his arrival to wherever he's heading.

"Now, let's continue," Faelwyn says with a polite smile.

CHAPTER
28

"I'M FINE, ASTER!" I gripe as my feet scrape against the cobblestone lane. Aster puts both palms up in supplication, stepping away from me as we walk.

"Yes, and I'm the Archmage of the Conclave," he quips dryly.

Snapping my head the other direction, I glare are Taigh when he lets out a dark chuckle. "And you! What are you even doing here?"

"I heard you collect little brothers. I'm offering myself for your collection." He smirks and waggles his brows. The mossy color of his eyes pops in contrast to his vibrant lilac shirt. The elf isn't afraid to stand out, that's a given.

Both of the men's clothing boasts their confidence and an air of "look at me." Typical blasted men. Not a care in the world if they're noticed and seen. Bunch of peacocks.

"I alrcady have a brother," I quip.

"Can't have too many," he says with a shrug.

Still grumbling, I pick my feet up a bit hopefully to stop their sympathetic glances. The winding market stalls give way to the open expanse of the canals with stone stairs every so often leading to docks for the gondolas and canal boats. Human and elf children float in shallow pockets where the canals widen into small coves while others toss balls between themselves or run down the towpath.

Flavorful spices drift through the air from the cafes that have taken up residence along the banks, utilizing the views and the passing boats to lure in customers. I eye the balconies longingly, having dreamed with Lachlan of sitting upon one enjoying a posh meal. Though our dreams diverged when I suggested launching crumbs to the birds or bits of food at passing gondolas—he looked at me outraged. He'd wanted to come in the golden hour to watch the sunset and the shadows take reign while enjoying a glass of red wine.

Sadness slithers its way into my heart again, but Aster breaks the spiral. "Did you know it took nearly the entire Conclave to conjure all of the Mage lights for the canals? It practically exhausted all of their resources, and each Mage had to spend a week with their designated affinity to regain their strength."

Aster's factoid shoos away the last of the heaviness. Sometimes he feels like an extension of my brother. As though Lachlan is guiding him.

"Is he always this…informative?" Taigh drawls.

"I cast the ones over the Garden District." Aster puffs his chest proudly, ignoring the elf's jibe. "Well, not all of them, of course."

"Since you have two—" I stop. Oh, gods. I'd almost blabbed his secret again. In front of yet another Ironhart. I hang my head, my woven hair swinging with the movement and the forced marching.

Aster bumps my shoulder. "Hey, I'm assuming there are no secrets between siblings." He's too good for me. He deserves a much better friend and surrogate sibling. I'm as likely to be a benefit to him as I am to get him killed.

"Are you sure you want to be my adopted brother?" I say with a half-hearted laugh.

Aster guides us in the other direction through a long stone tunnel. Taigh stumbles on my other side, trying to keep up with the Mage's abrupt direction change. Finally righting himself, Taigh confirms Aster's statement.

"Aye, Matthias rarely keeps things from me." The words are directed to Aster, but he focuses on me. Cool water sloshes through my limbs. Matthias' damn Grit seems to preen at Taigh's words. Of course, it does. How could it not with Taigh's smug confirmation?

I wrinkle my nose, and a knowing smirk blooms on Taigh's face. Narrowing my eyes, I contemplate probing to see how much Matthias has told him, but Aster finally stops his parading through the streets. I tear my gaze from the brother of the bane of my existence.

Purple-roofed buildings surround us. Planters filled with lush blooms and ferns float along the walkways, under the watchful gaze of Mage lights hanging suspended in the air. Robed elves, Humans, and Orcs scurry about. In a nearby patch of grass, a group of three Mages lob a ball of Arcane magic between each other in some sort of game, their laughter brightening the overcast day.

Aster parks us below a woven, wrought iron doorway, but it leads nowhere. It's a freestanding arch on a raised round platform.

"Did construction stop on something?" I ask him. I look toward him, but his eyes have taken on a purple hue with the Arcane Mana rippling through the copper, and the All Seeing Eye medallion on his chest glows in a matching shade. The vacant space in the arch ripples. Blues and whites undulate and swirl. A cyclone of the two colors whirls and spins, the eye of the storm growing larger and larger.

Eyes wide, I watch a picture paint itself in the center of the typhoon of magic. "Have you ever seen anything like this?" I mumble out of the side of my mouth to Taigh.

"Don't tell me you've never used a Mage portal in all your travels, Rogue?" He chuckles. "Your brother really made you travel on foot all those years?" I scrunch up my nose at him, but I manage to keep myself from sticking my tongue out too.

"Quiet, you two." Aster's voice echoes in a hollow-sounding reverberation. As though he's aged decades, centuries, and multiplied himself by hundreds, all of those copies of him speaking within a sprawling temple with high ceilings. "Take her through."

I glance back to the glowing portal. The center reveals puffy clouds in soft shades of gold and pink, but I inhale sharply seeing the floating structure among the billowing clouds. Filigree scrawls along the top and bottom of the round observatory-looking shape, like a bauble someone's gran might hang from a windowsill.

The view captivates me and—to steal Aster's favorite word—fascinates me. Taigh hardly gives me another breath to gaze into the portal before

I'm free-falling with my only anchor being the fingers wrapped around my wrist.

I can't figure out which way is up or what direction I'm plunging through space. Finally, I land prone on a spongy, verdant surface. Leaves and stems tickle my cheeks and arms, bared by my disheveled clothing. Pressing my hands against the plants, I heave myself off the ground, only to gape at my surroundings. We've landed inside the giant floating bauble.

Aster *pops* into existence next to me, and my Grit flares to life in my chest, pulling shadows from beneath nearby ferns and trees. He falls into step next to me as though he'd always been there. "Welcome to one of the Arcane Conclave's Skyward Solariums, also known as The Skies."

My mouth opens and closes while I try to find words. Lights and tomes float and flit through the air. One yellowed book whizzes by my head, and I jump to the side when it opens its cover to bat at my ear on its way by.

"Go on then, *Dwarven Politics Through the Ages*. You won't be needed this afternoon." Aster gestures me toward the center of the Solarium. I gawk unabashedly, trying to take everything in.

Planter beds flank the path, sprouting the same mana-fed plants Aster's always experimenting with in our dorm. A table of crystals in every shade here, a rack of potions and vials there. Some crystals float mid-air, and to complete the scene, a large cauldron stirs itself while a mortar cants over to pour some crushed substance into the cast-iron receptacle.

Lush couches and armchairs surround a blazing hearth, though only the gentlest bit of heat fills the space. Strange bits and bobs float and turn near the couches. A few shimmy and settle back into place upon the bookshelves weighed down with enough tomes Aster might be satisfied for a month or so.

A gentleman with a shock of white hair and deep-blue robes speckled with stars and constellations strides into the room. He enters from behind a large rotating sculpture, its round orbs oscillating around an even larger orb filled with fire. The swish of his robes echoes through the room. Wrinkles around his eyes and lips boast of a long joyous life, but his copper gaze hints at hidden knowledge acquired from his research within this Sky.

"My boy!"

A bright smile unfurls across the younger Mage's face. "Grando, it's been too long, hasn't it?"

Whose boy? Aster?

"You can bet your sorry ass it has! I've had to brew all these potions, tend to the plants, discipline the books—all by myself!" The older Mage throws an arm out and rips a zooming volume mid-flight before spanking it on the spine soundly and launching it back the direction it came.

My brows rise, and I find Taigh just behind the older man wearing an expression of fearful amusement.

"Leaving your poor grandpa here to fend for himself. How do you think I ended up with all this white hair?" His down-turned lips quiver so gently I barely catch the movement, but his echoing guffaw betrays any lingering intonations he's offended at his grandson leaving him in the Solarium.

"You never were good at guilting me into things." Aster's grin turns wry, and he finally strides forward to embrace his grandfather.

"Well," he says in an exasperated tone, "I never had to! You just came along willingly."

Their tender embrace leaves me with a sense I'm intruding on a familial moment, and I look down at the ground from the embarrassment. Taigh moves from his place near the odd floating spheres and gives my boot a light kick with his own before standing next to me, arms crossed. I peek up at him and stick my tongue out in response.

The elf pokes his tongue out to mimic me, slightly more than mine. Before I can think better of the action, I snatch the tip of his tongue between my thumb and forefinger. Taigh blinks his wide eyes at me.

"Holy Lumeris, you really are collecting younger brothers, aren't you?" I drop Taigh's tongue quickly to see Aster standing with one arm crossed against his chest, the opposite elbow resting on his fist with a hand cupping his chin. "Who's the middle brother?" Aster's question rings with indignation.

"Have you lost your mind?" I splutter at the same time that Taigh says, "We're twins, *obviously.*"

Nythraxis save me. I run my hand down my pant leg to wipe off the saliva then stalk past Aster. Extending my hand—not the one formerly holding a Night Elf tongue—I introduce myself to the white-haired man. "Kira, it's nice to meet you."

He offers me the same warm grin he had to Aster and clasps my forearm in the Arethian greeting. "The pleasure is mine, Kira. Aster's regaled me of your prowess and trials in every projection he sends me. Incredible, what you're doing."

I step back when he releases my arm. My brows furrow. I'm not doing anything incredible. Looking for answers hardly seems incredible. Just...logical?

"Thank you, sir," I say, my voice trailing up on the last word.

"Oh no. None of this sir business. Gershom or Gersh, if you prefer." He waves a hand to dismiss my formality. "No kings or lords here, eh? Just a few Mages, a Paladin, and you." He inclines his head.

I cock my head. I've never met anyone quite like this Mage, and that's saying something. Gershom takes a step forward, eating into the space I'd only just created. Slender fingers bearing scars from potion making reach out to push the last of my bangs that haven't shifted away. "Your marking?"

Without a sound, I dip my chin.

"Curious. You did not tell me she bore a crown of thorns." His disgruntled words startle me. Just how much has Aster told his grandfather? I shake my head, moving my hair back into place. With the tips of my ears still covered and my marking hidden, I can often pass for Human to the odd passerby, which suits me just as well.

"Nevermind that. She has a more pressing matter. Void injuries, Grando. What do you know of them?"

Reaching into the air, Gersh waits with an open hand while a book speeds through the Solarium. from a shadowy section lined with low bookshelves so not to obstruct the view outside. Behind thick clouds, the shine of filigree from other Skies glints in the sunlight.

The book nestled in Gersh's grip practically speaks for itself on Void-related topics. Smoke rolls from the pages, even while the book remains closed. Its black color saps the light from everything in reach. No cream or yellow hued pages line the sides. Onyx tips each page, and when Gershom finally peels the cover back, I gasp at the white ink used to write in some strange language. Runes and characters I've never come across run along each page in columns.

"It's Demonic. Only Locks, Demons, and Vaeroth himself speak it." Aster winks. "And Grando."

"Fascinating, isn't it? The Void?" Gershom supplies with a smile.

No. No, it is not fascinating. Having fought and killed more things than I'd like to count from that hellscape, I would say it is not even in the realm of fascinating.

"You two are bizarre," I find myself saying instead.

Gershom gives the tome a gentle toss, and his magic holds it aloft. It hovers alongside him when he approaches me. With an extended hand, he arches a questioning brow and looks at me expectantly.

"How exactly is this going to help? I don't want to point out the obvious, but none of us are Clerics here. So…" I trail off.

"I may not be a healer, but I've found magic can do a great many things when manipulated just the right way, Rogue. Haven't you noticed you can manipulate shadows the same way an Arcane mage can manipulate items? Have you ever thought about treating shadows like a portal? None of us are really that different, are we? Paladins and Berserkers are one step removed from each other."

The longer Gershom talks, the greater the resemblance between him and Aster becomes. The love of knowledge. More, the love of sharing that knowledge. For as much as I poke at Aster's odd facts, I appreciate that he never lords his intellect over anyone.

The Void book wiggles and dives toward me, pulling up abruptly when Gersh's magic leashes it and contains it upon a cloud of Mana. Gershom clears his throat quietly and dips his head to me before saying, "I'd rather not go searching for your injury, my dear. Can you show me where it is?"

Finally, I wordlessly dip my chin, indicating my arm. Scarred fingers trail down my bicep and linger over the spot that aches and burns on occasion. His brows pucker, and his other hand scratches at his short, tidy beard. When he asks if I'm wearing another shirt, I remove my leather armor and shirt, leaving me standing in my white undershirt crossing my arms to ward off the exposed sensation raising the hairs on the back of my neck.

Prior to resuming whatever it was he'd been doing, Gersh bends down to look at my forearm. Flowers litter my exposed skin, inked in by various artists from my travels. The older Mage rotates my arm, inspecting each bloom.

"All poisonous or ingredients for poisons, yes?"

My smile bares my small fangs. "Indeed."

"Why have you marked yourself so?"

I chuckle a humorless sound. "These are markings of my choosing. I make my own fate. Not whatever god controls these." I gesture to my pitiful Night Elf marking upon my brow.

He hums a noncommittal noise but returns to his original task.

Violet light entwines itself around my arm, leaving a warm tingle in its wake. Gershom's magic reminds me of fresh baked goods and a hearty stew after a hard day. I never knew my grandparents, but his magic rings truc with every quintessential grandparent stereotype I've been regaled about over the years.

"Lumeris shine upon us," he breathes. Gershom levels me with a heavy stare. "This lingering demon magic is the least of your problems. There's another magic that requires attention. It's woven itself into the fiber of your bones."

CHAPTER 29

I SAG, KNEES BUCKLING under the weight of Gershom's revelation. My body wants to reject the words, reject his assessment. Yet, I know it's anything but mere conjecture. Aster wraps an arm around my waist to hold me up.

"Looks like carrying all those books around in your pack has been good for something." My joke falls flat under the circumstances. Aster eases me over to the lush, green couch and settles me into a seated position, tossing the blanket from the back of the armchair around my shoulders for good measure.

Gershom's Mana flits through the sitting area, weaving through the bookshelves and into the fireplace. Heat blasts against my cheeks but quickly tempers to a more bearable temperature. "Sorry about that," he says, shooting us a sheepish grin.

Narrowing my eyes, I try to piece niggling thoughts together. "What designation of Mage are you exactly?"

"Best not to ask questions you aren't ready for answers to." He stands straighter, squaring his shoulders. Despite being more than a handful of decades older than me, his body shows no signs of deterioration, as though he trains at the Spire currently. "You've some sort of Lock-laced Grit that does not belong to you."

I blink, my mind shuffling through possibilities of what those words could mean. Individually, I understand each of them, but strung together in that order, I can't quite glean any sort of meaning from them.

Matthias' Grit? But why would he have Lock magic in his Grit. His has always felt pure. Then, the only other Grit he might sense stems from the brand, yet why would Laz' sigil be tainted by Locks. Even still, I can't help myself from offering that as a suggestion. "Lazrik's Shadowbrand."

Gershom hums thoughtfully. "Perhaps. There is a distinct Rogue shadow masking whatever this is. It is reminiscent of a parasite that has become one with its host."

I blanch. No. Lazrik wouldn't. *Wouldn't he?* A small voice asks inside. A voice I smothered because it asked too many questions that never had answers.

"Now. The process to remove Void essence from a host is unpleasant at best. It will burn—cutting two threads at once. This Lock-touched thread acts as a choke chain, a leash around your neck."

Delightful. "It's alright. I can assure you it's not been that bothersome." I shrug my shoulders, trying to dislodge the blanket wrapped around them, but Taigh clamps a hand around the fabric, stopping the blanket's descent as well as my attempt to stand.

And here I thought brothers were meant to keep me from experiencing pain.

Continuing on as if I haven't said a thing, Gershom details the process of removing the Void essence. "The Void latches onto your worst emotions. What you keep hidden inside. Pain. Heartache. Guilt. *Grief.*"

"And if I just...leave it?" The question escapes before I can stop it.

Gershom's lips flatten into a grim line. "Then it will keep feeding. Parasites grow hungrier with time. It'll twist what's left of your magic. Make it volatile, unpredictable. Then your mind. Give it months, maybe less, and it won't just whisper your worst memories; it will wear them like skin until you can't tell what's you and what's the Void anymore. Or maybe it will create them. You'll live inside nightmares."

Lovely. Just what every girl wants—demon-induced identity theft.

Agony flares in my chest, but Gershom continues. "It seems you may know what it may be latching onto. Unfortunately, you're going to have to confront that particular emotion. I can draw it out, but it will draw out the Void essence as though it is a demon. Lesser demon at least, but it will be a very real, very corporeal thing. It may fight. It may lash out with words. To destroy it...well, that I cannot tell you how to do."

Uncertainty coats my skin, weighing down my limbs. How can I face grief like a demon? How do you destroy that?

If I destroy it, will—will it destroy whatever's left of Lachlan too? Will his soul, be it with Lumeris or Nythraxis, be gone also?

"Come now, dallying won't stop this nor will it help." He leads the way to the shadowy part of the Solarium, and my friends haul me along with them. "Figure the shadows might help you regenerate should the Void essence be a bit feisty, eh?"

Aster chimes in, "We won't be able to do it for you, but we can offer some assistance." While the words lessen some of the tension lining my muscles, it doesn't alleviate the apprehension roiling in my gut.

Digging my heels into the cobblestone paths through the Solarium sounds like a much better option than continuing with this mad plan. He's a Mage, for Nythraxis' sake. What am I doing? *Getting rid of the Void*, Lachlan's voice murmurs in the back of my mind. The Void could be considered a shadow, could it not? Basically the same thing.

Kira. You're trying to rationalize keeping a piece of a demon inside of you.

I shake my head, trying to clear out the fact that I'm arguing with a voice inside my head. A voice long since dead.

Dead.

The word clatters around my head like the echoing of a temple bell. He's right. If he is even real or if my subconscious has created a version of him to keep him alive inside me.

A large gold plate circles around the outside of the Solarium, acting as a shade. Rich soil squishes beneath my boots with each trudging step, until we come to stop beneath a towering oak. Its branches stretch out like a shepherd protecting its flock. Leafy ferns and tall grasses litter the area around it. My lips tilt up when I spot a cluster of foxgloves and lily of the valleys, both inked into my arms.

Standing beneath the oak, a sense of protection washes over me. A motherly caress of my cheek with a touch like the soft leaves of a well-tended plant. Elyndra? I've never claimed the goddess before, but she's become increasingly present in my life. Her show of support leaves me off-balance.

"When I channel Mana into you, it will forcibly remove the essence. I understand you are no stranger to torment and suffering, but Vaeroth's torture bears no competition in its severity." Gershom gives me no time to recover, and when he claps his hands together, deep, amethyst-colored Mana explodes in a starburst. The rays of magic arc and dive into my chest.

When his spell flares, I feel it — two screams in one: the Void's shriek of hunger and Lazrik's brand hissing as it's consumed. The smell of char and salt fills the air. The mark on my skin glows red, then white, then nothing at all.

Gritting my teeth against the instantaneous eruption of agony and terror, I collapse to one knee. I can't even spare a thought to be thankful for the soft ground, as every molecule of my being homes in on remaining conscious. Nothing Lazrik or any opponent I've faced can compare to the sensation of my very soul being sundered.

I bite back the sobs, clamping my teeth into my lower lip to stop myself from begging the Mage to stop. Black smoke coils and slithers around me, approaching the center of the circle we've formed with Taigh and Aster standing on opposite sides between Gershom and me.

The smoke stacks and builds in the same unnerving way the wooden constructs from Faelwyn's lesson did. With each passing moment laced with my whimpers and misery, a form takes shape. Tall boots giving way to the loose breeches Lach favored, his belt with nearly as many pouches and hidden compartments as my own. His lean torso builds and sculpts, his shoulders adorned with the damned violet cloak he loved unfurling like a ship's sail.

I try to tear my gaze away once the smoke carves his face into the form, but I'm bound by a connection that holds me in its grip. Lach's violet eyes, twin to my own, stare back at me, only the slightest hint of writhing onyx behind them. His skin bears the barest of purple hues, the perfect arched ears, a single violet mark through one brow, down a cheek, and an almond shape upon his brow all lend to his Pure Night Elf passing appearance.

It's him.

My brother.

Lachlan.

Releasing my lower lip from its place of captivity between my clenched teeth, I cry out for him. When I try to stand, to get to him, my knee gives out as I falter to the ground. Reduced to crawling to him, I scrabble in the direction of his figure amidst the creeping smoke.

"Kira, no! It's not him!"

It is. How can they not see? It's him. He's been inside me. I've heard his voice, and now he's here.

"*You* let me die." Lach's lips move, but the words echo all around the Solarium. "How could you? You didn't come for me!"

Tears stream in hot tracks down my cheeks. Shame left in their wake, burning me from the inside out. He's right. I should have forced Laz to send me instead. He'd never sent Lach into such high-risk situations like this before. My brother researched and crafted runestones or finagled his way into political alliances and parties. A diplomat as much as Aster is.

I should have demanded Lazrik tell me where Lachlan had been sent. Tortured answers out of him if I had to.

"He never told you because you weren't strong enough. You still aren't. You're little more than a dog chasing her tail."

My heart crumbles, but I nod. "It should have been me on Vaeroth's Crimson Scale, not you. I'd trade places in a heartbeat."

"Hard to do something in a heartbeat when mine stopped a long time ago, Kira."

Collapsing back onto my haunches, I stare into his violet eyes. Smoke rings the edges now. Something's not quite right with him. Why is he being so cruel to me?

"Focus!" I snap my head to the right, seeing Taigh with one palm splayed toward the sky, the other dragging down his raised arm and arcing toward the specter of Lachlan. A concoction of confusion and panic urges me to my feet. A brilliant white light strikes down just behind where Lachlan strides in my direction. The bolt of Light splits straight through Lachlan, but it leaves no carnage in its wake.

"She must do it on her own!" a voice calls out.

But I can't. I can't do it alone. I can't do it without him. I reach for my Grit anyways, surging forward. Unsheathing two daggers, I launch my assault. Silver flashes in tight arcs. The blades meet *something*, but each slice and stab meets the same resistance as slicing warm butter. Too soft, too yielding. No blood spurts. No shrieks of pain. Only a singular shivering shadow curling from the useless cuts before it weaves itself back into the form of my brother.

A ferocious grin overtakes Lach's features. An expression so foreign I stumble away from him. I falter seeing the strange expression on his features and retreat a singular step, hating every inch I've given up.

His marking upon his brow, the one resembling the All Seeing Eye, glows, and Void-touched shadows whip out from it. One catches me upon the cheek, wrenching my head to the side. Pain licks up the side of my face. The world spins on its axis, and I fight the temporary blindness from the bite of the shadow.

He doesn't even bother to follow up with a blade—just watches, as though my struggle is sport.

Remembering Gershom's earlier words, I try a new tactic with my Grit. Instead of gathering them to me, I use the magic to shove and ram the shadows, propelling them away from me. Satisfaction lends a temporary relief from the pain.

"They should have drowned you in the river, sent you off to be food for the leviathans for all the good you've brought our family."

Any lingering warmth from the successful Grit experiment dissipates. Dead. Better off dead. My hands drop to my sides. One dagger and then the other slips from my grip, landing point down in the soft dirt. A vise squeezes around my chest.

"You left me alone to die. You promised to be by my side always." Alone. That word again. Alone in the Void. Fitting he's left me alone to face the world now.

You are not alone. I am here. That voice again. But it's not Lachlan. It was never Lachlan.

A forceful wind whips my braid back and forth, the spikes hidden within catch my other cheek. Matthias' cerulean Grit in my chest cascades out in a tsunami over my own.

The specter flies back through the air in a wicked projection before slamming into the glass wall of the Solarium.

Sever the connection, pisúlë. You bear no guilt in this.

Sever—my hand flies to my belt. The benefits outweigh the risks, but I can only imagine Aster and Taigh may murder me if this fails—if I'm not already dead. Without tearing my eyes from the specter righting itself from the collision, I select one of the vials from the holster of poisons. Focusing on the mimicry of my brother, I pull at what I know of him. Focus on his goofy demeanor that's lost to the specter's rage.

I waste no time and tear the stopper off with my teeth. Aster hollers at me to throw it, but I tilt my head back, only to pour the liquid down my throat while still biting down on the cork. The cool poison leaves prickles in its wake, but its effect leaches all emotion from my body.

Numb. I am numb. The perfect Rogue. Nothing matters. My limbs loosen as the rigidity flees with my emotions. Waves crash behind a wall in my mind with unmatched rage. Every strike erodes at the forced deadening of my emotions.

We'll be having words about this.

I prowl toward my prey. His features flicker from Lachlan's to a horrific visage, eyes with no lids, a hole where his nose should be, rows upon rows of jagged teeth. Gnarled, holed, taut skin over exposed bone.

The specter flickers. "You'll never escape me. Escape your guilt. Escape the hand you played."

"You do not exist," I state flatly. A skeletal hand wraps around my neck, but I remain rooted in place. The scent of burning flesh permeates the air, but inside me, nothing lives. "I will mourn the Lachlan who dreamed of owning a cafe with a bookstore, who baked but couldn't make anything more than slightly burnt bread, who brought home every stray cat. I will not hold grief in my heart. I will live for him, while you burn in Vaeroth's pits."

The essence of the Void flickers with every word, but finally, it winks out of existence when I spit the last sentence. For a heartbeat, I swear I hear Lazrik's voice whisper *mine* before the mark burns to ash.

Stunned silence remains in the wake. My eyes rove over the three men left gaping at me. Gershom finally hums.

"Duskthorn and hollowkiss, if I'm not mistaken. Ingenious. Reckless, but ingenious." He tilts his head in that way only a parent can. "The brand may have left remnants behind, but another day we can attempt to flush out the rest of its poison—er, perhaps that wasn't the best word choice."

I nod and float back to the sitting area.

Duskthorn numbs—pain, memory, even fear if you take enough. Just what I needed during that fight. Hollowkiss is its cruel twin; it scours, burning away what clings too tightly. Alone, they dull or sear. Together . . . they hollow you out. Leave a space where the wound used to be.

Now, I'm merely a deadly husk.

Something drips onto my undershirt. The garment bears enough red stains that fade to sweat to resemble an ominous sunrise. My thoughts are sluggish, and I recognize the cloudy haze; all I can do is endure the fog and the freedom from emotions until it's out of my system.

More and more waves pound against the barrier in my mind and soon cannon fire joins the barrage from the ocean. You'll just have to wait, Ironhart. I can't deal with the swirling questions when whatever is between us lies dormant.

Is this what a necroti feels when it's reanimated?

The lack of emotions leaves me feeling whole, somehow. The strange dichotomy has me waffling between emotionally drained and staring at the wall around my mind blocking me from my feelings.

A warm teacup suddenly fills my hand. I blink down at it then look up, startled to find Gershom standing before me. His gentle hands urge the cup to my lips, and I drink it down, the heat beating away the icy blankness within me. Emotions of every sort worm their way through the barrier, but chief of all is rage. Though, this rage is foreign to me. Simmering yet threatening to be all consuming.

Poison! That's your solution? To try to kill yourself too?

"How are you in my head, Ironhart?" I growl, gripping my temples.

Taigh makes a choked sound. "I'm not?"

"Not you, your blasted brother."

The rage eases, and my hands suddenly unclench. Lifting them, I look at my palms. Half moon indentations line each. Inwardly, I can feel the rage still lingering in the harbor of Matthias' Grit, but he must have it on a tight leash.

Leash. Lazrik leashed me. I cast the thought out to be dealt with later, along with all the other things I'm choosing not to deal with.

"I will deal with you later, Matthias. Keep your emotions to yourself," I bite out.

Aster leans toward Taigh to whisper, "Why is she talking to your brother when he's clearly not here." Looking to his grandfather, he adds, "Is this an effect of the poison?"

Gershom shakes his head, but his face gives away nothing of what he's thinking. Taigh, though, wears an expression of weary acceptance. "Not my den, not my wolves."

Aster runs a hand through his hair, looking bewildered by Taigh's words. The Paladin throws his arms up. "You want to know more? Ask her tomorrow or in a few days. I have a feeling she'll understand by then."

"But you already know?" Aster's words hold a bite I'm unfamiliar with hearing from him.

"Unfortunately." Taigh sighs heavily.

I turn toward the elf, steeling myself for the answer. "Taigh, what does vael'astor mean?"

"Nope. I am not a dictionary. I am not a relationship counselor. I am a Paladin. I am a little brother. I am a *Night Elf.*" He emphasizes the last words, like they should be some sort of hint to me.

"I know!" I cry. "I know it's Elvish, but I don't speak it!" I'd really like to have that numbness back. The walls have completely dissolved, and I'm left struggling to stay afloat in the storm.

Taigh heaves a weighty exhale. "My lost star. Like a wandering constellation."

CHAPTER 30

DAYS LATER, GOLDEN LIGHT gilds the trees on the island in the river in an ethereal glow, leaving the world with the last bits of warmth before it tucks itself away for the night and allows the moon reign of the skies.

The overcast sky has given way to interspersed puffy clouds that sail like ships through the vast expanse. Flat on my back, I stare up to watch them go by. Exhaustion settles into my body like an old friend. A weariness weighs upon me, and I sigh.

"I could stay here forever."

"You want to sprawl on wet sand outside the Spire for the rest of your life?" Aster's aghast question makes me giggle. Though by the wary glance he sends my way, he likely thinks I'm hysterical.

Crunching boot steps reach my ears just before Aster swivels to see who's approaching. "This should be enlightening." My friend summons a hunk of ice and a blade that resembles a carved icicle. I startle, both from his words as well as the ice and knife he's created.

"I didn't realize you carved the statues too." I roll my head skyward again, resuming my watch over the sunset.

"Idle hands and all that. They never turn out as well as if I sculpt them with Mana, but hopefully one day I'll have mastered doing it by hand." An ice chip lands on my neck, and I squeal from the sudden sensation.

A heavy weight settles on the damp bank beside me. "Hoarfrond."

"Captain." Aster dips his chin, but his eyes remain on the tail of whatever creature he's unveiling from the brick of ice.

"Ironhart." I push up from my reclined position and dust off the sand from my back.

"Thorne."

Aster snickers quietly, but I bite back my own chuckle since the simmering rage from Matthias rolls off him as well as causes his Grit inside me to roil.

"Great, now that we've established we all know each other—"

"Pound sand, Mage." Matthias cuts Aster off with a low growl and bitten words. Matthias' Grit crackles around us.

Aster peeks down at me, and I offer him a reassuring smile. He tosses both the hunk and the blade into the air where they wink out of existence.

His family's handle on magic astounds me. It would have been far more pleasant if our trip into the Skyward Solarium had been one of idle tea with his grandfather rather than an exorcism.

"I'd say send a shadow if you need me, but I hardly think you will." He nods to where my belt rests in the sand. Three daggers sheathed along with vials of poisons stashed within, the duskbloom and hollowkiss having been replaced already.

Aster stands and marches off without another word. Crickets chirp and a whippoorwill trills in the distance. The longer the silence stretches, the louder my heartbeat sounds in my ears.

"Here to regale me with more nonsense about the constellations, *my lost star?*" I clench my jaw shut and glare into the inky waters of the river.

"I have nothing to do with you using that word." He shifts then stretches out his legs.

"What's happening, Matthias?" I whisper. "Why is your magic inside me? Why can I feel you? Hear you?" I want to ask why he attacked his brother the last time we were on this riverbank, but I seal my lips before the words escape.

I turn to him and study the harsh lines of his face, tracing the lines of his marking. His glacial gaze watches me in return. Heartbeats pass, and he says nothing.

But with every breath, the kernel of his Grit in my well of shadows grows. Shock ripples through me when it changes and blends. My shadows take on a watery tinge, becoming a mist, somewhere between air and liquid.

Matthias' apprehension and trepidation wash over me. The emotion much clearer than anything I've experienced from him before. The emotions tightening like a fist around my lungs.

A word filters through my thoughts before I can shove it away. No. This cannot be *that*. Lachlan said those bonds were beautiful. All consuming. Papa adored Mama, their bond unshakable. They never mentioned pieces of the other living inside their magic. No hints that feelings and thoughts passed freely between them.

Pride warms me. But it's not my pride. My hands fist at my temples.

Keep going down that thought. It's close, but it isn't that word.

"Stop doing that!"

*You did it once with me. Well…*his words take on a wry tone. *You did much more than simply send words to me, didn't you?*

"I saw you in the pub *one time*." I roll my eyes, trying to even remember details about that encounter. He'd been with his friends, but the fact I'd been in his head made focusing on anything else difficult. My thoughts drift to when he'd hovered above my bathtub, but I push that away. I know I imagined that.

Smug amusement ripples through me. His? I look at him and a predatory gleam flickers in his eyes. Definitely his. Goosebumps ripple across my skin from that look alone, and I realize I most certainly had *not* imagined him at the bath house.

"I don't know what you're talking about," I say, my annoyance clear. But I can't help wanting to know more. "Does it get easier, telling your emotions from mine?"

Matthias tilts his head back and forth. "Yes, but that doesn't mean you can avoid what this is, Kira."

I fiddle with the knife sheath on my thigh. "You say that, but it's quite literally my plan."

His sigh is heavy, full of resignation. "I cannot force you to face it, but I can provide you information that may help you to decide." I open my mouth, but he holds up a hand. "I'm not pushing you one way or the other. You will always have a choice, even if they're hard ones.

"We aren't mates in the Elven sense of the term, where lineages and compatibility play a part in the selection of bonds. It goes beyond that. You call me vael'astor because there is a divine aspect. This bond is governed by the stars. Our souls were forged from the same star, planet, whatever it is that Zorvyn and Nythraxis chose when they forged our connection."

The world drops out from beneath me. I'm trapped in a free fall with no control, no end in sight. The implications send me reeling. The gods themselves chose this? Why? What do the two of us have to do with anything?

Images of my parents dancing in the kitchen, holding hands on the way to the market, choosing each other after every fight, all of it disappears. The idea of having a choice at all floats away. Even if a mate bond flares, they can still say no, go in search of love elsewhere and face no consequences.

I grasp for a safety line. "But what of Elyndra? She seems highly invested in this." I think of the Lunar Frenzy. His reaction at the greenhouse. Her hands have been deep in every instance of this bond flaring.

"I'd assume she bore witness to our patrons forging this bond." Matthias stares across the river. His words bear no unkindness, but they have all the emotion of a professor reading from a book on a subject they find no value in.

"What are we, Ironhart?" I ask, each word uttered singularly without any possible room for error.

"Celestial Mates."

I blink, waiting for my brain to process his words, to provide a nugget of information on what those are. But nothing comes.

Taking pity on me, he continues. "Since our souls were forged from the same celestial body, they were destined to find each other. We would have lived lifetimes over and over again until we found each other. Celestial Mates are rare, existing in times of either great need or when Gods decide change is in order. This kind of bond is not solely about love and affection. We become a team."

"What do you mean it's not about love?" Something shutters in my heart, closing its doors to this possibility I've found a mate bond only to discover love is not on the table for me.

I thought mates meant love. Mates meant a partner in your heart. Mates meant never walking this earth alone, someone to have your back, to hold your hand, to rub your back when something wasn't right, to shake you when you were being obstinate, to laugh with you when you make a mistake. Mates meant forever.

"Love comes in many forms, pisúlë," he murmurs, finally turning his head to me. I can sense a lingering sadness within him among swirling apprehension. His shoulders rise toward his ears. "You can love a sibling, a mother. You can love someone with every fiber of your being. You can love someone at the wrong time or wrong reasons. You can love them too much and stifle them. Love is a weapon just as much as it is a gift. Do not mourn that love does not have to be part of this bond."

An aching sorrow fills me with every soft word he speaks. He won't love me. I'm destined to be alone. I shove at the idea. Shove at his growing Grit within me. Like a tick, it just burrows itself deeper. If I'm going to be alone, I want it to leave me the fuck alone!

You are not alone. I am with you always.

"It's not the same."

Matthias inhales deeply, the weariness revealing his decades over me. As he opens his mouth, he hesitates, tossing his head back and forth, choosing his words carefully. "I did not say I would not love you. But I will not tether you to me if your affections lie elsewhere. That, however, is not the pressing issue here. Unlike Elven mate bonds, rejection of a Celestial Mate bond results in...unfavorable outcomes.”

“We die?” A fire ignites in my chest. No matter if he loves me, we’re stuck with each other or Vaeroth claims us?

“If only it were so simple.” A wan smile stretches his grim features. “To reject the bond courts madness. Harmony versus chaos. If we reject it, or fail to build the connection, pain, madness, and the fibers of our souls tearing will follow. Death would be a more savory alternative.”

“Great.” I flop back against the sand once more. “You won’t love me, but somehow we have to *nurture* this bond or else we’re going to go barking.” I turn my focus to the sky. “Nythraxis,” I holler. “I didn’t sign up for this, you old goat!”

Matthias’ solemn expression turns affronted. “Do you often talk to him like this? Zorvyn would drown me with my own Grit.”

“Don’t start with me. Would you have even chosen me if it weren’t for this handshake deal we’re caught in the middle of? I’m sure there are plenty of Pures that have caught your eye. That you’ve just waited for a bond to snap into place for.” I bare my teeth at him.

“Don’t you think I’ve already tried to fight this, Kira? And who says Elyndra wouldn’t have blessed us with a traditional bond had Nythraxis and Zorvyn not stepped in?” So many emotions swirl in his eyes, mirroring my writhing Grit, beckoning shadows to us.

Aster’s words about constellations and stories written in the stars float back to me—threads of fate knotted in distant light. Had Matthias read those same stars, long before I even knew to look?

“When did you know?” I whisper. This may be the one time I don’t actually want to be left in the dark. It’s usually my safe haven, but today that haven has become a blindfold.

"I saw it in the stars years ago. I didn't know for sure until…I nearly lost control on the beach."

With a shake of my head, I try to clear all the swirling thoughts from my head. It's all too much.

A shadow scampers to me, pulling me from the tempest raging inside. It forges into a small animal, and I realize its Araya. She wiggles her rump and pushes her cheeks out in a smug look. "He sent you, did he?"

Her tail flicks in response, but she turns from me to inspect my "Celestial Mate." That one will take some time to get used to.

"Your god sent you a pet with the Wanderer and the Sentinel constellations on its side?"

"She is a she, and she is not a pet."

Though, I sit dumbfounded when she climbs into his lap. I wait for his reaction, but he stares at her then looks at me panicked, almost asking what he should do. I shrug, the only affection I get from her comes from the occasional petting or her crawling into bed with me in the Guild. She doesn't typically snuggle me outside of bed.

"As for her constellations, those are new. She showed up the other day with them. Prior to that she's always been shadow."

A grunt is the only response Matthias offers me.

Irritation bubbles inside of me. At him. At the gods. At the situation. I fiddle with the knife sheath once more, exacting too much pressure in order to cause the tiniest bite of pain to ground me.

"What change exactly are the two of us meant to bring about? We're—what—just supposed to fall in line with whatever fate they've chosen for us?" I jut my chin out. "I am the master of my own fate, Ironhart."

"Already forgetting the part where we go mad if we decide not to go along with this?" He scoffs. "Lingering effects of the blasted poison you decided to shoot like a glass of Dwarven stout?"

"We're going to go mad anyways." My smile borders on manic at this point. "You think the pair of us are going to manage to *bond*?"

His solemn, removed demeanor morphs, fangs baring in my direction. Brows drawn down in harsh slants, the words he spits my way fall like hammers. "Bond? You think we won't bond, pisúlë? Why do you think you feel my emotions, send yours to me? Why do you think you can enter my head? Your Grit is no longer just yours, just as you've created a shadowy boat within mine that's set up shop and made a port in my ocean. Best to get on board now, Thorne, or the gods will leave you to drown." Flames lick out from the kernel of his magic, nearly searing my well of magic. I shrink back from his anger, shocked at the intensity of it.

Matthias growls one last time in my direction and pushes off the ground. Araya leaps from his lap, looking between the pair of us. The elf stalks away from me, but cursing and swearing reaches my ears with every step he takes. Araya snorts in indignation and follows after him.

Bitter loneliness replaces the warm companionship I'd experienced just moments before. Something I hadn't realized existed between us. I lay down on the sandy shore and close my eyes, trying to focus. Shoving the emotion back under a trapdoor to handle later to examine when things were less raw, I tunnel into my Grit. I call out to the piece of Grit that resides in Matthias, and much like before, it has the same result—nothing.

I am done. I'm done with the loss of control. I slam my eyes closed to shutter out the world around me. Reaching out mentally for the piece, I grip onto the connection and yank like a sailor hauling on a line. I heave with all the mental strength I can summon, but my magic has taken on a life of its own within his ocean. It's created a dock for the original boat I'd seen, which now resembles a large galleon rather than the small dinghy I'd found.

Use your words if you want me to come back next time, rather than yanking me to you.

Come back? Of course I don't want him to come back.

Then stop forcibly dragging me back to you.

I release the connection between our magics, but the damage can't be undone. Barely cracking an eye, I find Matthias looming over me. I accept the hand he extends down to me, shivering when our skin meets. He pulls me to my feet and steadies me with the other hand when I rock from the force of his tug.

Silver moonlight cascades over his features, giving him an ethereal glow. My heart pounds in my chest as I take him in. I waffle between enraptured and enraged at his beauty.

The crinkles around his eyes hint he's experiencing every thought and emotion going through my mind right now, and the desire to throttle him surges. His lips quirk. One tiny tip of a fang flirts with me, and my tongue drags uncontrollably over my own much smaller canine.

"I think I hate this bond." I glare up at him, but my eyes flare. Wrapping my fingers around his forearm, I yank him down to inspect his face. "Your markings."

"Yes, I have those, as do you."

"No, not your Night Elf markings, moron. You have a—" I trace the new markings with my finger. The design gleams silver in the moonlight, a beacon in the dark. "A crown of thorns? Why do you bear my marking?"

His eyes flutter close while I stroke along his brow. A ghost of a touch trails along my own brow. My lips part at the odd sensation of my own fingers on his skin. "One of us has apparently accepted the bond enough for it to form."

Questions swirl, but I refuse to give them voice.

"You'll have to ask at some point."

Not tonight I don't. Too much information has been thrown at me. Gods playing chess with our fate, the looming threat of madness if I don't properly connect with Matthias, Araya bearing the constellations—not to mention the crumbling hope I hadn't realized I'd held onto for a genuine mate bond.

"Can Megora kick me out for this?"

"*That's* what you're worried about? I can find the codex, I can help with whatever it is you're doing here even if you get kicked out." Our eyes catch since I still hold his face in my palm, but I yank my hand to my side. An earnestness fills his eyes, and I quickly divert my own, unsure of how to handle his willingness to help. And how to handle his apparent mood swings. He stretches to his full height, his gaze never leaving my face. It leaves a tingling in its wake as he roves over my face.

"Megora sort of threatened to either send me to Aldros or the Dread Flats if I stepped out of line, so..." I shrug.

"Death by Vaeroth's creatures or death by starvation and prolonged labor. Pleasant."

"What exactly does 'stepping out of line' mean to him?" I ask quietly.

Bewilderment crosses his face before his cool masks slips back over, my marking upon his brow fading into nothingness as he hides his emotions. "You didn't ask him when he was laying out your ground rules?"

"Best to beg for forgiveness, and all that." I wave a hand flippantly.

Matthias mumbles something about my being the death of him.

That is a very real possibility.

"Kira, you don't just stroll on into the restricted archives like you're hunting for a bedtime story," Aster bites, sending a lance of ice through a mocked-up training dummy Faelwyn left in the sparring ring for aspirants to use on our own time.

"I won't stroll then, I'll sprint and keep going until I've disappeared from Arethor," I wink and adjust my grip on the staff I hold. It's a strange weapon—one I haven't used prior to my time in the Spire—but I can't pass up the opportunity to train with a weapon I don't usually have access to.

Aster sighs—long, theatrical, and dripping with annoyance. His next spear of ice goes wide. I snort.

He throws his arms up and strides forward. "What in the Void are you doing?" I ask.

Aster draws his leg up and kicks out at the training dummy, his boot planting in the center of what would be his enemy's chest. The thing sways violently, and before Aster can hop back, it smacks him upside the head.

"I should have stayed in the bloody Archives," he mutters to himself. He turns to me, hair askew from his fight with an inanimate object. "You want the codex so bad you're blind to the risk, or have you become so numb to risk you'll lay yourself on a silver platter for Aldros?"

"Think I could poison him with my blood if he took a bite while I'm on that silver platter?"

He's not wrong though. Lachlan was hunting for this book. A book dated back to when the Gods walked upon the land. It holds secrets. Ways to sever destiny. Spells to change the very makeup of magic.

I shake my head before I can think too hard about why Lach wanted it.

Aster rolls his lips inward, but the apples of his cheeks rise, bunching the corners of his eyes.

"You can laugh. It's okay. You can find me *wholly amusing and amazing* while also being the stern, stoic Archivist," I tease.

He cocks a brow and opens his mouth to reply, but a low whistle cuts through the sparring ring. My braid thunks against my armor as I whip toward the sound.

"If we're planning a lethal dinner party with Aldros, I'd like to be invited," Taigh drawls, leaning against the low fence of the ring.

"Eavesdropping is unbecoming of a Paladin, you know." Aster brushes nonexistent dirt from his vest. He picks a piece off and flicks the imaginary dirt toward the lithe elf.

The smile that unfolds on Taigh's lips in response is devastating. "It's a good thing I aspire to be unbecoming, but you want to know what's even more unbecoming: getting your ass handed to you by a stuffed dummy."

"Lumeris take you," Aster snipes like an irate child.

Sticking the butt of the staff into the dirt, I lean my weight into it. Their game of volleying back and forth makes my lips tilt.

"*Anyways,* what is this about a codex and strolling into the restricted archives, and how do I join?" Taigh finally swaggers toward us.

Aster throws him arm down like a knife between the three of us. "You don't. No one is joining because no one is going."

Taigh scrapes a hand over his jaw in a move that's eerily reminiscent of another Ironhart Night Elf. "Funny," he says, circling the training dummy Aster just lost to. "That's exactly what people say before doing something stupid."

I bark out a laugh, unable to help myself. "It's a good thing I specialize in stupid."

Aster's sigh seems to echo in the arena. "And I unfortunately specialize in cleaning up after you. If we're caught—"

"We won't be," I cut in. "Besides, you're probably the only one in Arethor, save the Solariums, that can even read the codex, and we need to find whatever's in there before the Locks have a chance to."

The Mage's jaw tightens in rapid succession. Loyalty wars with logic in his amber eyes. For half a heartbeat, I regret allowing myself to befriend him.

"Fine," he sighs at last, pinching the bridge of his nose. "But when this ends with us in the stocks, I'm telling them it was all your idea."

"Wouldn't dream of taking that from you," I say with a wink.

Taigh grins, slinging an arm over my shoulders. "Good. Then it's settled. We'll meet after nightfall."

Aster groans. "I hate both of you."

"You say that a lot," I call as he stalks off toward the gates.

"Because it keeps being true."

CHAPTER 31

DRESSED IN ALL BLACK, Aster, Taigh, and I creep through the corridor, only to hesitate at every sound and sigh the Spire makes. Plucking the tiniest thread of Grit, I wrap us in shadow to hide us from everything but magical sight. I send up a silent thanks to the Guild for the years spent perfecting the minimal usage of magic to conceal ourselves.

"Can we hurry this along? I have an Orc kitchen girl's bed to warm at some point tonight." Despite his whisper, Taigh's cheeky tone rings clearly.

"What a catch you are. Blessing the ladies with your presence when you deign it suitable." I can't help the snarky comment, though I cringe knowing I should be silent to lessen the chance of discovery.

Creeping along behind us, having traded his robes for trousers and a black shirt, Aster pops both of us on the back of the head without a word. Taigh and I share a sheepish look and continue to the oversized arched doorway.

Peering back at Aster, I nod. This plan would either be a great success or go to the hells in a handbasket. While Aster chants something behind us, the words barely a flutter of air across my ears, I send up a prayer to Nythraxis.

An icy blade chills me to the bone when Aster's simulacrum walks straight through me toward the door. I split the thread of Grit into two and hurry after it. The strain of holding the second thread to keep Taigh and Aster's physical form concealed twinges, but I stay focused on ensuring I open the door to match the projection's movements.

From Aster's subtle questioning within the Archives in the Spire—asking as a former Archivist—there should only be one Mage sitting behind the desk. Key word here being "should."

The creaking door opens, shrieking through the otherwise silent library. My heart pounds, blood roars in my ears, and I fight to keep my breathing quiet while I watch the vision of Aster stride with confident steps to the desk.

The Archivist on duty for the night appears only slightly younger than me, somewhere around Aster and Taigh's ages. Close cropped orange hair stands out against his deep-green skin. His long-curved tusks gleam in the

Mage light. Luminous gold designs twist and twine over the top of his mulberry robes.

A curious delight overtakes the boredom creasing his handsome face. Their words are lost to me in hushed tones, but the Archivist waves his hand and strides off in the opposite direction of the staircase we need.

Pressing a hand to the inside of the arm I have hovering over the hilt of my dagger, Taigh urges me forward. With the three of us holding our breath, we creep toward the stairs then start our ascent, but just before I place my foot on the next tread, Aster grips the back of my belt.

"Not that one!" he whispers, alarmed. "It's spelled." His fresh, icy Mana wraps around me when he points to the step ahead of me. A red flicker winks back at us in a complicated rune.

Carefully, I avoid that one and move to the next step on the staircase, as does Taigh, checking with Aster before proceeding.

Once we've reached the top, Aster gives me a wicked grin. He moves his hands in a gesture I recognize from when he used it in the hallway weeks ago, and my ears pop once the sound shield forms.

"Restricted tomes are warded," Aster murmurs. "Most who seek them will walk right past, their hunger blinding them to the path." His eyes twinkle with glee as they dart from shelf to shelf, like a child trying to decide which sweet to try first at a feast.

"Anyone else feel like the air is thicker up here?" Taigh asks, voice raising comically at the end of his question.

Aster's face morphs into a look of confusion. "Technically speaking, air becomes thinner the higher you go, but perhaps we should find a Cleric for you if you think going up one flight of stairs is enough to change the makeup of air."

"Not like that, you blasted know-it-all. I feel...weighed down, like I'm being dragged somewhere." The Paladin waves his arms in wide arcs.

Aster rolls his eyes and steps away from us, toward the row of classified historical accounts, but I tug his sleeve. "You can look at those once we've finished."

His shoulders slump, but he turns toward the display cases, books he'd said were so forbidden, so controlled and controversial they required lock and key to even be held. Dozens upon dozens of steel cases with thick glass house the kingdom's most illicit books.

"Who exactly decides if a book is forbidden enough to warrant a jail cell?" Taigh whispers, gawking at the rows of locked away books.

"You don't have to whisper, Paladin." Aster sighs. "The Overseeing Archivist from the Conclave decides. And the King, but mostly the Conclave. Knowledge should not be locked away. Held hostage from the people." My brows raise at the fierce anger within his words.

Though I realize he's right. Having been squirreled away within the Underbelly for most of my youth, I'd gobbled up every speck of information I could with every mission Laz sent me on.

The thought of the Guild Master ratchets my shoulders up. I can only hope finding the codex Lachlan was looking for will help me piece the puzzle together so I can get the hells out of here.

My throat clogs with the nearly unbearable weight of it all. There's no way I can do all of this alone. The threat from the Guild looms over me. Aldros. The Locks. The damned hilt I gave to Laz.

You are not alone.

The words ring through my head, though I can't tell if they're memory or I'm projecting to Matthias again. Both? Probably both.

Aster and Taigh have each moved down the rows, searching for the tome we came for, and I move to the next row to join the search. With each passing breath, nerves coil inside me, ratcheting tighter and tighter. I'm a spring under too much load, ready to explode out of my own skin.

"Here," Taigh calls quietly. We scurry to where he stands three-quarters of the way down his row. Inside a case rests a thick tome with a scrimshaw cover; the design glows red. A skull in the upper corner leers up at us. A gnarled skeletal hand sits where the clasp should be, gripping the whalebone cover and the pages shut. "I can't read the runes, but it—it's speaking to me. The same phrase over and over: *When the veil is thin and the void calls forth.*"

Aster's Mana surges. Violet runes appear in the air above the case, each shifting to a dripping bloody sigil the longer they hang in the space. A stiff wind picks up, sending his blonde hair in every direction. The All Seeing Eye medallion glows like a lighthouse beckoning lost sailors with its vibrant hue.

His gaze cuts to mine, wild and bordering on unhinged. I pull my lockpicks from my belt pouch, kneel before the case, and set to work. I close my eyes and send a shadow into the lock alongside one of my picks to jimmy and shift the tumblers. Aster's Mana stirs, and I peek an eye open to check on him.

"Should you drop the sound shield?" I have no desire for him to burn out simply to allow us the ability to converse while he also pushes back against any magical barriers that may lay in wait once we open the lock. He shakes his head, but still, I search his face for any signs of his Mana depleting.

Once I'm satisfied he's being truthful, I return to my task. Finally, the lock gives way, and with the go ahead from Aster, I push open the case.

"Your magic is divine. Twisted. Mixed. Delicious." I recoil from the haunting voice. Aster's Mana blazes around me, ready to pour into the tome at the slightest hint of danger. After all, books should not be sentient. I recall a few stories from childhood about books that started speaking back to their writers. Those tales did not end well.

Taigh whips his head back from his position keeping watch of the staircase, eyes wild.

At least we're all in agreement about the utter wrongness of this book.

"Freedom. We seek the same thing. We can offer it to each other. A simple blood exchange should suffice," it croaks.

"Hard to offer an exchange of blood when you have no veins," Taigh calls, though his impertinent words lack their usual perk.

The red glow dims, and in the lines of the scratched design, a dark substance wells. Even from where I stand, the coppery tang of blood wafts through the air. Gripping the dagger at my thigh, I wrench it from the sheath and plunge forward. The motions are jerky, uncontrolled. Certainly not controlled by my own choices. My blade arcs down but stops a hair's breadth from my target: the beady eye sockets of the skull.

But instead, my blade hovers above one of Aster's wide, unblinking honey eyes. Somehow I'd turned around and aimed the dagger at him. A tremor wracks his body. I slacken. I'd almost taken his eye. Oh gods. Aster drags a hand down his face, tracing over the eye I'd almost pierced.

"How?" I breathe. I whirl back to the book. No longer laying upon its back, the book rests on end as though the skull wanted a front row seat to my maiming and dismemberment of my friend. The fingers curling around the pages tap one by one, each knuckle joint popping and cracking.

"Accept my offer, open my cover, and see what secrets I hold. What is it you'd like to sever? A life, a reign? Or perhaps a bond?"

I stiffen. Could it? Could it sever the Celestial Mate bond?

Free. I'd be free to choose my fate once more. Sheathing my blade, I run a hand over my forearm where my chosen markings lay hidden.

"Aha. Unhappy with your mate? You'd like a new lot in life. The Paladin could be a lively choice. Perhaps you prefer brains, a mate that can stimulate your mind as well as your body."

I flush. Embarrassment and rage well within me. No, I didn't seek a mate bond with either Taigh or Aster; just one that I could choose. One that resulted in a mate who would love me because he chose to. Not one that stemmed from a forced connection because the alternative was death.

"But I tell of so much more. You could sever the gods. They came to me once. To sever a blade, a prophecy. But they created a new one instead. Everything comes at a price, you know."

I suck in a breath and step closer.

"The Shardblade. You showed them how to sever it?" Aster asks.

"A price young Mage. What can you offer me?"

Aster's eyes flick back and forth wildly, the gears in his head turning and spinning. Thick silence fills the space while he thinks. "Knowledge. I can offer you knowledge. You've been locked in that case for nearly a century, no?"

His resemblance to his grandfather shines in his thought processes. Only a hum of agreement returns from the book.

"Queen Reyvna of the Dwarves. I can offer you a snippet of information on her."

"Yes, yes, I think I'd like that. A secret. I do love to hold secrets."

Aster bites his bottom lip, and I catch the slightest hint of the smug smile he's warding off. "Queen Reyvna found her third husband increasingly boring and began to dose him with the smallest amounts of sleeping draughts in order to avoid his company, until he died a mysterious death of unknown causes."

The skull's eyes flicker, but it says nothing. We wait, and Taigh shifts from foot to foot, checking between our conversation with the skull to the staircase again and again.

"Not world shattering, but I do like her craftiness. I accept your secret." A beat passes. *"You'd like to hear the true prophecy of the blade? The one the gods reforged?"*

I dip my chin.

"When the veil is thin and the void calls forth,

A tethered soul shall bear the stars.

Bound in light, yet shadow-born,

A gatekeeper forged, but never refired.

Two shall stand where none should pass,

One shall wane, the other last.

Blood upon steel, a choice to sever,

Loyalty sworn or lost forever.

The door must close, yet not by hand,

No mortal touch, no godly brand.

The price is set, the toll must take,

Lest the world be left in the Void's wake."

"Thorne?" Taigh's voice breaks the silence, but I shake my head. Even as the words fade, they echo along my subconscious. The original version, if this codex is meant to be believed, doesn't even come close to what this one insinuates, though my brain still struggles to wrap around each line.

Aster shuffles next to me, moving one hand while the other taps his lower lip, as he parses through each line, his mouth forming each word deliberately.

"Thorne?"

"Tethered soul? Gatekeeper? Who or what were they trying to stop?" I direct the question to Aster, but his eyes have glazed over with a purple hue. Grit stirs and shifts within me, unsettled by the words, the lingering power they hold.

"Kira?"

Whirling around, I glare at Taigh. "Are we about to die—oh."

Matthias stands next to his brother, an imposing figure towering over the lithe Paladin. Arms crossed and a thunderous look on his face, matching the turmoil shifting within our linked Grit.

Aster steps next to me, his eyes returning to their usual color. His face pales, and he whispers to Taigh, "Did you?" The elf shakes his head, looking equally alarmed at the appearance of his brother.

Hot anger cascades over me, so much my hands tremble under the weight of it. They itch to fight, to snatch up my blade and drive it into something, someone. Flicking my eyes around, I search for a threat to throttle, to destroy. My breaths heave faster and faster to match the race of my heartbeat.

In a blink, the anger burns out, leaving a hollow void where it consumed me. Dropping his arms, Matthias has the good sense to flash an apologetic grimace in my direction, though he sends no other emotions or words through our bond.

"What is it you think you are doing?" He masters his temper, the even words never betraying the rage I'd experienced rolling off him.

I jut my chin out and plant my hands on my hips. "What I came here to do." Shouldn't be a surprise to him. Hadn't we just discussed my need to find the codex and finish whatever Lachlan was here for?

"Yes, we did discuss that, but I believe there was a clause where I said I'd help you. Instead, you replace me with my brother?"

In a futile show of dominance, I bare my fangs at him. "Can't replace you when you weren't invited. Plus," I hold up a finger, "he just showed up and demanded to tag along. I figured you sent him."

Something flares both in his eyes and the link between us as I stand there asserting myself. He prowls forward, closing the distance until he overshadows me. His lip curls away from his teeth. I shiver, but even as anxiety vibrates through my limbs, heat pools deep in my belly. It takes every bit of focus to fight the instinct to submit, to curl into him, to accept whatever's between us.

Teeth clacking together, I force my lip to remain peeled away from my small canines. Silver bleeds into the icy blue of his eyes. "Submit, pisúlë. I can't fight the Frenzy forever just because you want to play games." His words are rough, but they only remind me of his callused skin upon my own. I burn with the thought. Any fear from him looming over me has vanished, leaving only the hot, honeyed lust.

Matthias sucks in a breath and groans. "Whatever you're thinking, you need to stop." He drives a hand into my hair, fingers tangling in the previously tidy strands pulled back into my braid. Two fingers curl around the back of my neck in possession. He leans over me so his lips caress the small points of my ears.

My lip falls over my fangs as I suck in a breath, vibrating from the foreign pleasure stemming from such a small caress. "If you don't submit, I am going to take you up against a shelf in front of Aster and my brother, and the only reasons I won't kill them for seeing you impaled upon my cock will be because they will know you are *mine* and the Mage's sound shield will let you scream my godsdamned name loud enough it will ring in their ears until they day they die."

And that, pisúlë, is why I didn't want you touching my ears in that tavern. Even then I would have fucked you on a table. Rutted you to alleviate the throb in my cock that touching an elf's ears causes.

I blink up at him. All but the smallest sliver of blue gone from his eyes. I struggle to remember why letting him follow through on his threats would be bad. My tongue slips out to wet my lip, and in a flash, Matthias dips his head and nips my lip hard enough to taste the copper tang of blood.

Just as quickly as it happened, he straightens and stalks past me. His emotions swirl too fast within our bond for me to decipher any of them.

"I want to joke that I need to smoke a pipe after that, but you being my brother and all makes it weird." Matthias' animalistic snarl startles all of us. My ears pop in rapid succession with Aster losing focus and his Mana momentarily slipping from the sound shield. "Right, yeah. Too weird."

Matthias yanks the cloth from the case where the codex had been kept and tosses it over the book. Out of our sight, the red glow fades away. Its whispers fall silent. "This atrocity is a weapon. Forbidden by our people." He glances at Taigh. "The old gods, dead and gone, wrote this. They imbued it with their power."

With deft hands, he wraps and secures the fabric around the book to ensure no light can sneak in. "Vaeroth seeks it. Aldros desires to possess it. The power has corrupted over the years. No one has ever been able to destroy it or void its magic."

Aster's head tilts. "If everyone wants to possess its magic, why is it just laying in a case up here?"

"Think, Mage. Which of the three of you found the book?" Aster looks to Taigh. "The one who just *tagged along*, who had no desire to find it? The Conclave cast protections around its case. Only someone who had no desires toward the codex can find it. Only someone who had no inclination to use it could stop the magical barrier. And only someone blessed by a deity can unlock the case."

I scoff. "And somehow we just happened to meet this trifecta of requirements?"

"Still think the gods don't have a hand in your fate, pisúlë?"

CHAPTER 32

Unlike his predecessors, King Wilder does not rule from the gilded throne of Crethor's Grand Hall but from the war chambers beneath it. A warrior before he was a king, he believes strategy and steel hold more power than ceremony and tradition. Some say this makes him a strong ruler. Others whisper that it makes him a dangerous one.

T AIGH HAD ARGUED TO take the codex to the Paladin Sanctum, stating the Light there would protect any from being swayed by its corruption, but Matthias won out believing the Night Elf High Priestess and her council were best equipped to handle it. Though he wouldn't be able to take it to her for another fortnight. In the end, Aster created a portal realm to store the codex in.

No matter how deep we dive into whatever this is, the answers slink away with every discovery we make.

I glance around the small room just outside the arena—the same one we'd been in for the first trial—as I adjust my tooled-leather bracers for the fifteenth time. My gut roils when I think about the last trial. They wouldn't be so blatant as to target me again in a trial, right?

You put too much faith in logic.

I scrunch my nose at the intrusion. I'd thought myself safe since he's meant to be with the other instructors on the dais. Faelwyn and Luella watch over all the aspirants this time. One offering words of support. The other prodding each aspirant with backhanded compliments just before they pass the threshold into the colosseum.

The stronger our connection, the greater distance we can talk like this.

Talk, he says. As if I can pop into his head the way he can mine.

Accept this for what it is, and you'll be able to do it.

But I refuse a bond that chooses my path for me and then provides no love in return. Annoyance flares from his direction, and I grit my teeth against it. It's quickly overpowered by a beaming pride.

You're getting better at recognizing my emotions from your own.

Does he actively seek me out to harass me, or are my thoughts just a constant stream for him?

The latter.

Taigh and Tharava lean against the wall near the other Paladins, and I sidle my way into their conversation. Taigh looks me up and down, surreptitiously checking all of my armor, daggers, and vials.

"Try not to end up covered in blood and gore this time, Thorne."

"You should try taking your time this go 'round, baby Ironhart."

He waggles his brows at me, leering. "You can call me baby, and you can call me Ironhart, but you can only use them together if you're saying, '*Ironhart, baby, give me more!*'"

Tharava's barked out laugh draws the attention of the other Paladins, who shoot a baffled look at Taigh.

My fingers curl around a dagger hilt and the slick sound of it being drawn silences the bark of laughter. I'll kill him for that comment. He has no business speaking this way.

How dare he act as though what's mine is his. I step toward him. Alarm shines in his green eyes, brows raised, lips parted.

"I didn't mean it!" he pleads and quietly adds, "Matthias, I would never. You know I'd never."

I stop short. Matthias? Why is he—oh. Gods damn it all, Ironhart. Get out of my head. If you can't keep your temper in check, I'm going to end up murdering someone and having to explain that it was your fault. Megora will happily send me to the Locks no questions asked if I send my dagger through a Pure.

With more force than needed, I shove the blade back into its home. Cursed fucking bond. I could have just as easily avoided this entire situation if I'd broken into the Spire to find out what Lachlan had been up to and slipped away without a backward glance.

No, you'd still need to get the book somehow, and then you wouldn't have had Taigh and Aster with you.

At least this bond would still be just something written in the stars instead. We could have met in the next lifetime, which might give me a few lifetimes break since he'll outlive me by several centuries. Hells, he might be free of me after today.

Don't even joke about your death today. His growl ripples down my spine in a delicious vibration.

This trial groups us into pairs, though we still fight alone. Should our partner fall, their opponent can attack the remaining aspirant. On the other hand, if our combatant is slain or surrenders, we can assist our partner, if we so choose.

They say it's meant to test judgment — whether we value victory over loyalty, self-preservation over mercy. To see what kind of blade we become when the choice cuts both ways.

I've yet to decide which option they want us to choose if we're the aspirant to succeed first: help our peer or observe to see if they're meant for the Guard? Either way, they'll never be my backup in the real world, as I have no intention of graduating this place or taking up a post within the city.

Luella opens the door to the arena and turns to call the next victims. "A Cleric, any of you will do. I don't care which. Stop wasting time," she huffs impatiently. "You, with the orange hair, Wood Elf. Yes, come here."

A slim elf whose limbs look fragile enough to break scampers forward with her hands brushing down the front of her ill-fitting leather armor. New to her, but likely from some armory trunk and dug out for this trial.

"And Thorne." Luella waves me over with only the barest of looks in my direction. As I approach the Mage and the Cleric, I realize the latter is a half. My lips part, but jealousy spikes in my chest. Wood Elf halves can hide their status much easier with their lack of Markings and their much shorter tapered ears. Human and Wood Elf heritage mix easier than Night Elf and Human, or Orc heritage and any other race.

Though I remember Tharava mentioning halves in the Orc culture do not suffer the same stigma Human and elven halves do. It also helps that the more rural the town Halves are born into, the more accepting the people are of their blood status. Not many folk care who someone's parents are if their patronage or their work puts food on the table.

The small woman shoots me a timid but no less warm smile, and I regret that I've never taken the time to learn her name. Her orange hair matches the sunny tone of her skin and rusty eyes. Wood Elves' ever-changing eye color has always intrigued me, but the idea of asking someone why their body does something is just a little too out there, even for me. Though, the curiosity of whether the nearest forest has anything to do with the change does linger. Would they still change if they were within the Dread Wood?

Faelwyn nods to both of us as we stride through the door. My eyes struggle to adjust to the change in light with the sun shining directly overhead. I groan with the suspicion my selection at exactly midday was deliberate, since there are no shadows present.

"Alright?" The Cleric's lilting voice snaps my momentary pity party.

Two figures stand in the middle of the arena. A tall broad male in full plate armor, his helm covering the entirety of his face and head. Rules out him being a Night Elf, his ears wouldn't fit in that helmet. Too tall to be a Human, so he's either a Wood Elf or an Orc. The armor sparkles in the sun's rays, appearing to have come from the king's armory itself. He grips the long brutal sword already, waiting for our approach.

The other's stature mirrors the small elf next to me. Our heights are all within inches of each other's, but his garb has me forcing my feet to continue moving alongside the Cleric. Black pants dotted with hidden sheaths. A fitted black shirt beneath obsidian armor with blood-red stitching. A full hood and mask with matching thread weaving through it. The uniform of a young Rogue. One without enough coin to purchase their own armor, their own kit.

Was he here as a message? Had Laz decided I was out of time? I stumble, only to have the Cleric grab my arm to steady me. What moon phase happens tonight?

New moon.

Gods, I'd ask why you track the moon, but I'm going to assume it's some cultural thing I was left out of as a half.

Or, he drawls the word along the bond, causing me to shiver. *I've already had the same thought you just had since I've been sitting here watching these two wait for you. There's something not right with their Grits. That Berserker feels...polluted somehow.*

My eyes dart between both figures, and the same clouded magic Matthias had described hits me. Our combined Grits recoil into my well of magic, not wanting to touch or exist in the same space. The utter wrongness of the oily magic in the air turns my stomach.

Dread pools in my gut, leaving my limbs feeling heavy. Sweat prickles at my hands, and I swipe along the front of my pants.

"Cleric?" Without speaking too loud, I attempt to get her attention before we reach the center of the arena.

"Sasha," she replies, not unkindly.

"Kira. Fancy working together? Fuck, their rules. Keep me alive, and I'll try to keep them away from you."

Without a single moment's hesitation, she nods. "Absolutely. End goal of this whole thing is to work together, right?"

Use my Grit.

No. I can't.

You've used it before.

Not intentionally, and not when even more Locks than the last trial were lurking about. On the balcony with Megora, Matthias leans with one of his friends from the vision in the tavern against a pillar, conversing with each other as if he wasn't also popping into my head. As if his own stress levels weren't ratcheting mine higher and higher, coiling like a spring under a severe load.

Aldros looms at the front of the platform, hands gripping the railing with his fingers curling up from the underside. His cloak billows in the gentle breeze, long hair floating out in finger-like tendrils. Dazek lounges in one of the ornate, carved and gilded chairs, looking as if a funeral would be more interesting than the trials. Six other Locks lurk about on the platform, but their magic stems from the Demon Threads tied to their familiars also lounging and floating about.

The sheer number of Locks and demons in the arena gives me pause. Why are they so fascinated by the trials? None of them are instructors within the Spire, save for one. I can't imagine all of these Locks have become so invested in their acolytes' progress to have shown up here today. And the rest would have no business with the Spire except for their search for the Shardblade and the codex. One of which they need me for information I don't have.

My thoughts stop short when pounding footsteps charge in Sasha's direction. She abruptly backpedals away, throwing her Mana into a bowling ball of power. The blue energy collides with the Berserker. He stumbles but recovers his feet with a shake of his head. The Rogue has all but winked out of sight, though I can sense him circling us, the hairs on the back of my neck standing on end as he creeps in an arc behind Sasha and me.

Focus on that Berserker. I can mind the Rogue while he bides his time for you.

I don't waste the attention and lost focus to respond to Matthias and drive forward, unsheathing the longer serrated dagger at my back and a small one from my hip. The longer dagger bears a vicious poison made from nightshade and corpsedust. If I can manage to nick the Berserker deep enough, the poison should do most of the work for me. But as I assess the thick plate armor, doubts creep in.

Finding a gap to slip my knife in seems impossible. Miraculous timing and luck will be the only way I manage to achieve that. Plan later, act now. Sasha hurls a spear of energy this time, but the Berserker only changes course, sidestepping to avoid injury.

I dive between him and his quarry, planting my feet. The Berserker's eyes flare at my serrated blade before his emotions flee entirely. Without any prompting, Matthias' cool Grit pours into my legs, bolstering them. The Berserker swings his weapon overhead and brings it down in a heaving blow. Sparks fly when I parry my crossed daggers against his sword. The blow rattles my arms, but thanks to Matthias, my legs remain steady.

Without its assistance, I'd likely be on my knees.

"Little shadow," he coos. My eyes widen, and the distraction costs me. I fumble, and he bears down, seizing the opportunity. It doesn't take long to realize trying to recover my position will result in his blade lodged in my neck.

Changing tactics, I use his momentum to send us falling to the ground. I hook a leg around his and push off to change the trajectory, leaving him on the ground with me straddling his hips. He bucks and thrashes, abandoning his sword in favor of swinging his massive hands in wild haymakers.

My earlier thought about them not trying something in the second trial filters through my brain. No, Sasha and I have been marked for death.

My stomach drops out from beneath me. No, not mine. Matthias'. Like magnets, my eyes find him leaning forward on the platform. Long fingers wrap around the hilt of his sword in a white-knuckle grip.

Incoming.

Sasha snatches the sword off the ground, and betrayal lances through me. But as she scurries backward facing me, holding the sword aloft, my head is yanked backward by a fist around my braid. Through the pain, delight roars within me when the Rogue yelps from the spikes I weave in.

A sharp blade bites into my skin. I steel myself, waiting for whatever effects of poison may be on the blade. Silk wraps my throat instead. Sasha's chanting reaches my ears. Thank Nythraxis for Clerics.

Sasha's blockade between the blade and my throat saved me, but I'm trapped between two assailants. The ground rumbles and shakes, and the chanting stops. Pain lances my scalp when my braid is tugged once more, but the presence behind me is gone. A hard thud sounds from somewhere across the arena, but I redouble my efforts to end the Berserker.

Darting forward, I urge my Grit into the motion, praying Nythraxis offers me some luck to find an opening. I aim my dagger for the small gap between the helmet and his gorget. Nythraxis smiles upon me because not a breath later the blade slips into the soft flesh under the Berserker's chin.

Peering through the slit in his helmet, black eyes stare back at me. Black with a vast nothingness behind them. I scramble off the male, terror at what those eyes could mean coursing through me. A glow emits from below his eyes, but winks out as the life fades from the Berserker.

Crimson drips from my blade as it slips out of the Berserker's body with a slurp. Each droplet sizzles against the pale sand, and a tendril of smoke flares out from the splatter. Behind me, Sasha retches, and though I commiserate with her, the small amount of guilt wanes with the idea that the Berserker had been corrupted somehow.

The Rogue springs forward, and I stumble back, already off-balance from the revelation of demonic eyes in a Berserker. My opponent lunges again and again, driving me back, using the same blade strikes I've mastered over the years. With every surge of Grit one of us uses the other's responds in kind. We dart and dance across the sandy arena.

"You know why I'm here." The distinctly raspy feminine voice gives me pause. Feminine. Not a male like I'd initially thought.

I grunt in response. "Working with the Locks? Did you forget what god you follow?"

"You've been gone a long time, Kira." Hasn't it only been a few months? We circle each other in a stalemate, puffs of air streaming through our lips. Before coming to Arethor though, I'd been in Baustantia, then somewhere on the western coastline, and prior to that lurking through caves along the mountain ranges looking for treasures on Laz's orders.

"Laz would never let them take the Underbelly." I leap forward, the hiss of my blade through fabric brings a satisfied smirk to my lips.

"Is it letting them take something when they were invited in?"

My heart stutters. Invited? But why? Why would he invite them in? Heaviness lines my limbs, and I waddle backward in a pathetic attempt to escape her onslaught. My movements are futile though. Her sharp dagger catches the soft skin of my belly between the waist of my pants and the bottom edge of my leather jerkin.

Sasha's magic can't stop it in time, can't create the same barriers she had for my neck. Hot blood oozes out of the long laceration. Pain shoves its way down my throat, and my stomach roils, threatening to expel everything in it.

"And look what they've given us. The key to everything. The key to power." She advances against me, head tilted in a condescending angle. "All we need now is that pesky hilt you've got."

No, that's not right. I shake my head. I don't have the hilt. Laz put it in the vault or sold it or whatever he deigned to do with the blasted thing. My fingers lock one by one, stiffness sliding up my arms that hang lifelessly at my sides. A paralytic poison. The Rogue makes no move to end me though.

I chance a peek at the balcony where the Locks and Spire staff hover above us. Aldros' pale face bears no emotion, but next to him Dazek gleams with enough glee for the both of them. Though I don't wish to see the concern and sadness I'm likely to find on Matthias' face, I flick my eyes his way.

His jaw clenches and unclenches in rapid succession, but his pale blue eyes bore into whatever stands behind me. Sasha. Gods, hopefully she's prepared to end this.

Stop fucking giving up and trust someone else for a goddamn minute.

Silk wraps around my fingers, pushing the poison out.

Did you forget what Clerics are meant for on a battlefield? Quieter than his raging and I'm not sure he intends for me to hear it, he whispers, *This is why Rogues are a disservice to themselves, locked away in their sewers.*

We'll be discussing that particular comment later, but a silver chain materializes around the other Rogue's waist and link by link stretches to me, hooking around my hips where the wound gapes.

Both of us rooted in place, Sasha's voice gains strength as she chants. Warmth blooms over the wound, and my eyes widen when the other Rogue doubles over, dropping her blades to grab at the fabric of her kit. She yanks the shirt up, and murmurs ripple across the balcony. Her skin rips and tears, redness cascading out of the opening wound on her belly. With every breath that passes, strength bolsters in my limbs while she crumples to the ground.

I'm frozen for a heartbeat, but the other Rogue—she'll be frozen for the rest of time. Her body remains still on the ground, and the chain pops out of existence. Eyes flaring, I whirl around and push my legs to get to Sasha. She sways on her feet, appearing smaller than she had walking into the arena. Her knees buckle, but I manage to scoop my arms under her shoulders before she cracks to the ground.

Instead I ease the pair of us to the ground, kneeling facing each other. She smiles gratefully at me when I smooth a few stray orange hairs away from her eyes and mouth.

"We make a decent team," she whispers.

"We do. You saved my ass enough times I think you're the real winner here." A shy pride fills her eyes. "How did you do that?"

"It's meant to link a Cleric to another fighter, to offer them the support of our strength if they're flagging. I wasn't sure it would work, but I linked the pair of you and sort of forced the spell to exchange strength for weakness." She shrugs as if she manipulates spells to do her bidding everyday.

"Incredible. You are incredible."

Not a single word comes from the balcony, but our attention diverts to the doors opposite us. They creak open, an inky darkness waiting for us with no indication of what's on the other side.

More waiting.

More swirling thoughts.

More questions.

No answers.

CHAPTER 33

A CHILL LINGERS IN the air, seeping into my bones making my joints ache like I've lived centuries instead of decades.

"Nythraxis' bleeding shadows, at least the damp air in the Underbelly had the decency to be *warm*." I can't stop the grumble before it's out of my mouth.

"What about this place screams warm and cozy to you?" Taigh teases from his spot on the dark fabric couch in the Mage common area.

I open my mouth to respond, but Aster beats me to it. "She did grow up in the Underbelly. This is probably brimming with fuzzy feelings for her."

"There aren't any rats to keep you company here, though," Taigh lobs back.

I roll my eyes. There have been rumors that because the entrance to the Underbelly resembles an entrance to the labyrinthine tunnels below Arethor, we must all live in a sewer. Some people even claim we bathe with the mythical crocolisks from the canals.

"How are you feeling after you almost lost your 'lickies and chewies'?" Taigh drawls the last three words, making them sound much lewder than they should.

"For the last time, 'lickies and chewies' has nothing to do with your cock and a lady's mouth." I huff a breath and divert my gaze out the window overlooking the harbor.

"Kiralin," Taigh starts. "I feel like I should ask this for my brother's sake. You do know there are no teeth involved when your mouth is near a man's dick, right?" He looks to Aster for confirmation.

Aster shrugs. "I kind of like the scrape? Plus, a well-placed nip on a hip bone? Makes a man go feral."

Taigh gapes at Aster like he cannot believe Aster didn't agree with him. "What? I'm all about knowledge. Can't know what works and what doesn't if you don't try it."

A long moment passes before a wicked grin overtakes Taigh's bewilderment. "That is the type of research they should have made us do in school."

My lips tilt thinking of my own research during my younger years. It hadn't been as extensive as Aster's shocking revelations, but I dabbled with a few of the boys ahead of me in training. Before Lachlan had scared them all off, threatening to shrivel their cocks if they even thought of touching me

"Ooh, looks like we caught someone thinking about having a man's hands on her. Shall I fetch him for you?" Taigh swings his legs over the end of the couch, making to get up. Summoning a sliver of my Grit, I wrap a shadow around his torso and toss him back onto the cushions.

"Please, he's probably out picking up some female to handle him." I hate the jealousy lining my words. When my thoughts divert to wondering if I could peer into his mind, I yank them back into submission. "The real question we should be asking is how the two of you managed to be paired up together and barely managed to survive a Berserker and a Cleric."

Aster looks at me solemnly. "That was a large Berserker."

"Do you think they sign up for these trials? Maybe they're criminals...I can't imagine the Crown wants us killing other magic users for the sake of training."

Footsteps round the corner leading to the alcove hosting the sitting area we're occupying. "Is this really what keeps you entertained? Discussing the morality of training?" Luella's nasally voice grates on my nerves.

Would it have been too much to ask to avoid her for the rest of the day?

"They're past recruits that failed out. Poor. Useless. Can't feed their families. In exchange for their sacrifice in the trial, we compensate their families. The no-name cretins that they've become. They'll be licking the ground for scraps in a year though. Can't manage their money, poor sods"

Aster's horrified face matches the disgust I fight to keep off my own features. Luella either doesn't notice, or she chooses to ignore them.

"Are participants aware that they'll be touched by Lock magic for the trials? I imagine that could be concerning." Aster's voice is clinical, but clearly he's digging. I recognize the tone. On the surface, however, it could seem like he's asking for research purposes.

"I'm sure I don't know what you mean, touched by Lock magic," she says with a careful mask sliding over her previously smug features. "We're very thankful among the faculty here to have Aldros and his very skilled Warlocks to assist us in the training of the Guard." Luella's eyes dim the longer she speaks on the Warlocks until only a vacant stare remains.

Fabric rustles as Taigh shifts on the couch and struggles to keep his features neutral. The same uneasiness rises within each of us, but the uneasiness in me comes to a head when those devoid eyes focus on me.

"In any case, that *halfbreed vigor* must be strong in you. An army of halfbreeds might be good for the infantry. At least their deaths wouldn't require a funeral."

I'm out of my chair before she can finish the thought. Screeching echoes in the small sitting area as I launch forward to wrap a hand around her throat. I drive forward until her back collides with the cold stone of the wall next to the window. In my peripherals, both Taigh and Aster have also leapt to their feet, but neither move to stop me.

"I'll help you hide a body, but we have to be smart," Taigh says.

"If you do this, we're going to push a domino I'm not sure we're ready to handle," Aster hedges. Nails dig into flesh. Both of their statements roll off me without a change in my course. Luella's fluttering pulse beneath my fingertips sends a chilling thrill down my spine. My lips curl savagely.

"Do it. End me," she goads. A second hand wraps around her slender throat, joining my first. The supple skin gives easily beneath my clenching fists, but I stand locked without making a move to finish her off. A purple flash flares from her irises. "He's never going to fall for you. Not when he had me first. Felt his hot length stretching me. Has he even touched you?"

I bare my fangs at her, leaning forward to growl, but she never flinches or even acknowledges my show of aggression. "He tastes just as delicious as a cold ale *sucked* down in the heat of summer."

Red tinges the edges of my vision. Pinning the blonde Mage with one arm, I reach for a dagger with the other, but something snags my wrist.

I turn, half expecting the object of all my rage to stand behind me, but instead his brother stares down at me. "She's egging you on. She wants you to do this." He lowers his head to murmur in my ear. "Or whoever's controlling her. Her eyes are not her own. She's never been with him. I swear it to you." Taigh makes the symbol of his god upon his chest.

I suck in a deep breath, but the red around my vision remains. "Let it go, Kira. Let his magic go or else he'll be down here next. If you hold onto his fury much longer, you're going to go into his Lunar Frenzy."

Aster chimes in next. "Elyndra's already focusing on us here. Her presence is growing stronger." He shifts restlessly on his feet, glancing between me and the smug woman I hold.

Let go before Megora has a reason to court martial you and send you to Aldros' dungeon.

One by one, my fingers unwind from her neck.

That's it, pisúlë.

My hand drops to my side, but the elf behind me keeps his wrapped around my wrist. With a tug from him, I step back from the Mage, her eyes flickering between her own and that purple tinge.

Taigh finally drags me to the hallway, and after a last look, my eyes catch on my own reflection in the window. I suck in a sharp breath.

My marking has changed. In addition to the onyx crown of thorns upon my brow, another set joins it with an ethereal silver glow. "Aster?"

"I saw it. I don't know," he says calmly, walking alongside us.

I wish he did. I wish he could explain why Matthias' marking now paints my face as well. I haven't accepted the bond the way Matthias has. I shouldn't bear his mark. Because I refuse to let the gods steer my fate.

Celestial Mates aren't always meant to survive. The sentence haunts me. A sentence I didn't even read with my own eyes. Matthias had finagled his way into the upper level of the Archives with his status as captain. Sometime after Taigh and Aster dragged me back to Taigh's solo room in the Paladin Quarters, I'd blinked and slipped into Matthias' mind. It was long enough to see that one sentence and then I fell back into my own body just as fast.

I've spun enough trouble for one night, so I haven't mentioned this to either male before me. I lay here on Taigh's floor, staring at him while he rubs a cloth over the shield I've never seen him use; Aster shaves chunks off a miniature tree made of ice. But I can feel Matthias' turmoil raging within his Grit. More concerning though is his anxiety rippling along my spine and filling my lungs with lead.

Outside of rage and jealousy, none of his other emotions have trickled down our connection without him actively pushing them my direction. I can't stop myself from wondering if his marking upon my skin has something to do with it. A marking no longer inlaid on my skin I discovered, after the countless times I've checked my forehead and cheeks in Taigh's mirror.

Before spending the last few months with Aster, I'd have been jealous that the Paladin doesn't have to share his space; but I'd happily keep my closet of a room with Aster over a dank room somewhere below the Spire, like in the Underbelly. I shoot a smile toward the Mage. I'd have survived without him, but I wouldn't be a better person for it.

Movement within the damn bond pulls at me. He's left the Archives, but still his emotions drag at me. Pull at me to find him. Do I want to follow that path? A path that's been cleared for me to walk down? It's that or stumbling through the weeds until madness and death claim me.

"Going somewhere?" Aster peeks up from his whittling.

"I—I don't know." Even as the words escape, my feet turn to the door and carry me from the room.

Taigh's reassurance follows me as I walk out the door. "She'll be alright. I have a feeling I know where she's headed."

The tug in my chest urges me faster and faster, up staircases and down hallways I've never explored, until I stand with sawing breaths before a nondescript wooden door.

He's on the other side of the barrier. Just steps away. The bond cajoles me to just turn the knob. Go in. Reduce the space between us to nothing.

The bond might be something forged by the gods, but I don't want to fight it anymore. I need him. Our path together might not have been our choice initially, but I'm choosing it now.

Damn him if he thinks we can avoid feelings in this bond. I grip the doorknob ready to force my way in if I have to, but I'm yanked into the room when Matthias pulls the door open.

"Hi," I say lamely, still gripping onto the handle. Master of potions and blades, and all I come up with is "Hi"?

"Hey."

We stare at each other for a long moment. Neither of us move. The air crackles and ripples, raising the hairs on my arms. Our eyes remain locked, hostage in some connection neither of us entirely understand.

"You're in your sleep clothes," I finally utter.

He looks down. Bare chested and clad in only a pair of low-slung linen pants. I peer down with him, eyes scrambling past the way his pants cling to his groin and note his bare feet. The fact that he stands with no shoes, no armor, no weapons feels too intimate.

Somehow his bare toes shake me from the hold of our bond. "Oh, Gods. I'm so sorry. I shouldn't be here." I rip my hands off the door and step back into the hallway, only to be hauled back, colliding with Matthias.

Hard planes of muscle tighten against my body. Terrified to look up into his eyes, I keep my gaze trained on the vast expanse of his chest. Runes dot one side, inked in by hand rather than written by the gods.

His hands wrap around my waist and fasten me to him. "It's my fault you're here anyways." It's a struggle to lock away the nervous chuckle threatening to bubble out.

I trail my fingers over the foreign symbols written across his chest. My nail leaves goosebumps in its wake and Matthias shivers, only to shake like a dog relieving stress. "Sorry," I mumble, but I don't mean it. I enjoy his hot skin under my touch. I bolster myself for my next words. "Why are we fighting this? It seems like death awaits us whether we go along with it or not."

Silver lines his eyes, Elyndra still making her presence between us known. What I wouldn't give to have a moment without the gods lingering. To be able to navigate whatever's building between us without the constant weight around our necks that we don't get to choose any of this.

"How much of my research did you see?" He eyes me with a grim trepidation.

"Only that some Celestial Mates aren't meant to survive. Which, Matthias, if we're going to die either way, shouldn't we choose which path we go down?" I lift my hand from his chest and drive my fingers through my hair. His eyes flutter closed for a moment before he snaps them back open.

"Aye," he drawls. "We should choose our fates. Are you sure you want to hear what I would choose, though? You're so worried about loving and being loved, but have you stopped to consider the rest of the bond?"

I open the distance and stride away from him, toward the warm hearth with its brick mantel and lean against the rough stone as I watch the flames. "What do you mean?"

"Our joined magic will make us a threat."

"People have been hunting me for decades. It's you that would need to consider that."

I look back and find him shaking his head in exasperation. "No, not just the crown or the Locks will hunt you. Every faction will hunt us. Joining our Grits will make us a step below the deities but above the rest of the magic users. The only safe place for us would be an island in the sea somewhere."

I quirk a small smile at him. "Couldn't you find one for us? Surely Zorvyn has a few tucked away."

He doesn't return my smile, just gapes at my glib. "Our status as target number one for every faction aside, we are linked to a prophecy, pisúlë. The codex shared that with you for a reason, played with you until I, too, heard the words for a reason. Not to mention Lazrik's tight hold on you—" he nods to my brand "—and his refusal to provide you with any worthwhile information."

Tears prick my eyes. He's goading me into saying I want to walk alone. He doesn't want to choose me. Turning to face him fully, I lean against the wall only to allow myself to sink onto my ass on the hard floor. I land with a muffled thud. All the while, I keep my eyes glued to the elf.

Standing before me with the pained look upon his face, he could be one of the statues hewn from granite along the path to the Spire. Even in nothing but a pair of tattered pants, he appears as beautiful as Zorvyn. His patron offers him all of the strength and solidity of a true Berserker.

A single teardrop escapes and rolls down my cheek then drips upon my navy shirt. The moment it falls, Matthias falls to his knees before me. Two great callused hands grip onto my face and tilt it up to look at him, knees on either side of me.

"Pisúlë," he breathes.

"Why do you call me that?" Matthias hesitates at my question. "Please. Is it something you chose? Something that just falls from your lips the way I cannot help but call you vael'astor?"

The moment the elven word slips out, his eyes flash and he gently presses our foreheads together. He closes his eyes and takes a deep inhale before he begins. "Do you remember the legend of the Wanderer and the Sentinel? Vael'astor has long been linked to their love, once translated to 'wandering star' rather than 'my lost star.' Súlë was long ago thought to reference the bond between them also. It refers to when they are allowed to be together during an eclipse, literally translating to the word eclipse."

I greedily tuck away the information, but he still hasn't answered what the word fully means or even if he's just as compelled to use it. "Vael'astor," I grit out.

He finally smirks, enjoying my annoyance and opening a little distance between us. "Patience, love. Pisúlë was the first thing I thought when I saw you perched on that roof, hiding from demons and Locks. Shadows twining around you trying to keep out of sight but even still lusting after the sweet treats of the market."

My eyes flare. I hadn't realized he'd seen me even before we'd made eye contact. "Pisúlë is just...who you are. A darkness rimmed with light. My eclipsed shadow who takes over my vision. Eclipses everything in me. Looking at you is like when the moon covers the sun and allows us to see something incredible, something that is hidden from the world. Something only to be seen for a brief moment by those who stop to enjoy it."

Finally, he crashes his lips to mine.

CHAPTER 34

Celestial Mates share more than just a bond of souls—it's said that when they finally give in to their connection, their magic briefly synchronizes, creating an aura only they can see. This phenomenon, called "Starfire," manifests as fleeting constellations flickering across their skin, unique to each pair. Ancient texts claim that these constellations reveal hidden truths about their fate, though the meaning is often obscured. Some believe it's a glimpse of the cosmos acknowledging their union, while others warn that if the light ever fades completely, the bond is at risk of breaking.

S TARS TWINKLE AROUND US. Real. Imagined. I can't find it within me to care. His lips move urgently, as though he's trying to convey just how he feels. As though he didn't just completely devastate me with his words.

I suck his lower lip into my mouth and drag my teeth over the sensitive skin. Hands pull at my hair, strands slipping out, and he wraps them around his hand to tug my head back for better access. I don't have time to marvel at the care he took to avoid the spikes in my braid.

Heat sears between us as our Grit writhes and undulates. Is it his lust? My own? The bond flares in bright blues and golds, rippling across my skin. I gasp into Matthias' mouth. Seizing the opening, he plunges in with long stroking lashes. He growls into my mouth, a sound I feel as much as I hear.

"Ironhart," I whimper against him. In a blink, he wrenches away from me, sitting back onto his haunches.

His eyes narrow and he bares his fangs at me. "You will not call me that name when it is the two of us, do you understand me?"

I can't help my lips quirking when I tilt my chin in defiance. "Is that so, Captain?"

He releases my hair and hauls me onto his lap. With my chin between his thumb and the knuckle of his forefinger, he guides me to look at him. "Aye, pisúlë." Shivers wrack my body at the low threat in his voice.

I lean into him, our faces nearly level in this position, but I pass by his waiting lips and stroke my tongue along the careful arch of his ear. His hands fly to my hips and grind me against the growing bulge barely concealed in his thin pants.

"Oh gods," I gasp. He's huge. Thick. Fuck, it's been so long since I've felt the thick ridge of a cock against me, but knowing it's him sends me higher. Teeth scrape across my pulse point, eliciting a moan.

"Tell me you need me like I need you." He slips his fingers beneath my shirt, exploring—teasing. I writhe against him, unable to even think about stopping, about telling him I don't need him. I nip and lick along his neck, up to his jaw, until I capture his lips again.

We're a flurry of tongues and teeth clashing against each other. I want to live in this moment forever, feeling him against me and along our growing bond.

Up and up, he pushes my shirt, taking my breast band with it. He rips it over my head and launches it somewhere behind him. The cloth hasn't even touched the floor by the time he's leaned forward to take one pert nipple into his mouth. Crying out, I arch into him. Deft fingers creep along my ribs, only to grip my other breast and roll my nipple between his fingers, all while still laving at my skin.

I grind down, rocking and seeking the delicious friction his cock offers me, but it's not enough.

I know it's not enough, pisúlë. Patience. My moan is the only answer I can give when his teeth clamp down at the same time he bucks his hips into me.

Off—I need his damned pants off. I want to see him in all his glory. To touch him. I want my mouth on him. Threading my fingers through his hair, I tug his head back and nip at his lower lip. Before he can deepen the kiss, I slide off his lap and tug him to his feet.

With him standing, I have perfect access to the broad expanse of his chest I didn't nearly appreciate enough when he first held me against him tonight. Using my tongue, I trace along the runes tattooed across him and then nip one nipple gently.

His hand shoots out to brace against the stone wall behind me.

I trail my fingers down the ridges of muscles, swirling along several scars I file away to ask about later, and come to the band of his linen pants. Through my lashes, I peek up at him.

It will crush me if he tells me no, but I'll take whatever he gives me tonight. I trail a finger along the hard length of him through the thin material. His cock jumps, so I do it once more.

Suddenly, Matthias laces his fingers around my hand and shoves it inside his pants, dragging the waistband down. "I am no boy to be toyed with, love. Play with me like you mean it or do not play at all."

He uses his own grip to wrap my fingers around his hot flesh. His features turn smug when I gasp. Steel balls ridge the otherwise smooth flesh. He removes his hand as I slowly finger each piercing so he can shove his pants the rest of the way off.

"Why?" I breathe and stare down at the proud length of him, studying each rung in the ladder of piercings. They line the considerable span, ending at the mushroom tip. His purple tinged skin tone seems deeper on his cock, more reminiscent of the night sky, and I can't help but think the piercings almost resemble a constellation.

"You'll see." He watches me but makes no move to urge whatever this is forward. Instead, he reaches up to stroke the tip of my ear. Euphoria coils through me, puddling in my core. "I'll bet I could make you come just from stroking your ears. Tell me, do you feel it in your clit when I do this?" He leans down and drags his hot tongue along the short arch and punctuates the move with a nip to my ear.

I roll my hips against him, seeking friction to relieve the ache he's building within me. "Again, please. Again," I beg. My fingers wrap around him and tug, as though I can tug him down to me once more, but he remains where he is. His eyes smolder, but any sign of Elyndra's Lunar Frenzy has disappeared.

Satisfaction blooms knowing all of this stems from him, from his need for me. Not some Goddess-driven lust. Though, our bond is apparently forged by the gods anyways.

His massive palm anchors around my neck. "Stay with me." Mutely, I nod and push away thoughts of deities interfering with us. "Go on, touch them. Feel them."

So I do.

With one finger, I stroke along each metal ball. His cock jumps with each swirl of my fingernail. A growl builds in his chest, and I revel in being the one to elicit that noise. His length is heavy in my palm, but I enjoy the girth of it, picturing just how he'll stretch me and how that ladder of rods will rub deliciously against me.

I go to fall to my knees, desperate to feel him against my tongue, but his hand still holds the column of my neck. Using his free hand, he unfastens my belt and pushes my pants and underthings down, the weight of my daggers carrying them to the floor with a clank of sheathed metal against the tiles.

Matthias releases me, only to step back and let his gaze rove over my naked skin. His lips tilt up in a soft smile, so at odds with the feral beast lurking beneath his skin. With a defiant tilt to my chin, I stroke my fingers down my body and let some of the annoyance at his slow perusal shine through.

Moaning when I tweak a nipple, I savor the feel of his eyes watching me. It's difficult to keep my eyes open when all I want is to drop my head back, especially when my fingers reach my sex.

"Stop." The word drips authority and raw dominance, but still, no traces of Elyndra show in his eyes. My hand falls still, and I wait with trembling breaths for what he'll do next.

He steps forward. I step back. We play the game until my back collides with the cool stone. I suck in a breath at the shock to my system. His fingers dance along my bare skin until I'm begging for him to put me out of my misery.

Finally, he drags a single rough finger through my dripping sex. I roll and moan against him. Gods, let the walls be thick enough to contain the echoing cries.

The wet sounds he draws from my pussy lips spur him on, and he switches between circling my clit and teasing along the seam of me. Never entering, yet still driving me higher, coiling me tighter.

Just as I reach the edge of the cliff, ready to drop, to free fall into him, he pulls his fingers away, nudging his thigh between my legs. Locked on my gaze, he sucks on each finger one by one, which shouldn't be as erotic as it is. I grind against the corded muscle of his leg, not caring at all how wet I am and how badly I'm marking him with my arousal.

Matthias closes the distance and captures my lips with an urgency I match. Hooking both legs around him, I grip the back of his neck to trap him against me. It's as though I will explode if he so much as moves even the slightest bit away from me.

"Please, Vael'astor. Please, *please,*" I chant against his lips, grinding and rocking against him. The pleasure ratchets me tighter and tighter, burning inside me. With every twist and tilt of his hips, he drives me against the wall, rubbing those delicious metal piercings against me.

"Please what? What is it you need?" He nips at my jaw. "To be stretched? Filled so tightly and fucked so hard you'll fear you might split at the seams? Do you need my come to drip down your legs as I fuck you again and again until you don't remember your own name?"

"Yes," I sob. All of it. More. Everything.

He draws back just enough to notch the head of his cock at my entrance, but it's too much space between us. I scrabble at his back, nails raking down his skin. Inch by decadent inch, he slides in, each ball rubbing against me, sending shockwaves through my system.

He stretches me in the most divine way, the pain almost giving way to a blissful pleasure. "Zorvyn's balls. Love the way your pussy is strangling my dick. Fuck, I want to live inside of you." Without any further hesitation, he bottoms out, shoving me up the wall.

My eyes close of their own volition, and a moaning sob tears from my throat. Matthias' hand finds my cheek and cups it tenderly, his thumb stroking just under my eye, coaxing me to look at him with a gentleness that has tears pricking my eyes.

"You are mine, and I am yours, *pisúlë.*"

Any docility he'd shown in the slow plunge in disappears when he draws back and slams in straight to the hilt. Every bit of that wicked piercing kisses along my sex. Matthias thrusts hard and long, and I savor every inch he feeds me over and over again. His grunts and groans mix with my moans to fill the room with a chorus of divine ecstasy.

I speed toward the same cliff he drove me toward with his fingers, and through the bond, I can feel him hurtling right along with me. I wrench my eyes open to look at him and capture his cheeks between my palms. He gazes down at me, a ferocity lining his features, but the second our eyes connect a blazing glow ripples across his brow.

I blink against the light, struggling to focus between the pleasure coursing through me from his savage fucking and the blinding glare.

A crown of thorns adorns his brow. My crown of thorns. My marking.

All my thoughts stutter to a halt. But Matthias continues. He ducks his head to the juncture of my neck, sucking viciously. At the same time, he plunges his hand between us to find the apex of my thighs and swirls his fingers around my clit.

The second I tip over into a free fall of pleasure, his teeth sink into my flesh with a pained roar. "Matthias! Oh gods, oh gods, oh fucking gods," I moan and cry as I kiss and lick and bite any bit of his skin I can find, leaving teeth marks in my wake.

His hips hammer once, twice more before his body seizes as he shouts my name and I feel him spill inside me. His hips continue a torturous, erratic roll as we ride out each pulse of our shared climax.

Finally, he stills. We stay like that for a long moment, heads bowed to the other's shoulder, hands clinging, and joined. Contentment washes over me through the bond, a warm feeling, a feeling that all is just as it should be.

Slowly, he guides my legs down and slips his softening length from me. I whine at the loss of our connection but can't tear my eyes away from the sight of him pulling out of me. His piercings ignite the smoldering fire within me as they each nudge my sex on their retreat. My whine gives way to a moan when Matthias drags a finger up my inner thigh to collect his cum that's slipped out and shoves it back inside of me. He leaves two fingers dipped within my pussy.

"I take the suppressants," I whisper.

His answering growl stops my words. "I don't give a damn. That belongs inside of you. My cock belongs inside of you to keep it in." His eyes flare in a possessive hunger, but more shockingly, my sex clenches at his words.

His lips curl in a slow, sexy grin. "You like that? You like the thought of my cock plugging you, keeping my cum locked tight in your cunt? Oh fuck, the way you clamp down when I tell you what I want to do to you."

Matthias pumps his fingers in and out. Oh gods, I'm so sensitive. I can't. I can't take it.

You can, love. You're going to take it until my cock is hard again and I'm going to fuck you again.

He grinds his palm against my clit, and I give up trying to do anything other than my fuck myself on his fingers. Matthias finds the spot where his fangs punctured my neck and laves over the wound with his tongue. "I'll mark you here one day. When you're ready for it. When you truly accept this. We'll wear each other's marks."

I nod. I'd agree to anything right now, as long as he keeps talking to me in that gravelly tone, keeps plunging his fingers into me.

His cock rubs against my hip, lengthening. Hard and hot and stiff. Reaching down, I take it in my hand, pumping roughly.

"That's it, work me over. Get me ready for you."

I cup his balls, and my eyes flare when he tosses his head back and groans. Batting my hands away, he wastes no time filling me up again.

Instead of pounding me into the wall again though, he cradles me in his arms. Every step he takes away from the wall sends delicious shocks of electricity straight to my sex. I cry out with every movement.

With a tenderness so at odds with the first time he fucked me, he lays me upon his bed. The navy coverlet soft and cool against my skin. It smells like him. Like a summer's day upon the ocean with the barest hints of pine and smoke.

Heat flushes my skin as he strokes my cheek with a loving caress. Cherished. I feel cherished and adored. I want to live inside this feeling the way he wants to live with his cock inside me. His thrusts are slower this time, languid.

It's a lazy fuck where we practically crawl to a joint explosion of pleasure and ecstasy. Different from the first, but no less perfect.

I expect him to collapse on top of me. Prepare myself for his crushing weight, all the while knowing I'll enjoy it, but instead, he rolls with me and perches me over him.

He sighs contentedly and tucks my head into the crook of his neck, wrapping his arms around me.

"Sleep, love."

CHAPTER
35

HOW AM I SUPPOSED to sleep after that? I feel as though I've found as many answers as I have questions. I try to shove them all down, to tuck them away beneath the trapdoor I lock everything under.

Matthias carefully unwinds my braid and the spiked strap. "I can feel your turmoil. Why don't you just ask and share the burden?"

I *hmph* in a faux-dainty sniff. "It's my burden, not yours."

"There is no mine and yours anymore." He resumes unweaving my hair and sets the spiked strap to the side. "Clever, that strap."

"Laz always said I'm vain for keeping my long hair." I shrug and push up onto a forearm to stare down at him. He truly is beautiful.

Seemingly realizing I'm not going to divulge any questions, Matthias' gaze drops to the arm I have resting on his broad chest. He strokes a finger down one of my tattoos. A pink flower with flared petals. "What's this one?"

"Oleander. Thrives on neglect. But, even the smallest bit can do a decent bit of damage." A hum is the only response he offers me. Curiosity lines our connection, but I don't offer up any further information. He doesn't press. I both hate and love that he's learning when he should and shouldn't press me.

His fingers drift over more of my ink, but he doesn't ask about any other flowers. I arch a brow and he looks back at me before saying, "If I make you tell me all about each one now, I won't have an excuse to trap you in bed with me."

I don't fight the chuckle his words cause, but I shake my head at the absurdity of his two natures. One sweet and charming, the other savage and wicked. I can't say I dislike either, and I can't say I like one more than the other.

"Are we fated to die?" I duck my head to nuzzle into his chest, whispering the question against his hot skin, the steady heartbeat offering me a sliver of comfort.

"Perhaps." I appreciate that he doesn't offer platitudes or empty reassurances; they don't make the pill any easier to swallow. "But would it be worth it if it meant the halves had a better lot in life? If the denominations weren't so segregated among each other as well as halves and Pures?"

"How can we possibly effect that change? A captain and a thief?" I shift my legs anxiously, but he traps them under one of his own, stilling my restless fidgeting.

"All it takes is one. One thought. One action. One person. A single seed can grow into a forest if you let it, just like a single spark can turn into a wildfire. Perhaps we're meant to be the wildfire."

His solemn look shifts something inside of me, slotting it into place. "You want to burn it down?"

"Aye, and I want to watch the new growth of a better forest, pisúlë."

Silence fills the space between us, but the electric charge leaves me picturing the world he speaks of. A world where Paladins and Clerics are raised together, taught to share their Light and Mana. Where Rogues are not cloistered away in the Underbelly. Where halves are just as valued as the Pures. Where the king celebrates with banquets and festivals for the entire kingdom, instead of just part of it.

He gently tucks a hair behind my ear, kisses my forehead, and says, "We may die. But for now, choose to live with me. Together."

After dozing for an hour or so, a hammering jolts through the silence in Matthias' quarters. He lays on his back with his head rolled toward the door, glaring at it like whoever stands on the other side can bear witness to the impressive slant to his brow and lips.

The knocking pauses, and Matthias exhales a relieved whoosh of air. His relaxation is short-lived when the pounding resumes moments later.

"Captain, we have a problem!" calls a vaguely familiar voice, his voice frantic.

"Is someone actively dying, Lieutenant?" Matthias hollers through gritted teeth.

A pause.

"Actively dying, no. Most likely on the verge of actively dying, yes."

That...doesn't make a lick of sense to me. I reach for my Grit, the same way Matthias instructed me in the pub months ago and slip into the shadows just outside his door.

I can see Milsap standing in full regalia, though the gleaming armor I'd expect hides beneath a layer of grime and drying blood. Soot streaks his handsome face, and his helmet has been lost somewhere, leaving his hair standing on end in every direction.

Oh gods. Has Baustantia actually attacked? Have the Dwarves made good on their threats to usurp King Wilder?

Vaguely, I feel the shift of the bed as Matthias slips from underneath me, though I remain tied to my Grit in the shadows of the hallway. I slide from patchy shadow to patchy shadow, gathering information. Pandemonium exists at every turn, but I can't decipher why or who is behind it. The sound of the door opening jolts me back to my body.

Matthias stands at the door in the same thin pants he'd been wearing when I'd showed up hours ago. Milsap peers from Matthias to me. I discreetly attempt to slide a shirt over my head, but the feel of his eyes lingering pauses my movements.

"Take your damned eyes off me, Lieutenant, or I'll remove them from your head." My voice rings out steadier than I feel, standing in just my underwear and a shirt halfway down my body.

"I ought to haul you in for insubordination, half." Before he's even finished the word, Matthias has him pinned against the door frame, his fingers pressing into the soft flesh of Milsap's neck.

"Need I remind you of your place," he snarls. Milsap's eyes widen, and with how close the pair had seemed in the pub during my interlude in Matthias' mind, I can imagine the Human's never been on the receiving end of that snarl.

"Cap, I didn't mean it like that," Milsap chokes out with pleading eyes.

Milsap's salvation comes in the form of a Paladin as Taigh comes tearing down the same hallway I'd been lurking in the shadows of.

"As much as I enjoy seeing you scare the piss out of insubordinate bastards, brother, we have *slightly* bigger problems—like the fact that the Spire is about to be riddled with Warlocks and their newest Void-cursed creations."

The smaller elf's voice draws Matthias' attention away from Milsap. As soon as his hand falls from the Human's neck, Milsap sucks in air, grasping at his own throat.

Taigh pushes past his brother into the room, completely unbothered by the lingering tension between the two Guards. When he comes to stand next to me, he sighs and stops short. With a speed that would be comical if I wasn't sure he was scenting what his brother and I had just done, he whips his head in my direction. The smirk that unfurls across his mouth is both sinful and amused.

"Don't. Just fucking don't." I bark out at him. His eyes flick down, and I realize my legs are still bare and I'm still clutching my shirt halfway down my body.

I shove him and snatch my pants—belt and all—off the ground to yank them on.

"We're out of time." Taigh's amusement morphs into urgency.

My vision wavers. Nythraxis, no. Not now. Torchlight flickers, and the pounding of footsteps echoes through my mind. My hand shoots out, locking around Taigh's forged bracer. Burnt flesh dives down my throat when I suck in air and sends my stomach into a churning vortex.

"Hold the line!"

"Who!? Hold what line," I plead with the voice. Dimly, I feel Matthias' presence in the bond and Taigh's attention on me. I don't have time for their concern, someone needs help. Or do they? Gods, is this even real or have the poisons finally addled my brain so much I've got lasting damage.

Shaking my head doesn't clear my vision though; it only amplifies the dissonance. The cozy bedroom falls away, replaced by a courtyard with stone everywhere. A crest I don't recognize adorns a flag half torn from its place of pride. It seems every door has been thrown open and armored figures pour out like ants leaving their colony.

My fingers tighten around Taigh's wrist.

"Nythraxis' bleeding shadows, retreat! We can't hold the line."

"Matty, what did you do to her?" Taigh sounds as though he's speaking through canal waters, distant and muffled.

At the head of the company of soldiers bearing down upon me, one figure seems to stand out amongst the crowd. A figure with a broken tusk with flaming-red skin. A Blooded Orc. The commander from my vision.

Whose commander though, I still haven't pieced together.

"You've brought us to our deaths. Zorvyn drown you, Commander," I spit, but the voice drifting back to me isn't my own. It's too deep, too gritty.

Matthias' Grit surges in my well of shadows, pushing out the scene. His sea salt and leather smell brings me back to his quarters.

Taigh holds onto my shoulders as I blink hard, watching the room become clearer. "Focus, Kira! We'll deal with whatever *that* was when we're not concerned about dying. Locks have been lurking, and those corrupted dropouts we faced?" Taigh looks to me. "That was just the beginning. Rogues with the same altered Grit are crawling through the Spire."

Matthias stares at Taigh for a brief moment, but then he's bounding for his wardrobe to yank and tug his gear on.

"Kira," Taigh says, and I eye him warily. "The Rogues are asking about you. From what I can tell, they're tracing your Grit the way Void Demons can."

"What do you mean the way the demons can?" I hedge.

"It's almost like a Void Demon's essence is inside of them, guiding them while they still use their Grit and training."

Fuck. Fuck. Fuck. The word repeats like a bard stuck trying to come up with the next line.

Matthias forgoes his battle axe and snatches two double-ended war glaives from the wall. Each gleams a deep-blue, and at the center, they narrow for his hands to slot in behind a large sapphire. The blades curve wickedly in a mirroring arch. Standing on end, they're taller than I am.

A sharp recollection beats in my chest. Those glaives—I'd seen them before. The engraving on the blades gleams in a hue to rival the seas around the southern islands. Waves and ships. An ancient magic ripples off them. It skitters across my skin, my own Grit curling out to slip around the sensation. A thought hangs in the air, but Matthias' voice sends it away like the tide.

"Who let them in?" Gone is the male who had asked me about the flowers on my arms, who had stroked down my cheeks and tucked me into his arms to doze. Replacing the tenderness is a captain I've only seen glimpses of. Not even Matthias in his instructor capacity matches the level of intensity rolling off him.

"Just like your little eclipse here, they slipped in through the cracks," Taigh quips.

Matthias tosses an extra sword to his brother who catches it without sparing it a second glance and straps it to his back, alongside his broadsword. "Full report, Milsap."

"That—that is all I have. Taigh had more information than I did," he mumbles nearly inaudibly. A harsh breath puffs out between Matthias' teeth. Can't say I blame him for his displeasure.

He strides for the door. Just as he crosses the threshold, he casts a look back to Taigh—to me. "Get yourselves out. Use your shadows and get out." He focuses on Taigh. "I'll meet you beneath the gaze of Rianta Kai."

"Oh get the fuck over yourself," Taigh barks back at his brother. "Do you honestly think we're going to run with our tails between our legs?"

"I don't picture you running with a tail at all, since you're not a Druid," Matthias' lazy drawl battles with the tension lining his muscles. He looks to me, shifting the war glaives in his grip.

"I've been through worse," I say cooly.

Milsap scoffs, but wisely chooses to keep his thoughts to himself. Good boy.

Without another word, the lot of us charge into the fray.

The fight to keep pace with a Berserker on a mission, one with access to Rogue Grit, proves challenging as we slice, jab, and kick our way through the spire. If corrupted magic users weren't enough of a problem, the Locks had also sent necrotis alongside their new creations.

The corrupted magic and the utter wrongness of the risen dead sticks to my skin like sap, trying to weave their way into my pool of Grit to siphon or infiltrate. I'm not sure which they were going for, but I lock a thick stone wall around my well of magic, relying on blades and poisons to do the trick instead of magic.

Matthias leads us down several flights of stairs, winding in directions I'd never thought to explore in the Spire. Watching him with those ruthless glaives sent a thrill through me. The art of it takes my breath away. A necrotic soldier charges him, and without a second thought, Matthias hurls him over the side of one of the sky bridges. I stare at the runes on the bridge, then peer over the side. The fuck? I'd tried to effectively do the same thing to Thara, but the runes had flared and sent her back into me. He shoots a smirk my way, enjoying my disbelief, I assume.

"The wards won't save what's already dead."

Smug bastard.

Powering through an arched doorway, Matthias draws up short. A shimmering purple dome hangs over the room. My ears pop when I barrel through the magical barrier, unable to stop myself from following the silver-haired elf through.

I blink rapidly, trying to take in the scene before me. From outside the dome, the chamber appeared empty; but just steps inside its ring, chaos reigns. Shouts come from all directions as maps spread on tables, clusters of Guards arguing, and messengers running in and out of the dome.

Mages line the outer edge of the chamber, arms outstretched with their palms at elbow-height, facing up. The sheer amount of power rippling through the room almost cripples me beneath its weight. Across the way, I spy a familiar Mage, the only one with his eyes open. He winks at me and closes his eyes. Knowing the power within him, I can't imagine he's draining himself for the barrier, nor does he need to close his eyes to focus.

Matthias storms to the table in the center of the room where other Guards and higher-ranking Spire officers ring a round table. I recognize Megora, Luella, and Faelwyn, but most of the Guards are strangers.

My eyes snag on a Paladin two Guards over from Faelwyn. Christofer Traw, one of the most decorated Guards. The poster-elf of the Guard. Some Wood Elf farmer or something, but he joined the Guard—or was forced, *semantics really*—and reaped all the benefits of falling into line: a large manor atop a hill, all the spoils of going to war for the king, and the cushy job of sitting inside the keep pushing figurines around on a map like an oversized child. Sounds like a snoozefest to me.

Luella points a finger at one of the higher-ranked Clerics, growling something I can't hear over the din of the Mages' magic and the rest of the hollering between officers and Guards alike. The Cleric cocks her head with a frown and snarls something back.

"Enough!" Megora's booming voice rises above the noise and the room quiets in an instant. "We don't have time to squabble and point fingers at each other like children. Someone give me the facts, *now.*" Megora snaps his fingers, commanding the room's focus.

Drawing himself up to full height, Matthias steps up to the table, holding both war glaives in one hand and resting their sharp tips upon the stone floor. "Warlocks are trying to take the Spire. They're using some sort of Demon Thread to corrupt failed recruits. They've turned them into vessels of corrupted void magic. A step above necrotis. We saw it in the last trial."

Gasps resound around the table, several Mages peeking open their eyes. A few show signs of recognition, as though a piece of a puzzle has slotted into place with that tidbit. Megora narrows his gaze on Matthias, tusks pulling his lips into a harsh frown.

"Why is it you failed to bring this information forward previously?"

The abrasive tone draws me forward. Rage simmers in my belly, and I manage to keep my thumb tracing the sheath of my dagger instead of whipping it out to lodge in the commandant's throat. Taigh steps ahead of me though, blocking my leg's movement with his own.

Before I can spit any fire in Megora's direction, Taigh opens his mouth. His tone as sharp as my own would have been. "Forgive us, Commandant, for not assuming the Academy's walls were paper-thin to a demonic invasion. For believing the brass was fully aware of everything the Locks were doing."

Red creeps up Megora's neck, tinging his mossy skin. The Orc gnashes his teeth, ready to call upon his patron god to smite Taigh, who appears as calm as if he were seated in a pub having a drink.

"Ah, right," Luella cuts in. "Because if there's anything this institution should prioritize, it's the word of a half supporter and a Rogue pretending to be a soldier. Tell me, does it ever get exhausting being the common denominator in every disaster?" She directs the last part to me.

Fist tightening around the hilt of my dagger, I step forward. "Trust me, nothing I do is as taxing as the constant, tiring work of believing you're the center of the universe."

Her magic wraps around the room as she flips her palm to summon an orb of arcane magic. The song of my dagger being unsheathed punctuates Luella's thrust of the orb in my direction.

I brace to summon my Grit, but the magic never reaches me. Faelwyn and Gwyn weave their magic around the pair of us. Gwyn bares her teeth at Luella with a savage roar as Faelwyn says, "Luella, this is neither the time nor the place for your grievances. If Matthias and Taigh are right, then we need to act now, not waste time playing politics."

Faelwyn shoots me a chiding expression, and I have the wherewithal to look properly chastised. Luella lets go of her Mana, but refuses to take her scathing gaze off me. She smiles, completely unbothered by anything occurring around her.

Ignoring our antics, Matthias addresses Megora once more. "The corrupted soldiers—they're looking for something. This isn't just mindless destruction." After a breath of hesitation, he turns his head to look at me. A lock of hair falls to cover his brow where the mark twin to my own lays hidden. I nod for him to continue. "They want the hilt of the Shardblade. And they're willing to burn this place to the ground to get it."

Unease ripples through the room, the murmurs grow and build until I can't hear myself think. Guards shift from foot to foot, their hands reaching for their weapons. Almost as though it realizes we speak of it, the hilt of the blade slotted along my spine warms to a blaze that rivals the brand that's been suspiciously dormant the last few days.

Megora's brows raise, but his eyes flick to me, cold and calculating. "If that's true, then we have a much larger problem than we realized. But even if the Warlocks know about the hilt, why do they think it's here?"

"Because it is." My words echo like a gong in the suddenly silent chamber. They hang in the air as Spire instructors and Guards' expressions shift in rapid succession. Disbelief, anger, suspicion.

Luella's delighted giggle rends the silence. Unadulterated glee warps her features into something twisted. "There it is! A confession. Tell us, little shadow, are you keeping it to destroy the Pures? Or were you holding it for *safekeeping?*"

I hadn't been positive, but Luella's leading words confirm it. The strange blade at my back—the one given to me by Laz—for a random mission completion is the Shardblade hilt. Though it looks nothing like its initial form, if he's working with the Locks, I doubt changing its appearance lays outside of their capabilities.

Matthias' grip on the edge of the table tightens, and a crack fills the room. Stone crumbles from between his fingers and rains to the floor. A rumbling growl erupts from his chest. If he can't keep it together, we're all headed for the morgue.

Taigh steps around me to rest a hand on his brother's shoulder. His tone shows none of the anxiety rippling off him when he says, "You already know this isn't just a matter of who holds the blade. The Warlocks are here, in the walls of the Spire, and you're letting these fools distract you with a scapegoat."

Faelwyn seizes the moment to redirect Megora. "The Warlocks have never wanted the Academy to stand strong. If we hesitate now, we'll be fighting a war inside these walls before the day is out."

Matthias glances over his shoulder at me then at Taigh. Within the bond, anger bleeds away into a resolute determination. A readiness for whatever comes next, and for that, I appreciate him, even if an underlying conflict simmers. I look about the room and realize these are his peers. People he's trained or fought beside for years. He's turning on them for me.

Not just for you, pisúlë. I'd burn the world for you, but to keep the world whole for you—to make it a place where you are safe, I'll do what I must.

The commandant wavers in his anger and suspicion directed at me. His eyes spare Faelwyn an assessing stare. He glances at each instructor and Guard standing at the table. His words are careful when he fires them. "Then we have only one choice—we cut out the rot of the halves before it spreads." Drawing his sword, he levels it at me. "Starting with you."

In Eldrath, wars are seldom forged in steel—they begin in whispers.
And that's when everything went to hells in a hand basket.

CHAPTER
36

D RAWING A DAGGER WITH one hand, I grab onto Taigh, who still grips Matthias, and tug both of them backward. I reach for my Grit to collect shadows toward us, encouraging them to act as a barrier rather than concealment.

Time to go.

Luella cackles in sheer euphoria, but she holds her place leaning against the table. Watching as each member of the war council draws their weapons or summons their magic.

The amount of Mana, Grit, and Light swirling in the room threatens to suffocate me, but I keep pulling shadows and the two elves in front of me away from the table. The Paladin to our left slashes out with his axe, only to be met by one end of the war glaive Matthias holds. Step by step, I drag us away from the horde hellbent on taking out the rot. Shoving my blade back into its sheath, I grab onto one of the vials at the front of my belt. Without bothering to unstopper it, I hurl it toward the center of the table. The glass shatters, and a green mist erupts from the vial. Two of the Guards watch, mystified, as it swirls and creeps toward them.

The Cleric shouts for those closest to back away. I feel a sick sense of accomplishment when the first victim falls paralyzed to the ground. Unfortunately, it will wear off, but it offers a smidgen of assistance for the moment.

But then I realize there may not be a way out of this. I only have so many vials of poison and so many daggers. Three of us against more than a handful of them did not have great odds. Even if Matthias and I both use his Bloodlust and combine that with whatever frenzy Elyndra incites in him, it still may not be enough.

His rage already simmers along the bond, coaxing me to give in to his Berserker nature. Before I can delve in, an explosion of fuchsia and indigo blinds me. A hand snakes around my bicep, and I try to wrench away. I grip onto Taigh tightly, refusing to let him leave my side amidst the madness. Another pop bursts in my ears, and everything descends into darkness for a moment. My body tumbles in on itself, and my stomach threatens to expel its contents.

The band wrapped around my bicep releases me, and I rub furiously at my eyes, making more stars dance across my vision.

"Easy, easy. You'll be dazed for a moment." Aster's calm voice settles some of the panic clouding my thoughts.

"What in the ever-loving fuck was that?" I utter, my voice breaking as I try to remember how to breathe.

"Short distance portal travel. Also referred to as a blink or blinking. Similar to what we did in the observatory, but farther."

I suck in a calming mouthful of air. "Ast, I love you, but I don't ever want to blink again."

He chuckles darkly. "It was that or one of you was dying."

I finally take stock of where we are. We're in the courtyard just a few hallways away from where we'd been.

"I couldn't take us far since I only had a grip on you and if you'd have let go, well we can't be sure where those two would have ended up." Matthias leans on a stone pillar doing far better than Taigh, who's bent over, reacquainting himself with his last meal.

A snarl rips from Matthias and he's on the move, storming toward me. If I wasn't experiencing his emotions, I'd be terrified he fell victim to some kind of Warlock corruption. But it isn't rage directed at me. An instinctual terror and need to protect me lines the bond.

He's just steps away from my side when doors behind Aster slam open, nearly falling off their hinges from the force applied. Two figures stalk into the courtyard.

Nythraxis? This would be a fine time to lend some assistance in offering us a boon.

The god remains silent, and the figures continue their advance. So much for being chosen by the deities.

Dark whipping robes swirl around the taller, thin Warlock, a devilish-looking imp frolicking behind it. The shorter figure strides along in measured steps, each calculated and controlled. A corrupted Rogue, if I had to guess.

Despite Aster's brave face, I know his Mana reserves are depleted from portalling all four of us out of the council chambers. Taigh has collapsed to his knees, still trying to recover from the magical transport. I move ahead to place myself between them and the corrupted magic users. Every movement I make, Matthias mirrors as his body attunes itself to mine.

The clatter of blades being pulled from sheaths and an imp screeching fills the open space, but no words are exchanged. Warmth flares in my hand when Matthias brushes his grit against the back of my knuckles.

With a pounce, the imp jolts into action, its bony limbs flared out and claws at the ready. Matthias lunges only a moment after to intercept the demon's course. A second later, the Warlock descends next, the two of them timing their strikes one after the other.

Before I can move, a dagger comes flying in my direction, having been thrown by the Rogue. I pull my gaze away from Matthias and his fight and concentrate on the corrupted assassin. A mask covers the top half of the Rogue's face, but the soft lines of the lips and jaw hint at a young Rogue, possibly female?

I stumble back as soon as she reaches for her Grit. Sigils glow upon her cheeks. One in a faint red and the other a sickly green. My gaze locks onto the first sigil, one I recognize after tracing its lines on the back of my neck day after day, year after year. Lazrik's personal sigil branded into my own skin.

The Rogue sprints toward me, a new blade in her grip. Reaching for my own Grit, I tug a shadow, weaving it through the other Rogue's feet. She stumbles when she steps into the trap I've laid, but still manages to avoid the blow I've aimed for her throat as she dives forward.

Popping up from her roll, she counters quickly with a flurry of strikes. I bob and duck and parry, narrowly missing the edge of her blade. I jolt when her fist catches the underside of my jaw.

Stars dance across my vision when my head snaps back. I shake off the blow, but in my peripheral, I catch sight of Aster locked in a battle of Arcane magic versus the Warlock's Demon Threads. Taigh still struggles to stand, looking almost drunk.

Panic courses through me, though not my own. The unmistakable sound of a body collapsing to the ground follows.

The other Rogue seizes my faltering attention and lands a kick to my stomach. I careen backward and land flat on my back. Air whooshes out of me, and I try to suck in oxygen while my lungs spasm.

"Go!" Taigh cries. Vaguely, the soft presence of his Light casts over me in the direction of the Warlock Aster battles.

Shadows wrap around me when a figure approaches. I reach for them with my Grit, but the other Rogue already commands them. They wind around my legs and arms to pin me in place.

"Did you truly think he'd only send a single Rogue after you?" she says, triumphantly pulling off her mask.

Holli.

The night Rafe and Laz gave me my blade was the last time I'd seen her.

When there's finally enough air in my lungs, I choke out, "You were missing. Laz said you'd died." Shock ripples through me. He'd sent word on my travels back to Eldrath that Holli had been taken and was presumed dead. That she'd gone out on patrol and never returned. He'd received a note...A note he never showed me.

"The Holli you knew died. Laz and Aldros made me more. More than you could have ever been."

I blink at her. Not because I don't believe what I'm seeing, what she's saying—but because deep down, I do. I always knew Laz would keep a trump card. I just never thought it would be her.

I buck and thrash against the bindings, but they only wrap tighter around me. My fingers tingle the longer I'm pinned.

Matthias' Grit flares hotly in my chest, and Holli looks down at me. I startle at how vividly red her eyes have become. Unnatural. Unholy.

"Yes. Yes, we need to deal with *her*," Holli growls. Confusion steals my focus for the briefest second. The sharp glint of steel driving down winks in my eye. Boots crunch. A skid. Rocks scatter across the stone.

Then a crushing pain followed by blazing agony.

A rift tears open next to Holli. The Lock, having abandoned his fight with Matthias, steps through. He extends a hand to Holli. Taking the offered limb, the pair fall back into the open Void rift.

Holli's shadows release me, and I press up to my knees. What in Nythraxis' shadows was that? Holli's alive. She also just willingly took a step into the Void? Where the fuck does that even take her? How the fuck is that even possible?

I stumble toward where the others should be.

Finally seeing Matthias. Seeing the root of my pain. Holli's second dagger protrudes from between the juncture of his armor. Where his lickies and chewies, his vital organs, were left unprotected. Because I didn't stop Holli. My hesitations on taking a killing blow. My own shame bleeds through his pain, masking nearly all of the hurt.

I scramble toward him, catching him as his knees buckle. Matthias falls back into me, lids closed over his glacial stare. A stare I'd give anything to see. Thick crimson seeps out from between the heavy plates of his armor.

"Hells yeah! We did—oh fuck," Taigh's joy changes in an instant. Boots slap against the stone and he crashes to his knees next to Matthias. Horror twists Taigh's face, and he stares at me. Tears line his mossy eyes, and it hits me in the gut. Another death that's all my fault. Another loss to add to the tally.

"Do something!" he pleads with me.

"I can't," I cry. Tears stream down my cheeks. What am I supposed to do? I reach for my Grit, for the very essence of myself to shove down the slowly withering bond. Not nearly as solid as it had been just moments ago.

But nothing happens.

Aster looms above us and swears violently, fixing Taigh with a weighty glare. "Did they not teach you a bleeding thing in your Paladin combat classes? You're a godsdamned battle healer too, Paladin." The bite to each word shocks me.

"We hadn't gotten that far yet," Taigh mumbles, tears streaming down his cheeks.

Ignoring the defensive comment, Aster forges on. "Reach for your Light. You can't fully heal this, but maybe you can give your brother a fighting chance."

In that single moment, the resemblance between Gersh and Aster shines. No nonsense and straight to the point. Taigh's Light reaches toward Matthias, slipping through the plates of armor.

"Good. Kira, when I tell you, you're going to pull that dagger—"

"You're not supposed to remove something impaled," I protest with a cry.

Aster gives me a thin smile. "And I'm sure you didn't have a Paladin or Cleric at your disposal when you were taught that. Taigh, send all of your

Light into stopping the bleeding and fixing the hole in his lung. What else do you feel damaged in there?"

Taigh's silence stretches on long enough that I open my mouth to snap at him, but he finally answers, "His heart. Ast, his heart's been punctured."

Aster nods as though he expected that and fumbles with the pouch on his belt. He pulls out a vial and pops the cap off. "On my count, Taigh. One. Two. Three. Pull, Kira!"

I maneuver the dagger out of his ribs, the sucking sounds turning my stomach. The only thing worse than the slurp of the dagger is Matthias' pained groan.

Taigh's Light flares, and Matthias' body stiffens in my arms. A glow erupts from the cavern between his armor. Aster pries open Matthias' clenched jaw and pours the gleaming red liquid down his throat.

"It'll keep his heart going, but not indefinitely."

Even as he says it, Aster's hands shake. The first time he's shown an ounce of fear in any of this. Aster casts a weary gaze over each of us, then again. And one more time like he can't make sense of something.

"Fuck!" The curse tears from Aster's mouth. Both Taigh and I stare at him stricken. "Faelwyn! We fucking left Faelwyn." He spins and paces a few steps away from us and whirls back. "I can't—I don't think I have it in me to blink back to get her and blink here and then portal all of us out." He swears several more times.

My forehead drops to the crown marking on Matthias' head. Nythraxis. Zorvyn. Anyone, I'll even take Elyndra. Send something, someone, anything to help.

A calm settles within me as Matthias' breathing evens out to a steady rhythm. A solution slowly starts forming.

"Can you send her a message somehow?" I ask Aster.

He nods weakly. "A brief one, yes."

"Tell her to meet us near Lefendor. We have to get Matthias to a Moon Pool. It's the only way to save him." Aster nods again and creates a bubble of Mana, murmuring into it before it swirls in on itself and pops.

"Will he make it?" Taigh's eyes plead with me.

"Only time and the gods will tell," I say, bringing a hand to his tear-stained cheek.

Shadows writhe and slink toward us from the corner of the courtyard, converging into a small fox—Araya. She nudges Matthias' limp hand and whines when he doesn't react to her.

I sniff. "I knew you liked him better." She waggles her tail in agitated flicks, as if to insinuate my fault in this. "You're right. It's my fault. I let our history with the Guild cause me to falter and my mate is dying."

Pain lances through me at the knowledge. *Celestial Mates aren't always meant to survive.* Gods, if I'd known I'd have exactly one day to accept the bond and enjoy it, perhaps I would have relented sooner. We could have had more time.

"That's the first time you've acknowledged him as your mate," Taigh whispers, still holding his brother's hand. I nod. It's all I can manage. I have nothing in me when the shrinking bond consumes my entire focus.

The threads holding us together begin to fray in the middle, slowly letting him drift away from me. Panicked, I dive into my well of Grit to search for his magic. The safe harbor his magic had built falls away, dock coming apart board by board, rock by rock of the breakwater.

No. No no no..."He's fading."

Araya nudges my knee cradling Matthias. The constellations on her side have changed, shifted, moving closer together. She nudges me again and nods upward.

"You want me to stand?" The fox hops once. "With him?" She hops again. "Nythraxis, I hope this means you're sending help."

Taigh helps me pull Matthias up once I'm on my feet, the two of us bearing his considerable weight with the armor and extra weapons. Aster scoops the lethal war glaives from the ground. In any other moment, the sight of him holding them at such an awkward angle would make me giggle. Now? I can't seem to find a shred of joy within me.

I fight back the snappy comments to urge Araya along. She trots away from us then moves in a complicated pattern. Silver light flares around her, making the edges of her form blur. She repeats the pattern again and again.

With every pass, something above her flickers into the plane of existence.

CHAPTER 37

Two tall pillars build themselves up made of stone, wood, and the fabric of the world. Araya continues her careful padding as the pillars converged into a sharp peak. The next pass she makes has me gripping onto Matthias' waist tighter. I watch as ancient runes start to appear, lining both uprights.

Once the uppermost runes glow a steady red, shadows crawl from every corner of the courtyard to swirl in the newly formed opening.

"Kira, what is that?" Taigh's voice wavers.

I had no answer. Araya had never done anything like *this* before. I'd had no inkling she could do more than poof into and out of existence.

Aster whistles in a grim appreciation. "That's a hell of a portal. Do we trust it?"

"Do we have a choice?" Taigh asks.

No, not really. But all the same, where exactly does Nythraxis want to send us?

"How far can you portal us?" I ask Aster, shifting Matthias on my shoulder.

He sighs. "Possibly the canals. At worst, the end of the avenue with the statues."

Taigh and Aster both look to me. I grit my teeth, wanting to curse Matthias for leaving me to make decisions.

Guilt quickly replaces annoyance when I remember exactly why we're in this predicament. The damn hilt on my back. A blade I rarely draw but couldn't get rid of.

Wondering how angry my patron deity will be if I shirk his portal, I glance to Araya. Her patterns have stopped and she sits at the base of one of the pillars, tail wrapped around her paws.

"We vote on it. Aster, you first since you'll likely be close to drained afterward."

I flick my eyes to the door, anxiety rippling. We've been lucky thus far that no one else has come into the courtyard, but luck always seems to run out for us.

"I've never seen a portal like that. And I only trust things I've tested and can—"

"Agreed. Thanks to your god and all, Kira, but I trust him." Taigh nods to Aster. "Sorry, we didn't have time for a whole hypothesis and results conversation."

Araya bounds away from the base of the pillar and rubs against Matthias' leg. With a final glance at me, she dissipates along with the dark portal.

Aster extends both hands to me and Taigh. I clap my hand into his clammy one and grip tight. His reassuring squeeze offers me little comfort, but I send a grateful smile his direction.

"I'd make a full portal if I could, but you'll have to withstand another blink." Taigh grimaces, and that same falling sensation takes over.

We did not make it to the canals. Nor did we end up in the avenue of statues. Slamming to my knees, I manage to stop an unconscious Matthias from landing face first on the cobblestones.

Taigh thankfully manages to keep his stomach this time, though that may be because he doesn't have anything left to throw up. As unsteady as he looks, he snatches Aster, whose eyes have rolled back in his head.

Taigh groans and looks between the two unconscious males. "Trade? I can carry the brute, and you can take Ast."

Even as I nod fervently, I already mourn the impending loss of Matthias' presence; it feels too much like goodbye. Matthias stirs, lips parting around a rasp like wind through dry leaves.

"Leave me." His quiet rasp has the same weight as words hollered across a great distance. They echo and reverberate through me. Matthias cracks open his blue eyes to catch mine as I snap my gaze to him. "Pisúlë, live. For me. I'm out of time."

Tears stream freely down my face. "Damn you, Ironhart. You do not get to say goodbye like this. You told me to stop fucking giving up, and now I'm telling you the same thing."

Taigh's broken expression warps into a defiant rage. "Fuck that. You don't get to die in some back alley because of some fucking Roguc. You're supposed to live long enough to climb Rianta Kai. To help me when I fuck up with my mate. Thalos knows you'll have enough experience with that by the time I'm shackled."

Matthias' eyes have shut by the end of Taigh's rant, but the corner of his mouth shifts the smallest amount.

Silver hair tickles my cheek when his head lolls against me, his forehead bumps my chin, and the cobblestones disappear, replaced by the cozy warmth of Matthias' quarters as a vision takes over.

I'm promising myself right now: Once we've escaped, I'm finding a Cleric to look at my head with all these hallucinations.

"She deserves to choose her fate, Matthias. Not be bound by it." I know that voice. One I shouldn't be hearing. One I haven't heard in far too long.

"If you truly believe this prophecy surrounds her and the Shardblade—" Matthias' words are hushed. The words rumble my chest and slip past my lips.

"Swear to me you'll help her if I fail," Lachlan pleads. He drives long fingers through his mop of hair. "You came here to stop the corruption in Arethor. Because that corruption decimated the Sea Berserkers. It's spread and it's going to take out the halves and everyone else with it. Lumeris tells me you'll be in the eye of the storm. Take Kira with you. Pull her out of this chaos."

"Stop talking like that, Lach." Matthias' low growl rattles my bones. A thick fist raises to gently rest against the cream shirt Lachlan wears. "We'll figure out a way to get you out of here."

"We both know my death has been set in stone, especially since my nose has been poking around where I most certainly don't belong." Lachlan manages a hollow grin—one I recognize as his sister but full of enough false joy it might fool Matthias.

The bond flares and Matthias' Grit surges, pulling me back from the vision. I'd have to thank him for holding together my sanity even on the brink of death. Because I refuse to believe Vaeroth has any claim on him. Matthias will be eternal. He has to be. He can't die without answering my lingering questions from seeing this last vision. Have they all been his memories?

I shake my head to clear the last dregs of Matthias and Lach from my eyes. My heart pounds, from the sight of Lach and Matthias together or the fact that Vaeroth's fingers are creeping closer to beckon Aster and Matthias to his Crimson Scales or the fact that this corruption runs deeper than I could ever have imagined, I don't know.

Taigh reaches for his brother, concern etched into every blood- and dirt-covered feature. We shift Aster and Matthias between us, and I dip to throw Aster over my shoulders in a carry our instructors taught us early on in the Guild.

Before I can heave him into the correct position, something small thuds against the cobblestones. A book. Of course it's a book.

Aster's nose drips blood onto the surface of the book, and a red light explodes in the alley we're tucked into.

Oh gods. The codex.

Silent as the grave, the cover whips open. Pages ruffle though no breeze exists within the city. As suddenly as it started, the rippling of pages silences.

Taigh settles his brother against a brick wall and leans down, careful not to touch the book.

"The Gatekeeper's blood seals the path between gods and mortals. If the bond is broken, the Gate will open," he reads. "What in the hells does *that* mean?"

My head pounds. We don't have time for riddles. We need answers and a way out.

Aster wheezes over my shoulder, chest rattling. "Can't let him die." He sucks in another tired breath. "Can't let them have it."

Bond. Our bond. But what gate? What path? I open up a pocket of shadow and use a tendril of Grit to toss the book unceremoniously into it. I seal the thing in there so it can't toss any more problems our way with no solutions in sight.

I settle Aster back over my shoulders and anchor him against me, leaving one arm free to grab at a dagger. Taigh pokes his head out of the alleyway and trots back to grab Matthias from his slumped position.

"Come on. We can steal some horses from the stable over this way."

I set off behind Taigh with Aster's head bouncing against my arm. I peek back at him and catch his sleepy gaze. Aster manages a chin jerk, and I turn in time to watch Taigh push himself to a brutal pace, keeping to the shadows.

CHAPTER 38

For a hefty price, certain Mages within the Conclave can create stones that return their user to a certain location. Be wary though, they have a finite number of uses before they might return the user to the Void.

EVERY STEP SENDS PAIN through my joints, and though I know he's tried to minimize his grunts, Aster's body reaps the punishment of overuse.

"Two more blocks. Pick up the pace, Kira," Taigh grunts over his shoulder.

A shock of magic trips up my feet, and the stumble sends Aster and me to the ground. Taigh's footsteps pause, and I look up at him to see a look of horror cross his face.

The eerie, distant sound of stone crumbling behind me sends shivers up my spine. Hairs raise on the back of my neck, and I turn back just in time to see the very tip of the Spire falling.

"The Warlocks. They've taken the Spire," Taigh whispers in a shocked awe.

King Wilder—does he know? Is he part of whatever coup just happened? Or is he still too lost in the grief from his son going missing?

The Locks, the Guild, and the crown? Eldrath could never survive. As if thinking the word drew attention, the brand that still remains sears in a ghost of what it once was. I can't muffle the sob in time, and Taigh glares back at me.

"We're going to figure out how the fuck to handle that too."

I stand and pick Aster back up, following behind Taigh past another two buildings where lights begin to flicker on, the shock wave seemingly rousing the sleeping city. Urging my feet faster, I duck into the open doorway.

The scent of horses, leather, and hay bombards me as soon as I pass the threshold. Taigh has already propped Matthias on a trunk against the wall.

Taigh staggers over to the stalls to take stock of the horses. Two draft horses poke their heads over the half doors to their stalls, sleepy eyes peering at us curiously. Neither of them have the speed required for the trip.

I lean Aster against the pillar in the center of the stable, the lantern hanging above him casting a warm glow over his pale skin. He's recovered enough to hold himself to the beam without my assistance.

A paint horse with one blue eye joins the crowd of onlookers. Taigh stops in front of that stall.

"Only three of them can make the run." He runs a hand over his brow. "Do you think you have enough Grit to store his armor in one of your little shadow bags?" He waves a hand in a circle.

I nod and set to stripping Matthias of his plate armor while Taigh saddles horses. "Ast, if we get you on that horse, will you stay on it?"

You're shaking. Matthias opens his eyes slightly, focusing on me. Tears well again in mine. I can hardly feel him. Our bond holds on by the barest of threads.

You're dying. His mouth quivers in the smallest of smiles. I did it. Successfully sent him a thought without him having to read it from my thoughts.

Not...yet.

Taigh suddenly slams a saddle down on a wooden rack. "Do you even know if this Moon Pool will work? Will the Druids even let you use it?"

"I'd like to see them stop me." He eyes me as he continues to saddle up the horses. "What do you want me to do, Taigh? Let him die?"

Light crackles around him. "No," he growls. "I just want you to start thinking with your damned head and not your heart."

"She...doesn't have...a choice...brother."

Taigh's anger bleeds away and his shoulders slump. Looking back to Matthias, the barely-conscious elf's brow gleams.

Between us, something slots into place, wrapping around the last few threads of our bond and holding fast. Elyndra. Her verdant magic holds us together. Holds Matthias on this plane.

His crown of thorns settles but remains marked upon his skin. Resigned, Taigh peers at his brother's slackened features. Then looks to me. His nose wrinkles. "At least you don't bear his marking yet. *This* we can cover."

Magic crackles from the open doorway. "Hurry," Aster whisper-shouts. A flash from the magic outside the barn blinds me momentarily, but I start shoving Matthias' hair forward over his brow.

Footsteps sound just outside the door. *"Find them,"* comes a hissed snarl.

"Kira," Taigh snatches Aster around the waist and hauls him into one of the stalls, tucking him into shadows. I build the shadows around the pair of them, thanking Nythraxis they chose one of the draft horses stalls. The giant beast offers them a bit more concealment.

Another pair of footsteps creeps closer to the open doorway. Reaching into my shadow pocket, I yank out an old mask from my initiate kit. I wrench it down, but the size difference poses a minor problem when it barely covers his forehead and none of his eyes like it's meant to.

Nythraxis. I send up a silent prayer to my patron when scuffing stops outside the door and they step in. I make Nythraxis' symbol upon my lips, praying for secrecy.

He's seemingly left me out to dry though.

Luella appears through the doorway. She's changed, opting for deep-blue trousers to go with a white blouse that highlights her favorite plunging neckline. Mage light flickers above her, giving her an ethereal, eerie glow.

I'd expected Warlocks. Even instructors from the Spire. Perhaps one of Matthias' comrades. Luella had not been on my list to expect.

"Going so soon?" The patronizing innocence in her voice grates upon my ears. As she leans upon the door frame with her arms crossed, tension brackets her lips set in a fine line.

Small movements shift my hand still resting on Matthias' shoulder. He's fumbled to grip onto one of the daggers I hadn't removed from him yet. He's losing touch with reality if he thinks he'll be able to do anything in this state.

Light slithers around me, waiting to pounce, and I can only hope Luella can't feel Taigh's magic.

"Shouldn't you be evacuating if the Spire is crumbling?" I search for words to buy us time and only come up with that dumb excuse. Forgoing more words, I step toward her, snatching the dagger from Matthias' grip.

"Ah, ah. I wouldn't do that if I were you." She holds up a flat, round stone about the size of her palm. A purple rune gleams in the center, when she flips it one of Laz's runes—the shadowbrand rune—winks at me. "Would be a shame to cripple you when we could turn you into something so much greater."

Air whooshes out of my lungs, leaving me winded like I've been kicked in the stomach. Luella's thumb caresses just the edge of the brand rune. The rune's light shivers, and my own skin prickles in response.

"You honestly believe he merely wanted to keep track of you?"

"Both—both of you sold us out? All of us." I splutter the words, my brain whirring.

"Hard to sell someone out when they've been groomed and cultivated for what's at stake. And before you start moralizing," she flips her hair, "I'd like to remind you—I'm the only thing keeping you from being dragged before Aldros in chains. Lazrik still wants what's his... and he wants you intact."

Fingers wrap around my thigh. Support. Restraint. Could go either way, but in any case, Matthias uses his meager strength to anchor me—or hold me back. With a roll of my shoulders, I try to hold onto anything stable. But a question bounces around my thoughts. Did Laz select me and Lachlan because he knew of the prophecy and the Celestial Mates?

"You think Laz would let anyone else have you? You're his and his alone, Thorne."

My stomach lurches. Not just trained—*owned*. Not just tracked—*chosen*. A chill creeps up my spine as her gaze flicks to Matthias. Oh gods. Laz knows. Luella knows. What are they going to do with that knowledge?

Nothing we can do about that now, short of killing her. We need an out.

"Just hand over the hilt, Thorne. I don't particularly relish in killing, so I'll even help your little Mage with a portal once you give it to me."

Aster chokes in the stall. His head suddenly appears over the half door alongside the chestnut beast. Owlish eyes blink in rapid succession. She sighs at his surprised expression. "Where she goes, you go, Aster. Can't force me to believe Taigh isn't lurking in there with you. The hero worship for his brother is almost sickening."

Taigh surfaces, leaning next to Aster's head on the wooden door with a scowl. "Hero worship? A little sense would serve you better than that smug mouth. Something you clearly lack if you think we'd just hand over the hilt like a bumble of witless recruits."

Unperturbed, the Mage clicks her tongue like a disappointed mother. "So predictable. So protective. You could have made things a little more *exciting* for me." Her words turned to a mocking whine, and my anxiety ratchets up a notch. I catch Taigh and Aster both swaying despite the support of the stall door in front of them, but I'm not the only one.

Luella's grin grows, eyes sparkling. Behind me, Matthias adjusts his grip on my thigh, and I peek down at him. "She doesn't get it."

Luella seems equally confused as I am. "And what is it you think I don't quite get?" she asks.

Two points peek out when Matthias grins. "You think Lazrik trusts you."

Something flickers across her features. Something that I haven't seen yet. Doubt. Fear. Concern. All of them? "Laz trusted me with her, and that's all that matters. But trust? No, Matthias. Trust is for fools. We are only as useful as what we can give." Her knuckles turn white as she intensifies her grip on the spelled stone. "And you, darling, have plenty to give."

CHAPTER 39

A SURGE OF MAGIC from the stone glares and flashes through the barn. My stomach drops out when the blast directs itself in a single blaze toward Matthias. Red shadows fly but thankfully leave the stone crumbling in Luella's hand. Luella flails, and the redirection of the shadows go wide.

My eyes flare. Gershom's handiwork must have severed the tie the rune stone had over me. Without an outlet, the magic must have consumed the stone.

I lunge in front of Matthias, taking the full force of the web of shadows in a direct blow to my throat. Pain sears along every nerve ending. I land in a heap on Matthias' lap. Luella's angered curse barely registers as I thrash against the pain, all of it converging within my brand, searing like never before.

Another blast of light nearly blinds me, though this one flares as actual Light. Taigh's Light. Uncontrolled and raw. It lashes out of him, barreling directly toward Luella. A mask has dropped over her face though, no sign of fear or any of the other emotions that had played out just moments ago.

She merely rubs her fingers together to rid herself of the dust from the rune stone. Taigh's unadulterated power collides with her violet shield, and despite her confidence, a sliver of his power weasels through; he beams with pride as the Light slices across her face. A hand flies to her cheek as she stumbles back, her shield traveling with her.

I attempt to sit up from my heap on the floor when the thunk of the stall door latch sounds. Aster crushes his fist and snorts whatever it is while stepping around the threshold. His lips move too fast for me to catch, but his hands soon join in a complicated dance. The very threads of the realm seem to buck and sway with every movement.

Pushing ahead of Taigh, the great draft horse walks alongside the Mage, seizing the opportunity to snatch up some of the hay and grain upon the floor of the stable. It's somehow completely unphased by the entire fiasco unfolding before us.

Aster continues mumbling and muttering, striding out of the stall, the effects of whatever he'd inhaled taking hold of him to drive away the weariness of battle. The threads pull away from each other in a jagged tear. His pain emblazoned across his features, but he refuses to stop, still planting one foot ahead of the other. Forcing his hands out, his magic begins to tear and pull at the air at the back of the barn, pulling open a portal.

Luella stands within her protective shield, her shock and awe plain as day. She reels back, moving her own hand into a swirl, collecting her Arcane Mana into a ball. Just as she plants her foot so she can launch the magic in Aster's direction, she stumbles on something, pitching forward. The Mana plummets into the ground just ahead of her. A squealed whinny bleats from the horses within the stable.

Rocks and soil rain upon us, skittering along every surface. At Luella's feet a gaping hole remains. My eyes widen when I finally see what caused her to stumble in the first place.

Oh, gods. Nythraxis, send me to the Void before you do this to me.

Long red curls pulled into a tail at the back of his head whips in the wind coming from Aster's forming portal. Chocolate-brown eyes find mine with little hesitation, his plush lips pulled into a smirk.

Rafe.

"Hello, sweetheart." His voice drips in sickly sweetness, just as syrupy as the last time he'd said those words to me. When I found him balls deep in a Warlock all those years ago.

He's almost exactly the same as he was then. Thick straps lined with daggers and throwing stars across his chest. Facial hair shaved and neatly trimmed. Scars still lining his palms where he'd stupidly decided to try to catch my blades while dueling.

It's all so familiar. Except...

Nearly hidden beneath his perfectly sculpted beard, two runes flash on each cheek. The runes from the trial with the failed aspirants.

Carefully, knowing Rafe can also sense others' magic, I prod about to feel for his and recoil when I discover the same oily, Lock-tinged Grit I'd felt from the others.

What is he? What have Laz and Luella entwined themselves with?

"Playing with your food or pretending you have the upper hand, Lu?" Rafe arches a thick brow at the smaller Human. Looking back to me, his eyes glint with delight. "Glad you've held onto my gift for so long. Such an easy little halfling to please. Never questioning her lover or her master."

"Shut up and do your job," Luella snips at him. I flick my eyes back and forth, unable to determine what the fuck is going on. Rafe's all but confirmed he and Laz have been playing a game this entire time.

Without any further preamble, Rafe lunges for me. Palm outstretched, intent on leaping across the pit between us. I recoil farther into the wall behind me, but I have nowhere to go. But before I can try to react, another body moves, startled by the sudden movement. A great hind end launches a single blow backward. One bulging, chestnut back leg connects with Rafe's stomach, sending his momentum backward...and into the pit Luella made.

In the next instant, I push myself off the wall and look down to Matthias, but see Taigh hefting him over his shoulder. The hulking Berserker groans with the movement, his already sodden shirt dripping blood, the potions and magic now worn off.

Taigh stumbles and pulls his brother toward Aster and this new tear in the world, a moonlit forest visible through the gap. Taigh shoves Matthias' body through it, tumbling in after him, but just as he disappears from sight, an Arcane bolt strikes true to his spine.

Aster pulls at me, still chanting ferociously, and all but kicks me through, moving to dodge another Arcane bolt and climb through just as I clear the edge.

A resounding thud echoes through the cavern of time we fall into to reach wherever Aster's sent us. I don't know if Taigh's alive. I don't know if Matthias will wake. But I do know one thing: Rafe is here. He's been corrupted by the Warlocks and their mission. And we are not ready.

CHAPTER
40

I THOUGHT BLINKING TOOK the cake for worst form of travel. No, no. Full portal is now my least favorite way to travel. My limbs quake like leaves in a breeze, right alongside my stomach clenching. My brain rolls, momentarily unable to form thoughts, leaving me off-kilter.

Gods, where has Aster sent us? A dark green field fills my gaze, rustling and branches cracking accompany the gentle wind. Humidity dampens my skin, adding to all the sweat I've accumulated from running across what feels like the Void and back. I suck in air to ward off the uneasiness building in my chest. We've landed in a dense forest, vines tangled in the undergrowth. Closing my eyes, I refocus. Who cares about the location? With an ungraceful flail, I push myself to my knees. Where is Matthias?

He'd been bleeding when Aster snatched my hand and tugged me through. A heap of bodies and tangled limbs catches my attention. I attempt to stand but only end up crumbling, barely saving my chin from meeting the ground in a painful collision.

Neither Taigh nor Matthias move. My heart seizes.

I call out Matthias' name. Nothing.

Taigh. Nothing.

Gods. Please. Please.

I drag myself on hands and knees, not caring about the pitiful method I'm using. I will crawl to him. I will shimmy like an inchworm. Vaeroth himself cannot stop me from reaching him.

"Vael'astor." The tangle of limbs rises, but only just. I struggle along a few more feet. Mud squelches beneath my knees. "Vael'astor." The word tumbles out on a sob, wrenched from my soul.

A groan comes from the pile, and with a great heave, a silver head emerges. His features taut with pain, but even still, he pushes his brother's limp form from him to move in my direction.

His lips move, but no sound reaches me. Again. Nothing. He moves his lips over and over with the same result, but though no sound comes, my heart still knows the word. Still feels the plea, and so I drag myself through mud that grips at me like millions of tiny vines lashing against my skin.

Aster, still on his feet from whatever it was he snorted—I'm going to need to ask him what that was so I can keep it on hand—reaches both the elves much faster. He grips Taigh's shoulder and pulls him to a seated position. In a grim move, the unconscious elf's head lolls at an odd angle.

"Bleeding Eye! As if one dying Ironhart wasn't enough." Aster snaps. I drag my eyes to him, hating every minute I'm not looking into Matthias' intense stare.

"D-dying?" My shoulders rise around my ears, my hand flying to my mouth. Mud flings with the movement, but I ignore the gritty feel of it against my skin. I watch Aster dig once again through the pouch on his belt.

He removes another set of vials and gently pulls Taigh's mouth open. He pours one then the other down Taigh's throat.

"Will that—"

"No. Fuck no. That's just going to tide him over until we find the Druids. Need I remind you again, I'm a blasted Mage not a Cleric. Just like *that* is going to need more than a potion this time." He nods at Matthias.

I reel back, shriveling into myself. Have I put too much on him? He never intended to join a war when he reported to the Spire. His kindness has reaped what? Problem after problem.

"Lumeris fucking take me. Stop blaming yourself. I'm an adult not a child, you're not responsible for my actions. I chose to leave the Archives. I chose to open my mouth on the way to the Spire. I chose to insert myself. Are you hearing me, Kira? I *chose* this. I *chose* you and this friendship." Aster's chest rises and falls like the great bellows the smiths use for their forges.

"Kiralin." Matthias' soft call brings my gaze back to him. He's shimmied himself closer to me, his hand extended.

I clasp onto it and revel in the delightful shock at the contact of our skin. My joy dissipates into concern as my hand slips along his slick palm. Looking down, blood covers his forearm down to his fingertips.

Elyndra's magic on the bond flares, and I gasp at the wild flare of magic in my chest. Only a single thread remains between us. Her magic is the only thing holding us together. Holding him in the realm of the living and saving him from Vaeroth's Crimson Scales.

Magic pulses within me. Not my doing, though. The sensation is ferocious, uncontrolled, untamed. Matthias' Grit lays dormant and I jolt, realizing my well has stirred on its own.

Wild Grit uncoils like a whip being snapped. Shadows writhe and undulate around us. Slinking closer. Flaring taller. Wrapping around everything they touch.

Two wisps drift into the clearing, soft and phosphorescent, their glow cutting through the gloom. The Grit in their undulating forms mixes with Elyndra's touch. They are souls she's claimed that aren't ready to pass on but have no ill will. Souls that have traded service to her for their allowance to roam her Groves.

Verdant magic yanks on my own. Elyndra pulls on our threads, weaving our fate into a tapestry. Seems Nythraxis wants to share me with another deity.

My Grit sucks in, a gale force wind ruffling my hair. All of my Grit gives a massive exhale. Shadow pockets I'd forgotten ever creating pop out of existence, dropping their contents across the sodden grassy ground.

"Who knew you were such a hoarder?" Taigh's raspy jibe brings a chuckle to my lips.

I adjust my position, hand running over a strange texture. Slimy with the blood on my hands against cool leather. Before I have a chance to respond to Taigh, a red glow sparks terror in my chest. The codex.

I'd tucked it into one of those pockets. The codex now sitting between my knees, covered in a smear of blood. Steam curls up from the book, and the air grows cold around it. A ghastly blink from the skeleton on the cover sends a shiver down my spine.

"Oh. Oh, that is delightful, isn't it?"

Aster's hand falls to my shoulder to grip it tightly. The codex gives a contented wiggle, scraping against the reedy weeds.

"I haven't been blessed with a Gatekeeper's blood in years."

Matthias. He's the Gatekeeper?

"What is a Gatekeeper?" Aster leans over me. The trees around us sigh in a collective whisper of air on a warming breeze. With a loud snap, the cover whips open and pages ruffle just the same as they did in that alley.

This time, words from the page scrawl in the air in a golden script.

The Gate stands between the ending and the beginning.

A soul unbound, a tether severed, yet still the lock and key.

Only blood may name the Gatekeeper, but blood alone will not unmake the price.

He who walks in two worlds shall hold the door ajar—

But beware, for the Gate does not ask. It takes.

"I'm about ready to send this book to the damned Void," Aster growls.

"Never thought I'd see the day," Taigh barks with a laugh. I look up to see him slowly standing, swaying on his feet like a newborn calf.

Aster frowns and I can tell the Mage is fighting the urge to stick his tongue out at the elf. "You've known me less than a year. Let's not act like I've never harmed a book."

Taigh cocks his head in question.

"I threw a book when the ending wasn't satisfying once," Aster jokes.

I throw my hands up, dislodging Aster's hand on my shoulder. "Enough!" I shout. "I don't have time—Matthias and Taigh don't have time to be worrying about wandering words from a book that only feels like sharing when it's sufficiently pleased."

I wrench my hand out of Matthias' feeble grip and open a pocket of shadow to toss everything littering the ground into one pocket.

"Doesn't it get exhausting having so much in one of your little hidey holes or keeping them tethered to you?" Aster asks.

I grunt a response, but the silence that meets it tells me he's not satisfied. "I forget it's even there. Especially now that Matthias' Grit sort of takes the place of my missing magic."

He *hmms* in response.

I shove things haphazardly all into one shadow pocket, but I leave a pile of clothes I'd forgotten I'd been storing where they are, hopefully some wood rat can use them as part of her den. Nythraxis, I really am a hoarder.

Together, Aster and I heave Matthias between our shoulders. We stumble toward the edge of the clearing, toward a wall of trees.

"Do you know where you're going?" Taigh asks, causing a hacking cough to wrack his body. He doubles over and spits a glob of blood to the ground.

"No," Aster and I say at the same time. Matthias chuckles darkly.

"At least we'll die among the trees beneath the moon, brother."

Stomping forward with Matthias' weight dragging along beside me and Aster trying to keep up, I stride for the end of the treeline again.

A rustle stops me. Taigh turns toward the sound, eyes narrowed. If it's another appearance of Luella or the Locks, we're all as good as six-feet-under. I take stock of our haggard group.

Aster with his thirst for knowledge that will never be quenched at this rate. Taigh and his snappy comments, never shying away from offering a shoulder or a hand. Matthias. My honorable Matthias, turning away from everything and everyone he's fought alongside for decades to follow a prophecy and a bond.

Two paws step out of the treeline. Black paws. A writhing, shadowy outline. Araya. The wisps that had been circling the clearing dance around her in flitting bounces in and out of her shadows.

The heavy elf dips when Aster and I sigh in relief. She bounds forward, butting her head against Matthias' legs then shoots me a glare. Her fox feature twisted with a glare, a hiss whispering between her bared teeth.

"Listen, I'll happily step through one of her dark portals this time," Taigh says. With several hops and pounces, she bounds toward the other side of the clearing, waiting for us to follow.

Taigh bows his head and shuffles after her, taking his time to avoid roots and overturned logs. "Lead on, little constellation." Araya's tail flicks rapidly, and she hops in a circle, seemingly delighted with her new title.

Taigh stops suddenly. The chestnut horse stands grazing on the grass at the edge of the clearing. "Well, I should say it's no wonder Aster's drained. He sent a mammoth through that portal."

Instead of creating a shadow portal, Araya weaves around the horse, who pays her no mind. It snuffles her direction for a heartbeat then munches along. She wants us to use the horse? The small fox sidles forward and places her brow to where she can reach above the draft horse's muzzle. They remain locked together like so, both animals' eyes falling shut.

Finally, the horse saunters over to us and stands, bringing her head around to gesture to both Taigh and Matthias.

"Can she carry both of them?" I ask Araya.

The question causes both animals to cock their heads at me in a united front.

"Yikes, sorry I asked."

Aster and I heave both males onto the horse's back in a joint effort, nearly taxing both of us. Taigh perches behind Matthias, utilizing whatever concoction Aster gave him to cling both to his brother and the thick mane in front of them.

Araya, finally pleased with our actions, sets off at a quick clip through the trees.

"Lumeris, if you can see me now, guide this vulpes."

Preferably to the Druids, I add silently to Aster's plea.

CHAPTER 41

W E WEAVE BETWEEN TREES, over roots and logs. Ferns kiss upon our ankles. The farther from the clearing we get, the thicker the foliage becomes. The air weighs upon my skin, but it's restorative. As though the air itself wraps around my body like a bandage, trying to root out where exactly my ailments hide.

Suddenly, Araya stops beneath a great willow tree, leaving us to pull back the weeping branches for the horse to nose her way through. She follows along dutifully, presenting her head high next to Araya, who comes to sit next to her new friend, leaning her shadowy form against the horse's foreleg.

A soft hoot echoes through the cavern created by the weeping willow; the sound ripples along the branches, and each one lights up in an effervescent glow. I gaze at the light in awe, unsure why we've stopped here.

The moment my hand touches the horse's flank, a large prowling bear emerges from behind the drooping limbs. Standing taller than the draft horse at the shoulder, the bear lumbers toward us, head held high. Glowing yellow eyes dart between each member of our haggard group, finally landing upon Araya.

Silver-tipped, brown fur covers most of the creature, and mossy green fur stems from between its ears and down its neck almost like a lion's mane. Pieces of the mane fall in thick braids with beads clasping the ends together.

Two bands of woven branches and wildflowers wrap around each foreleg, highlighting paws larger than serving plates and arced claws longer than my forearm. In the same glow as the tree's gleaming blooms, a rune pulses on both of its shoulders.

My heart pounds within my chest, threatening to burst through my rib cage. If this evening's events haven't shaved off years—decades—from my life, I would sell my favorite daggers.

The very ground itself sighs with each step, plants reaching toward the great ursine, while I fight to keep myself from shrinking away. A Druid, that was for certain, but my experience with Druids has not been extensive. On top of that, other Rogues in the Guild would joke that Druids lost all parts of their civilized minds when they shifted, taking on the animalistic nature of the creatures they traded their souls with. The bear heaves a great sigh, bordering on a quiet growl.

The sound of flapping sends my attention skyward, and a great owl-like bird snaps open its wings before descending next to the bear. The bird's head is level with my own, and it ruffles its milky-white feathers interspersed with deep indigo as it settles next to the bear.

Gold bands around its feet clink together as wide taloned feet spread into the thick dirt. Clacking its hooked beak at us, the same haunting hoot peals like church bells. Pine-colored light flashes, and an elf taller than any I've seen stands where the owl once perched.

My eyes widen, and Aster's gasp matches my own surprise. My fingers grip the horse's flank in an attempt to steady myself, to find something to anchor me while I take in the mystifying sight in front of me.

The elf's bare chest, broad and corded with muscle, is a living canvas of inked beasts. Stags leaping across his dark skin, owls stretching their wings across his shoulders. But it isn't his markings that steal my breath. His ears arc back, long and proud as any Wood Elf's, and above them rise two great antlers, twisting like an ancient elk. Ivy coils up their ivory tines, stark green against pale bone.

Curls black as onyx frame his face, threaded with strands that catch the lantern glow in mossy green, like the forest itself has touched his hair with its seasons. Two glowing cerulean eyes regard us with unblinking curiosity, no whites or pupils in their depths—only the raw light of magic.

He rolls his shoulders, as though remembering how to be flesh again. From each arm, beginning at the shoulders and tapering down to his wrists, layers of owl-feathers fan outward from his skin, forming the illusion of wings. His claw-tipped fingers clasp together before his chest, halting my wide-eyed survey of all the ways the wild has claimed him.

"Araya," he purrs, voice low and warm as midnight. "I'd wondered where you slipped off to."

The shadowy fox barks at the strange Druid, but instead of taking offense, he chuckles, cocking his head in an affectionate tilt.

"Yes, I figured Elyndra had work for you to do."

Elyndra? Araya belongs to Elyndra...not Nythraxis?

Araya barks at the Druid again, flicking her tail in an agitated pattern then looks up to Taigh and Matthias.

Finally, the Druid steps closer to see around the great draft horse's head. He sucks in a sharp breath seeing Taigh with his arm wrapped around his brother. With a wave of one feathered arm, the willow tree parts, revealing a winding path down into the Grove.

"Come."

The Druid sets off at a brisk pace, and I urge the horse forward. She needs no guidance though, following along behind the Druid as if sensing the urgency in the air. The leaf-lined path twists down into a copse of twisting trees with purple, green, and orange leaves. As I give a second glance, I realize the gnarls in the trunks almost look like doors.

I don't have time to linger though, because as we get closer to the center of the Grove, animals, Orcs, and elves step out of the trees and bushes to peer at us. Bears, owls, elk, stags, foxes, wolves, and everything in between.

I notice Aster stopping to stare, and snatch his hand to pull him along behind me. From the gleam in his eyes, I can tell his mind is already whirring. "Later," I murmur with a smile.

Hopefully.

He hurries on after the Druid leading us to the very center of the Grove. Flat stones form a ring large enough to fit all of us inside. A silvery-blue light shines up from inside the ring, twinkling as though the night sky winks from within the ring.

As we draw closer, I realize the ring is full of water. Lush plants push through the cracks between rocks. The hum of magic vibrates along my bones, and I thank whatever god is listening for sending us to the Moon Pools.

Araya perches along the edges of the pool and dips her front paw in the water then licks off the water like a cat. The tall Druid looks down at her with a sardonic cant to his lips.

"Are you quite finished?" Araya dips her paw again and he chuckles again before turning to me. "Seems Elyndra has plans for you if she sent Araya to collect you. We've little time to waste. The only thing tying the Sentinel's soul to the realm of the living is Elyndra—to you."

Aster helps Taigh down from his perch, easing him into the Moon Pool. A relieved sigh falls from his lips the second the water touches him. He melts in a languid slump once Aster releases him.

The Druid reaches past me to grab onto Matthias, gently pulling him off the horse. In a blink, I've shoved myself between the pair, baring my fangs at the elf. Help does not come without a price, I've learned, and trepidation sinks any hope I've felt since our arrival.

Despite knowing bliss covers Taigh's face, I stand between the Druid and Matthias. "What is it you want in return?"

"The same thing Elyndra wants," he answers cryptically. "Her gift of the Moon Pool costs nothing more than you are already willing to give. If he does not enter it soon, more than his life will be lost."

I sag but relent. The elf eases Matthias' slumped form off the horse and into his embrace, careful of his claws with every move. Instead of simply setting him within the water's grasp as Aster had with Taigh, the Druid steps down in with him.

Blood droplets splash from Matthias' body into the pool. The water churns with every drop, lapping against the Druid's ankles, as though begging to work their magic. He steps farther into the pool and kneels in the healing waters, carefully cradling my Berserker against his chest.

The twinkling above the pool surges as Matthias' body submerges into the pool. Chimes ting in a soothing rhythm, pulsing like heartbeats, though none of the other Druids seem to notice the music.

I step onto the rim of the pool, dropping to my knees. I can barely hold myself back from diving in alongside thc Druid, but with every breath I take, I can feel fibers weaving between the unconscious elf and me. His breath links with mine, chest rising and falling alongside my own.

"Elyndra, Everlasting Light, your servant calls upon you. Lend your breath, your grace, your mercy to this devoted Sentinel. If my instincts do not mislead me, his path is not yet finished—his purpose, not yet fulfilled. His steps are bound to the fate you have woven, the balance you seek to restore. I beg you, Lady of Verdant Souls, grant the Gatekeeper another thread of life, lest the world slip further into shadow without him."

Light swirls around them, a figure reveals herself before the Druid kneeling in the pool. A waif-like woman stands in the water, clad in an emerald dress with gold stitching, the sodden hem flowing about her. Coiled horns like a ram arch up from her head, her dark, tight coils reaching nearly past her hips.

She focuses upon the Druid, eyes like the brightest green grass. With a dip of her chin, she says, "Anduin, your devotion is heard, and your plea is felt. But know this—it is unnecessary."

I shift closer, peering down into the water reflecting a sky not of this world. I glance up through the canopy of trees and back down to gape at the puffy clouds and blue skies shown on the water's surface that should be showing the night sky.

Fresh flowers and petals float across the breeze, bringing their fresh scents along with them. A splash calls my attention. Elyndra kneels before

Anduin and Matthias and reaches a hand to his brow. Gentle fingers remove the ill-fitting Rogue mask, and the crown of thorns blooms an ethereal glow. I feel her ghostly touch whisper across my own brow, leaving a warmth in its wake.

"My imprint already lingers upon him, woven into his very being. He is not here by mere chance, nor by the force of your will alone. His tether remains because fate demands it—because he is not yet done."

Elyndra's gaze lifts to meet Anduin's. Something gentle passes between them. "Your heart is noble, your sacrifice commendable, but I have already granted what you ask. His thread will not be cut this night."

My heart stutters, and I have to force myself to hold steady when she casts those green eyes upon me. "But hear me, all of you—what binds him now is no longer only mine to give. His path is his own to walk. The price of defying the beyond is steep. Guard him well."

Elyndra's form shimmers around the edges, and before she fades, she casts one hand upon Anduin's cheek.

CHAPTER 42

Long before the rise of the governing bodies of each denomination, there existed an ancient pact known as the Celestial Accord—a binding agreement between the gods and mortals. Those who swore the Starforged Oath were granted the ability to channel divine power, but at a cost: their fate was no longer fully their own. Over time, knowledge of this pact faded into legend, but remnants of its influence still linger in rare bloodlines, manifesting in Berserkers and Mages with uncanny resilience and purpose.

A NDUIN RELEASES MATTHIAS' BODY. Though instead of sinking as I'd expected, his body floats on the surface. Anduin steps away from Matthias, wading toward Taigh's languid form at the edge of the pool.

He extends his hand down, and with heavy limbs, the Paladin lifts his own to grasp the mighty paw. Anduin hefts Taigh to his feet and guides him out of the pool.

"Ought not linger too long once you've healed," the Druid offers.

With every step Taigh takes toward my perched spot on the rocks, he gains strength. The looseness in his muscles falls away and fills with the same vigor I'd seen from him during the Void Demon trial.

He offers me his hand in the same way Anduin did for him. Taking it, I stand beside him. We both watch as the water undulates around Matthias, but he still doesn't stir.

Anduin calls to us from the nearby pavilion. "Your Sentinel will rise when he is ready. Come. Introductions are in order." As Taigh and I pull ourselves away from the mosaic stones ringing the pool, we walk the path toward Anduin. Light filters through an overhang laced and looped with hanging vines and swaying flowers. Druids in various forms and Rangers along with their bonded take our place, sitting and laying upon the stones. They cast their gazes upon Matthias, the runic tattoos on their bodies aglow.

Though I'm loath to step away from him, knowing that our bond has woven itself back together brings me comfort. I turn inward briefly, feeling for Matthias' Grit. Relief floods me when I brush against the steadily growing magic in my well, feeding magic into me.

Only the building of his magic and our bond allows me to focus upon Anduin and the same large bear from before.

His deep warm voice cuts through the dense air. "Whispers of your existence has reached us even tucked away as we are. The Wanderer and Sentinel have joined us again. What's more, whispers of the hilt you carry and the balance it threatens have stirred us." His features turn icy, sending a chill through me. "Why have you brought the Gatekeeper here? And why have you brought that forsaken hilt?"

He nods to the hilt of the blade peeking out from behind my shoulder, one I thought had only been a sentimental gift. A muscle in my jaw flickers. Anduin obviously holds weight in this Grove, but who is he to lay judgment? He knows nothing about the situation.

Ivy on his antlers shifts when he tilts his head. "I see you do not trust me. I understand these sentiments, but you must see where I come from as the Archdruid. Elyndra and all of the Druids and Rangers have entrusted me with their care and protection. *You* are a threat to that."

I rear back as though he's slapped me. "Take it then. You save the damned continent and put things back in balance. I don't want it. You can stop Aldros and Lazrik and King Wilder on every front. You know what I want at this point? To take my mate, our friends, and the horse we ended up with and fuck off to an island where no one is trying to kill us."

With a violent yank, I draw the blade and throw it to the stones between us. The clattering from my throw echoes around the clearing. Anduin's eyes fall to the blade and then connect back with mine. He opens his mouth, and I brace against whatever he's preparing to spew at me.

He halts, turning to the bear. A flash of emerald light blinds me and a man appears—standing naked as the day he was born.

Black waves loosely frame his face, a thick braid drapes down his back to match the thick beard covering his upper lip and cheeks. Bulging muscles line each limb, a sharp V directing toward a considerable—I tear my gaze away from him, cheeks flaming. Warmth tingles within my bond to Matthias, and I flush further.

I'm unconscious for less than a day and not only did you run into an ex-lover—yes I caught that—but you also check out a naked Druid?

Kind of hard to avoid that when it's just out there. And proud. And...there.

Yes, you said that.

How are you talking to me? Rest.

I'm in a forced sleep, but I'm watching through you.

His magic wriggles against mine, filling me with a cool strength. During my conversation with Matthias, someone has offered the Human Druid a pair of loose linen shorts.

"Good evening," he offers, tilting his head and bending ever so slightly at his waist. He turns to Anduin. "Anduin, the Wanderer has not sought the blade. She came in desperation to save her mate, fed her own life force down her bond. Elyndra herself has guided her for years. Perhaps she is the wielder that blade requires. A wielder able to withstand the struggles alongside the Gatekeeper."

Anduin shifts, feathers rustling as he rolls his shoulders. Finally, he dips his chin in a grudging acceptance. "When was the last time deities converged in such a way, Elder?"

Aster steps forward, having pulled himself away from gawking at the Moon Pool, only to prevent Anduin from answering. "I'm sorry, Elder?" He turns to the other man. "I missed your name, I believe."

Aster's comments have me biting back a smirk, knowing full well he didn't miss the name, and this is his polite way to force an answer.

Cheeks bunch when the man smiles and simply states, "Names carry weight, some more than others. Some weights are not meant to be shouldered by all at this time."

Aster stares bewildered while Anduin nods sagely at the man's words. "Please, enjoy our hospitality. I have been shown the error of my ways by my young charge." My brows raise at the word young. "When is the last time any of you have eaten? Drank? Enjoyed a moment of peace? Let us show you how Druids treat our guests."

Men, women, and animals of every shape and size imaginable prowl and stride forward. They coax and beckon to each of us. Taigh, refreshed as ever, grins seeing the beautiful women approaching and leaves gladly when two snatch up his hands.

I shake my head, chuckling. Regains his strength and his libido in the same breath.

Aster looks on, questions dancing in his eyes. A mink and a man with nearly violet hair cautiously make their way his direction. "Would you like to see our temple?"

The Mage accepts without hesitation, following along and chattering with the Druid excitedly. His hands flail with every back and forth they share.

Anduin approaches me. "I apologize for questioning your motives."

"I can appreciate your wariness of outsiders. Though, this blade—it's not something I wanted. This bond, as I'm sure Elyndra has shared, is not something I sought out. I went in search of answers about my brother Lachlan's death and ended up at the center of more than I could have ever imagined. I will accept whatever debt you feel necessary for your boon of the Moon Pool, and I can assure you we will leave before we can bring more problems to your door."

Anduin's eyes spark at Lach's name, but he says nothing about it. "Leave tomorrow's burdens for the sunrise. Go, rest. Matthias will require more time in the Moon Pool. Elyndra has left him in the hands of more than one force."

He leaves me standing in the pavilion, staring after him as he joins the fray of Druids offering food and plucking instruments.

CHAPTER 43

Beyond the eastern edge of Eldrath, past the ruins of long-forgotten empires, lies the Hollow Veil—a stretch of land where the boundary between the mortal world and the Beyond wears dangerously thin. It is said that the Daggered Lands, named for their jagged, obsidian-like terrain, are home to lost souls and beings that slipped through the Veil. Few dare to travel there, save for exiled Warlocks seeking forbidden knowledge, and the rare Seers who claim the land holds glimpses of futures yet to be written. Legends say that if one stands at the highest peak during the eclipse, they may hear whispers of what was, what is, and what will never be.

T HE MOON HANGS LOW in the sky, flirting with the treetops before the dawn comes. I sit upon the same rock I'd been perched on during Elyndra's blessing. Matthias still floats in the waters. He's not reached out since he caught me staring at the unnamed man but worry courses through me.

His presence dimmed, but I put it off as his body resting, regenerating. How many of those potions had Aster shoved down his throat? How much of my own life force did I push down the bond? I trail a mental finger along the pathway joining us. I'd never thought I would be as attached to it as I am. I'd been angry to have it at first, and now—anger vibrates through me at the thought of anyone trying to take it from me.

Matthias stirs, his hips drooping below the water, leaving him in a seated position. His eyes flutter open. Silver lines the glacial blue for a beat, but he blinks slowly and I wonder if it was only a play of the light.

"Care for a dip, love?" His voice scrapes along every nerve ending I have. It leaves every hair standing on end. He sounds stronger than he should. Stronger than he looked, even moments ago. Relief fills me with the coolness of an icy drink after a long day. Just hearing him speak. Especially with the strength I've come to expect from him. A thick sleepiness still lines his words, but I nearly sob just seeing him awake, seeing him not an inch from death.

I shouldn't—these waters are blessed by Elyndra herself. But isn't all of this because of her? She pushed us together in front of that greenhouse. Caused us to twirl as though we were petals floating in the breeze. She's the force behind my magic nestling within his Grit's soothing embrace.

I suppose I never did care about what I should and should not do. I slowly wade in until the water laps around my waist. The fabric of my cream tunic turns sheer, billowing around me. I step farther into the Moon Pool.

Matthias' previously hazy eyes smolder, locked in on my every move. His body remains rigid, save for the gentle rise and fall of his chest.

A hazy vision explodes from our bond.

Matthias and I stand upon a bridge over churning, violent black waters. Ahead of us, a structure built of bones hanging at odd angles, picketed by skulls at the top, blocks our path.

It's a gate.

Shadows lick along the sides, but the shadows are not alone. Demon Fate Threads weave through the bones. Holding it together? Pulling it apart?

Constellations wink above us. I find the Wanderer and the Sentinel easily, but they aren't in the positions Matthias had originally shown me.

Elyndra's voice echoes somewhere beyond the gate. "He is not meant to linger. This path is closed to him. His thread remains, but the tapestries fray at the edges. Let go, Gatekeeper. You are needed elsewhere."

Her last sentences sound almost as though she knows we listen on the other side like children locked out of their parents' room.

Another voice, one full of rumbling thunder, speaks in return. "You cannot hold what is no longer yours alone to command, Elyndra."

A shadow of something larger than life appears on the other side of the gate, something with hulking shoulders and wild, windswept hair.

"He has never been only yours, brother." Elyndra bites the words back.

"The Gatekeeper walks two paths. The price is paid, the balance disrupted. And what has been taken must always be replaced." The second voice brooks no argument.

An icy wind blows, and I have to grip onto Matthias' arm to keep from slipping off the bridge, realizing there is no barrier between us and the sheer plunge into the churning waters. When I look back, nothing of the two arguing figures remains. Only the macabre gate and lingering shadows.

Shadows that take on a life of their own and slither toward us—no, toward him. I shrink away from the shadows for the first time in my life.

Matthias ignores my tugging, standing like the breakwater his magic has formed for me.

The shadows lick against his form, but still, he remains locked in on the gate. Waiting.

Sweat slicks my palms and my hands tremble even as I grip his arm. Knees quaking, I reach for Grit that doesn't exist in this plane. I cry his name, but the wind steals my breath before the sound ever forms.

Matthias turns.

Pale eyes find mine. Not glacial. Silvery. Unending. A pool of molten metal, lines of something ancient weave through them. He blinks and it's gone, vision and all.

My entire body seeks out Matthias where he slumps at the edge of the pool, elbows resting upon the stones. I push through the water, despite the resistance it gives, rushing to get to him. To feel his solidity beneath my fingers. To remind myself we're not standing atop a bridge. That no churning waters wait for us below, ready to suck us into the current.

"Pisúlë, I need you. I need your skin beneath my fingers. Remind me what's real." He reaches out a hand, beckoning me to him.

He spreads his knees wide, allowing for me to stand between them. His hands come to grip the backs of my thighs.

I wasn't ready for you to die. I send the thought to him, still reveling in the ability to actually send things down the bond intentionally.

There is no me without you nor you without me. As long as you breathe, so will I. There is nothing that will stop me from reaching you, in this realm or the next.

My heart stops nearly all together. Warmth blooms down the bond, and he tugs me into his consciousness.

Black hair streams from my head at all angles. Fresh scars and new cuts litter across my cheeks and nose. Matthias peers down, appreciating the view my now-transparent shirt offers him.

My pert nipples peak beneath the fabric. He tugs me closer, and I straddle his lap, bracketing his waist with my knees. He rolls his hips beneath me, and I toss my head back on a silent moan. But when I bring my gaze back to his, I finally notice what he pulled me over to see: his markings. Two jagged, whirling patterns now bloom through my brows and down my cheeks.

I trace over the marking on his cheek and feel it as though it were on my own.

"Does this—"

"We are one soul now. You've accepted me as I've accepted you."

Matthias releases my consciousness back to me, and I hurtle back into my own body. Crashing my lips down to his, I let go of anything else. Anything that isn't him. My fingers dive into the strands of hair at the back of his head, loving the rasp of the shaved sides.

He groans into my mouth, nipping at my lower lip. I gasp when his hands drag me down against him, the hard ridge of him creating a searing friction I want to chase. My knees find purchase on the bench he's sitting on, leaving me with most of my upper body out of the pool. The cool breeze bites into my skin, a respite to the heat blooming between us.

Water laps at the edge of the rocks, splashing over into the thick ferns.

"Matthias," I breathe out. "We're—*ah*—a bit exposed." He sucks on my pulse point and drags a single fang tip over it. His fingertips find my shirt ties just above below my collarbone and he begins unlacing. I stare, mesmerized, as he pulls the string through each eyelet, all the way to my navel.

Devious eyes flick up to find mine, and he gives me a boyish grin. "Tell me to stop, then." Painstakingly slow, he runs his finger along the edge of the plunging V to expose each breast. "I can't hear you, pisúlë."

Matthias pinches one nipple and rolls it. Stars dance along the edges of my vision, and my teeth find my lower lip to stop the sounds from escaping. I rock against him with reckless abandon, chasing the coiling feeling that's just out of reach.

"Easy, splash too much and you'll draw the priestesses' attention." Matthias ducks his head and sucks the other nipple into his mouth. Hot and wet, my attention narrows to only that point of contact. His tongue flicks expertly against the tight bud.

I forget his warning, moaning and grinding. He releases my nipple with a chuckle, the air against my wet skin leaving goosebumps in their wake. "Unless you want an audience, which by all means, let them see."

Heat flushes my cheeks. When he'd made the comment in the Archives about fucking me in front of Aster and Taigh, I hadn't put much thought into it. But here, with my breasts exposed and need pooling inside me, a reckless abandon fills me. After having almost lost him, I don't give two shits who watches. I pull back to work at the laces of his breeches. Soaked as they are, I'm seconds from finding a blade to cut the damn things when he bats my hands away.

Finally, he frees himself from his pants, but he doesn't dislodge me to take them off, keeping one arm wrapped around my back, stroking me in long, luxurious drags of his fingers. His cock juts up out of the water, only the very base of it hidden by glowing liquid.

Like a fucking blessing from the gods—all for me.

Beads of the blessed waters drip down it. His piercings glint in the light. Nythraxis' shadows, he's got the most gorgeous cock I've ever seen.

And how are you going to worship the most gorgeous cock you've ever seen?

I slip off his lap and nestle my knees on the shallow stone floor in front of him. He groans as he watches me. I stroke a finger along the underside, following a bulging vein all the way to the flared head of his length, scooping up a bead of his liquid.

An intensity burns between us when I bring my finger to my lips. His cock jumps when I dart my tongue out to taste him. Fresh. Vibrant. Smoky. Vael'astor. My vael'astor.

Finally, I duck my head to drag my tongue along the same path my finger had traced. He groans with no regard for our exposed position, the sound filling the space. Fingers thread through my hair, and I peek up at him as I flick my tongue around the crown of his cock.

He guides me down with a tenderness filling his gaze, and I greedily suck in everything he gives me, hollowing my cheeks. The metal of his piercings gives me pause at first, but he doesn't shove or force it. The added sensation has me thinking of the last time I felt them. When they dragged against my lower lips and rubbed the inside of my pussy.

I moan around his thick shaft, my hand snaking down the front of my trousers. I easily slip in a finger, the water making my center completely wet.

"If you make yourself come, you won't like the punishment," Matthias growls. I swallow him down to the hilt finally, my nose and lips submerging to reach the base of him. For a brief moment, I find myself stolen of breath when his grip tightens to hold me there.

Bubbles ripple around my head when I moan beneath the water.

Fuck, that's so good. You're so good. I won't let you drown, love.

My lungs burn, and he lets me up. I find a rhythm, enjoying every buck of his hips and reckless groan.

All too soon, he cups my cheek and pulls me off. Matthias dips his head to kiss me, probing my lips open to lick into my mouth. I pull away; he can't enjoy the taste of himself on me, can he?

Putting his forehead to mine, he puts my doubts at ease. "I find it delectable to know your tongue has been on me. To know I've stuffed my cock in two of your holes and only your virgin asshole is left for me to take."

My eyes widen, and he takes that moment of surprise to pick me up under my arms and lay me back on the stones behind him. He tears at my pants, leaving me in just a splayed shirt.

Matthias' chest heaves as he stands in the pool, water cascading off of him in thick rivulets, cock protruding up and toward me. He stares down at me.

"Such a perfect pussy." Teasing fingers trail down my inner thighs, halting before they reach the apex. Where I burn for him. I turn my head to one side and jolt when my eyes find another pair watching back. A bear lurks forward and settles onto its belly to watch. "Looks like we'll get to show off your pussy, won't we?"

Say the word and he's gone.

I—I... Matthias' fingers finally swipe up my slit. "Oh, fuck. Let him watch. Please, gods. Again."

I look back at the Berserker over me, and his gaze remains locked on the spot between my legs. His fingers swirl around my clit, sending pleasure throughout my entire body. When Matthias ducks his head to swipe his tongue in the same pattern, my head falls to the side again, locking eyes with the Druid, who's transformed back into his Human shape.

The unnamed Druid, naked once again. He lounges with both legs extended. His thick cock doesn't have the length of Matthias', but the girth is just as impressive. With every swipe of Matthias' sinful tongue, the other male's cock grows harder.

"T-touch—*unh*—touch yourself," I moan the words to the Druid. His beard moves in a ghost of a smile.

You dirty little girl. Do you want him to play too? I don't mind sharing if it brings you pleasure.

My thoughts stutter to a halt, and I whip my head down to him. *Share!?*

Matthias inserts two fingers with one hand and leans over me to use the other to guide my gaze back to the Druid who wraps his fist around his cock. He pumps in lazy strokes, as though not to bring himself too close too soon. I moan and arch at the visual along with my mate's thick fingers sending me higher.

His fist is huge. His body a work of art. What would it be like to have two males?

You're sure? I ask down the bond, hesitantly. *It wouldn't bother you? Send you into a bloodlust?*

The only lust we're at risk of is cunt lust. I want to see you full of cock, choking on cum. If you're lost to pleasure, I'm lost to it. But remember, you belong to me, *as I belong to you. He may please you, but he will not own your soul as you own mine and I own yours.*

"What do you say, Druid? Willing to put your hands to work?"

The Druid swipes his thumb over the head of his cock and studies us. He stands and lumbers our direction. Pleased with the turn of events, Matthias dips his head and renews his efforts, inserting a third finger, using his palm to grind along my clit. But just as I approach the cliff of my orgasm, he backs off.

With hazy eyes, I look into the dark gaze of the Druid. He's sat himself on the stone beside me.

"May I?"

I nod. He trails a thick digit along my collar bone and drags it down to my exposed breast. His hands are rough, like someone who works outside doing hard labor. He palms my breast and gives it a rough squeeze. I buck between the males, rolling my hips into Matthias and arching up into the Druid.

"Play with his cock, pisúlë. Don't leave the poor man neglected." Matthias growls the command.

Almost shyly, I peek up at him. Only the second time encountering him, and I'm spread out nearly naked with my mate's hand in my pussy, and seeking permission to touch another's length. The length I'd admired in front of the Archdruid.

The Druid breaks my thoughts with his rough, deep voice. "Go on. You liked it earlier. I smelled your arousal. It's what drew me back here." His words draw a moan from my lips. The Druid adjusts onto his knees, and I reach over to take his cock in my fist. My eyes widen when I realize my fingers don't quite fit around it. He flashes me a wild grin in response to my shock.

Pumping my hand, I watch his face contort in pleasure, filing away whether he likes a twist or squeeze.

Matthias' approval slips down the bond, the praise raining over me, and I wiggle like a pleased puppy. I chance a glance back toward my mate and smile shyly at him.

It's okay to like having both of us.

Relief pushes away some of my trepidation, and I shimmy away from Matthias' fingers, not wanting to come so I can keep playing.

Flipping onto my forearms and knees, I take the Druid's cock into my mouth.

It's probably a crime how much I enjoy seeing you take another male's cock when you're my mate. I'd have torn Taigh's head off that day by the river. But now you're mine. You bear my markings. He may get to play with us, but you belong to me.

Just as you belong to me, Vael'astor. Just know, though, I love your pleasure but we're not bringing any one I have to share with to bed.

The Druid bears none of the tenderness Matthias had. He thrusts his hips forward, and I gag on his cock. Matthias seizes this opportunity to plunge into me from behind. The rungs on his ladder-like piercing drive me wild in a whole new way from this angle.

I moan around the Druid, tears streaming down my face. The Druid takes my hair and wraps it around his fist. He uses it as leverage to pump in and out of my mouth with reckless abandon. Matthias moves in tandem, thrusting in and out.

All I can do is take what they give me, spiraling, climbing to new heights with every thrust and pump. Matthias curves one arm around me to rub my clit.

That's all it takes to send me over the cliff. I writhe between them, but the Druid shoves his cock down my throat to muffle my screams.

Both males slow their paces, and I peer back at Matthias who exchanges a devious look with the Druid.

The hulking man pulls his cock from between my lips.

"Do you trust me?" Matthias murmurs in my ear as he tugs me back against his body. I nod and let him carry me out of the water, laying down on the rocks and positioning me on top of him. Matthias reaches back down and fills me up with his thick length. The Druid comes around us, kneeling behind me between Matthias' spread legs.

His thick finger traces my pussy lips between my puckered hole and Matthias' thick cock.

"Oh, fuck. Those piercings are going to kill me." He chuckles darkly.

Relax, pisúlë.

Fingers trail down my spine in a gentle caress, and I sink into the embrace of both males. The crown of the Druid's thick cock pushes next to Matthias'. He eases in, and my pussy greedily accepts every inch he feeds me. Full, I'm so fucking full.

He stretches me, allowing me time to adjust with every bit he pushes in.

"You're doing so good. You're such a good girl for us," the Druid praises.

"Aye, you've got such a tight, wet cunt. Made for us. Made for two cocks."

I whine when the Druid finally seats himself to the hilt. After a breath, Matthias and the male move in sync with one another.

"Fuck, that piercing. I'm gonna come from that alone."

Pleasure I didn't know was possible coils tighter and tighter in my belly. The fullness is something I never knew I needed. Matthias wedges his hand between us to strum at my clit and I cry out, the moan echoing and bouncing off every surface in the glade.

The males pump again and again, sending me into a tailspin of ecstasy. I sob and moan incoherent words. One after another they finally roar their own pleasure and fill me with their cum. Slipping out of me first, the Druid places a kiss to my shoulder.

"Elyndra's tits, seeing our come drip out of you is enough to get me hard again," he growls, watching Matthias' softening cock pull free.

In a move all too similar to one Matthias had done in his quarters, the Druid scoops up their combined cum and stuffs it into me, holding it in place with his finger.

"If I had a plug, I'd shove it in you. Force you to keep it in."

A rumble sounds from Matthias, and I look at him, afraid the Druid's overstepped and Matthias might teeter on the edge of a frenzy. But only interest fills his eyes.

"Perhaps we can just use your fingers for now," I tease.

I think we may have to keep him, Matthias hums along the bond.

With his finger still in my pussy, the Druid settles in next to us. I drape my arm over him. My hand finds his beard, and I stroke the soft strands of hair.

"Can we keep him?"

Air blows across my wrist when the Druid laughs. "Me? You don't even know my name yet."

"Don't need to. I know your cock," I mumble, sleepily.

CHAPTER 44

D AWN BROKE NOT LONG after my eyes fluttered shut having been thoroughly fucked and satisfied. Stretching my legs, I bite my lip when my skin scrapes along two pairs of legs.

He stayed.

I had figured the Druid would slip away the minute Matthias and I fell asleep. A sinful ache burns between my legs, but I don't regret any of it. I'd felt powerful. Desired. Like a queen.

Peeking my eyes open, I look to my mate first. Sleep softens his features, easing the hard lines of his cheeks, his lips parted slightly. The glinting crown of thorns still emblazoned across his brow brings a smile to my lips rather than the panic I felt the first time I saw it. We truly did belong to each other.

I look over to the sleeping Druid, curled on his side into where I lay on my belly. One of his legs hooked over mine to mirror my own leg hooked over Matthias'.

A Human Druid is a rare thing in the world, which makes him all the more curious. I'd once believed it to be impossible, but it seems my absolutes aren't quite so firm. He didn't appear to be a half, but that might explain his reluctance to share his name—his lineage.

I frown, looking down at the Druid's body. He bears only one tattoo upon his skin. Two numbers and two letters. Coordinates? Only the most noble families used the coordinate system on their maps. Sailors following stars and the rest of us just relying on landmarks.

Something creaks, and I snap my head in that direction. Taigh sits in a wrought iron chair, holding a steaming mug as his lips curl in a wicked grin. Aster lounges opposite him with a purple book boasting an elven script on the front.

"Mornin'," Taigh drawls. "I see someone's recovered."

I bury my head back down into the Druid's arm beneath me, heat flooding my body at the realization all three of our bare asses—well, dick in Matthias' case—are on display for Taigh, Aster, and whoever else has happened through the Moon Pool this morning.

"Tea, coffee, potion to relieve some pain?" Aster quips without looking up from his book. I groan at their jibes, and the Druid shifts. His cock hard against my hip sends a shiver through me, but I stuff it away.

His nose dips down to my neck. "Your cunt smells like it's weeping for us again." Fingers trail across my backside and dip between my thighs. Mortified, I scramble back away from both naked men, trying to right my shirt to cover my exposed breasts and tug it down while going in search of my pants.

The Druid lolls his head and flops to his back. "Mornin', fellas. I reckon you're the reason she's so shy this morning?" Not an ounce of shame or modesty in sight as he lays there with his entire body on display.

Matthias sits up, leaning an elbow on his bent leg. "Might be the fact that one of those idiots shares my blood."

Once I've found my discarded trousers, I shove them on, glaring at the naked males conversing like old friends.

Taigh chuckles. "Oh, Matty, don't pretend like this is the first time you've been caught in a *delicate* position. It's the first time you haven't had the decency to be decent."

I blink owlishly.

Aster sets his book down. "He's right. The shame isn't the act itself, it's the public showing. The Goddess's Grove is known for its...fluidity. The only thing they care about is propriety, not whom you share a bedroll with."

"Many females take Elyndra's Vow and choose to stay celibate during their service to her. Many serve for their entire lives. However, you can imagine how prolific it can be to live within a Grove of a goddess that grants life. So many males...many related..." He looks at me waiting for me to catch on.

"Oh. *Oh.* Ooh!" My eyes flick to Taigh.

"You already played with my ears once," he teases. My mind whirls with ideas, but I put the stop to all spinning. Not the time.

We'll need to discuss you touching elves' ears.

"Now that we've stirred that pot, Kalesh, this came for you."

The Druid—Kalesh—whirls to Aster, who extends a folded missive in the man's direction.

"You've known who I am this whole time?" His eyes narrow on the parchment held out to him before he snatches it, wrinkling the edges in his tight grip.

Aster closes the book with a quiet *thwap* and regards Kalesh carefully. "Before my time at the Spire, I was an Archivist. One who had a tendency to research things outside of my scope. I had a bit of an obsession with history and lineage, you see."

Kalesh nods. "I assume you saw the birthmark upon my shoulder and did some simple math, then."

Coming to stand next to Kalesh, I watch him turn the missive over and break the seal bearing a crow. Brow furrowed, I look back to Aster. "And whose lineage exactly does Kalesh fall under?"

Aster looks back to the man reading the missive, but surprisingly, he doesn't offer me the answer I seek. Looking back to Kalesh, his lips turn down and scrubs a hand over his beard.

"King Wilder's lineage." The words are soft, bearing none of the gruff rasp or playful jibes he's offered since finding us last night.

I startle, and he tears his gaze away from me, his eyes downcast.

"King Wilder's...son? The missing heir? The one he forbade Eldrath from speaking of?"

With a tragic heaviness, Aster nods. "The Crown Prince."

Kalesh's shame clear as day on his face. Any betrayal or sense of distrust flees with how readily he provides the information. How shamed he seemed to even have to say the name.

"You're taking this well," he attempts a joke.

"I slept with the Crown Prince," I say with a wink. I try to match his levity and shimmy my shoulders.

Matthias comes to stand at my shoulder, fully dressed. His brow furrows. "The Crown Prince? You've not been heard from in years, nearly a decade." Matthias searches Kalesh's face. "We were told you killed your tutors and then fled."

Kalesh laughs, but the sound is a haunting hollow thing. "I killed them? Naw," he shakes his head, peering down at me for a breath. "The king sent a group of mercenaries to kill me. My tutors held them off as long as they could. But, yes, I did flee. Not my proudest moment, but as a young buck, I'd never have been able to hold off a squadron of trained Rogues, Berserkers, and some Baustantian rebels.

"The Archdruid, he was an Elder then, found me wandering the forests, eating whatever I could find off the ground. He brought me to the Grove and raised me as one of his Druids. Turns out Paladin Light isn't so different than Druid Mana." Kalesh shrugs as if he hasn't turned everything we know about magic inside out with a single sentence.

"In any case, it sounds as though you left quite the wake of destruction," Matthais says.

"Us? We're just in the crossfire, blame the damned Locks," Taigh huffs with indignation.

An easy smile falls back over Kalesh's features. Magic pops, and Aster reaches over with a pair of shorts. "Here. It's hard to talk business when your *business* is hanging out."

"Regardless of who caused it, Aldros has taken the Spire along with Laz. The Guild's fallen."

Kalesh's words rattle around my head without registering more than *fallen.*

Did it fall or was it given away? How could the Rogues have gone along with what he has been doing? My heart all but stops. My father. Oh, gods. What's happened to him?

"Hey, hey," Matthias calls my attention. "We'll get your father out. Whatever's happened with the Guild." He looks back to Kalesh. "Whether you're his son or not, the war isn't waiting for us to decide how to proceed—waiting for us to have a council meeting about how to proceed. If anything, time is slipping away faster than we can expect."

Kalesh heaves a great sigh. "I renounced my claim to the title, but if you'll have me, I'll lend you my strength, my title, whatever it is you need." The Druid claps a fist to his chest in a sign of allegiance. I give the barest of nods, lost at the turn of events.

Matthias slips a hand into his pocket to pull something out. A key made of bone. Twisted and gnarled bone. I'm yanked back to that horrific bridge, standing in front of it with Matthias.

When the Moon Pool took me into the vision, I'd been wholly focused on Matthias and the arguing figures. This time, my gaze snags on the center of the gate. A singular skull with rubies inset in the eye socks hangs with an open jaw. In the gaping maw, a keyhole winks.

A keyhole that might fit a wicked, bony key.

"Where," Aster hedges, "did that come from?" He leans over to inspect the key Matthias holds aloft. A tendril of raw Mana slithers around the key.

"I wouldn't—" Kalesh hasn't finished his warning before the key rejects the magical probing and a small explosion erupts in Aster's face.

The Mage blinks several times, the only white left on his face being that of his eyes. One eyebrow glows orange for a brief second before he bats at his face.

"Can you not feel the Void touching that key?" Kalesh asks, incredulous at Aster's clumsy mistake. "That key comes straight from the Void."

Probing out with my Grit, Matthias' Grit, Taigh's Light, and Aster's Mana all lay dormant, but before I can direct my attention to the key, I snag on Kalesh's strange earthy Light . He hadn't been lying when he said Paladin magic might not be so different than Druid's. White Light woven with ivy and branches and leafy greens.

"Incredible," I mumble. He looks down at me appreciatively. "Sorry." My cheeks heat, and I divert my attention back to the key.

Nothingness. The key reeks of an ancient nothingness, but something—*something*—lurks in that deep chasm. Something that hasn't seen the light of the world in an age. Yet even as I gaze into the void of the key, I realize something gazes back at me.

An icy chill creeps out from my chest. My breath puffs in a cloud in front of my mouth. I shiver, from the frosty sensation or the shock.

A consciousness brushes my own, and I rip myself back away from the key.

"Bleeding shadows, there's something very wrong with that." I clutch my arms around myself, warding off the chill leftover from the key's magic.

"I noticed it when I went to get my trousers—it wasn't there when I discarded them last night. This appeared instead. Have you seen anything like it before, Kalesh?" Matthias asks.

The Druid steps toward Matthias' extended arm but avoids touching it, keeping his odd magic tucked in tight to his body like the wings of the great owls the Druids the night before had shifted into.

Wind gusts, sending leaves, sticks, and blooms across the pavilion. Pebbles skitter across the stone. The Archdruid appears in the archway formed by a leaning tree.

"He is coming."

CAYLA CAVALLETTO

To be continued...

ACKNOWLEDGMENTS

I truly can't believe I've hit the point in writing acknowledgments. When I set out to write this book, all I had was a vibe and a single character idea. I didn't expect half the characters to show up, but more than that, the outpouring of support from so many people. First, thank you to my husband who was up for so many ups and downs in this process. I truly couldn't have hit the end without you.

To my brother and sister, I appreciate you two more than you know. Andy, for all the bizarre lore ideas I bounced off you and rambling thoughts and text messages you probably opened and thought "sis, it's 2am, go to bed," I'm only partially sorry. Cerra, I'm still dying that you read this book...idk if I will ever be able to look you in the eye again. Thanks for always checking in on my word count and watching murder documentaries with me during late night writing sessions.

Sam and Courtney: thank you both for being my first readers. I don't know that I would have had the courage to do a lot of this without you. My hype girls, my best friends, and the people I run to first for every idea. You guys are amazing, and I am so lucky to have you.

To my ARC readers, thank you so much for taking a chance on me and this wild idea I had one night. I couldn't do this without readers like you!

Lastly, to Gooser, son of Gooserson, of the Gooserson Clan, thanks for keeping my feet warm and my heart full during my midnight writing sessions. My favorite cave troll that sat under my desk while I poured my heart on the page and offered your support in the form of long howls and happy snuggles.

Sneak Peak

Turn the page for a sneak peek of Cayla's cozy romantasy...

Chapter One

Pink petals flit through the air out the window. They twirl and bounce as though the very magic of Elyndra herself carries each one. I sigh, blowing a strand of amethyst colored hair from in front of my eyes. I'd made the foolish decision to let Alina prepare my hair this morning.

"It's the Night of Whispers, Janikah!" Alina had cried when I told her I was going to simply wear my hair in its usual twist and my favorite and most comfortable emerald dress.

Instead of arguing with my best friend, I'd let her put her lotions and creams and whatever other potions she'd had into my hair. Alina had managed to make it fall in loose waves, but every time it fell into my face while I kneaded dough and prepared pastries I got closer to using a fork from the bakery to lock it into a knot on my head.

She'd kill me.

Absolute murder once I arrived at our meeting spot for the night.

So I left it down, and tried to keep my flour-covered hands from leaving white streaks in it. It'll be frizzed to hells and back though, not much I can do about that. The heat from the ovens and all the movement will leave me with curly wisps all around my face.

A tinkling from the chime above the door catches my attention. Stooped and shuffling, an elderly Human offers me a cheery grin and a wave of his cane. "Happy Whispers!"

"And you as well." I incline my head to him, that same strand of hair falling back over my face. I could shave my head, I suppose. "What can I get for you?"

The Human, with his silvery-gray hair and odd violet colored eyes, peered through the glass case I used for the day's pastries. Being the Night of Whispers, I'd spent the morning slaving over cakes and pies and loaves of sourdough. The intricately decorated cakes perched atop the shelf on pedestals.

Those violet eyes flicked to one cake in particular with its lavender-colored frosting. My pleasant smile deepened. It was one of my favorite cakes for the color of the frosting truly matched the hidden lavender ingredient I put into the batter. Odd some might say, but the lavender and honey fit right in with notes of almond and vanilla.

"Only the loaf and one apple pastry for the missus, if you please," he says. The note of longing and somber undertones evident in his voice.

Pulling his requested baked goods from the case, I turn to wrap them, mind whirring. Gods above, Lady Preshkin had ordered the lavender cake for the festival tonight.

I chew my lip, finishing the final fold of the intricate wrapping around the pastry. I have one more jar of honey in the cabinet. I could — before the thought fully has time to form, my hand has already snatched the knife from the block on the worktable. I set the knife down.

With a decisive nod, I pull the whole cake down, then open one of the cake boxes to fit it inside. A gentle warmth fills me, and though I am not blessed by any of the gods with magic, I send an inward smile to the elven goddess Elyndra, attributing the warmth to her.

I'll be late to the gathering tonight and Alina will have an absolute fit because I'll show up covered in flour, but the wrong kind since I should have flowers adorning my dress and hair for the festival.

Gathering the wrapped loaf and pastry atop the cake box, I turn and push them across the counter to the man. His white brows shoot up into his hairline.

"Happy Whispers, El'athar," I offer with a small smile. His head tilts at the Elven honorific for an elder.

"Oh, dear. I cannot aff—" I wave my hand, halting his stuttering refusal.

"It's no trouble. Please, keep your coin. Spoil your wife this evening." Pushing the cake once more, it nearly teeters on the edge of the counter. I could push it just a little more before it falls, but I don't have to. He snatches the pile of treats before they can topple over.

He thanks me profusely as he leaves the shop, the bell chiming overhead once more. Each time, I just wave him away. My heart swells, hoping he and his wife will enjoy the cake and perhaps pass on the good fortune to someone else.

Turning back to the worktable, I shake my head. I need to get started on the replacement cake if I want to avoid Lady Preshkin's wrath. Her husband is bit of a dolt — I ought not think such things — but the lady certainly makes up for his easygoing nature with her manipulation of high society.

I pull the flour, vanilla, and lavender out along with the other ingredients before returning to the cabinet to collect the honey. My fingers wrap around the jar at the same time the chime above the door jangles again. I turn my head, but before I can comprehend who stands at the door, the smooth ceramic pot slips from my fingers. Oh, gods. The jar—my last jar—dives to the ground. I dive after it, my hair filling my mouth, thundering drowning out any other sound.

I hit my knees, but the jar doesn't crash. It hovers for the briefest of seconds. The weathered wooden floorboards isn't beneath it any longer, but instead a broad, scarred hand—one that grips the very jar that would decide my fate with Lady Preshkin. A hand that quite literally holds my fate in its palm.

I dust my hands on my skirts after straightening and look up, up, up. Sweet Groves, this male is tall. Scars riddle one side of his face, as though he lost a fight with a Lefendorian panther. The side of his face I can see, I should say. Half of it lays beneath a neatly trimmed beard. His hair is cut close on the sides but left long and wavy on top in the style of most Berserkers, but even as a non-blessed Wood Elf, the Light that ripples off him curls around me. Though, it's tainted. Like Thalos, the God of Paladins has forsaken him. Odd that a Paladin would dress and wear his hair like a Berserker.

The male stood also, still clutching the jar of honey in his oversized hand that more resembled the paw of a bear than an elven male. How could a Wood Elf be so large? For he had to be a Wood Elf with those amber eyes that bordered on a molten honeyed orange. His ears didn't arc like those of a Night Elf, they were straight and pointed. Like my own.

I tear my gaze away from his face that is far too beautiful despite his scars with his full lips peeking through his beard and the waves I want to run my fingers through. Looking back to the jar of honey, a glimmer clings to it. Almost as if the honey jar mocks me, saying "I'm your last jar, how dare you mistreat me."

You're losing it, Janikah.

"Would you like me to set this on the counter?" His voice is warm though still reminiscent of thunder rolling in the bay before a storm.

"I—I—yes, thank you, sir," I stutter and somehow manage to stumble against the counter. The Paladin's other hand shoots out and grabs my waist, searing me through the fabric. Gods, is it that cold in here that his touch nearly burns?

With a shiver, I steady myself against the counter. The male steps back, leaving a chill in his wake. A cloud seems to hang around his shoulders as he steps back around the counter. He fidgets under my gaze, hands drifting from the pommel of a sword to dusting against a tarnished chest plate to dragging his fingers through his hair.

Gods, I've never seen such an uncomfortable male in my life. What has him so frazzled? I'll just add that to the list of questions I have about the male. The list that seems to be growing even though I'll likely never see him again. Maman scolded me as a child for how often my questions made her late for things or forget what she was doing.

"Groves, I'm so sorry about that," I finally say with a warm smile. "What can I do for you?"

The male shifts from foot to foot. He looks to the floor before meeting my gaze with those strange golden-orange eyes. "A sandwich? Er," he clears his throat, as if he's not used to speaking. "Do you sell sandwiches?"

"Oh!" The sound flies from my mouth without me thinking about it. I don't usually make sandwiches, but I have some roasted turkey and cheese in my basket I'd brought from home for lunch. Running through the list of ingredients I have mentally, I figure I can probably make some sort of sauce to go on top. Turkey, cheese, and cranberries? That would go together right? Could I put some sort of orange marmalade? "Of course, not a problem! Would you prefer one of the sourdoughs or rye? I have a few different varieties of sourdough?"

He shifts again, shoulders tightening around his ears. "Just plain is fine, thanks."

I pull down a loaf of onion and chive sourdough from the basket on the shelf and cut off two healthy slices. "Are you new to town? I don't think I've seen you in here before. Not that I know everyone in town. Arethor is rather large. Oh, perhaps you're here for Whispers? Big into festivals?

Hoping to leave a letter for Elyndra to grant you a mate? Or prosperity for the year?" I ramble on never waiting for an answer from him.

I gather the meat and cheese from my basket and assemble the sandwich for the male. Wrapping the sandwich in a cloth, I turn back to the strange Paladin. His hands reach for the coin purse on his belt, but I lean over the counter to stop his movements with a hand on his forearm.

"Please, keep your coin. You saved my tail when you caught that jar." I squeeze his forearm once more, the muscles beneath my fingers tightening in response. His features twist in conflicting emotions.

The chime above the door tinkles again. "Janice!" A high-pitched voice trills from the door.

"That's not my name," I mumble under my breath before I can stop myself. The male's beard twitches imperceptibly, as though he fights a smile. Oh. Oh no. It registers who the voice belongs to. Lady Preshkin. I'm so screwed.

"Pack my cake! I still have to gather my gown and have the sprites fix my hair." Lady Preshkin looks me up and down. "Looks like you could use a trip to the sprites with that rat's nest." I fight the urge to pat my hair down. Not much I can do about it at the moment.

"What are you waiting for? Where is my cake?" She demands. Lady Preshkin is neither tall nor terribly imposing, but somehow she is still formidable — and terrifying. Her hooked nose still somehow allows her to look down it at me, even though she's half a head shorter than I am.

I push the jar of honey behind the display of cookies. "It's still in the oven, Lady. Why don't you pop down to the sprites and come pick it up after? That way you don't have to worry about toting it to two other stores? I'll even toss in a few lemon curd pastries for your trouble," I offer, holding my hands up in a placating gesture.

"It isn't much of a 'why don't you' so much as it's my only option now, isn't it?" Lady Preshkin spits. "I'll take the pastries — and my coin. You'll have it finished within the hour, Janice."

The chime rings out once more. I fold over the counter and rest my forehead against the cool worktable. It's going to be a long afternoon. Gods, I need to start that cake. Two cakes I wouldn't be paid for and a sandwich. On top of that, I gave away my lunch. Two of those things I didn't quite mind. The older Human would have a wonderful night with his wife with that cake. The Paladin...well, I'm not sure what his story was, but I was happy to offer him some lunch.

Another chime pulls my attention, though this one seems muted almost slower. As though someone tried to stop the sound. Through the shop window, I can just make out the Paladin slipping through the crowd and disappearing.

Standing up, I pull the honey out from its hiding spot, only to find a stack of coins where the Paladin had been standing.